"A report?" Brognola said. "I'd like to see it."

"I misspoke. Call it a rumor, if you like."

"I don't like rumors," the big Fed stated. "Who are these valued contractors?"

The black eyes pinned him. "Let's cut the crap. State officially objects to any unauthorized Justice programs you may be running in Afghanistan. That comes from the top. I hope it's clear enough for you."

"It's crystal clear," Brognola said, rising to his feet. "I can assure you without fear of contradiction that Justice has no *unauthorized* programs running in Kabul, or anywhere else. And *that* comes from the top. Have a good one."

Brognola felt them staring daggers at him as he left. He had a problem now, a leak, and he would have to deal with it before he and Bolan landed in a world of hurt.

# Don Pendleton's Mack Bolan®

## Altered State

A GOLD EAGLE BOOK FROM

# WORLDWIDE®

TORONTO • NEW YORK • LONDON
AMSTERDAM • PARIS • SYDNEY • HAMBURG
STOCKHOLM • ATHENS • TOKYO • MILAN
MADRID • WARSAW • BUDAPEST • AUCKLAND

Recycling programs
for this product may
not exist in your area.

First edition October 2009

ISBN-13: 978-0-373-61532-2

Special thanks and acknowledgment to
Mike Newton for his contribution to this work.

ALTERED STATE

Printed in U.S.A.

We have to condemn publicly the very *idea* that some people have the right to repress others. In keeping silent about evil, in burying it so deep within us that no sign of it appears on the surface, we are *implanting* it, and it will rise up a thousandfold in the future. When we neither punish nor reproach evildoers...we are ripping the foundations of justice from beneath new generations.

—Alexander Solzhenitsyn

It's time to reproach *and* punish evil, once and for all. Beginning here and now.

—Mack Bolan

For Corporal Jason L. Dunham, USMC

# PROLOGUE

*Badghis Province, Northwestern Afghanistan*

Black helicopters *do* exist.

After all the fervid speculation among UFO-watchers and conspiracy theorists, despite all the official denials and earnest assurances, unmarked whirlybirds of ill omen *are* seen on occasion.

And they always bear bad news.

The two aloft this morning, shortly after dawn, had lifted off from Murghab, heading northwest toward the border of Turkmenistan. They did not mean to cross the border, although such a violation of the law would not be out of character for anyone on board.

Their destination was a mountain village called Uzra, inhabited by peasants who had caused more trouble than their tiny lives were worth. This day, the men who called the shots were settling old accounts.

The black choppers were both Sikorsky UH-60L Black Hawks, each with a two-man crew and complement of twelve troops aboard, capable of cruising at 173 miles per hour with a top-end do-not-exceed speed of 222 mph. Their combat radius was 368 miles, but this morning's jaunt covered only a fraction of that distance.

Each Black Hawk was armed—one with a door-mounted 7.62 mm M-60D machine gun, the other with an M-134 Minigun that spewed armor-piercing bullets from an electrically driven rotary breech at a rate of 4,000 rounds per minute.

Beyond that basic airborne armament, each member of the strike team carried either some variant of the M-16 assault rifle or a Mossberg 590-A1 12-gauge shotgun loaded with No. 4 buckshot—averaging seven hits per round on a man-size target at fifty yards. Most carried pistols of their own selection, chambered for 9 mm Parabellum or .45ACP, and all were packing grenades.

Just in case.

Most of the villagers in Uzra were awake and eating breakfast when the war birds fell upon them, dropping from the newly risen sun to skim at rooftop level, starting with a solid strafing run to soften up the target. The M-60D was brutally efficient, spitting death at a cyclic rate of 550 rounds per minute, but its stutter was eclipsed by the high-tech buzz of the Minigun shredding roofs, walls and bodies below.

Uzra was on the smallish side, for an Afghani village. Its population estimates waffled between 150 and 200 residents in winter, when the sheep stayed close to home. But this was spring, so an even hundred would be a closer count.

The inconvenience caused by Uzra's citizens was out of all proportion to their numbers and position in Afghan society. Someone had not impressed them with their innate insignificance, and now they had to pay the price for stepping out of bounds.

Ten seconds, circling once around the place with weapons spraying in full-auto mode, turned Uzra into a chaotic shambles. Men, women and children ran or staggered from their riddled dwellings, seeking shelter they would never find, some of them dropping in their tracks to rise no more.

"That's plenty," said the strike team leader to his pilot. "Put us on the deck."

Phase Two was mopping up and making sure that no one lived to profit from the lesson they had learned that morning.

Uzra, after all, was not a classroom.

It was an example.

Touchdown was a gentle bump in the midst of a dusty whirlwind whipped by the Black Hawk's spinning rotors. Rising from his seat, the strike team leader faced his soldiers and reminded them, "No prisoners!"

They rushed past him toward the open bay, some snarling, others smiling as they jumped off into Hell on Earth.

# CHAPTER ONE

*Kabul, Afghanistan*

Mack Bolan turned his rented car off Jadayi Maiwand, putting the Rudkhane-ye-Kabul River behind him as he entered the Old City, Sharh-e-Khone. He started looking for a place to park after he passed the giant Abnecina Hospital, aware that driving through the Old City without a guide could get him lost, despite the maps he carried.

It might even get him killed.

He found a fenced-in public parking lot, paid the young attendant one hundred Afghanis up front—about two dollars, U.S.—and received a numbered ticket in return. The young man smiled and seemed to wish him well as Bolan left the lot.

How did you say "good luck" in Dari or Pashto?

Bolan didn't have a clue.

There'd been no time for him to study either of Afghanistan's official languages, much less the other forty-five in use throughout the country. He would need a skilled interpreter and guide, which brought him to the heart of old Kabul, with soldiers in the streets.

Some of them were American, still hunting Taliban and terrorists nearly a decade after the invasion that was meant to punish those responsible for 9/11. Bolan had a diplomatic passport in his pocket that should answer any questions asked by U.S. soldiers who might stop him on the street.

As for the native military and police, if they tried to detain him, he would have a simple choice: either resist or bluff it out.

He definitely needed that interpreter.

The simple map of Sharh-e-Khone that he had memorized included streets and major landmarks, but it didn't give the flavor of the Old City. It didn't simmer with the tension Bolan felt around him, didn't indicate the spots where bullets, fire and bomb fragments had scarred ancient walls.

Passing along the old wall that had once defended Kabul from its enemies outside, Bolan was conscious of the irony. This day, no matter which side you were on, the city's enemies were all *inside*. Whether they strapped plastic explosives to their bodies or wore military uniforms, they were combatants in a struggle dating back, at least, to the Soviet invasion of the country in the latter 1970s.

Or should he take it further back, into the early nineteenth century, when British troops had made themselves at home here, in the midst of a society they never really understood? Where did the grim cycle of kill-or-be-killed have its roots?

Passing a line of busy market stalls, Bolan watched for tails, even as he was scouting for his next landmark along the route to locate his interpreter and guide.

The man he sought wasn't supposed to be alone.

It was a two-for-one deal, this time, which compounded Bolan's risk. Without even addressing trust issues, two contacts made it twice as likely that they would be followed to the meeting place. If Bolan's guide was not under surveillance, then it stood to reason that the guide's control—a DEA spook from the States—would be.

Bolan could only hope that one or both was smart enough

to watch their backs and deal with anyone who tried to crash their rendezvous in Sharh-e-Khone.

In case they weren't, he'd come prepared.

The pistol slung beneath his left arm was a Jericho 941, the simple but elegant Israeli-made 9 mm semiautomatic. It was slightly shorter than his usual Beretta, held one extra Parabellum round, and had its muzzle threaded for a sound suppressor.

Of course, the supressor was back in Bolan's car, along with all the other martial hardware he'd acquired upon arrival, prior to seeking out his guide.

A soldier had to deal with first things first.

Now, as he passed a bank of aromatic food stalls, keeping track of each turn in his mind, he hoped the day that had begun with jet lag wouldn't end with blood. A simple meeting and agreement to collaborate would suit him fine.

The killing would come soon enough.

It was, after all, his reason for being in Kabul to start with. The land that his country was making "safe for democracy" still had some serious problems. Negotiation might solve some of them. As for the rest…

Enter the Executioner.

"I WAS AFRAID HE MIGHT be late," said Edris Barialy.

Deirdre Falk replied, "He isn't late. Your watch is fast. Again."

It was a challenge for him, working with a woman. Make that, working for a woman, since the slim brunette American was certainly in charge. She told him where to go and what to do, approved his weekly pay and judged when it was time for him to risk his life.

Like now.

As a strong Muslim—well, an adequate Muslim—Edris Barialy recognized the subordinate state of womankind established by God when He said, "Be" and created all things. Men were supposed to be the rulers of their homes and of the world, but things had changed a great deal in the world outside Afghanistan.

When Barialy had joined his first protest against the growing Afghan heroin trade, he had not expected covert contact from the American Drug Enforcement Administration. And when he accepted the DEA's offer of part-time employment, using his freedom as a licensed tourist guide to gather intelligence on smugglers, he had not expected that his control officer would be female.

It was strange how things worked out sometimes.

Now here he stood in Sharh-e-Khone, waiting to meet yet another American. A specialist, as Deirdre Falk had described him.

But in what?

Nervous as he was about the meeting and whatever might ensue from it, Barialy had armed himself with a venerable Webley Mk IV .38/200 revolver. It weighed nearly three pounds and pulled down his slacks at the rear, where he wore it tucked under his belt, but Barialy felt better for having the gun close at hand.

He also prayed that he would not be called upon to use it.

Deirdre Falk carried a pistol, too, of course. Barialy had seen it but could not identify the weapon as to brand or caliber. It was some kind of automatic, presumably she had been trained to handle it.

Unlike Barialy himself.

He had served two years in the Afghan National Army, but his firearms training had been limited to practice with Kalashnikov assault rifles. After the basic course, he had been posted to a clerical position in Lashkar Gah, the capital of Helmand Province, and had never fired another shot.

Still, he knew guns as most Afghanis knew them, having

grown up in a nation with one of the world's highest concentrations of firearms per person—one gun for every two of Afghanistan's twenty-three million citizens, according to estimates from Oxfam and Amnesty International. It had been simple to acquire the Webley and a stash of cartridges.

But as for using them, well, he would have to wait and see what happened next.

"Who is this man, again?" he asked.

"I told you," Deirdre Falk replied.

"A specialist, I know," Barialy said. "Could you be more specific?"

"Are you getting cold feet now?" she asked.

"I'm simply curious."

"I'm told he's someone who can cut red tape," she said. "We're blocked on this end, going nowhere. If he helps us break the jam, more power to him."

Barialy understood and shared her natural frustration, but the "jam" she spoke of seemed to be, at least in part, a product of the very government that had dispatched her to Afghanistan. Could Barialy trust another agent from that government to set things right? Or would the *specialist* succeed only in making matters worse, perhaps increasing Barialy's risk?

Give him a chance, he thought.

And then, the small voice in his head amended, *But keep close watch over him.*

And then, what, if it seemed that things were getting out of hand? Should he resign, break with the DEA? Or was that even possible?

At least he had the Webley, Barialy thought. And they had taken care not to be followed.

Still, in Kabul's teeming streets it was impossible to guarantee security. For all he knew, the enemy might be observing them right now.

"I'M GETTING BORED," Farid Humerya said. "They don't do anything."

"They brought us here," Red Scanlon told him. "And they didn't do it for the tourist thing. Keep watching."

If the circumstances had been different, Farid Humerya might have told the rude American to do the job himself but Humerya had his orders.

Not from Scanlon and the pigs he served, although their interests coincided with the wishes of Humerya's master. And Farid Humerya knew enough of life—and sudden death—to follow orders from the man *he* served.

He did not wish to think of the alternative.

"You think that they are meeting someone?" he asked Scanlon.

"Why else come down here, together?"

"We would know if they were seeing someone from the National Police or the Special Narcotics Force," Humerya said.

Both agencies were riddled with corruption from top to bottom. They leaked information as if it was water poured into a sieve.

"Most likely," Scanlon granted. "But we need to find out if it's someone new."

They sat watching their targets from a Toyota Prius, with two armed men in the backseat. Two other cars containing four men each—a Camry and a Volkswagen Passat—had the target zone boxed.

Despite their manufacture in Japan and Germany, the Toyotas and the VW were all emblazoned with maple leaf flags, marking them as "Canadian cars." Imports from Canada were highly prized in Kabul, regardless of their original source or the fact that some had been refurbished after homeland accidents before finding their way to Afghanistan.

If their cars were mock-Canadian, the weapons carried in

those cars were strictly Russian. Each man had an AKSU-74 assault rifle with folding metal stock and shortened 8.3-inch barrel, otherwise identical to the standard Kalashnikov assault rifle. The twelve of them together could fire 360 rounds without reloading, all within ten seconds.

And wouldn't that cause bloody chaos in the Sharh-e-Khone?

"What shall we do if they *are* meeting someone?" Humerya inquired.

"See who it is, first," Scanlon answered, none too patiently. "Identify them, if we can. Then make our move."

"To capture them?"

"To do whatever's necessary. Are you getting squeamish on me now?" the American asked.

"Of course not."

It was an insulting question. Farid Humerya was certain he had slain more men than the American had ever dreamed of killing.

Then again, he might be wrong.

These grim-faced mercenaries were a breed apart. Like Humerya himself, they killed for money, but this lot also seemed to possess—or be possessed by—an evangelistic zeal. It seemed almost as if they thought their acts were sanctified he some exalted power beyond cash or earthly politics.

"Whatever happens," Scanlon said, "we'll have the edge."

"I simply thought that with the soldiers all around, perhaps we ought to follow them and find a place less public."

"It's a thought," Scanlon agreed. "But either way, we nip it in the bud. This bitch has caused too much trouble already."

"Will eliminating her cause further problems for your people in the States?"

"That's not my worry," Scanlon answered. "And it's sure as hell not yours."

Humerya bore the rudeness, understanding that the arrogant American was simply following the dictates of his character. Coming from a culture fueled by sex and greed, he knew no better.

Which would not prevent Humerya from exacting sweet revenge, if the opportunity presented itself.

They were allies of convenience, which should never be confused with friends. Humerya had his orders to collaborate with Scanlon and the others while it served the purpose of Humerya's masters. When the day came—and it would come—that the mercenaries served no further purpose in Afghanistan, the soil would drink their blood.

But in the meantime, he would watch and wait.

BOLAN KNEW THAT HE WAS getting close. His briefing on the ancient city had included detailed maps, plus satellite and ground-level photos of Kabul's crowded streets. He recognized landmarks in passing, even if he couldn't read their signs or tell exactly what trade they pursued.

The Sharh-e-Khone was a riot of colors and smells, the latter ranging from enticing aromas of food that made Bolan's mouth water, to auto exhaust, raw sewage and a general musty odor of decay.

He could imagine the Crusaders marching—riding—through the very streets where he now walked, meeting the same looks of curiosity, suspicion or hostility that faced him now. The native clothing would have changed, at least a little, and the weapons that they used against him if their mood turned would be more advanced, but otherwise....

Bolan was well aware that many Muslims, in Afghanistan and elsewhere, still recalled the ancient conflict of religions during the Crusades, the same way many U.S. Southerners still brooded over stories of the Civil War. Throughout the Near East, though, grim memories of the Crusades were aggravated by a Western military presence—in Afghanistan, Iraq, Saudi Arabia—and by the saber-rattling on both sides that was too often cast in terms of Muslims versus Christians.

Bolan wasn't a religious man, by any standard definition of the term, but he knew well enough how faith could bleed into fanaticism with a little push from pastors or imams who had agendas of their own and didn't mind using their "flocks" as cannon fodder.

Not my problem, Bolan thought, as he drew closer to the designated meeting place.

Despite the setting, his primary targets on the present mission were Americans and self-styled Christians, not Afghani Muslims. Still, it was naive to think that he could pull it off without certain natives who collaborated in the traffic that was poisoning the West.

Come one, come all, he thought. And half smiled as he added to himself, But don't come all at once.

More soldiers passed, in vehicles painted to match their desert cammo uniforms. They all wore sunglasses, and if they noticed Bolan, none gave any sign of it. Some of the natives watched them pass, scowling or showing poker faces, but the great majority ignored the military vehicle and men in uniform as if they had no substance.

In the long-term scheme of things, Bolan supposed, that was the truth.

He marked a pharmacy ahead and on his left, which meant that he had two more blocks to go. Aside from checking to make sure he wasn't followed, Bolan now began to watch for indications of a trap.

The problem was, he wasn't overly familiar with Kabul or its Old City, couldn't tell whether its normal rhythm was disturbed or right on track. Cars raced and swerved along the narrow streets, parked anywhere they liked, apparently without regard to anything resembling traffic laws, and many of them bore anomalous decals that seemed to mark them as Canadian.

Another mystery.

Nearing the rendezvous, Bolan first checked the obvious. He saw no snipers on the nearby rooftops, no one leaning from an upstairs window with a rifle or an RPG launcher in hand. No one at street level displayed a weapon, and there was none of the war-torn country's "secret" gun shops within view, where anyone could snatch an AK-47 off the rack.

So far, so good.

Bolan carried no photos of his contacts, but he'd memorized their faces prior to takeoff on his transatlantic flight. The native, his interpreter, was Edris Barialy, twenty-seven, an ex-soldier working undercover with the DEA.

The Yank, and Barialy's boss—at least, in theory—Deirdre Falk, age thirty-five, with twelve years on the federal payroll. Bolan didn't know where-all she'd served, but rookies who had never stained their hands with dirty work wouldn't be posted to Afghanistan.

Well, not unless the brass in Washington was hoping they'd be killed or simply disappear.

Another dozen strides and Bolan had them spotted. They were standing just where he'd been told they'd be, outside a theater whose faded posters showed a wiry old man with a dragon. Bolan couldn't tell if the old man was feeding the dragon or threatening it with a spear, and he couldn't care less.

Showtime, he thought, and stepped into the street.

"THIS COULD BE HIM," Deirdre Falk said. "I think it must be."

Edris Barialy turned to face the same direction.

"Who?" he asked.

"How many Yanks do you see heading this way?" she inquired.

"Sorry." And then, "But there's another one."

"Say what?"

"Across the—"

"Don't point, damn it!" she snapped at him as he raised an arm. "Just tell me!"

And for Christ's sake think!

"Across the intersection," Barialy answered, sounding chastened. "In the black Toyota. I believe the passenger in the front seat may be American."

Trying to seem as if she wasn't searching for the car, Falk found it anyway, and even with the windshield glare she saw four men inside it. Sitting there and watching… what?

Had she been followed? Had the men trailed Barialy separately? Were they here for some entirely different reason, mere coincidence?

Falk didn't like the feel of that, and now that she'd had time to scope him out, she thought the husky white man in the black Toyota's shotgun seat most likely *was* American. She'd found that there was something in the Yankee attitude abroad that set Americans apart from Britons, Frenchmen and Scandinavians before they spoke out loud.

So, an American, a native driver, and two backseat friends she couldn't really see.

So what?

Afghanistan was crawling with Americans, from servicemen and -women through a laundry list of spooks and law-enforcement officers, reporters and photographers, corporate people and their bodyguards—even some freaking tourists, if you could believe it.

Money-seekers, story-seekers, thrill-seekers, mixed up with warriors and manhunters. Afghanistan absorbed them all, and if some never made it home…well, what was life without a little risk?

The man she'd marked as their contact was one block out and closing fast, as Falk played catch-up with another quick scan of the scene. Behind her, parked outside a grocery across the street, a Volkswagen with four men in it sat, immobile, waiting patiently for God knew what.

Eight men, if they were working with the guys in the Toyota. And if any of them even knew Falk was alive.

Because she planned to stay that way, she would assume that they were enemies and act accordingly. But what, precisely, could she do?

The tall pedestrian, her maybe-contact, had closed the gap between them to a half-block now. She thought he had his eyes on her, although the mirrored aviator's glasses made it hard to say for sure, but there was nothing she could do about it.

Wave him off? Ridiculous. If she was right about him, and he was her contact, she would just be marking him for anyone who hoped to take him out. And if he wasn't there to meet her, nothing that she did or said would make sense to him anyway.

"There's a Toyota," Barialy said.

"Saw it the first time, thanks," Falk answered.

"No. Another one."

"Don't point," she snapped. "Just tell me."

Barialy did, and there it was. A *third* car with four men inside, just sitting there, triangulating on the spot where she and Barialy stood. Thus making hash out of her futile hope that they were in the clear.

The tall, not-so-bad-looking stranger was almost on top of them. Falk hoped she wouldn't spook him, reaching underneath her lightweight jacket for the Glock pistol that rode her hip.

"Matt Cooper," the stranger said as he stopped in front of her.

Falk stared into his mirrored shades, ignored his outthrust hand and answered, "Pleased to meet you, Matt, but I'm afraid we're in a world of hurt."

"ARE YOU SURE?" Bolan asked, shifting gears within a heartbeat.

"Sure as I can be, until they nail us. Three cars, four men each, triangulating."

"You were followed, then," he said. Not quite an accusation.

"They were here ahead of you," she said. "So, yeah. Unless they got a tip somehow, they followed one or both of us."

She didn't try to dump it all on her companion, which showed class, but Bolan had no time to parse the etiquette of laying blame. It didn't matter, at the moment, how twelve hostile men had found him.

All that mattered was evading or eliminating them.

"My ride's a quarter mile behind me," Bolan said. "Who's got the closest wheels?"

"That's me," the DEA agent replied. "Four blocks, due north."

"Past the VW," he noted.

"Right."

"Okay. We'll let them earn their money. Are you packing?"

"Absolutely."

Bolan shot a sidelong glance toward Edris Barialy. "You?" he asked.

"Me?"

"Are you armed?"

After a fleeting hesitation Barialy nodded, and caught the glare from his control agent. He blushed beneath his rich olive complexion.

"Right, then," Bolan said. "Try to ignore them as we pass their car. If they get out, let me make the first move."

"There are cops and soldiers all around the—" Falk began.

"None of them can help us now," he interrupted her. "Our first priority is getting out of here, alive and in one piece."

"Okay," she said.

Her native sidekick bobbed his head in mute agreement.

Bolan led the way north, toward the waiting Volkswagen. He didn't eyeball any of the men inside it, kept his scan of them peripheral and unobtrusive as he closed the gap, seeming to chat with Falk and Barialy about nothing in particular.

One of the men in the VW was talking on a cell phone, now, asking for orders or receiving them. Whatever happened in the next few seconds would depend upon those orders and the ultimate intent of the watchers.

If they'd been sent to take their prey alive, Bolan would have an edge. If they were simply triggermen, he'd have to put his trust in speed and hope that Falk, at least, could back his play effectively.

He put himself at curbside, with Falk on his left and Barialy beyond her, farthest removed from the street. Whatever broke within the next few seconds, Bolan was the front line of defense, trusting an agent he had never met before that day to watch his back.

Ten yards, and there was stirring in the Volkswagen, to Bolan's right. As he drew level with the car, both doors came open on his side and two men heaved themselves out of the vehicle. Behind and beyond them, flowing traffic briefly blocked the driver and his starboard backseat passenger from exiting the VW.

A flash of metal told Bolan that one of his assailants had a weapon held against his right leg, not quite out of sight. The man was speaking to him now, Midwestern accent ruling out a Briton.

"Hey, you!"

Bolan drew the Jericho 941 as he turned, squeezing the pistol's double-action trigger as he found his mark between the stranger's eyes. The shot slammed home at point-blank range and snapped the dead man's head back, shattered skull rebounding from the car's door frame behind him as he fell.

The second target was Afghani, trying for a crouch and bringing up his automatic weapon as the Jericho swung toward him, already too late to save himself. Bolan's next shot wasn't precision-perfect, but it did the job, drilling his target's cheek below the left eye, angling downward through the sinuses to clip his brain stem, heading off the mental signal to his trigger finger.

Bolan crouched and lunged, firing twice more into the Volkswagen. He caught the backseat gunner rising through a half-turn, punched a slug through his rib cage but knew it wasn't lethal, even as the man dropped out of sight.

The driver fumbled with his weapon, tried to swivel in his seat, but found the steering wheel a deadly obstacle. The fourth round out of Bolan's pistol struck him just below the right nostril, slamming the driver to his left and likely knocking him unconscious, even if it didn't kill him.

Bolan spent a precious second scooping up the AKSU rifles that his first two enemies had dropped as they were dying, then straightened to find Falk and her Afghan agent gaping at him. Somewhere at his back, tires screeched on pavement, the Toyotas peeling out.

"We're done here," Bolan snapped. "Move out!"

# CHAPTER TWO

They moved.

Bolan had no idea where he was going, but he ran as if his life depended on it, which it did. Deirdre Falk kept pace with him, Glock drawn and held in her right hand, while Edris Barialy lagged a step or two behind.

"Another block," Falk told him. "Left on the side street."

Bolan's four shots had unleashed pandemonium around the Volkswagen, where he'd left two men dead without a doubt, two others badly wounded at the very least. So far, no shots had answered his, but growling engines and the cry of tortured rubber told him that pursuit was under way.

They reached the side street Falk had indicated, turned left into it, their weapons scattering pedestrians. Cars lined the curb on both sides of the street, narrowing two slim lanes to one and change, but Bolan didn't have a clue which vehicle was Falk's.

She solved the riddle for him when she palmed a key and pressed a button that unlocked the doors on a new Ford Focus that might have been silver or gray. In passing, Bolan noted that the agent's car did not display a crimson maple leaf.

Falk threw herself into the driver's seat, while Bolan

claimed the backseat for himself and left Barialy to ride
shotgun. If they got a running start, Bolan knew that the
primary danger would come from behind, and his two liberated assault weapons gave him an edge for repelling attackers.

Unless they were trapped at the curb where they sat.

"We should go now," he said as Falk revved the Ford's L14
Zetec-E engine.

"We're going!" she told him, reversing to butt her way clear
of an old car parked too close behind them. "It's damned tight
in here."

"And about to get tighter," Bolan said as one of the Toyota
chase cars swung into their street.

Bolan leveled one of his hot SMGs at the charger, but Falk
spoiled his aim with a lurch that put the Ford in motion, bar-
reling along the narrow street in a general northerly direction.
Bolan kept the chase car in his view and saw its mate approaching seconds later, just as Falk cranked through another
squealing turn.

The backseat of the Focus wasn't coffin-tight, but it was
cramped: four feet two inches wide, to Bolan's six-foot-plus
stature, with three feet, eight inches of head room. It was
awkward for defense, but Bolan blessed the windows that gave
him a clear 180-degree view of his unfolding battleground.

"Is this car registered to you?" he asked.

"Some kind of lease deal through a paper company," Falk
answered.

"So, you won't mind if I make some alterations, then?"

She didn't ask what Bolan had in mind, just shot a hard
glance at him from the rearview mirror and replied, "Do what
you gotta do."

The lead Toyota was almost on top of them, its backup
car running some thirty yards behind. Bolan wanted to get
them off Falk's tail—or, at the very least, to slow them
down enough for Falk to try some fancy footwork, maybe

lose them in the maze of Sharh-e-Khone without a higher body count.

He wasn't squeamish, but every extra body added heat. Or would, if those he killed were men with influential friends.

"So, what's the plan?" Falk asked him when they'd cleared another block.

"You drive," Bolan replied. "I'll shoot."

And as he spoke he squeezed the AKSU's trigger, shattering the Ford's rear window into flying beads of safety glass.

"GET AFTER THEM, goddamn it!"

"I am trying," Farid Humerya stated.

"Then try harder! Christ! We're losing them!"

Red Scanlon might have said that he'd seen everything during his years of soldiering, but he'd been startled—make that shocked—when the tall stranger shot his four men just like that.

*Bam-bam-bam-bam.*

Four up, four down.

Scanlon knew two of them were dead, for sure. He'd seen the head shots strike, and there was no mistaking how their bodies dropped like puppets with their strings cut. That was brain death, even if their hearts and lungs kept pumping for a few more minutes. On the other two, he wasn't positive, but they were down and showed no signs of rising as the Prius passed them, following the Camry that was closer to the shooting scene.

The bastard was quick and cool, Scanlon would give him that. Most shooters hesitated for at least a fraction of a heartbeat in a face-to-face encounter, and some of them—especially Americans—were still hung up on John Wayne etiquette, giving the other guy a chance before they drew and fired.

Fuck that.

Scanlon had stayed alive this long by shooting first and generally not bothering with any questions afterward. Somebody threatened him, or seemed about to, and he hit them with a terminal preemptive strike.

When in doubt, take 'em out.

The men he'd handpicked for this job all had the same philosophy, all had sufficient notches on their guns to qualify as shooters *and* survivors, but the stranger had dropped four of them like it was nothing, cutting Scanlon's force by thirty-three percent in something like two seconds flat.

That was embarrassing.

It simply couldn't be allowed to go unpunished.

"There!" he snapped. "They've got a car now!"

"Yes, I see it," Humerya said.

"Shit! What's Eddie doing?"

Eddie Franks being his second in command for what had been envisioned as a relatively simple job. Follow the bitch from DEA, using a GPS tracking device that one of Scanlon's men had planted in or on her car, find out who she was meeting and take care of them.

Easy.

With twelve men on the job, it should've been like swatting gnats with a sledgehammer.

Now the whole damned thing had blown up in his face, and Scanlon had begun to worry that he couldn't make it right.

Scanlon was leaning forward in his seat, willing Humerya and their car to greater speed along the narrow crowded street, when someone in Deirdre Falk's car opened fire on Eddie Franks's Camry with an automatic weapon. Scanlon couldn't actually see it, but the rattling sound of a Kalashnikov was unmistakable.

Humerya seemed to flinch at the first sound of gunfire, then stomped on the Toyota's accelerator to compensate for his flicker of weakness. The Prius surged forward, sideswiping an aged pedestrian and leaving him sprawled in their wake, his packages scattered from curb to curb.

"Closer!" Scanlon barked at his driver. "Get me a shot!"

But that meant two lanes, at the very least, and Humerya couldn't widen Kabul's streets, regardless of his skill behind the wheel.

Humerya didn't answer Scanlon, but he kept his foot down, speeding on in hot pursuit of the Camry and Deirdre Falk's Ford. Whether he'd ever catch them was a question Humerya couldn't answer at the moment.

But he knew one thing beyond a shadow of a doubt.

He couldn't go back and report that he had failed, until he had exhausted every trick at his command.

THE FIRST BLAST from Matt Cooper's automatic rifle sounded like one of those 20 mm Gatling guns, inside the narrow confines of the vehicle. Deirdre Falk wished for earplugs but had none at hand, so she focused on driving the Ford like a bat out of hell.

She checked the rearview, trying to see if Cooper had scored any hits, but the chase cars were weaving as much as they could between vehicles parked on each side of the street, while the point car's shotgun rider tried to aim a weapon through his open window.

Cooper fired again, but Falk had to focus her gaze on the roadway ahead. She felt more than saw Barialy crouch in his seat to her right, his hideout revolver now clutched in his lap.

"Don't shoot yourself with that," she chided. "And for God's sake, don't shoot *me*."

"I won't," he promised, and forced a nervous laugh that could have been incipient hysteria.

Another burst from Cooper, as she made a sharp right turn and watched startled pedestrians scramble for safety. They would soon be leaving the Old City, roaring into the Chindawol district one of Kabul's poorest neighborhoods, where overcrowding and horrendous sanitation made cholera outbreaks a daily fact of life.

"Where are we going?" she asked Cooper, speaking to the rearview between bursts of autofire from the back window.

"You tell me," he countered.

"Not the office," she replied, thinking aloud. "And sure as hell not to the Ministry of Justice."

"No," he granted, and unleashed another short burst from his stolen SMG.

"We need to lose these guys and ditch this car, then find another one," she said.

"And pick up mine," he added. "All my gear is in the trunk."

"We're rolling into Chindawol," she told him. "That's a big-time slum, and Rika Khana is another one, just over Jadayi Maiwand. We won't find any decent rides there, but if we can dump these turkeys without winding up on foot, I know where we can make the switch."

"I'll do my best," Cooper replied, and fired another 4- or 5-round burst at their pursuers.

"Listen, Edris," Falk said to the man huddled beside her. "If we have to leave the car and separate, don't go back to your flat. Hear me? Somebody may be watching it."

"I hear you," Barialy said.

"And don't go wandering around the streets with that thing in your hand," she added.

"I am not a fool," he answered.

"Who told you to bring it with you, anyway?"

"Perhaps I had a premonition that we would be killed," the slim Afghan replied.

"Hilarious. You doing stand-up now?"

"Excuse me?"

"Never mind. Forget it. Just be careful where you're pointing that antique."

The city's odor changed as they drove into Chindawol, from market stalls and roasting meat to sewage and despair. The streets and sidewalks were as crowded as before, but not with vehicles, since virtually no one in the district could afford to buy a car or keep it running.

"What I need," Bolan announced, "is combat stretch."

"Say what?" Falk asked.

"Some room to move," he said. "At least to turn the car around, instead of leading a parade all over town."

"We've got some waste ground coming up," Falk said. "If we drive into it, I can't swear we'll get out again."

Bolan considered that for something like a second and a half, then told her, "Try it, anyway."

"Okay. It's a half mile up ahead."

The rearview showed her Cooper switching auto weapons as the first ran out of ammunition. Thirty rounds left, she surmised, and they were back to pistols. Against six or eight Kalashnikovs.

Better to end it while they had a chance.

If they still had a chance.

One last stand, coming up.

Falk focused on the road again, watching for vacant lots ahead and praying that she hadn't missed her turn.

SCANLON HAD TRIED a long shot through his open window, knowing it was risky, but he couldn't pull it off. It wasn't shooting with his left hand that defeated him—he'd trained himself to become nearly ambidextrous with weapons—but the weaving, rocking motion of his car and the obstruction of the Camry traveling in front of him.

Last thing I freaking need, he thought, is shooting Eddie or one of his people.

Scanlon ducked back inside the Prius, spitting road grit or some kind of garbage that was thrown up by the two cars running hot and fast ahead of him. He didn't even want to think about the garbage that was dumped in Kabul's gutters every day, or how a person actually inhaled tiny particles of everything he smelled.

It was enough to make him envy the people who lived in plastic bubbles, isolated from the outside world until something broke down and they died like fish out of water, gasping for air.

Another burst of AK fire erupted from the DEA Ford, and this time Scanlon nearly mastered the involuntary flinch that came with it. They're not shooting at me, he reminded himself. It's on Eddie.

But still…

The bastards *would* be shooting at him, if they had a chance, and if anything happened to Eddie, Scanlon's ass was next on the line.

"I need a better angle," he announced, already knowing that his driver couldn't manage it. The streets of Chindawol were so damned narrow, shops and housing crowded on both sides, that vehicles could only pass each other by mounting the sidewalk and threatening lives.

And even then, he knew it wouldn't be enough. There'd still be people in his way—at least, until the Prius flattened them—and he'd still have a moving target.

Need to stop that, he decided.

Scanlon palmed his cell phone, hit Eddie's number on speed dial, waited through two agonizing rings, then started barking orders as soon as he made the connection.

"Take out the driver!" he snapped. "If you can't do that, blow the tires!"

He cut the link before Eddie could answer or object that he was trying. *Trying* was a lame excuse that losers used to cover up inadequacy. So far, it hadn't lodged in his vocabulary.

A woman chose that moment, God knew why, to dart in front of the Toyota. Scanlon felt a surge of panic as her clothing fanned across the windshield, momentarily blinding him and his driver. Farid Humerya dealt with it efficiently, giving the wheel a little twist that jigged the car from left to right and dumped her at the curb.

It seemed to energize the driver, somehow, and Humerya put his full weight on the gas pedal, running up close behind the Camry.

If the lead car crashed now, could they stop in time?

Scanlon clutched the AKSU in his lap and offered silent prayers to a long-forgotten God.

THE PROBLEM WITH A RUNNING firefight was, of course, the running. Moving while you fired shots at a target that was also moving, maybe even shooting back, could spoil the most experienced marksman's aim. Throw in civilians by the dozen, ambling around downrange, and it became a soldier's nightmare.

"How much longer to that waste ground?" Bolan asked his driver.

"One block," Falk replied. "I see it now."

"Pull off, if you can, and turn around. We'll make them come to us."

"Okay," she said. "But if we get stuck—"

"First things first," he interrupted her.

"Got it."

And Bolan's first thing was one more attempt to slow the leading chase car's progress. Lining up his sights before the Camry's shotgun rider could unload on him, Bolan pumped three rounds through the Toyota's radiator.

"Here we go!" Falk warned, and then the Ford was swerving to her left, jumping a broken curb of sorts and bouncing over the topography of a large vacant lot.

Bolan had no idea if shops and houses once had stood there, or if it was undeveloped all along, nor did he care. His eyes picked out the mounds of rubbish dumped by passersby and neighbors, some still smoldering where they'd been set afire the previous night or by sometime in the recent past.

It was a little glimpse of hell on Earth, and kids were *playing* there, or maybe hunting rats. They scattered as the

Ford snarled toward them, with the Camry losing speed now in pursuit, a Prius bringing up the rear.

Bolan kept watching while he could, as Falk raced halfway across the lot, then worked wheel and brake through a sliding 180 that placed them between two looming piles of garbage, facing back the way they'd come through clouds of settling dust. He saw the Toyotas separate, one going right, the other limping to his left before it stalled. Doors opened, gunners spilled out.

Bolan did likewise, warning Falk and Barialy, "Use whatever cover you can find."

With Barialy's nerve untested and his skill unknown, Bolan treated the odds as four to one. It could be worse.

Would Bolan's enemies be edgy, since he'd dropped one-third of them in nothing flat, before they'd fired a shot? Or would it make them more determined to exact revenge? He could have tossed a coin on that one, but there wasn't time.

Bolan went to his left, saw Barialy trailing Falk off to the right, around the other garbage Matterhorn, and wished them well. His pile of cast-off junk was ten or twelve feet high, which seemed to be the norm. It smelled of dust and something rotten that he couldn't place, offhand.

Gunshots rang out behind him, but he couldn't focus on that now, much less retreat to help Falk and her agent. They were on their own, while Bolan faced the Camry's crew.

He heard one of them coming for him. Or was it only one? Footsteps on loose dirt could deceive the ear, and Bolan tried his hand at mind-reading, hoping that he could reason out what his opponents would do next.

Split up and flank the garbage pile from both sides? Send a man to check the Ford, and then circle around behind Bolan or Falk? The one thing he was reasonably sure they wouldn't do was scale the garbage piles, going for higher ground.

Two men suddenly appeared in front of him, both swarthy

Afghanis, looking startled. Bolan fired on instinct, from the hip, and caught the nearest shooter with a rising 3-round burst to the chest. The guy went down, while his companion bolted, ducking out of sight and shouting what could only be a warning in some language Bolan didn't recognize.

Damn it!

Now he would have to track the others down, while they were hunting him.

And hope that this time Death was on his side.

RED SCANLON LET THE OTHERS go ahead of him. He wasn't frightened, but he wasn't crazy, either. He had paid Farid Humerya and the others for their services that day, and so far all they'd done was ride through Kabul.

It was time they earned their money.

He'd been quick enough to see the Ford's three occupants bail out, knew two of them by sight but still had no name for the third. With any luck, he would be taking ID from the stranger's corpse before much longer, and he could deliver it to headquarters for further research.

Any thought of bringing Falk and her companions in alive had vanished when the unknown shooter took out four of Scanlon's men, then tried to do the same with Eddie Franks and his three backups. Falk and her Afghani stooge would have been killed, in any case, but now all three had to die without being subjected to interrogation.

Never mind.

By killing them, Scanlon would either cauterize the threat or, at the very least, require his boss's enemies to start again from scratch, inserting new players into Kabul. And when the new players arrived, they would find Scanlon and his people waiting for them.

There was too much money on the table to permit the DEA's fumbling investigation to proceed. Perhaps he should have killed Falk earlier—it was debated at the time, then shelved in favor of approaching her superiors with bribes— and next time Scanlon would be ready.

Even if he had to act alone.

But he'd take care of this mess first.

Gunfire, away beyond two mounds of garbage to his right, distracted Scanlon from the hunt for all of two heartbeats. He never lost focus completely—he was too good at his job for that to happen—but he had to wonder whether Franks had met the enemy or if his men were firing at shadows.

Scanlon lost sight of Farid Humerya as his driver moved around the garbage heap, scuttling after the point men Scanlon had dispatched ahead of them. He almost called Humerya back, then bit his tongue.

The more the merrier, if they ran into trouble.

And, as if in answer to his thoughts, there came a rapid *pop-pop-pop* of pistol fire. Nine-millimeter, by the sound of it, but swiftly joined by something heavier, maybe a .45. A strangled cry of pain raised Scanlon's hackles as he waited for Kalashnikovs to answer the challenge.

And heard nothing.

Three down, that quickly? Was it even possible?

Hell, yes, he thought. In combat, damn near anything was possible.

Scanlon reviewed his options, listening to autofiring from the second, farther garbage heap, and made his choice. Someone had to survive this fucked-up set and carry word to headquarters, or it was all in vain.

Cursing and flushed with shame, he turned and ran back toward his car.

BOLAN MIGHT HAVE chased his three remaining enemies around the garbage heap all afternoon, but the retreating shooters met someone who put steel in their backbones, snapping orders at them in a fair approximation of demonic rage.

"Where do you think you're going, damn it?" stormed the unseen man in charge. "Both of you get your yellow asses back in there and fight!"

It could have been a trick to stall him, keep him waiting while they circled to his rear and came up on his blind side, but he didn't think so. There'd been too much anger in the loud, commanding American voice. If that was fake, the speaker ought to take home an acting award for Best Performance by a Heavy Under Fire.

So, Bolan waited. Kneeling in the shadow of the refuse mountain, hard against it on his right, he sighted down the barrel of second hot Kalashnikov and covered the approach that was their only way to reach him from the front. He counted the seconds, feeling sweat bead on his forehead and begin the slow crawl downward toward unblinking eyes.

Two of them came at him together. Bolan recognized the leader as the one who got away, and saw that he was none too thrilled about returning to the fight. His leading adversary clutched an AK in a white-knuckled death grip. The second in line was almost duck-walking, crouched to present the smallest possible target.

Bolan gave the first one two rounds through the chest, punching him back into his waddling companion. Both fell together, the live one struggling to extricate himself from the other's deadweight. Bolan waited until he'd almost reached his feet again, raising his gun, then shot him in the neck, with one more through the face to make it stick.

And now, a cautious rush to find the one who gave the orders, wondering if he would stand and fight or cut and run. Would pride outweigh the man's survival instincts when it counted?

Bolan heard the sound of heavy footsteps crunching toward

him, froze in place and had his shot lined up before the husky target stepped into his line of fire. The face and accent of his speech made him American, though Bolan couldn't place where he'd been born and raised.

No matter. He was dying here.

A 3-round burst surprised the mercenary, dropped him on his backside in the dust with an amazed expression on his face. He clearly hadn't planned to die that afternoon, but now he had no choice.

It took a moment for the dead man to collapse backward, and by the time he'd managed it, Bolan could hear an engine revving on the far side of the garbage mountain. Snatching up the merc's AKSU, he ran around the pile and was in time to see the Prius barrel across the waste ground, toward the street.

Bolan fired after it, peppered the trunk and took out half of the rear window, but the car kept going. He had missed the driver, and a sharp left turn at the next intersection put his target out of range.

"I missed him, too," Falk said, approaching with her Glock in hand.

"And I," Barialy added, sounding glum.

"It was his lucky day," Bolan replied. "And ours, too."

"He'll report back to the man," Falk said.

"No doubt," Bolan replied. "While he's running, we can ditch the Ford, pick up another ride. And then, we need to talk."

# CHAPTER THREE

*Chesapeake Bay, Two Days Earlier*

Standing on the dock at Tilghman, Maryland, Mack Bolan felt as if he had gone back in time, not merely to some past familiar day but to a bygone century. The ticket in his hand entitled him to one two-hour cruise aboard the skipjack *Rebecca T. Ruark,* departing at 11:00 a.m. and returning at 1:00 p.m.

It might as well have been a time machine.

When Hal Brognola had proposed the cruise, suggesting that a sail would grant them maximum security, Bolan had not known what a skipjack was. He'd looked it up online, discovering that it was a type of nineteenth-century sailboat, developed by fishermen on Chesapeake Bay for oyster dredging. Despite modern advances in technology, the boats remained in service because Maryland state law banned use of powerboats for oyster fishing.

The *Rebecca T. Ruark,* built in 1886, was a classic skipjack, with its V-shaped wooden hull, low-slung freeboard and square stern. A dredge windlass and its small motor—the only mechanical engine aboard—were mounted amidships, but conversion of the ship to tourist cruises had given the Chesapeake's oysters a long, welcome respite.

Bolan boarded with a dozen other passengers and made a brief walking tour of the ship—all fifty-three feet of it—trying to forget that a freak storm had sunk it in 1999, trusting that its owners had refurbished the vessel and kept it seaworthy since then.

If not, he reckoned he could swim to shore from any point where they went down, but Bolan had his doubts about Brognola.

Speaking of Hal, where was he? They had five minutes before the ship set sail, and if the man from Justice had been stuck in traffic or distracted by some crisis, Bolan was about to waste two hours on the briny deep.

He spent the time remaining in a futile bid to read the big Fed's mind. Brognola often presented mission briefings at Stony Man Farm, in Virginia's Blue Ridge Mountains, or on walking tours of Arlington National Cemetery. The vast graveyard of heroes offered ample solitude, and with the exception of a single disastrous lapse, Bolan had never questioned the security at Stony Man.

"Too many ears around these days," Brognola had explained, without really explaining anything. "A sail sounds good."

And so it had. Bolan had no problem with seasickness, no fear of open water or the gliding predators that it concealed. A cruise had sounded fine…but he still wondered why the change in their routine was necessary.

*Ears,* of course, meant *spies*—but whose?

The Department of Homeland Security had risen from the 9/11 rubble, tasked with coordinating intelligence collection and defense against all manner of enemies, both domestic and foreign. It was supposed to end the age-old bickering and backstabbing that put the CIA at odds with FBI and NSA, and sparked unhealthy feuds among the several branches of the U.S. military.

Note the qualifying phrase *supposed to.*

In reality, no branch or bureau of the government had ever given one inch to a rival without bitter resistance, sometimes verging on mutiny. Bolan knew, as a matter of fact, that tension was rife throughout all of America's intelligence and security agencies, each on tenterhooks from fear of another terrorist raid—and each determined to expose that plot, whatever it might be, before "the other guys" could vie for a share of the glory.

It was the same old story, made potentially more dangerous by the official mask of peaceable cooperation that concealed the dissidence and subterfuge within.

But was it what Brognola had in mind?

Or was there something—*someone*—else?

One minute left until the ship cast off, and Bolan had begun to think that the big Fed was cutting it too close for his own good. A panting sprint along the dock would only call attention to him—which, presumably, was the last thing Brognola wanted.

Bolan drifted to the dockside rail, shook hands in passing with the ship's captain and settled into the countdown.

If Brognola did not appear, he had a choice: jump ship and eat the thirty-dollar ticket's cost, or take the cruise alone and hope that his old friend was waiting for him when the skipjack berthed again. He had his cell phone, for a point of contact, but a ship-to-shore briefing made absolutely no sense to him, when a thousand different listeners could snatch their words out of thin air.

With forty seconds left, a black sedan appeared and coasted to a stop at the far end of the dock. Bolan saw Brognola exit the shotgun seat, dressed in a sport shirt, nylon windbreaker and jeans, surmounted by a shapeless fishing hat, with size-twelve deck shoes on his feet.

Compared to Brognola's habitual dark suits, it might as well have been a clown costume, but Bolan realized that no one else aboard the ship would notice the discrepancy. Hal was a total stranger to them all, and dressing in his normal Brooks Brothers' attire would have raised caution flags among his fellow travelers.

The big Fed didn't sprint along the pier. Rather, he walked "with purpose," as the drill instructors used to say in boot camp, and he reached the gangway just as crewmen were prepared to take it up. He muttered an aw-shucks apology for being late, which was dismissed with airy smiles.

Eye contact from the dock told Bolan that Brognola knew exactly where to find him. They would seem to meet by accident, fall into casual discussion of the ship, the bay, whatever, and conduct their business at a distance from the other passengers who jammed the rails or lingered near the loudspeakers to catch the captain's commentary.

No unwanted ears aboard the skipjack, unless some demonic master of disguise had learned Brognola's plan and come aboard with Bolan and the other passengers who'd paid their fares at dockside.

The big Fed waited for the lines to be cast off and let the vessel find its course before he drifted toward Bolan, walking with hands in pockets, still testing his sea legs.

"Nice day for it," he said.

"Seems like," Bolan agreed.

"I'd buy a round of drinks, but the sloop's BYOB."

"Skipjack," Bolan corrected him.

"What's the difference?"

"Sloops were warships, intermediate in size between a corvette and a frigate," Bolan said.

"You live and learn."

"With any luck."

"I haven't been out on a boat in years," Brognola said. "I used to like it, but you own one, it's a money pit. As far as friends go, I felt like a barnacle, you know? Just going along for the ride. Anyway, who's got the time?"

"And yet…" Bolan replied.

"You're wondering why this, instead of meeting at the Farm?"

"It crossed my mind," Bolan admitted.

Brognola nodded, his shoulders slumping just a bit.

"I may be getting paranoid," he said. "But you know what they say, right?"

"Just because you're paranoid—" Bolan began the old slogan.

"It doesn't mean nobody's out to get you."

"Right."

"So, this is *delicate,*" Brognola said. "I thought a little extra buffer couldn't hurt. Hey, if I'm wrong, we're only out a couple hours and sixty bucks."

"Okay."

Brognola scrutinized the other passengers, as far as possible, then said, "Let's head back toward the stern."

They made the shift, and no one followed them.

"Okay," he said at last. "What do you know about a group called Vanguard International?"

"They do private security worldwide," Bolan replied, "on top of various government contracts. They guard oilfields, corporate offices—anything, anywhere, from what I understand."

"Assuming that the customer can pay their going rates," Brognola said.

"I didn't think it was a charity."

"I guess you've heard about the controversy in Iraq?"

"Only what CNN reported," Bolan said.

He was aware that three Vanguard employees had been kidnapped and executed on camera by Iraqi terrorists in 2005. A few weeks later, Vanguard commandos had raided an Iraqi village said to be hometown of the kidnap team's ringleader, gunning down three dozen unarmed men, women and children. An FBI investigation found that the victims were slain "without cause," but Iraqi officials and State Department spokesmen mutually ruled out any criminal charges.

Some people wondered why.

"Well, what they ran was the tip of the iceberg," Brognola said. "We've got allegations of Third World gun-running, and half of the UN is up in arms over supposed violations of the Mercenary Convention."

"Makes sense," Bolan said.

He couldn't quote chapter and verse from the International Convention against the Recruitment, Use, Financing and Training of Mercenaries, approved by the UN's General Assembly in 1989, but he understood the gist of it. The declaration defined mercs as private soldiers recruited expressly for profit and condemned their employment either in general warfare or for specific projects, such as toppling governments. Companies like Vanguard and its handful of competitors skirted the rules by posing as "security consultants," or simply ignored the UN's declaration in full knowledge that it was a toothless order, virtually unenforceable.

How could the UN stop America, Britain, or any other country from hiring private troops to guard facilities abroad? And if those "guards" should run amok, committing acts that qualified as war crimes if performed by soldiers of a sovereign state, what was the legal remedy?

In Vanguard's case, apparently, there wasn't one.

"We wouldn't normally concern ourselves with anything like this," Brognola said. "Hell, Stony Man was founded to reach out and touch the bad guys when the law can't do it. And the gun-running, that falls to State or Treasury, if either one of them decides it's worth their time."

"So, what, then?" Bolan asked his oldest living friend.

"So, heroin," Brognola said.

"Explain."

"You know we keep track of the traffic, right?"

Bolan nodded, waiting for the rest.

"Well, what you may not know is that Afghanistan surpassed Turkey in heroin production during the nineties. In 1999, the Afghanis had 350 square miles of opium poppies under cultivation, with smack refineries running around the clock. A year later, the Taliban moves in and takes control of the country, declaring the drug trade 'un-Islamic.' Whatever else we think of them, hiding Osama, treating their women like slaves and the rest, they reduced Afghan poppy cultivation by ninety-odd percent in one year, down to thirty square miles in 2001."

"What's the bad news?" Bolan asked.

"That would be 9/11," Brognola replied. "Down come the towers in New York, and we invade Afghanistan. Boot out the Taliban and supervise elections. Never mind missing Bin Laden. Anyone can have a bad day, right? Or eight bad years? The trouble is, that with the Taliban deposed, the drug trade started up again, big-time."

"So I heard. But, what's the most recent data?"

"Right now, opium cultivation is back up to three hundred square miles and climbing. The UN's International Narcotics Control Board says Afghanistan produced 3,500 tons of heroin last year, up from 185 tons in 2001. That's an increase of nearly two thousand percent. Scotland Yard says nearly all the heroin in Britain comes from Afghanistan now. They've frozen out the China white and Turkish product, underselling their competitors because they deal in bulk. It isn't quite that bad, stateside, but I can promise you, we're getting there."

"I'll take your word for it," Bolan said. "But where does Vanguard come into the picture?"

"It's looking more and more like they may *be* the picture," Brognola replied. "Or, anyway, the transport side of it."

"I'm listening."

"They aren't just in Iraq, okay? That little blow-up got the company its first global publicity, but they've got outposts everywhere you go. Saudi Arabia. Bangkok. Jakarta. Take your pick."

"Afghanistan," Bolan said.

"Almost from the start, back in 2001," Brognola said. "They weren't front-line, but they moved in behind the coalition troops, guarding oil pipelines, corporate HQs and CEOs, the usual. And somewhere in the middle of all that, we think they hooked up with the poppy growers and refiners."

"When you say *we think,* that means…?"

"We know," Brognola said. "We have surveillance tapes of Vanguard personnel guarding the opium plantations, running convoys on drug shipments, piloting some of the planes."

"So, lock them up and shut it down," Bolan replied.

"Ah, that's the rub," Brognola said. "So far, nobody's caught them with a shipment anywhere in U.S. jurisdiction, or in Britain. They've been able to evade surveillance for the hand-offs, and they let the buyers run with it from there— wherever *there* is, for a given load."

"We must have pull inside Afghanistan," Bolan said. "With the Army, FBI and CIA in place? A president we basically appointed to replace the Taliban? You're telling me nobody can arrest drug dealers operating in plain sight?"

"It's all about 'democracy,' these days. Democracy and *appearances,* okay? Afghanistan was on the economic ropes when we moved in, back in 2001. The government, such as it was, was drowning in red ink and weird religious proclamations from the Taliban. Now they're on track again—or seem to be—but tossing out the zealots left a vacuum. And who fills it? The same characters who were in charge before the Taliban started its holy war. Oil men and heroin producers. The DEA calls it a 'heroin economy.' I won't say that drug smugglers own the president, but draw your own conclusions."

"So the job is what, exactly?" Bolan asked.

"We can't wipe out the poppy farms or the refineries," Brognola answered. "No one can, unless the Afghans managed to elect a government that's more concerned with law and common decency than profit."

Bolan smiled ruefully and said, "Good luck with that."

"Meanwhile, we need to shut down our part of the pipeline. Vanguard's crossed the line, but we can't touch them legally. Between the jurisdiction thing and their connections from Kabul to Washington, arrests aren't happening."

"Connections," Bolan said. "Whose toes will I be stepping on?"

"Vanguard has friends in Congress and around the Pentagon," Brognola replied. "They serve huge corporations, which means lobbyists are at their beck and call. As far as opposition on the ground, watch out for people from the Company."

Bolan suppressed a grimace. Elements within the CIA had dealt with organized criminals from the Agency's inception in 1947. Espionage was a dirty business, but some of the CIA's allies were filthy beyond redemption: French heroin smugglers in the late 1940s and early '50s, Asian traffickers during the Vietnam War, and South American cocaine cartels throughout the Contra mess in Nicaragua. Each time they were caught, the spooks cried "national security" and vowed that they would never touch another load of contraband.

In each and every case, they lied.

"I see a problem going in," Bolan remarked.

"Which is?"

"I'll need a guide, interpreter, whatever," he replied. "We

usually use a native who's been working for the Company. But if they're on the other side, this time…"

"You're covered," Brognola replied. "The DEA's been working overtime on this. In fact, most of the information I've just given you came straight from them. One of their agents will provide a native contractor to meet your needs."

"We're in the middle of a bureaucratic civil war, then," Bolan said.

"No one in Washington will ever call it that," Brognola stated. "Vanguard's the target. Do it right, there'll be some backroom grumbling, but no politician's going public to defend drug smugglers who've already been accused of killing innocent civilians. They can spin the killings seven ways from Sunday, but there's no way to explain shipments of heroin."

"And if the Company steps in?"

"Wrong place, wrong time," Brognola said. "Do what you have to do. They bury their mistakes. It's one thing they know how to do."

"I'll need more background on the targets," Bolan said.

Brognola took a CD in a plastic jewel case from an inside pocket of his windbreaker and handed it to Bolan on the down-low.

"Everything's on there," he said. "Including info on your DEA contact. Just wipe it when you're done, as usual."

"I'll check it out tonight," Bolan replied, and made the CD disappear into a pocket of his own. "When do I leave?"

"Sooner the better," Hal replied. "You'll have to fly commercial, I'm afraid. A charter where you're going raises too damn many eyebrows, but the CD has some addresses in Kabul where you can pick up tools of the trade. In fact, from what I hear, guns are the one thing in Afghanistan that's easier to find than heroin. Come one, come all."

"So, it's Dodge City in the middle of a bureaucratic civil war."

Brognola smiled. "Picture Colombia, devoid of any self-restraint."

"Sounds like a blast," Bolan replied.

As PROMISED, the CD contained all of the information Bolan needed, and then some. There was a capsule history of opium and heroin production in Afghanistan, spanning the period from British domination in the nineteenth century, through Russian occupation, modern civil wars, up to the present day. Bolan skimmed over it and focused chiefly on the maps and satellite photos depicting known heroin trade routes.

The background on Vanguard International demanded his closer attention. The company had been founded in 1995 by present owner-CEO Clay Carlisle and a partner, improbably named Thomas Jefferson, who had dropped out of sight after selling his shares to Carlisle in August 2001. Carlisle was the undisputed king of Vanguard, fielding a private army larger than those deployed by some Third World nations.

As for Carlisle himself, he was the son of a self-ordained evangelical minister, born in 1964, who had graduated "with honors" from an unaccredited parochial high school, then volunteered for the U.S. Marine Corps and served with distinction in Grenada. After eight years in the Corps, he'd pulled the pin and entered corporate security as a hired bodyguard. In 1994 he'd shot it out with kidnappers who tried to snatch his client—a Texas oil billionaire—and had suffered a near-fatal wound in the firefight. The grateful client, who emerged unscathed, was pleased to bankroll Carlisle in creation of his own security firm, Vanguard, which claimed the oilman's vast empire as its first client.

And the rest, as someone said, was history.

An odd footnote to Carlisle's dossier described his fat donations to various far-right religious groups and his membership on the board of Hallelujah Ministries, which sponsored revival meetings and kept a small staff of attorneys on retainer to defend ministers "falsely accused" of various crimes, including embezzlement and child molestation. At a private Hallelujah gathering in 2002, Carlisle had described the 9/11 raids as "proof that the Second Coming will occur in our lifetime."

How all of that squared with drug smuggling was anyone's guess.

Carlisle's second in command was Dale Ingram, a twenty-five-year FBI veteran who had ended his run as chief of the Bureau's Counterterrorism Division. September 11 had caught Ingram and his G-men by surprise, despite warnings from several FBI field offices that Arab nationals with suspected ties to al Qaeda were training at U.S. flight schools. Whistleblowers produced memos bearing Ingram's signature, dismissing the warnings as "red herrings," whereupon he was invited to retire two years ahead of schedule. Meanwhile, he had become acquainted with Carlisle through contacts still unknown, and Ingram found retirement from the Bureau very lucrative indeed.

If smuggling heroin into the States bothered the former G-man, he had learned to conceal any qualms. In fact, judging from the photos Brognola and Stony Man had supplied, Ingram seemed to be laughing all the way to the bank.

Bolan scanned the reports of Vanguard mercenaries seen on Afghan opium plantations and convoying heroin shipments. The CD included numerous photos and several video clips—one of Carlisle and Ingram together at a Kabul hotel, meeting a native identified as Basir Ahmad-Shah.

Ahmad-Shah's CD-ROM dossier identified him as one of Afghanistan's four largest heroin kingpins. Within his territory, he enjoyed a vertical monopoly, from poppy fields through processing and export from the country. He had agents scattered all over the world, but Ahmad-Shah himself had never left Afghanistan, as far as anyone could say. Imprisoned briefly by the Taliban in 2001, he'd been released and lauded as a "prisoner of conscience" after coalition troops drove his persecutors from Kabul and environs. His number two was a cut-throat named Jamal Woraz, identified by the DEA as Ahmad-Shah's strong right hand and primary enforcer.

That left the file on Bolan's DEA contact, one Deirdre Falk. Bolan had worked with female Feds before and found them more than capable, but he was still a bit surprised to find a woman stationed in Afghanistan, where brutal violence was a daily fact of life and male officials of the Islamic Republic were predisposed to treat females with a measure of disdain.

The good news was that she'd been handling it for nearly three years now, and showed no signs of cracking up. She'd built some solid cases, although only one of them had gone to trial so far, sending a second-string drug smuggler off to prison for three years. The big boys were protected, and Falk had to know it.

Which perhaps explained why she was willing to collaborate with Stony Man—or the organization "Matt Cooper" said he represented.

There was no reason to suppose she'd ever heard of Stony Man Farm or the covert work it performed. If she *had,* then the Farm's security needed a major tune-up. The flip side of that coin might be shock, when she realized that Bolan hadn't come from Washington to help her put the Vanguard gang on trial.

Officially, the U.S. government did not engage in down-and-dirty vigilante tactics. Since the 1960s, when the CIA's clumsy attempts to kill Fidel Castro had backfired with disastrous, embarrassing results, no federal agency was authorized to carry out "executive actions"—otherwise known as assassinations.

Scratch that.

No agency was *publicly* authorized to do so.

Stony Man had been created expressly to do that which was forbidden. A former President, beset by enemies on every side, domestic and foreign, had realized that every nation had to defend itself, by fair means or foul. When the system broke down, when the law failed, clear and present dangers had to be neutralized by other means.

Deniability was critical.

If Bolan or some other Stony Man agent—the troops of Able Team and Phoenix Force—were killed on a mission at home or abroad, they did not officially exist.

If worse came to worst, if one of them was caught alive and cracked under torture or chemical interrogation, providing verifiable details of Stony Man's operations, the buck stopped with Hal Brognola at Justice. He'd been prepared from the start to fall on his sword, confess to launching and running the program on his own initiative, financing it covertly, without the knowledge or approval of superiors.

It was a fairy tale that might be hard to swallow, but the Washington publicity machine would sell it anyway. The corporate media—so far from "leftist liberal" that Bolan had to laugh each time he heard the talking heads on Fox News rant and rave—would ultimately join ranks with the state to cover any tracks that led beyond Brognola's office to respected politicians higher up the food chain.

The trick, on Bolan's part, was not to get captured or killed. So far, he'd managed fairly well.

And this time?

As he started to erase Brognola's CD-ROM, he knew that he would have to wait and see.

# CHAPTER FOUR

*Kabul, Afghanistan*

They ditched Falk's bullet-punctured Ford near the Park-e-Timor Shahi, on the River Rudkhane-ye-Kabul, and found another waiting two blocks over, thanks to one of Falk's associates who asked no questions when she'd called him on the telephone.

"The other one will be reported stolen," she told Bolan as they drove across the city to a safe house in the Shash Darak district.

"You've done this kind of thing before?" he asked.

"We're living on the edge, here, Mr. Cooper. No one really wants us in Afghanistan. We get that message from the beat cops, right on up the ladder to the president."

"Which one?" Bolan inquired.

She smiled at that and told him, "Take your pick. Ours has to talk about the 'evil scourge of heroin' to get elected, but I swear, sometimes it feels like it's *all* talk." She frowned, then added, "Hey, forget I said that, will you? I still need this job, and I don't even know who sent you."

"Someone who agrees with you and wants to make a difference."

"Well, anyway, we gave someone a wake-up call," she said.

"They knew where we were meeting," Bolan countered. "How do you suppose that happened?"

"Damned if I know. I could swear I wasn't followed, and I'd guess Edris will say the same."

"Indeed," Barialy said from the backseat. "I was very careful, following all necessary steps of tradecraft."

Tradecraft?

The last time Bolan could remember hearing that was in a movie from the late eighties.

He let it slide and asked Falk, "Do your people sweep their cars?"

"We do," she said. "But that's not saying someone couldn't slip a homer past us. It would mean access to the secure motor pool, but with Vanguard, anything's possible."

"And will this car have been checked?" he asked.

"You put it that way, I can't swear to anything," Falk answered.

"Then we need a rental office, stat."

"Jesus. Okay, I know a couple places we can go. I've got a credit card, and—"

"This one is on me," Bolan said. "If you're under a sophisticated shadow, using plastic is like sending up a flare."

"Shit!" she said. "Do you always shake things up this way?"

"It wouldn't be the first time," he replied.

Falk found an auto rental agency and Barialy went inside with Bolan, translating his bid for a midsize four-door sedan. They left with a Toyota Avalon, rented by Bolan in his alternate identity as Brandon Stone. The Visa Platinum he used was paid in full and had a $20,000 credit line.

"No tail on this one," Bolan said as he slid in behind the steering wheel. "About that safe house, now…"

"You're thinking that it might not be so safe," Falk said.

"It crossed my mind."

"All right. It's not the only place we have in Kabul, but if one of them is compromised, we can't trust any. Can we?"

"No."

"This sucks."

"Welcome to my world," Bolan said.

"Hey, mine was bad enough, thanks very much."

"The good news is, you have them worried," Bolan told her.

"Great. They want me dead now and they almost pulled it off, first try."

"It wasn't even close," Bolan replied.

"Were you and I at the same party?" Falk inquired. "They shot the hell out of my car."

"And we all walked away," Bolan reminded her. "Their side sent twelve men out to do a job and lost eleven. I'd say we're ahead."

"Except that now we're fugitives," she said.

"That's only if police are looking for you," Bolan said. "We're going underground. There *is* a difference."

"Care to explain it, Mr. Cooper?"

"Call me Matt, if you feel like it," Bolan said. "As for the difference, a fugitive is always running, hiding, constantly on the defensive. When you're underground, you have a chance to be proactive. Bring the war home to your enemies."

"When you say war—"

"I mean exactly that," Bolan replied. "The men who staked you out today were there to kill us. They don't know me, but they thought a public hit was worth the risk to keep you from revealing what you know to an outsider."

"Maybe it was just supposed to be a snatch, before you started shooting," she replied without conviction.

"What's the difference?" he asked. "You think they planned to warn you off or question you, then let you go?"

Instead of answering, Falk asked, "So, then, what's your plan?"

"I told you—take it to the enemy. Rattle their cages. Disrupt operations. Blow their house down."

Falk was staring at him now. "You mean, just go around and shoot them, like some kind of hit man?"

"I imagine there'll be more to it than that," Bolan replied. "But understand, before you take another step that I'm not here to serve warrants. You've already tried that route, and you can keep on trying if you like. Just tell me where to drop you off."

She spent another moment staring at him, then replied, "Screw that. I'm in."

"And you?" Bolan met Barialy's dark gaze in the rearview mirror.

"With misgivings," the Afghan said, "it appears that my best prospects for survival rest with you."

"Okay, then," Bolan said. "The first thing that we need to do is see about my gear."

*Vanguard International Branch Office, Kabul*

"LET ME GET THIS STRAIGHT. You ran away?"

Clay Carlisle's voice carried no hint of animosity, despite the seething anger that he felt inside, the acid churning in his stomach.

"I withdrew," Red Scanlon said, "and broke off contact with the enemy in order to report, so you would know what's happened, sir."

"I'd know when the police called me to view your body at the morgue," Carlisle replied.

"That wouldn't help you, sir. A corpse can't give you any information."

"Right, then. Enlighten me, by all means. Share the information that entitles you to leave your men behind."

"My men were dead before I left. I saw them drop."

"Dead, but identifiable," Carlisle replied. "You've put me in an awkward spot with Eddie Franks. I have to disavow him now, and *still* pay off his family to keep their damned mouths shut."

"I'm sorry, sir."

"I'm waiting," Carlisle said.

Scanlon swallowed, his Adam's apple bobbing, then pressed on. "I saw who Falk was meeting, sir. In fact, he set the whole thing off."

"Explain."

"Two of our men stepped up to brace him, and he shot them both, then popped two others in the car before they could defend themselves."

"He's no procrastinator, then."

"Some kind of pro, no question," Scanlon said. "He took a couple AKs from the first two that he dropped. Without that extra firepower, we would've had him, sir."

"I wonder." Carlisle studied Scanlon's face and said, "I understand that one of those this man of mystery gunned down in Shahr-e-Khone is still alive. Not talking, I presume?"

"He *can't* talk, sir. Shot in the face. I'm taking care of it."

"And this bitch from the DEA. We've found her car?"

"Abandoned, sir. The GPS tracker was still in place, but by the time I called up reinforcements—"

"She and her playmates had disappeared."

"Yes, sir. They got another Fed mobile then dropped that one after a couple miles. They're getting wise."

"I'd say they were already wise enough to run rings around you," Carlisle observed. "The question now is, whether you're entitled to a second chance, or if I ought to cut my losses. Starting with your throat."

Carlisle had no fear of the younger man seated across from him, with nothing but a teakwood desk between them. Scanlon was unarmed, defeated, a spent force. He also had to have known that any move against his boss would bring an armed security detachment charging into Carlisle's office through the door immediately to his left.

"I saw the shooter, sir. I can identify him, and you know I'm motivated."

"Motivation's good," Carlisle replied. "But he's already kicked your ass. You lost eleven men and barely got away alive. That kind of failure is expensive *and* embarrassing."

"Yes, sir," Scanlon replied through clenched teeth. "Let me make it up to you."

Carlisle considered it, then said, "Call me a sentimental fool. I'll give you one chance to clean up your mess, but use it well. And do it quickly. If you fail a second time, you would be well advised to die trying."

"Yes, sir!"

Scanlon rose from his chair, snapped to attention and saluted before leaving Carlisle's office. Carlisle watched him go and wondered if he'd made a critical mistake by letting Scanlon live.

No sweat.

That kind of error, if it was an error, could be easily corrected any time he had the urge. A simple order, and Scanlon would never see it coming.

More important at the moment was the task of covering his tracks and Vanguard's on the mess that Scanlon had created.

Carlisle would explain that he'd fired Eddie Franks for insubordination and produce back-dated paperwork to prove it, if push came to shove. As for the local talent, Eddie could have found them anywhere. There were no Vanguard payroll records for them, certainly no canceled checks or any other kind of paper trail.

His word would be accepted where it mattered. That was where the bribes Carlisle had paid to various Afghan officials—and his contacts at the U.S. embassy in Kabul—served their purpose. He was an established man of substance, with connections all the way from Afghanistan's Republican Palace to Pennsylvania Avenue, and adversaries who forgot that did so at their peril.

There was nothing for Carlisle to worry about.

Not just yet.

*Shahr-e-Khone, Kabul*

THE RENTAL CAR with Bolan's hardware stashed inside was lost to him. He knew it when he reached the parking lot where he had left it, in the Old City, and found police milling about like ants on spilled sugar. He waited long enough to see one of them exit with a heavy duffel bag he recognized, then put the Avalon in gear and drove away, not looking back.

"I guess you're short on gear now," Falk suggested.

"Not for long," Bolan replied.

He couldn't use the same dealer again, in case the cops had traced his hardware or were on their way to doing so, but Brognola and Stony Man had given him directions to four weapons merchants in Kabul, trusting Bolan to find alternatives if all of those went sour.

And as Hal had told him, there was never any hardware shortage in Afghanistan.

He skipped the second armorer on Brognola's list, no clear reason other than gut instinct, and went on to number three. The dealer's cover was a pawnshop in the Shar-e-Naw district, near the intersection of streets called Shararah and Shar Ali Khan. It meant driving back across town, to the northwest quarter, but the trip gave Bolan time to question Deirdre Falk in more detail.

He learned that she'd been tracking Vanguard's operation for a year and change, collecting evidence that no one in authority would take time to review. Her boss in Kabul was a thirty-year man with the DEA who faced compulsory retirement in the fall, and he encouraged her to forge ahead, while warning Falk that he could not protect her, short of sending her back to the States.

So much for the omnipotence of Uncle Sam.

She still seemed ill at ease with Bolan's plan of action, not that he'd provided any details, but he thought she'd keep her word and go along.

If not…well, she could pull the pin and split at any time, unless the heavies took her down.

He found the dealer's shop and made a drive-by, trusting Falk and Barialy to help him spot anything odd, out of synch. They told him that the busy street looked normal, so he found a parking place and all three of them walked back to the shop.

Inside, a man who looked like Gandhi with a port wine birthmark on the left side of his face greeted them enthusiastically. He introduced himself as Izat Khan and listened carefully as Barialy translated for Bolan, spelling out his needs and specifying that the payment would be made in cash.

If dealing with a group of total strangers bothered Khan, he didn't let it show. Smiling, he locked the front door to his shop, reversed a dangling sign—presumably changing Open to Closed—and led them through a screen of softly clacking plastic beads to reach a storeroom at the back.

Bolan saw no weapons in evidence, and had already braced himself to shoot his way out of a trap, when Khan opened a door in the west wall, revealing stairs that vanished into darkness. Finding a switch beside the door jamb, he illuminated bright fluorescent fixtures that revealed a spacious basement. The familiar scent of gun oil wafted up to Bolan's nostrils from below.

Bolan let Khan go first, followed by Barialy, then himself,

with Deirdre Falk watching their backs. He no longer suspected that police or Vanguard mercs had found the shop ahead of him, but there was still a chance that Khan might plan to double-cross these strangers who had showed up without warning on his doorstep.

In the dealer's spotless basement, guns were mounted on the walls and racked in standing rows across the floor, with crates of ammunition, magazines, grenades, and other such accessories positioned like the specials in a supermarket. Bolan took his time, examining Khan's wares, and told Falk she could pick out something for herself, to supplement the Glock.

At length, bearing in mind that he couldn't predict what situations might still lay ahead of them, Bolan chose a range of weapons suitable for all occasions.

They already had the captured AKSU automatic rifles, but he took a third one, plus spare magazines, and stocked up on the 5.45 mm ammunition they devoured. With distance work in mind, he also chose a 7.62 mm Dragunov SVD sniping rifle, fitted with a Russian PSO-1 scope whose features included an elevation adjustment knob for bullet-drop compensation, an illuminated range-finder grid, a reticle that permitted target acquisition in low-light conditions, and an infrared charging screen that served as a passive detection system. He found spare 10-round magazines for the Dragunov, and picked up more 9 mm Parabellum ammo for his pistol. While he was at it, he added hand grenades for balance.

Bolan reckoned that he was done, then changed his mind and selected a 40 mm MGL grenade launcher, the South African spring-driven, double-action weapon that resembled an inflated 1920s Tommy gun. The launcher measured twenty-eight inches with its folding stock collapsed and weighed thirteen pounds empty. Its revolving 6-round cylinder could launch two rounds per second in rapid-fire, with an effective range of four hundred yards. To cover all eventualities, Bolan picked out a mix of HE, thermite, smoke and triple-aught buckshot rounds for the launcher.

Falk was prepared to settle for the second AKSU rifle, then decided Barialy might need it to supplement his vintage wheelgun, so she chose a mini-Uzi for herself, with a suppressor and a stack of 32-round magazines, plus more 9 mm Parabellum rounds.

Pleased with his payday, Khan furnished the duffel bags required to carry their new acquisitions at no extra charge. He counted Bolan's money, smiling all the while, then led them back upstairs and showed them to a rear exit that let them walk most of the distance back to the Toyota Avalon along an alley hidden from the street.

When they had stowed the gear and Bolan had the car in motion, Falk said, "That was strange, you know?"

He smiled at her and said, "You ain't seen nothing, yet."

*Vanguard International Branch Office, Kabul*

"YOU LET RED HAVE a pass?" Dale Ingram asked.

"He's on a leash," Clay Carlisle said. "He isn't going anywhere, except to clean up his own mess."

"And then?"

"Then, nothing. If he does the job, he'll have redeemed himself. If not, he pays the price."

"Which doesn't help us, either way," Ingram replied.

"It settles his account," Carlisle said.

"But we're still out eleven men, three cars, the lost hardware."

"The locals are a dime a dozen, Dale. Their paychecks stopped when they quit breathing, so they cost us nothing. Eddie Franks had no dependents, just a barfly brother in Kentucky. If we can't find him, we scrub the life insurance payment. I regret the cars, of course, but we have others. Most important, we've preserved deniability."

"Which helps us how, with the DEA problem?" Ingram asked.

"I'm on it," Carlisle said. "I've got a call in to Russ Latimer at the embassy."

"And you think hc can yank the reins on this narc and her boss? He hasn't done us any good, so far."

"Let's say that I've enhanced his motivation," Carlisle said.

Ingram knew what that meant. The damned spook had his hand out for more money, promising the world and paying off in peanuts.

"We could deal with him, you know," he told Carlisle.

"Don't start on that again."

"I'm serious," Ingram said. "Why don't we take advantage of the situation while we can? Civilian casualties are higher in Afghanistan than in Iraq these days. They headlined it on CNN. Who'd be surprised if insurgents took out the CIA's head of station in Kabul or greased the DEA's front man? I'm surprised they haven't done it already."

Carlisle stared him down and let the silence stretch between them, making Ingram nervous in the knowledge that he'd overstepped his bounds.

"You know we have a firm, long-term relationship with Langley," he replied at last. "We get thirty percent of our gross from the jobs they can't handle, everything from diplomatic coverage to wet work. I don't plan to foul our nest with an impulsive and unnecessary action, nor do I plan waging war against the U.S.A. I hope we're crystal clear on that."

"I hear you," Ingram answered.

"And to hear…"

"Is to obey," Vanguard's vice president replied, feeling the angry color rising in his cheeks.

Carlisle put on a smile. Ingram wished he could reach across the desk and slap it from his boss's face, but that would be the next best thing to suicide.

"Dale, you're a valued member of the team," Carlisle pressed. "You know I cherish your connections to the FBI, but sometimes I think you inherited old Hoover's pathological aversion to cooperating with the other agencies of government. Langley is *not* our enemy. We're in this thing together, for the long haul. Terrorism and the heathen hordes of Islam will be crushed in our lifetime. And if we turn a profit on the deal, so much the better. No one loses but our enemies."

"You're right, of course, Clay."

"Thanks for that. Humility becomes you," Carlisle said. "Now, if you only had a closer personal relationship with our eternal savior…"

"I've been working on it," Ingram said, "but when you've been out in the wilderness as long as I have, it's a problem."

"He forgives us everything," Carlisle said. "All you have to do is ask, but you must be sincere."

"I ask Him every night," Ingram said, lying through his teeth.

"Then your place in the kingdom is assured," Carlisle replied. "Now, if you'll just excuse me, Dale, I have to touch base with our friends and see about kicking some heathen ass."

"IN THERE," FALK SAID as Bolan drove along a street of office buildings on Jadayi Sulh.

He looked in the direction she was pointing and beheld one structure that stood out among the rest. It had been walled off from the street with concrete barricades along the curb to frustrate car bombers. The wall itself was eight feet high and topped with shiny coils of razor wire. Behind the black steel gate, an armed guard watched pedestrians and traffic pass.

"Looks like a bunker," he remarked.

"It is," Falk said. "Clay Carlisle may be a religious crackpot—or, at least come off like one in public—but he's grounded well enough to know that thousands of Afghanis would be thrilled to take him out. His apartment's inside there, along with Dale Ingram's."

Bolan glanced briefly at the other nearby buildings, then scratched Vanguard HQ off his mental list of targets. Infiltrating one of Carlisle's neighbors for a shot over the walls of his command post seemed too risky to be worth the effort it would take.

But he would find another angle of attack.

Turning southward, they drove past the historic royal citadel built by Amir Abdur Rahman Khan in the late nineteenth century, which presently housed Afghanistan's president, his chief of staff and national security adviser, and the president's protocol office. At a glance, Bolan guessed that stronghold would be easier to penetrate than Clay Carlisle's headquarters, two blocks farther north.

They passed the Prime Ministry, then the Republican Palace, while Bolan put his thoughts in order.

"Carlisle won't be fielding mercs from a CP that close to the president's office," he said. "Where does Vanguard keep its mercs and hardware?"

"Next stop on our tour," Falk said. "We've got another quarter mile or so to go. It's by the Plaza Hotel complex, in the Pol-e-Shahi quarter."

"Lodgings for his visitors?" Bolan asked.

"Right again," the DEA agent replied. "He has a steady stream of drop-ins from the States, Britain, some places you might not expect."

"Such as?"

"Last month, there were some gentlemen from Bogotá," Falk said. "They're wanted in America for cocaine smuggling—a couple of the so-called 'Extraditables' that no one ever gets around to extraditing. Booked in at the Plaza under phony names, but you can recognize them from the Wanted posters."

"Anybody tip the local law?" Bolan asked.

"Absolutely. And the cops showed up to question them… the day after they flew back home. But, what the hell, you can't expect them to drop everything and do their jobs."

"Who else comes calling?" Bolan asked her.

"It's a regular *Who's Who*. We've spotted Corsicans, a nice Sicilian delegation, Russians, Turks, some Yakuza."

"All in the smack trade," Bolan said, not asking this time.

"Those were," Falk agreed, "but Carlisle has all kinds of shiny, upright friends on the flip side. Think of a CEO from any petro company that's doing business in the region, and he's been here. Diplomats stop by, after they touch base at the embassy, sometimes before. We even had a stateside televangelist swing by and press the flesh, before he shot a TV special in the Holy Land."

"You check them out?" Bolan inquired.

"As far as possible," Falk said. "They all have public faces, but we try to dig a little deeper. Still, we don't get much. The really big oilmen have more security around them than the President. Diplomats, forget about it. We couldn't arrest them if we caught them with a limo-load of kindergarten prostitutes. The preacher may have trouble, when the IRS gets through with him this year, but don't expect the dirt to rub off on Carlisle."

"You're frustrated," Bolan observed.

"Who wouldn't be? The prick's untouchable."

"Not anymore."

"I wonder."

Bolan couldn't fault the lady Fed for being skeptical. Her own superiors had undermined her efforts against Carlisle and the Vanguard set, while the Afghan authorities played ostrich and banked their payoffs. Now, Bolan dropped in from out of the blue, and drafted Falk into an illicit war that might well get her killed.

If she'd wanted to bail, Bolan wouldn't have argued. And he knew it still might come to that. Meanwhile…

"We've got the Plaza over there," she told him, pointing to the left. "And coming up a half block farther down, that's what I call the Vanguard Hilton."

It was different from the company's headquarters, not so reminiscent of the Führerbunker in 1940s Berlin, but still secure enough with heavy gates and lookouts guarding entryways to the lobby and an underground garage.

"What kind of vehicles does Carlisle stash downstairs?" Bolan asked.

"Just the normal," Falk replied. "You want to see the hard-core motor pool, with APCs and all, we'll need to go west, to the Bala Kohi deh Afghanan district. Out by Kabul's big TV tower."

"Let's see it," Bolan said. "And then I need to find out when Carlisle is moving freight."

# CHAPTER FIVE

*Park-e-Zarnegar, Kabul*

The mausoleum of Abdur Rahman Khan stands in Zarnegar Park, near Kabul's city center. Once, it was a palace, converted to a vast tomb by the king's son when Abdur Rahman died in 1901. Its red dome mounted on a white octagonal structure, surmounted by small minarets, still ranked among the finest examples of nineteenth-century baroque architecture in Kabul.

Clay Carlisle loved beautiful things. He had booked the mausoleum for a private tour soon after his arrival in Kabul, but at the moment he had no eye for antiques. His thoughts were focused on the future, both immediate and long-term.

Zarnegar Park was the hub of Kabul, located near Embassy Row, overlooked by the stylish Kabul Serena Hotel and Afghanistan's Ministry of Communications. None of those features had drawn Carlisle to the park, however. He was not a tourist, and his visit on this fading afternoon was strictly business.

His limousine stopped at a newspaper kiosk on the park's western boundary. One of Carlisle's four security guards stepped out of the car and returned seconds later with a new passenger in tow.

The man was fortysomething, with a long face under thinning sandy hair, his slender form clothed in a tailored suit of charcoal-gray. Black wingtips made his feet seem overlarge and heavy. Opaque sunglasses concealed his eyes, which Carlisle knew from past experience were washed-out bluishgray with a tendency to squint.

"Strange days," said Russell Latimer, the CIA's deputy station chief in Kabul.

"Getting stranger all the time," Carlisle replied. "What can you tell me about our dilemma?"

Latimer cocked one eyebrow behind his shades. "I'm not sure that I'd call it *our* dilemma just yet."

"Wouldn't you?" Carlisle made sure his practiced frown fell somewhere short of hostile. "My mistake, then. As an uninvolved outsider with no future stake in anything that happens to my company, what can you tell me about *my* dilemma, then?"

"Hold on a second, now."

"Hold on to what, Russell? Remember what our Lord and Savior said in Matthew 12:30: 'He who is not with me is against me.'"

"Hey, I'm with you, Clay. All right? I only meant—"

"Don't tell me what you meant. Tell me what whatever you've found out about *my* problem."

Sandwiched between two bodyguards who made him look emaciated, Latimer put on a brave face and replied, "You seem a little out of sorts today, my friend."

"Seeing eleven of my men gunned down has that effect, Russ. Call me crazy."

"I'd call it normal, in the circumstances. And I'm working on it, but—"

"I hope you're not about to disappoint me," Carlisle said.

"That's never my intention."

"But you don't know anything."

"We have a name, okay? Maybe we have a name."

"Let's hear it."

"Matthew Cooper. He left Baltimore for Paris yesterday, then caught connecting flights to Rome and into Kabul. Had a rental car waiting when he arrived. We have it now, impounded from the Old City around the time of your…unpleasantness this afternoon. Trunk full of guns and ammo, see? And I don't mean the magazine."

Carlisle ignored the feeble joke and asked him, "Is there more?"

"I ran a check on Cooper, stateside. He's got credit cards that bill him through a P.O. box in San Diego. Some months he buys nothing, other times he's in the high four figures. Always pays on time, with postal money orders. No luck running down a bank account or any kind of residential address in the time I've had, so far. It's looking like a classic legend."

Carlisle understood the Langley-speak. A "legend" was a false identity created to withstand at least a cursory examination, covering for…what?

"That doesn't tell me anything of value," he replied.

Latimer nodded. "I agree, and I'll keep digging. But I know already that he doesn't have a package with the Feebs or with the Pentagon. We're running prints they lifted from the rental car, but in the circumstances, I'm not hopeful."

"What's your gut saying?" Carlisle asked.

"It could go either of two ways," Latimer responded. "One, this Cooper is some kind of independent crook with business here in Kabul, unrelated to the incident this afternoon."

"Who shows up just before my men get wasted, with a carload of weapons parked near the scene? Then disappears and leaves his car behind, after the shooting? I can't swallow that kind of coincidence."

"Neither can I," Latimer said. "The second option is that he's a black-ops artist sent or summoned for a meeting with your nemesis from DEA."

"That sounds more logical," Carlisle said.

"I agree. Unfortunately, at the moment I can't tell you where he comes from, who he works for, what his orders are."

"All right. What *can* you tell me?"

Latimer frowned and replied, "Smart money says that he's official. The sophisticated cover tells me he's got juice behind him."

"And?"

"And I can't see the DEA calling a private shooter in, no matter how badly you've pissed them off."

"Could he be one of yours?" Carlisle inquired.

"From Langley?" Latimer appeared to be surprised by the suggestion. "I don't think so, but it wouldn't be the first time one hand didn't know what the other was doing."

"Can you check it out?"

"I'll definitely try, but if there's some kind of covert team-within-the-team, I may not have full access."

"This is critical," Carlisle reminded him. "I'll deal with the man when he comes up for air, but I need to find out who's behind him."

"Agreed. It's priority one."

"Then I'll let you get to it," Carlisle said. A nod to his driver and the limo pulled over. "This must be your stop."

"Looks like it," Latimer agreed. "Listen, about before—"

"If you want to impress me, Russell, earn your pay."

"I will."

One of the guards stepped out, allowing Latimer to leave the car, and then the limousine rolled on, leaving the CIA's deputy station chief to find his own way home.

*Nangarhar Province, Afghanistan*

JALALABAD LIES ninety miles due east of Kabul, in Nangarhar Province, where small farmers have traditionally supported themselves by growing opium poppies. Recent claims suggested that production had been slashed by ninety-five percent, but Bolan knew that those statistics were skewed.

In fact, while many of the local growers *had* been driven out of business, large opium plantations thrived in the Chaparhar, Khogyani and Shinwar districts.

Bolan was headed for Shinwar, with Deirdre Falk riding beside him and Edris Barialy in his now-traditional backseat observatory post.

"So, have you seen this farm before?" he asked her when they were a half hour from Kabul.

"Not the way I think you mean it, in the flesh," she said. "We have a ton of photos at the office. Hidden camera, flyover, satellite, you name it. I can draw a map of it from memory, if that's a help."

Sending Falk back to her office for whatever maps or photographs they might have used, in Bolan's view, had been too risky after their first clash with Vanguard warriors. He assumed the DEA office would be under surveillance, or might even have a paid-off mole inside who would, at the very least, tip off their enemies to Falk's movements.

"Maybe later," Bolan said.

In fact, he didn't plan to hit the farm itself. At least, not yet. It would be covered by seven ways from Sunday by a troop of Vanguard mercs, most likely with the Afghan National Police or army on speed dial, in case the hired hands couldn't cope with a particular emergency.

On top of which, Bolan was not equipped for razing crops in cultivated fields. He wasn't armed with napalm or defoliants, and even if he *had* been, their delivery required aircraft.

"You're after the refinery?" Falk asked him, frowning at the thought.

"I want to see it," Bolan answered, "but it wouldn't be my first move."

He'd destroy more drugs by taking out a heroin refinery, along with whatever equipment Vanguard might have to replace after he blitzed the plant. That *was* part of his plan, but not the first move that he had in mind.

Falk shifted in her seat, plucking her damp blouse from her damper skin. Despite the small Toyota's air-conditioning, the outside heat still made its presence felt with sunlight blazing through the windows, baking any skin it touched.

As with her office, Bolan had been forced to veto letting Falk go back to her apartment for fresh clothes or any other personal accessories. They'd done some hasty shopping back in Kabul, but he knew she wasn't thrilled about the merchandise available.

"Feel free to share," she said, a hint of irritation in her voice.

"They ship the heroin through Pakistan, correct?" he asked her.

"Right. It's just a few miles farther east, and Nangarhar's the next best thing to Pakistan, already. Most of the district uses Pakistani rupees when they pay their bills or bribes, instead of the official Afghanis. The provincial governor is kissing-close with Pakistan's Intelligence Bureau."

"And they move it how?"

"Depends on the size of the shipment. These days, most of the big loads roll by truck convoy."

"Well, there you are."

"I am?"

"A convoy isn't fortified. It doesn't have high walls or razor wire around it, and it's not next door to a police station."

"Aren't you forgetting something? Like twenty-five or thirty shooters who'll be guarding it?"

"I didn't say it would be easy," Bolan answered. "But it's still our best shot for an opener."

Grim faced, she said, "Okay. Give me the rest of it."

*United States Embassy, Kabul*

A TWENTY-SOMETHING SECRETARY smiled at Russell Latimer and said, "The vice consul will see you now."

The man from Langley thought about making some kind of smart-aleck remark, like James Bond in the movies, but his mood was too sour for levity. Instead of cracking wise, therefore, he gave the little redhead a low-wattage smile and moved past her, toward his contact's inner sanctum.

"Come in, Russell! Come in!" his contact said, beaming. By that time, Latimer *was* in, closing the office door behind him. "Can I get you something? Coffee? Tea? A nice cold beer?"

"Scotch, if you have it, sir," Latimer said.

"That bad, is it?"

Vice Consul Lee Hastings forced a chuckle. It reminded Latimer of dry bones rattling in a wooden cup. And yes, he'd heard that very noise some years ago while visiting a village in Angola.

"It's bad, all right," he said before thanking his host for the drink and tossing it down in one gulp. "I can't say how bad, at the moment, but it has *fubar* potential."

"Come again?"

"*Fubar.* Fucked up beyond all recognition."

The bony laugh again, as Hastings settled into his chair behind a standard-issue foreign service desk.

"In that case," Hastings said, "I guess you'd better fill me in."

Hastings was in his late forties, losing the battle of the bulge around his waist, but otherwise in decent shape for an American who'd spent the past three years in Kabul, fixing cracks and pinholes in the diplomatic dike and listening to bomb blasts in the streets outside. Latimer saw him slip one hand beneath the desk and knew that everything they said from that point on would be recorded, which was fine. He'd worn a wire, himself, prepared as always for the day when one of his superiors might try to sacrifice him for some personal advantage.

He began the briefing with a question. "Have you heard about the shootings in the Old City and Chindawol this afternoon?"

"Not yet," Hastings replied. "Anything serious?"

"Eleven dead, sir," Latimer informed him, giving Carlisle credit in advance for silencing his wounded soldier in the hospital.

"That's most unfortunate, of course, but—"

"Sir, it's not the number I'm concerned about," Latimer interrupted. "It's who they were."

"I see. And who were they?"

"Vanguard employees. One from stateside, that I'm sure of, and the rest natives."

Hastings was silent for the best part of a minute, then replied, "Were they...um... What I mean to say is, did the police find anything?"

In any other circumstances, Latimer would have considered it a strange question. But at that moment, it made perfect sense.

"Just weapons, sir. They weren't running a shipment."

He enjoyed the vice consul's dilemma, thinking of the tape and how best to avoid seeming to understand the reference to drugs. After another moment's thought, Hastings sidestepped the subject altogether, asking, "What do you suppose they were doing, Russell?"

"Some kind of surveillance, I take it. From what I've been told, there's a person of interest in town, just arrived, seeking contact with some of our friends down the hall."

He left Hastings to guess whether he meant the DEA or FBI. In either case, it had to be bad news.

"There was a meeting, then?" Hastings asked.

"So it seems."

"And Vanguard's people tried to...interrupt it. Isn't that a rash decision?"

"Rash depends on whether you're successful, sir. But in this case, I have assurances that they were simply watching."

What the hell. Latimer reckoned that another small lie wouldn't break the camel's back.

"How did the shooting start, then?" Hastings asked him.

"I suppose one of their men was spotted. Probably a local, since they're not the sharpest. Anyway, the other side starts shooting, and it goes downhill from there."

"And were there any casualties on the other side?"

"If so, they weren't left at the scene. None found so far, at least."

"What do you make of that, Russell?"

Meaning, *What's wrong with Carlisle's people, getting killed like that, with nothing to show for it?*

"Sir, I can't explain it, at the moment. If I had to guess, I'd say we're looking at imported talent."

"But, imported for what reason? That's the question we must answer, isn't it?"

"One of them, definitely. I'd be happy with a name and address, mind you, but we'll have to look at the big picture sometime."

"Someone underneath this roof," Hastings said, as if talking to himself. Then he asked Latimer, "How certain are you?"

"There's no question, I'm afraid. One of their personnel was seen. May have participated in the killings, but that is speculation. Anyway, she's disappeared."

"She?"

"I'm not sure how much more you'd care to know, sir."

"If we're threatened, Russell, I must know enough to mount a competent defense."

"All right. Her name is Deirdre Falk. She's DEA. You may have passed her in the halls, sir."

"DEA? Was this official?"

"I'm in no position to determine that, sir."

"No, of course not. I'll look into it, discreetly. In the meantime, someone needs to find her. And this stranger. What's he call himself?"

"Matthew Cooper. It's a cover."

"Damn it!" Hastings reached beneath his desk again, to kill the tape, then said, "I'll make some calls and see what I can do—or learn, for that matter. If you see Carlisle, tell him he's expected to clean up after himself."

Latimer smiled and said, "With pleasure, sir."

*Nangarhar Province*

THE POPPY PLANTATION was more or less what Bolan expected: acres of flowers in bloom, tended by peasants who stooped and shuffled along the rows, using razors to etch the plants' bulbs and release the sticky sap from which raw opium gum was derived. A sprinkler system kept the crop from wilting underneath the brutal Afghan sun.

Bolan saw all of that in passing, with the houses set well back from the two-lane highway running past the property. A glance through compact field glasses showed him two figures on the farmhouse porch—one carrying an automatic rifle and the other tracking the Toyota Avalon through glasses of his own.

The land around the farm, predictably, was flat and open. A direct approach in daylight, without air support or armored vehicles, would be a clumsy sort of suicide. The place was dwindling in his rearview mirror when he said to Deirdre Falk, "Okay. Where's the refinery?"

"Eight clicks ahead," she answered. "Jesus, I've gone metric without knowing it. Say five miles, give or take."

Bolan checked the odometer and memorized its reading.

"Any better access to the plant?" he asked.

"Hardly. For one thing, you won't even see it from the road.

It's set back half a mile, screened off by trees, only the one way in or out for vehicles."

"You've seen the layout, though," he said. "From bird's-eye photos?"

"Sure. You want a sketch? I'm not a draftsman, but the place is simple. Big square building like a mill or slaughterhouse. A gravel parking lot with half a dozen vehicles at any given time. A loading dock around in back, for trucks."

"They move that kind of weight?"

"I wouldn't be concerned about this mob, if they were pushing nickel bags," Falk said.

"Okay. Let's see the access point, then decide the best place for a hit."

"Terrific," Falk replied. "I've always had this secret dream to be a gangster. *Little Crackhouse on the Prairie* was my favorite book in school."

"We're fighting fire with fire," Bolan replied, unruffled by her sarcasm. "I'm here because someone upstairs was told you couldn't stop Carlisle through normal means. If that's changed, let me know right now. Write up your warrants, and I'll help you serve them."

"Rub it in, why don't you?" Falk responded. "I'm a failure. I admit it. Are we happy now?"

"Not even close," Bolan said. "And I don't buy for a moment that you've failed. Headquarters obviously sent you here believing you could help them close the pipeline. That tells me you've been successful in the past, and not just handling rookie jobs. You've made your mark and paid your dues. The only reason that you haven't closed the case on Carlisle is that he owns people higher up the food chain, in Kabul and back at home. On this one, you were beaten before you started."

Falk smiled at him, saying, "You're not bad at ego-stroking when you put your mind to it."

"I don't indulge in flattery," Bolan replied. "There's no doubt in my mind that you can pull your weight—or have, at least, so far. But I'll remind you that we're in a gloves-off situation, where the rules go out the window. Winning isn't everything in this game. It's the only thing."

"You're quoting Vince Lombardi now?"

"New game, same rules," Bolan said. "How we play it, only winners leave the field alive."

"I knew I should've bought that Kevlar girdle when I saw it in the store," Falk said.

"My point is, you can still bail, no shame attached. You didn't sign on for guerrilla warfare, and it isn't covered by your oath of office. If you want to pull the pin—"

"And do what?" she inquired. "Go back to my flat, where they're probably waiting to kill me? Check in at the office, where someone's been selling me out? Maybe catch a flight back to the States and retire? Write my memoirs? Who'd print it?"

"It's your call," Bolan said. "But go into it with your eyes open."

"They're open, Matt. Believe me."

"Right." He glanced at the odometer again and asked, "So, where's that access road to the refinery?"

*The Republican Palace, Kabul*

LEE HASTINGS WAS five minutes early for his appointment with Habib Zarghona, deputy minister in charge of Taftish, the Inspections division of Afghanistan's Ministry of Justice. Arriving ahead of schedule, then patiently waiting until Zarghona was five or ten minutes late, was a show of respect for the man and the office he held.

Or, in this case, for the strings he could pull.

Hastings had spent his whole adult life in the diplomatic

service of America. He'd met all types during his years abroad and in the States, from starry-eyed idealists and altruists to homicidal maniacs and simple-minded thugs who thought "negotiation" meant you asked for cash before you pulled a gun. He was accustomed to the world of double-talk, veiled threats and bribes disguised as foreign aid. He'd compromised his principles so often that he could barely recall what they'd been at the start.

Dealing with scum took up a fair amount of Hastings's time, and it had made him comfortably wealthy over time. But any way you tried to dress it up and douse it with perfume for parties, scum was scum.

Speaking of which…

"The deputy will see you now," a voice cut through his reverie. "Please follow me, sir."

Hastings did as he was told. Zarghona's secretary was a young man, although women had begun to make a sluggish comeback with removal of the Taliban from power after 9/11. Still, Zarghona would be sensitive to attitudes in his division, and throughout the government at large. He would offer gossips anything to talk about, since he had much to hide.

The secretary left him in a lushly decorated, empty office, but Hastings knew the drill. Another sixty seconds passed before a door opened between the flags flanking Zarghona's desk, against the southern wall, and the great man himself entered.

He wasn't smiling, which could only mean the news had found its way to him already.

"Mr. Hastings," Zarghona said. "Please, sit down."

Hastings complied. He did not offer to shake hands, which was regarded in some Muslim circles as intrusive and insulting. Some Muslim men held hands without attaching any stigma to it, but to shake hands with an infidel would set them reeling.

"I suppose that we must speak about our problem," Zarghona said without any of the usual preamble.

Hastings wanted to be sure which problem that might be. "If you mean—"

"The unpleasantness of earlier today, with Mr. Carlisle's late employees."

"Yes. We're on the same page," Hastings said.

"We take such violence quite seriously, as I'm sure you understand."

"Indeed. And so does the United States."

"But this did not occur in the United States," Zarghona said. "And while one victim was American, the rest were natives of *my* country, killed on *our* soil. Can you tell me why this happened, Mr. Hastings?"

Four years of collaborating on a range of projects, and they hadn't made it to first names. Hastings supposed they never would.

Which suited him just fine.

"A logical assumption would suggest some link to Vanguard International, its clients and the service it supplies. Of course, my people have no ready access to police reports about the incident."

"Don't you?" Zarghona asked, then forged ahead without waiting for a reply. "In that case, I should tell you that we have retrieved a hired vehicle, near the scene of the first shootings. There were weapons in the car, and it was registered to an American."

"Indeed?"

"You would not recognize the name of Matthew Cooper, I suppose?"

"Not personally," Hastings said. "It sounds like quite a common name."

"But not, I think, a common man."

"You believe that he's responsible for the shootings?"

"I will not say solely responsible," Zarghona replied. "In fact, aside from his name on a rental contract, I have no proof he even exists."

"We can assume that someone drove the car," Hastings said.

"Most assuredly. As for his true identity and what has brought him to Afghanistan, let us say that the matter is still unresolved."

"For how long, would you estimate?" Hastings asked.

"Who can say? If you possessed some knowledge of this man, and could perhaps enlighten me…"

"I would cooperate, of course. And I will make urgent inquiries. I believe you said the name was Cooper? Matthew Cooper?"

Zarghona nodded, frowning. "If, by some chance, he is known to others at your embassy in some capacity, you might advise them to cooperate, as well. Such incidents as this are not conducive to our common goals. Democracy, prosperity, the war on terrorism."

"I completely understand."

"If you should see Mr. Carlisle before I do," Zarghona said, "please offer my sincere condolences."

Reminding Hastings that the Vanguard team did business with both sides—and with a list of others that could prove embarrassing to many in high places, if those ties should be revealed.

"I will be pleased to do so," Hastings said. "And might your staff supply copies of the police reports?"

"Within the limits of the statutes that control such sharing, certainly," Zarghona said.

"In that case, thank you for your time," Hastings said. "I look forward to a swift solution, on behalf of all concerned."

"A swift and absolute solution," Zhargona said as he rose behind his desk. "Good day."

No handshake on the way out, either. Just the secretary waiting for him, guiding Hastings toward the exit.

Sunlight blazed at Hastings from the sky and from the pavement as he left the building, walking swiftly to his chauffeured vehicle. It made his head ache, made him sorry that he'd left his sunglasses inside the car.

Too late.

Zarghona had been toying with him, to a point, perhaps hoping that Hastings could step in and do his job for him. Wrap up this stranger, the enigmatic Matthew Cooper, and deliver him for execution as a sign of solidarity.

I might, too, Hastings thought. If I had any fucking idea who he was.

That was the rub, of course.

And Hastings guessed that it was only going to get worse.

# CHAPTER SIX

*Nangarhar Province*

The setup wasn't perfect—nothing ever was, in preparation for a battle—but it was the best Bolan could manage, in the given circumstances. And his people were as ready as they'd ever be.

The ambush site was five miles to the east of Carlisle's heroin refinery, located at a point where some ancient upheaval had raised rocky bluffs resembling a ruined castle. Ages later, when a road construction crew had come along, they'd laid blacktop beneath the rough stone face, with arid scrubland on the other side, never considering that it might serve some future warrior as a sniper's nest.

How could they know? Why would they care?

Bolan had thought about dividing his small force, then put it out of mind. There was no decent cover on the north side of the two-lane road, they had no time to dig a trench, and neither of his two companions had the battlefield experience to stay alive if he had placed them over there, exposed to hostile fire.

Instead he took advantage of the landscape Mother Nature

had provided, finding stony niches for himself and his draftees that would protect them, more or less, while they poured automatic fire onto the road below. He also used the crags to hide his Toyota Avalon, parked out of sight from the highway and pointed westward, back toward the refinery, the opium plantation and Kabul.

Before he'd gone to all that trouble, Bolan had confirmed and reaffirmed with Deirdre Falk that Vanguard sent a shipment eastward every Tuesday and Friday, bound for the Pakistani border and whoever might be waiting for it there. It was a thriving trade, and Falk vowed that she had the schedule memorized, out of frustration that she'd never found police willing to interrupt it.

That would change this day, albeit without aid from the authorities.

Falk told him that the convoys varied slightly from one shipment to the next, depending on the weight produced in any given period. A military-style Humvee—the famous M998 High Mobility Multipurpose Wheeled Vehicle—led each formation, packed with shooters, while a second brought up the rear. Between the the two carloads of guards ran a flexible number of 2.5-ton cargo trucks bearing the heroin, wrapped up in kilo bricks.

No scout cars, she assured him, would be sent out in advance. The Vanguard team, while never unprepared for trouble on the road, had grown complacent over time, relaxing just enough in their coccoon of safety purchased with extensive bribes, to give Bolan an edge.

Or so he hoped.

The plan was relatively simple. He would stop the point vehicle with his MGL grenade launcher, hopefully blocking the road in the process, then close the back door with an HE round to the second Humvee. That would leave the drug trucks in a lethal sandwich, under fire from Falk and Barialy while he dealt with their protectors then came back to torch their loads with thermite rounds.

No sweat—at least, on paper.

But experience had taught him that a thousand things could still go wrong, not the least of them a change in normal shipping schedules if Carlisle was unnerved by what had happened to his men in Kabul. He might double the shipment's guard, provide air cover, even take it off the road entirely until he decided on his next move in the game.

He might do that, but Bolan didn't think so.

Money was the smuggler's primary consideration, and if he was worried about moving heroin with unknown enemies at large, he'd worry all the more about stockpiling dope at the refinery. Better to ship it out and bank the proceeds than to offer tons of product as a sitting target.

No, if Carlisle changed his routine at all, Bolan was betting on enhanced security. That would increase the risk to his side, obviously, but would not protect Bolan's intended targets from a storm of automatic fire and 40 mm rounds.

Falk had her Glock and Uzi, with one of the AKSU rifles dropped by their first adversaries in Sharh-e-Khone. She could fire eighty rounds without reloading, and she had her spare mags within easy reach.

Barialy had the other AKSU-74 and his vintage Webley revolver, thirty-six rounds without pausing to switch out a magazine, and while his combat marksmanship remained untested, trucks the size of a deuce-and-a-half were hard to miss at twenty yards.

Hard, but not impossible.

Bolan made a conscious effort to relax, telling himself that it was good enough if Barialy made noise, kept their enemies' heads down, while he and Falk did the killing.

And it *should* be good enough. But if it wasn't.

Then, he'd find out soon enough. A soldier gambled every

time he stepped onto a battlefield, going all-in against an enemy who might outnumber him, might take him down immediately with a lucky shot before he had a chance to score at all.

Nothing was certain in a warrior's life, except for death waiting to greet him at the end.

This day, he thought, there would be death enough to go around.

BILL SCHULTZ WAS ANXIOUS to be on his way. The vehicles were ready, all his men were standing by, except for Tim Ross with the tail Humvee.

"Where is he?" Schultz asked Ross's driver, an Afghan named Bahram Najiya.

Najiya shrugged. "He says must use the W.C."

A goddamned bladder break, Schultz thought.

They'd had all afternoon to answer calls of nature, while the heroin was being parceled up and loaded on the trucks, but Ross still waited for the last damn minute, like some kid stalling departure on a family vacation.

Was the pressure nibbling away at Ross's nerve? Was he becoming unreliable?

Not yet, but Schultz was paid to spot the early warning signs of stress among his various subordinates *before* it caused a costly major problem. Tim Ross hadn't reached the point where Schultz needed to cut him from the team, but it could do no harm to jerk his chain a little when they finished up this evening's run.

One thing Schultz wouldn't do was snap at Ross in front of native hirelings. There would always be a sharp dividing line between the home-grown Vanguard team and any locals who signed on to fill the lower ranks. Even if he was forced to kick Ross's ass or fire him, there would be no Afghan witnesses.

Ross interrupted Schultz's train of thought, emerging from

the refinery's cavernous loading bay and jogging toward his Humvee.

"Sorry for the holdup," he called to Schultz, getting a curt nod in return.

"All right," Schultz bellowed at his people. "Saddle up and hit the road."

Each Humvee seated ten, and while they sometimes ran with fewer personnel aboard, the call Schultz had received from Kabul earlier that afternoon had emphasized the need for beefing up security. There'd been "an incident," Vanguard had taken casualties, and now HQ was nervous.

Fine.

He'd packed the Humvees, twenty men in all, even the drivers armed with SMGs besides their normal handguns. They had two trucks running, with a one driver and one shotgun rider each, plus two more he'd dragooned to babysit the heroin in each truck bed. That gave him twenty-eight shooters in all, with Tim Ross second in command.

If anything went wrong between the plant and Pakistan's frontier, Schultz figured they were ready for it. And if anybody planned to stop the shipment, bring 'em on.

Schultz would kill them and complete his mission, as he always had before.

Game on.

DEIRDRE FALK WAS SWEATING through her clothes again, and hating every second of it. She had rigged a headband to keep perspiration from stinging her eyes, blinding her when her life might depend on clear vision, but it didn't help the generally miserable way she felt.

All right, Afghanistan was hot. She'd come to terms with that, aided by air-conditioned offices and cars, by lightweight clothes, by cold showers and frosty drinks. But none of those was presently available.

When Matt Cooper spoke of going to war against Clay
Carlisle and Vanguard International, she hadn't pictured actual
maneuvers, lying on a slab of rock that felt like a barbecue
grill through her jeans and her wet denim shirt, waiting to
ambush trucks and shoot at men she'd never seen before—or,
maybe glimpsed as tiny figures in a photo taken from a satellite outside Earth's atmosphere.

She sipped some water from a plastic bottle, found it had
been heated by the sun to eighty-odd degrees, and made a sour
face. So much for any concept of refreshment.

Falk was worried about letting Cooper down, and more
specifically that she would make some blunder that resulted
in her own sudden and painful death. She'd done all right in
their first clash with Vanguard mercenaries, but that had been
more or less a case of self-defense.

This time, she was lying in wait for strangers, planning to
shoot them from ambush. Any way she sliced it, in the absence
of a war declared between two nations, that was murder.

And the odd thing was, she didn't feel that bad about it.

She was worried, absolutely, but her main concerns revolved around mechanical aspects of the ambush, her personal
ability to pull it off without getting killed in the process, or
endangering Cooper and Edris Barialy.

She could think about the legal and the moral aspects later,
if they managed to survive the hit and get away. It seemed
peculiar, not to be preoccupied with office politics and covering her own backside before she made a move.

Peculiar and exhilarating.

"Here they come," Bolan said at her elbow. He was nearly
whispering, although they had the rocky summit and the
stretch of lonely highway to themselves.

Or had, until this moment.

She could hear the vehicles approaching, running at speed
along the open road. The point vehicle's occupants would scan

for any obstacles or opposition, maintaining contact with the trucks and rear Humvee by radio. Cell phones were hopeless out there in the open, without towers to relay their signals, but the Humvees might have satellite phones as a backup system, for emergencies.

She watched the road, could see the little convoy now, and felt Cooper shifting beside her as he aimed the fat grenade launcher downrange. The first shot would be his, and after that it was each man for himself.

Or woman, as the case might be.

She waited, clutching her AKSU-74 in a white-knuckled grip, index finger taut on the trigger, holding the mini-Uzi in reserve and hoping that no close-range killing would be necessary.

"Here we go," Bolan said, as he sighted, squeezed, and sent the first round hurtling toward its mark.

BOLAN COULDN'T TELL at a glance if the Humvees were armored, or how extensive the plating—if any—might be. One thing he knew beyond a doubt, however: none of the Humvee's four wheels and tires was immune to a high-explosive charge.

His first round went in on target, slamming into the lead vehicle's right-front wheel well, detonating with a clap of smoky thunder that punched the boxlike vehicle's square nose sideways, to the driver's left.

The shock waves of that blast were still ringing in Bolan's ears when he leaped to his feet and ran twenty feet down the spine of the crag that he'd turned into his citadel. The second Humvee's wheelman would have seen and heard the first explosion, but reaction time was slowed by shock, even among the best professionals.

Still moving, hearing Falk and Barialy cut loose with their twin Kalashnikovs, Bolan lined up his second shot and squeezed the MGL's double-action trigger again, launching his second HE round toward the highway below.

It wasn't perfect, but it went in close enough, slamming against the tail vehicle's right rear door, within a hand's span of the fender, shattering the axle between the bushing assembly and geared hub of the wheel. The right rear wheel popped off, causing the vehicle to leave a trail of sparks before it wobbled to a halt.

The two trucks in between the Humvees had been taking hits, but neither seemed inclined to stop. Both forged ahead despite the smoking roadblock in their path, one swinging to the right, the other to the left, in an attempt to pass the lead Humvee.

Bolan took on the farther of the two trucks first. His next round in rotation was triple-aught buckshot, an antipersonnel cartridge containing twenty 9 mm lead pellets. He aimed from the shoulder, triggered the shot, and saw the windows of the cab vaporize. The truck lurched, shuddered and died with its driver.

That left one truck on the move, and it was rolling under fire from Falk and Barialy's automatic rifles. Bolan turned in time to see Falk shred the heavy vehicle's near-side forward tire with a 3- or 4-round burst, costing the driver control of his ride, while Barialy peppered the passenger's side of the cab. Another moment, with Falk firing at the grille, and then the juggernaut lurched forward, shuddered, died.

Better.

Their work was far from done, though, as revealed when someone in the lead Humvee opened a hidden sunroof, poked his head out and began to spray the tall escarpment with machine-gun fire.

Before he hit the deck for cover, Bolan couldn't tell if he was dodging from an M-60 E-3 or a Stoner 63, and it hardly mattered. The calibers differed, 7.62 mm versus 5.56 mm, but both had cyclic fire rates between 550 and 700 rounds per minute, well able to chew him up and spit him out again.

The sudden drop stole Bolan's breath, but he didn't let the jolt slow him. Another automatic weapon had begun to rake the bluff, most likely from the rear Humvee, and Bolan knew the shooters would be covering for their companions as they scrambled clear and took up firing posts behind their vehicles.

It was expected, but he couldn't let it pass.

While Falk and Barialy cringed from the incoming fire, Bolan crawled past them, back toward his original position, where he'd left his AKSU-74. When he reached the spot, Bolan risked a peek over the jutting ledge and saw what he'd expected: heads and gun barrels lined up behind the Humvees, with a couple here and there behind the crippled trucks.

How many men to start?

Say twenty max for the Humvees, unless they'd ridden in on one another's laps. Then figure two crewmen per truck, and how many concealed in back with the cargo?

Bolan rounded off to thirty, knew he didn't dare say that to Falk or Barialy, and prepared to whittle down the odds. Dusk was approaching, and it struck him that they'd soon need light to aim by.

It was time to start a fire.

His next round up, in clockwise rotation, was thermite. Bolan sighted quickly on the rear bed of the furthest truck, squeezed off, and ducked back under cover as the firing squad below cut loose with everything they had.

He didn't see the thermite canister explode on impact, but he heard the hungry whoosh of flames, followed by screams of pain and panic.

Better still.


BILL SCHULTZ SUSPECTED that his team was well and truly fucked. Most of them had survived the initial ambush, but their vehicles were trashed and going nowhere without wreckers to retrieve them. That meant questions, and perhaps examination of their cargo, which could only bring more trouble down the line.

But Schultz knew he had jumped the gun with that thought. None of them could be interrogated or arrested if they were already dead when the authorities arrived.

Before they left the plant, Schultz would have said his team was good enough to take on any group of bandits or guerrillas they were likely to encounter on the road. The Afghan mercs he had to use were no match for a homegrown Vanguard team, but they were fighters and they didn't get hung up on abstract questions of morality.

Now, here he was, pinned down and obviously fighting for his life with four wrecked vehicles, against an enemy of unknown strength who held the high ground with superior cover.

Not good.

Not good at all.

He heard the bloop of a grenade launcher, then flinched as one of the trucks burst into raging flames. Some kind of an incendiary round, maybe white phosphorous, and men were screaming where the flames or blazing chemicals had found their flesh.

There went half of the load up in smoke, and that posed further danger to his men. One way of using heroin, Schultz knew, was smoking it, and while he wouldn't recommend lighting your hookah or whatever with a thermite canister, he'd read somewhere that smoking was the fastest-acting method of ingesting any drug.

And one thing that he didn't need right now was for his shooters to get high and zone out in the middle of a firefight.

What he did need was reinforcements, preferably with some air cover, but reaching out for help would be a problem now. Each vehicle in the convoy carried a portable two-way radio, but one of them was toast now, while the second truck was nearest to the enemy and had no armor on its bullet-punctured cab. That left the Humvee walkie-talkies, and Schultz didn't have a clue where either of them was.

He hadn't thought to grab the radio from his car when it took the fatal hit and slewed sideways across the road. His only thought was to get clear before another rocket, or whatever the hell it was, came crashing through a window and exploded in his lap. Schultz guessed that Tim Ross had felt much the same, back at the tag end of the convoy, but if neither of them had a working radio in hand, then they were fucked.

Huddled behind his Humvee, trying not to breathe the cloud of oily-smelling fumes that roiled around them, Schultz snapped at his soldiers, "Hey! Who has the radio?"

One of the Afghans blinked at him and asked, "Don't you?"

Schultz cursed, opened the driver's door to smoky haze inside the vehicle, and cursed again as the dome light came on. He groped for the button to kill it, couldn't find what he was looking for, and concentrated on the radio instead. Rooting around the front seats and the floor, he couldn't find the damned thing anywhere.

Jesus! Where was it?

Finally his fingers found the oblong, boxy shape and clutched it. Schultz was backing from the vehicle, grinning in triumph, when an explosion rocked the vehicle and pitched him backward into crimson-streaked darkness.

EDRIS BARIALY SAW a pair of men run from the shadow of the burning truck, one trailing flames behind him like a banner, screaming as he ran. His rifle seemed to aim itself, his trigger finger clinching of its own accord, and he was startled when one of the runners staggered, pitching facedown on the pavement.

It was the first time he had shot a man—killed one, from all appearances—and while he had expected waves of nausea or vertigo to seize him, he felt nothing beyond the fear that had been nagging him since the first shooting in Kabul.

He wondered, now, if he would ever shake that fear.

But shooting helped.

It was remarkable, feeling the AKSU's folding metal stock buffet his shoulder, smelling the cordite while percussive gunfire numbed his ears. The rifle served to vent his fear and anger at the enemy, his bullets reaching out to punch through metal, glass and flesh.

Perhaps he would be sickened by it later, when he was no longer fighting desperately for his life.

Or maybe not.

Barialy glanced toward Deirdre Falk, in time to see her drop the rifle she was firing, lift the little submachine gun she had chosen at the arms dealer's establishment, and fire off its whole magazine in one long burst. She seemed to feel him watching her, returned his glance and answered with a shrug, then reached out for a fresh clip to reload her Kalashnikov.

Below them, their targets took turns firing up toward the bluffs, rising and dropping out of sight again like pistons in an engine. In that manner, they managed to keep up a fairly steady fire, and while the flying bullets worried Barialy, stinging him with chips of shattered stone from time to time, he kept firing at the vehicles and their huddled passengers.

He feared that they would reach a stalemate soon, and what would happen then? Would they be trapped here, dueling with their adversaries, until Vanguard reinforcements or police arrived? If that happened, it would mean death for Edris Barialy and his two companions, beyond any doubt. And he was not prepared to die.

Not here. Not now, like this.

At least Matt Cooper was not cowed by the incoming fire.

He moved along the crest of their escarpment, firing both his
AKSU rifle and the squat grenade launcher. Below the bluff,
both trucks were burning, and Barialy thought he smelled the
sweet stench of their cargo mingled with the smells of burning
rubber, canvas, oil and gasoline.

Could breathing in the smoke make him an addict?

Panic gripped him for an instant, then he shook it off.
Even injecting heroin did not create immediate depen-
dency—did it? Why had he not learned more about the
subject earlier? Would simple ignorance betray him now,
and seal his fate?

But Cooper did not seem to fear the rising clouds of smoke
from down below. He fired a last round from his launcher,
toward one of the Humvees, then knelt to reload it. The process involved opening the cylinder, extracting spent rounds
and replacing them, then winding a spring like that of an old
pocket watch. Barialy watched until a bullet struck the stone
beside his face and stung his ear with razor shards, reminding him that he was in a battle to the death.

"I'm going down to root them out," Bolan said, leaning in
so Falk could also hear his low-pitched voice. "Be ready when
they break from cover."

Edris Barialy nodded silently and watched the tall man go,
then wriggled closer to the precipice, clutching his gun so
tightly that his fingers ached.

IT WAS A SHORT JOG downhill, then around the western angle
of the bluff, to come in from behind the convoy vehicles.
Bolan was gambling with his life, but knew he had to break
the stalemate now, before a call for reinforcement brought
results.

He'd loaded the MGL launcher with six buckshot rounds
and folded its stock, turning it into a fat riot gun. The HE and
thermite were better at long range, but posed too much risk

to a shooter up close, where shrapnel, flames or shock waves might rebound and take him out.

Above him, on the crest, Barialy and Falk had ceased firing, the lull tempting Vanguard's mercs out from cover. The pros didn't rush to expose themselves by any means, but they were slowly rising, peering over vehicles, as Bolan's run brought him to level ground behind them.

Any second now they might decide to send flankers around the bluff on either side, to scope out what was happening. Bolan had thought they might've tried it earlier, but he supposed the shock of the ambush had slowed their reactions in the crunch.

He caught the nearest of them huddled behind the rear Humvee, half veiled from sight by drifting smoke from the two cargo trucks. Bolan gave no thought to the fumes, made no attempt to hold his breath as he came in on their blind side and caught them unaware.

He hardly had to aim his first shot, simply thrust his weapon's muzzle toward the clutch of men and squeezed the trigger from a range of sixty feet. The MGL's twelve-inch barrel was shorter than that of most sawed-off shotguns, allowing for maximum spread of the triple-aught buck, and Bolan employed a "sweep-shooting" technique to enhance coverage.

Three of the five men in his sights collapsed immediately, dead or dying from their wounds, while two more lurched and staggered, fumbling weapons, plainly injured. Bolan drew his pistol as he closed with them and fired one head shot each to finish it.

Then back to hunting, with his other prey alert as Bolan cleared the backup Humvee's nose and found his next targets. They loitered in the smoky space between the burning trucks, unsure of which direction they should choose for maximum security.

Bolan made the choice for them, firing a buckshot charge into their midst and driving the survivors in front of him, through the noxious smokescreen and out into plain view from the crest above them.

Falk and Barialy opened up on them immediately, stitching the runners with bursts of 5.45 mm fire from forty feet above their heads. Bolan hung back and watched the human targets twitching, dancing, crumpling to the asphalt as they died.

How many left?

He'd seen nine fall, and guessed that four or five were down before he'd left his post on high. Say six or seven left, at the outside, and they were all somewhere ahead of him, beyond the trucks, around the lead Humvee.

Waiting.

He needed visual contact before he opened fire, and that meant risking everything. If Bolan could see them, it followed that his adversaries could see him.

But would they be alert and watching when he came?

Bolan circled around the farther of the two trucks from the crest where Falk and Barialy watched the battlefield, alert for any hostile move. The Vanguard soldiers might expect him to come up the middle, where their friends had run and died, or to move along the south side of the road, where his two friends could cover him most easily.

He chose the third route, moving up the north side in a crouch, letting the MGL's squat muzzle lead him through the battle smoke.

And in another heartbeat, there they were.

All things considered, they were in a fairly tight formation, five men gathered in the Humvee's shadow, two watching the bluff, two covering the trucks behind them, while the fifth faced to his left, or eastward, covering all bets.

The westward-facing shooters picked out Bolan's movement, swung around to bring him under fire, but they were both too late. He squeezed the launcher's double-action trigger four times in three seconds, fighting the recoil, sending eighty 9 mm pellets downrange in a murderous storm.

The shooters seemed to blur before his eyes, red mist combining with the pall of smoke in a grisly illusion of souls taking flight. They fell together in a tangled heap, reminding Bolan of photos depicting old Chicago's St. Valentine's Day massacre.

He slung the MGL and drew his pistol, ready if the fallen still had any fight left in them, but nobody moved. If there were any final gasps of pain or desperation, Bolan couldn't hear them above the hungry crackling of flames.

He turned away, began his walk back to the car, trusting Falk and Barialy not to shoot him by mistake. They had been truly blooded now, he thought, and anything that followed would be something they could handle.

Right.

Unless it blew up in their faces and they all went down together like the trained men he was leaving on the killing field.

# CHAPTER SEVEN

*Laghman Province, Afghanistan*

"Something to drink?" Clay Carlisle asked his passenger.
"I'm having beer. You might prefer soda, some lemonade?"

"Nothing," Frozaan Sabeir replied, without a hint of grati-
tude for Carlisle's offer. "What I *want* is to be told why we
are summoned in this way."

Carlisle opened his beer, a stubby Foster's, sipped it, and
considered how he should respond.

On one level, the answer was so obvious he could have
laughed in Sabeir's swarthy, bearded face. The short, black-
turbaned Taliban warlord was filled with self-importance that
belied the personal humility demanded by his widely touted
faith in the Koran. He did not suffer insults gladly, and was
likely to imagine them where none had been intended.

So, no laughter, then.

The armored H2 Humvee limousine they occupied was
thirty-eight feet long and seated eighteen passengers in
comfort, although Carlisle and Sabeir had only four companions now, all seated at the far end of the stretch compartment.
Bringing any more along, in Carlisle's estimate, *would* be an

insult—to their host, not to Sabeir—and that might have grave consequences.

"We've been invited here," he said at last, "because our friend is properly concerned about the loss of merchandise."

"Your people were in charge of the delivery," Sabeir observed.

"And nearly half the guards were yours," Carlisle reminded him. "We're either partners in this operation or we aren't."

Sabeir stiffened, glaring. "I do not take your meaning," he replied.

"It's simple," Carlisle told him, pausing for another sip of beer. "You supply the local talent, for security or whatnot, and receive a share of gross receipts. The money serves your cause, presumably. I don't hear you complaining on payday, only when something goes amiss and you're required to shoulder part of the responsibility."

"You have insulted me!"

"If you're insluted now, imagine how you'll feel when Basir Ahmad-Shah gets started on us."

Carlisle saw Sabeir's shooters turn in his direction, glowering, but trusted his own men to take them out if they made any sudden moves. In that case, they would have to kill Sabeir, as well, and find another Taliban militia leader who'd play ball.

No sweat. Next to opium poppies, Afghanistan's fertile soil seemed most apt at producing religious fanatics with plenty of weapons and pent-up hatred. The Bush blitz of 2001 had stripped them of power, but otherwise left their private armies more or less intact, seething with rage and plotting for revenge.

The war and occupation had even managed to overcome Taliban disdain for heroin trafficking as a source of income and a weapons of subversion in the West.

Mission accomplished.

"I will tell Sheikh Ahmad-Shah what I tell you," Sabeir

replied. "My men, under *your* leadership, were ambushed and annihilated. I was neither present nor aware of the specific shipment details."

"But you knew about the killings in Kabul," Carlisle said. "And you damn well know the days when we run shipments into Pakistan, as well as I do. Playing dumb and innocent won't win you any points in this game."

Sabeir was on the verge of making some retort, but he thought better of it, frowning to himself, apparently considering his options and discovering that he had few.

"You have a plan, perhaps?" he said at length.

"I plan to listen and observe," Carlisle replied. "Let Ahmad-Shah vent, if he needs to. Then get down to cases and solve the problem."

"What solution will you propose?"

"I like to stick with basic common sense, whenever possible," Carlisle said. "You can only locate and eradicate an enemy once he's identified. It's pointless, running off in all directions, getting hysterical, looking for scapegoats."

"And have you identified this enemy?"

"I have two solid names and one made up for the occasion. We have people looking for the first two, but they've gone to ground. When I can pin a tag on number three, I'll know who's pulling strings behind the scenes. And then, I'll deal with them."

"But how?" the warlord asked.

"I'll terminate them," Carlisle said. "With extreme prejudice."

*Department of Justice, Washington, D.C.*

HAL BROGNOLA GAVE UP waiting for the call and dialed it on his own, using his private scrambled line. In theory, at least, no one inside the Justice building or at any point between his desk and Stony Man Farm, in the Blue Ridge Mountains of Virginia, would be able to eavesdrop.

And just in case they could, somehow, he'd keep it cryptic, as in days of old.

One of the Farm's young military operators picked up on the second ring and gave the number back to him without inflection, without salutation, making no inquiries.

Brognola gave back a shorter number, randomly selected by computer as the day's pass code, and told the operator, "Patch me to the Bear."

"Yes, sir!" the faceless operator said. "Hold, please."

He held, for all of ten seconds, before the baritone of Aaron Kurtzman—a.k.a. "the Bear"—came on the line.

"I was about to call you," Kurtzman said.

It was as close as he would ever come to chiding Brognola for being overanxious. In the daily game of life-or-death they played together, worry was a given. For the agents they dispatched to foreign killing fields, and for the outcomes of their missions, which were always high intrigue with even higher stakes.

"I was afraid I might've missed you," Brognola lied. "What's the word?"

"It's spotty," Kurtzman said. "We've had nothing direct from Striker, but we weren't expecting anything. Alternate sources on the ground tell us that he engaged within two hours of arrival, and he handled it all right."

Brognola wasn't sure which sources on the ground Kurtzman referred to. It might be the CIA or DEA, maybe the Afghan National Police or Counter Narcotics Police, the latter controlled by Afghanistan's Ministry of the Interior. In any case, he knew Kurtzman would not cite any sources he distrusted, for whatever reason.

"Can you give me specifics?" Brognola inquired.

"There was a reception committee," Kurtzman said. "It's

not clear whether they were there for Striker or his secretary from the local branch office. They had a disagreement. Striker settled it on favorable terms. Unfortunately."

"What?" Brognola pressed.

"There was a problem with his car and sample merchandise. He had to leave them in a hurry."

Brognola translated: shooters had jumped Bolan and his DEA contacts in Kabul. Bolan had disposed of them, but had to ditch his rented car and some or all of the hardware he had acquired upon arrival. Kurtzman couldn't say whether the opposition was expecting Bolan or had followed his contacts, but now his primary cover identity was compromised.

"Is he proceeding?" Brognola inquired, never doubting the answer for a moment.

"Absolutely," Kurtzman said with more enthusiasm. "He's already had a solid impact on the transport operation. We're expecting further progress soon."

"Okay then," Brognola replied. And added, knowing that it wasn't necessary, "Keep me posted, right? Regardless of the time."

"Will do," Kurtzman said just as Brognola severed the link.

He cradled the receiver, lifted his remoted control and tried the office television on a whim. It was preset to CNN, and they had coverage of Afghanistan, but none of it did Hal Brognola any good.

From all appearances, the troubled country was falling apart. Despite ongoing negotiations and supposed "settlements" between Kabul and the Pakistani government, Taliban guerrillas treated Afghanistan's western border as a revolving door, passing freely from one country to the other and back again, striking at will against coalition troops and representatives of the elected government. In the northern provinces, Taliban agents posted threatening "night letters" on the doors of countless villagers, threatening those who supported the state. Rebel violence claimed an average twenty to thirty lives per day, while Washington bemoaned "a growing insurgency, increased attacks and a burgeoning drug trade."

In short, the whole place was going to hell in a handbasket.

And Bolan was stuck in the midst of it, fighting opponents who represented the worst of all sides: the religious fanatics, drug barons and rank profiteers from the West.

It wasn't the first time that Brognola had regretted dispatching his friend on a mission that smelled to high heaven and might well be foredoomed to failure.

Not the first, but possibly the worst.

God keep, he thought, and switched off the depressing TV news.

*Sherzad, Nangarhar Province*

SHERZAD WAS AN administrative district of Nangarhar Province, analogous to a county in an American state. It claimed some 67,000 inhabitants, all Pashtuns, governed locally from Sherzad village.

Sherzad's true ruler was Sheikh Basir Ahmad-Shah, a man whose wealth and influence were recognized beyond Nangarhar Province and beyond Kabul. Informed observers claimed that in addition to Nangarhar, Ahmad-Shah also controlled the lion's share of opium and heroin production in the neighboring provinces of Kumar, Laghman and Lowgar. No one would risk a guess as to the limits of his personal ambition.

Sheikh Basir Ahmad-Shah was very rich indeed. He had a veritable palace outside Sherzad village, with a private army at his beck and call. He had survived the reign of Taliban extremists by corrupting some and terrifying others. Now he prospered through collaboration with Afghanistan's new democratic government, with officials of the coalition that supported that unsteady institution and with private contractors who served the common cause.

But this day he was not a happy man.

Ahmad-Shah greeted his two guests with courtesy, although without his normal warmth. Both visitors were well aware that he had summoned them to answer pressing questions. It was not a social gathering. No women would be joining them and no refreshments would be served.

Clay Carlisle did not seem unduly worried as he chose a cushion on the floor and sat. Beside him, Frozaan Sabeir was as sullen as ever, frowning through his ratty beard, eyes shifty beneath his black turban and beetling brows.

Ahmad-Shah normally distrusted zealots, but he dealt with Sabeir and the Taliban because their soldiers were more numerous and were distributed across a broader range than his. For now.

Carlisle had certain built-in problems, too. He was a Christian and a supposed fanatic in his own right, if Ahmad-Shah could rely on media reports, but from Ahmad-Shah's private observations, the American appeared to worship money over any other deity. Carlisle also had contacts in the West who might not deal directly with an Afghan narco-trafficker. He made the transportation and delivery of merchandise more economical.

Except this day.

Basir Ahmad-Shah broke the ice, saying to both of them at once, "You understand the purpose of this meeting, I believe."

Carlisle nodded, while Sabeir fidgeted, blunt fingers writhing in his lap.

"I wish to hear an explanation," Ahmad-Shah continued, "for the loss of merchandise valued at six billion Afghanis or 130 million U.S. dollars, wholesale."

"Sir, we all know what happened," Carlisle replied. "The convoy was ambushed."

"By whom?" Ahmad-Shah asked.

"We don't know yet."

"You have no suspects whatsoever?"

"There was an incident today, before the ambush," Carlisle said. "Sabeir and I lost several men in Kabul."

"And the matters are related?" Ahmad-Shah inquired.

"I don't have much faith in coincidence," Carlisle admitted.

"So. Explain."

Ahmad-Shah noted that Frozaan Sabeir stayed silent, letting Carlisle speak for both of them. The sheikh knew this was not indicative of trust, much less friendship, but rather of a wish to make himself invisible and be forgotten if some punishment was handed down.

A vain hope, from a foolish man.

"We put a shadow on an agent from the DEA," Carlisle elaborated. "That's the American—"

"Drug Enforcement Administration," Ahmad-Shah finished for him. "I am quite familiar with your country's law-enforcement agencies."

"Of course." Carlisle showed no embarrassment. "I had word from a source inside the U.S. embassy that she—the agent, Deirdre Falk's her name—was bringing in someone from the outside to help with an investigation she's been working on."

"Investigating *us,*" Ahmad-Shah said.

"My operation, more specifically. And probably Sabeir. But yes, your name would certainly come into it at some juncture."

"Continue."

"So the person she was waiting for showed up, but our men failed to take him out."

Carlisle was spreading the blame now, to the evident discomfort of Frozaan Sabeir, who muttered something to himself, his lips moving silently.

"And they were killed? Your men?"

"That's right," Carlisle replied.

"And now my merchandise is up in smoke, along with more of your supposed professionals."

"Regrettably that's true, sir."

"I shall assess a portion of the loss—say, one-third of the gross—to each of you," Ahmad-Shah said. "And I expect the situation to be remedied."

Carlisle blinked once but did not protest. Sabeir sat and fumed, his hands now clenched into double fists.

"Of course, we will resolve the situation to our mutual advantage," Carlisle said.

"I hope so," Ahmad-Shah replied. "If I am forced to intervene, some reconsideration of our contract may be necessary."

"That would be unwelcome and unfortunate," Carlisle replied.

"Indeed it would," Amad-Shah said, thinking, Unfortunate for you.

*Jalalabad, Afghanistan*

BEFORE 9/11 AND THE subsequent American invasion of Afghanistan, Jalalabad claimed 160,000 residents. It was the capital of Nangarhar Province and a major trade center, moving both legitimate cargo and contraband. Decades of war—against the Russians, then between the Taliban and opposition forces, now between western coalition forces and insurgents—had ravaged the city, flooding it with refugees from other provinces and nearby Pakistan.

As Bolan drove slowly through crowded streets, he saw the omnipresent signs of new construction supervised by the United Nations and NATO. Jalalabad was getting a face-lift, but the corrective surgery was being performed in the urban equivalent of a giant MASH tent, with hostilities continuing on every side.

Jalalabad had seen its share of warriors come and go, across the centuries, but few—if any—had seemed more unlikely than the trio who requested separate rooms at the small Mustafa Khan Hotel that evening. The desk clerk seemed confused, trying to pair off Deidre Falk with Bolan, then with Edris Barialy, finally scowling in disapproval as he handed her a key.

As foreigners, Bolan and Falk were both required to show their passports at the desk, but were not forced to leave them there, as some countries demanded. Bolan watched the clerk jot down the numbers and names—in his case, that of Brandon Stone—and knew they would be given up immediately, if police or other figures of authority showed up, searching for foreigners.

Barialy, as an Afghan national, was not required to show ID, but he'd be fingered with his two companions, guilty by association, if any questions arose. And his penalty, if the state determined that he was a spy, could be death.

"My room in twenty minutes," Bolan told the others as they separated on the second floor.

Despite the fact that they had glimpsed no other guests while checking in, two rooms separated Bolan's from Falk's, while Barialy's lay at the far end of the hallway, in the opposite direction. Bolan used his key—no pass cards in a place of this vintage—and stepped into a room that Dr. Watson might have occupied before he set off to the Battle of Maiwand, nearly 130 years ago.

Okay, the sheets and towels weren't *that* old, but the wallpaper was definitely vintage, and the whole room had a musty smell about it, as if it had not been aired for years. Bolan tried opening the window, found that it was painted shut and gave it up.

He'd used the washroom and swapped his dusty, sweaty clothes for clean replacements by the time Falk and Barialy came knocking. He double-locked the door behind them, while Falk looked around his room and said, "Hey, yours is way nicer than mine."

"Must be discrimination," Bolan said.

"I wouldn't doubt it," she replied. "You see the way that guy was looking at me?"

"Unescorted women," Barialy said, "are seen as, um, I mean to say they're not respectable."

"That weasel made me for a hooker?"

Falk seemed on the verge of marching back downstairs to settle it when Bolan called a halt to the festivities. "Before we go out and redecorate the place," he said, "we need to talk about what's waiting for us."

"Are we not finished?" Barialy asked.

Bolan had to smile at that. "Not even close," he said. "One shipment down won't stop Carlisle or his suppliers. We're just getting started."

"I suppose that there must be more shooting, then?" the short Afghani asked.

"Bet on it," Bolan said.

And briefed them on their next target.

*U.S. Embassy, Kabul*

RUSS LATIMER WAS RUNNING out of leads and out of time. His contacts at the Ministry of Justice, Afghan National Police and the CNPA weren't returning his follow-up calls, which meant they either possessed no new information or else they were sick and tired of talking to him.

Either way, the man from Langley figured he was screwed.

If he went back to Lee Hastings with nothing, Hastings might be moved to place a transatlantic phone call that would bring the curtain down on Latimer's career. The Agency's director wouldn't fire him outright, knowing that to do so might open an ugly can of worms. He might send Latimer to Greenland or some stagnant Balkan backwater, where all he had to do was answer e-mails about "national security" and watch the time to see if it was booze-o'clock.

So far, so bad.

But if he went back to Clay Carlisle empty-handed, then the shit would *really* hit the fan. His secret bank accounts, which had been fattened over years of clandestine toil, could vanish with a keystroke of some mechanic's laptop. Latimer couldn't complain, in that case, since his nest egg was strictly illegal and Latimer hadn't remembered to keep the tax people informed.

Exposure of his dealings with Carlisle and Vanguard would cost him his job and might send him to prison, assuming that Latimer lived long enough to stand trial. But if he crossed Carlisle, even the Company might not be able to keep him alive.

In fact, he was convinced that some higher-ups would be quick to sacrifice him, in their own best interest.

His best insurance was performance, which meant finding "Matthew Cooper," whoever he was, and serving the bastard up to Carlisle on a platter. Second-best would be if Latimer discovered who had sent Cooper to Kabul, and revealed *that* to Carlisle. The news might be unwelcome, but at least Vanguard's CEO would be forewarned the next time enemies came gunning for him.

Now, if Latimer could find Cooper *and* name the group or individual who'd sent him into Kabul, that would be the hat trick. Carlisle would be grateful, no two ways about it. He might even put a little something extra in Latimer's next covert pay envelope, to put away for a rainy day.

And it was raining pretty goddamned hard right now.

Latimer needed to make sure that he wasn't washed away

by the deluge. And if worse came to worst, he wanted to be the last man afloat on the life raft.

He'd often heard it said that winners wrote the history of wars and other conflicts, meaning that they had to be survivors. Harry Houdini had vowed to come back from the grave if he could, and his elderly fans were still waiting.

Latimer needed to go him one better, get out of this damned mess alive, and keep everything he could grab in the process.

Scowling at wrinkled maps of Kabul and northern Afghanistan, he muttered to himself, "Cooper, you prick, where are you?"

*Outside Mihtarlam, Laghman Province, Afghanistan*

"THE DAMNED AMERICAN treats me as if I was his servant," Frozaan Sabeir said. "A cursed drug dealer summons the pair of us, and I must sit in silence, like a child, while the American offers promises."

Karzai Parisa listened to Sabeir's complaints without comment or interruption. When Sabeir was in one of his moods, it did no good to counsel him, and might, in fact, have fatal consequences.

If he was to speak, Parisa might have offered a reminder that Sabeir had chosen to do business both with the American, Carlisle, and with Sheikh Basir Ahmad-Shah. He had involved himself with drugs and heretics, thus violating sacred principles of the Koran, because Sabeir believed that other Taliban militia leaders would step in and fill the void if he declined. They would grow stronger, as a consequence, and threaten Sabeir's influence in Laghman Province and surrounding areas.

Karzai Parisa had remained with Sabeir for the same reasons, weighing his soul and access to the sweet rewards of Paradise against what he believed to be his earthly mission.

"Now we have become the hunted," Sabeir told him, as if that was something new. "Not only by the state and the Crusader coalition, but by these assassins no one can identify."

"We know the woman from the DEA," Parisa said. "We know the traitor from Kabul who serves her."

"Yes," Sabeir agreed. "But where are they? Their names are meaningless if we cannot locate and kill the two of them."

"The agent," Parisa said with a shrug, "who knows? She has no roots in Kabul, only an apartment now abandoned. But the other, Edris Barialy…"

"You have located his family?"

Parisa risked a smile. "It was a relatively simple thing. Since they are likely unaware of his betrayal, they made no attempt to hide."

"He may not be in touch with them," Sabeir replied.

"In fact, I doubt that he would risk it, sir. But they still know him best, his secret life aside. Indeed, they may have valuable information without even knowing it. A simple comment may deliver him to us. A name, an address, anything."

"Have the police secured them yet?"

"They have detained his parents and a sister," Parisa said. "There are others we could try, in Kabul or at home in Fayzabad. A grandfather, uncles and so on."

"We could hold them hostage!" Sabeir said, beaming at the sheer brilliance of his notion.

"Sir, that might rebound against us," Parisa said cautiously.

"How so?"

"First, Barialy may not know we have the prisoners, unless he is in daily contact with his family. In that case, they provide no real advantage."

"So? Why not announce it?" Sabeir asked.

Parisa nearly grimaced, but he caught himself in time. "Sir, by announcing the abductions, we reveal our link to the events in Kabul and Nangarhar Province."

"But we—"

"Which, in turn, links us to Carlisle and to Basir Ahmad-Shah."

Sabeir had seen the trap, at last. He shut his mouth, went through the ritual of knuckle-cracking that Parisa knew to be one of his many nervous tics, and doubtless spent a moment thinking what would happen if his name was linked in print with drug-dealing.

It was one thing to furnish guards and pocket money for the service. But to be revealed as a narcotics trafficker—worse yet, acting in league with the despised Americans—could be the kiss of death.

Sabeir could not acknowledge an involvement in the drug trade *and* pose as a valiant warrior of Ged. It made no difference if each and every one of his opponents also smuggled heroin, as long as their transgressions were concealed.

The sin, at least in human eyes, was getting caught.

"What shall we do, then?" Sabeir asked long moments later.

"Sir, I recommend that we locate and question Barialy's relatives. Find out if they know anything, and use whatever information we collect to find him. He will not desert his new friends while the three of them are hunted."

Sabeir nodded slowly, then replied as if the idea had been his.

"So be it. Give the order in my name, and supervise the search yourself."

Parisa bowed to hide his smile, saying, "To hear is to obey."

# CHAPTER EIGHT

*Nangarhar Province*

Unlike the poppy farm they'd driven past, the heroin refinery was covered from the highway by a screen of trees including both old growth and new. Its single-access road was an inviting trap, but Bolan motored past and slowed to a crawl, seeking another exit from the two-lane highway that would let him stash his vehicle.

He found it three hundred yards past the refinery's entrance, ancient tire ruts disappearing into weeds and shrubbery, apparently a dead-end track to nowhere.

From its appearance, Bolan guessed that no one else had pulled in there for months, perhaps for years. Only the barest trace of former vehicles was visible, and that vanished when Bolan killed his headlights.

It seemed perfect.

"Let's try this," he said, and nosed the vehicle into the weeds before his passengers could offer an opinion on the subject. Bolan crept along at something below walking speed, ready to brake at once if he felt any major shifting in the soil beneath his tires, and stopped a hundred feet back from the highway.

No one in a passing vehicle would see their car before sunrise, unless they scanned the roadside scrublands with a spotlight. That would mean a hunter-killer team, and Bolan knew he would find nowhere to conceal his ride from someone who was both determined and professional.

He switched off the dome lights before he stepped out of the car and stretched, back turned to Falk and Barialy as they did likewise. Bolan had slept well during his flight to Kabul, and with seven hours on the ground felt fairly fresh, but he supposed the pace was wearing on his two companions.

"We can rest here, briefly, if you like," he told them.

"I'm all right," Falk said, her face masked by the moonless night.

"Perhaps we should proceed," Edris Barialy said, sounding not at all convinced.

"Okay, then. Rally 'round."

Bolan spread Falk's line drawing of the heroin refinery on the Toyota's trunk lid and used a penlight to illuminate it, screened by the half circle of their bodies.

"We're out here," he said, pointing beyond the left edge of the paper, "moving eastward. I'm assuming that your aerial recon photos are recent."

"Last week," Falk replied.

"Then we have no fence to cut or climb. That helps, but they still may have other security fixtures in place. Guards, for sure, but we don't know how many. Some may have been sent with the convoy, or that could be pure wishful thinking. Basir Ahmad-Shah and Carlisle have a sizable investment here. It won't be unprotected."

"So what can we do?" Barialy asked, sounding even less enthusiastic now.

"Scout first, then plan our move. I haven't seen the layout yet, except on paper. If it gels, I should be ready for a strike at daybreak."

"You mean *we'll* be ready, right?" Falk asked.

"This is a different ball game," Bolan told her. "Back in Kabul, when they tried to get the drop on us, I went on instinct. With the convoy, it was basic strategy. They have to pass a certain point. We line them up and knock them down."

"It didn't seem *that* simple," Falk replied.

"Compared to what's in front of us, it was. Believe me," Bolan said. "This time, I'm going up against the home team, on their own ground. Unknown numbers and security devices."

"But you're going in, regardless," Falk said.

"Absolutely."

"Then I'm going, too," she said. "Hell, I'm a murderer already. Why stop now?"

He had to smile at that, but only for a heartbeat.

"Right," he said, and turned to Barialy. "You?"

"It is a long walk back to Kabul, where they wait to kill me anyway," the Afghan said.

"Okay, then. Step one is to reach the target without losing anyone along the way or setting off any alarms. There's no rush, as long as we're in place and ready by an hour prior to dawn."

"Why then?" Falk asked.

"Part of it's psychological," Bolan said. "There's a natural letdown in defenses, maybe something going back to prehistoric times, when dawn meant safety from nocturnal predators. More people die in hospitals and nursing homes around that time, as well. In Italy, it's called the hour of the wolf. By any name, it seems to work."

"I'm hoping we're the wolves," Falk said.

"I hope so, too," Bolan replied. "But even wolves get caught in traps sometimes. We need to do our recon first, so we don't step in anything we can't get out of."

"So let's do it, then," Falk said.

The hike back to the heroin refinery from where he'd

parked the car was just under a quarter mile, with trees around them all the way. The undergrowth was mostly stunted grass and wildflowers, no thorns or tangle-foot to slow them or make unnecessary noise. They took it slowly, cautiously, and twenty minutes after starting out they had the dark bulk of the plant in view.

When Bolan spoke, he whispered, barely audible even with Falk and Barialy leaning into him.

"From here on," he informed them, "any careless step could be your last. Stay with me. Don't make any noise or sudden moves."

They nodded acquiescence and three shadows moved as one, circling the heroin refinery in darkness, one step at a time.

*Vanguard International Branch Office, Kabul*

"HOW'D IT GO?" Dale Ingram asked as he settled in the chair in front of Clay Carlisle's desk.

"Humiliation sums it up," Carlisle replied. "Bowing and scraping for that heathen bastard while he sat there, sneering. And the worst of it was that he's right. We let him down. Failed absolutely on security, which is supposed to be our specialty."

"We couldn't know there'd be an ambush," Ingram said.

Carlisle's fist slammed onto his desktop, jangling the nearby telephone, rattling a stylish pen-and-pencil set.

"Is that supposed to make it right?" he snapped. "Of course we didn't know. That's why it's called an ambush. If they advertised it in advance, no one would need security. We'd all be out of business."

Ingram blushed, saying, "I only meant—"

"And we'll *be* out of business," Carlisle interrupted, "unless we get our shit together in a hurry. Last night's blunder cost us twenty-eight men and our piece of 130 million dollars. I won't accept excuses for that kind of failure! I *will not* let such negligence be repeated!"

"No," Ingram replied. "You're right, of course."

"So, we're agreed. That's good. What's the progress in our search for Mr. Matthew Cooper?"

Ingram swallowed hard, hoping it didn't show. He kept his face deadpan and said, "No further progress, I'm afraid. His car's impounded and he hasn't rented any other wheels—at least, under that name. We're helping the police check out hotels in Kabul, but it's going nowhere."

"Can you tell me where he got the guns recovered from the rental car?" Carlisle asked.

"No, sir. They're generic military surplus, mostly Russian. Any covert dealer in the country could've sold them to him, *if* he bought them here."

"Well, that's a given, isn't it?" Carlisle replied sarcastically. "He got the car here, didn't he? You think he flew in with the weapons in his luggage?"

"No. I simply meant—"

"If you can't trace the weapons," Carlisle interrupted, "what about his little helpers? Falk from DEA, and this Afghani. What's his handle?"

"Edris Barialy," Ingram said. "And so far, we've got nothing more on either one of them. Falk hasn't called her office since the shooting in the Old City this afternoon. She hasn't gone to her apartment. Barialy hasn't been home, either. We have both their places covered."

"Maybe they've left Kabul," Carlisle said. "Maybe they took a little drive out past Shinwar."

Ingram leaned forward in his chair. "You think *they* pulled the ambush? Took out twenty-eight men on their own?"

"They handled twelve without breaking a sweat," Carlisle replied.

"That was a fluke," Ingram said. "There's a world of difference between fighting through a loose stakeout and taking down an armed convoy, killing more than twice as many men on full alert and torching a shipment of smack. Besides…"

He faltered, but Carlisle prodded him.

"Go on. Besides, *what?*"

"Well, think about it. If the ambush *was* this Cooper's doing, where'd he get the hardware? The police picked up his hardware with the rental car in Sharh-e-Khone."

"They got some of his hardware," Carlisle said. "We both know you can outfit a battalion without leaving Kabul, if you have the cash to spend. So Cooper bought more guns—or had them stashed already, as insurance."

Ingram shook his head, still disbelieving.

"Then," he said, "there's Falk. She's DEA, for Chri—for heaven's sake. A cop. You think she's out there, shooting up the countryside like Annie Oakley?"

"Annie Oakley was a trick-shot artist with a Wild West show," Carlisle replied. "I'm not concerned with ancient history, when we've got people meddling in our business, killing off our men and taking money from our pockets!"

Feeling defeated, Ingram said, "It was just a figure of speech."

"Well, if you're feeling clever," Carlisle told him, "think of some way we can find this Cooper person and his friends. Bag them, and we'll find out if they're the ones responsible for last night's fiasco. If they are, we've solved our problem and they'll tell us who's behind it. If they're not, they still owe us eleven lives."

"I'll find them," Ingram promised him.

"See that you do," Carlisle replied, and spun his swivel chair, turning his back to Ingram as his second in command stood and left the room.

*Nangarhar Province*

DEIRDRE FALK HAD DONE her fair share of stakeouts, and then some, but she'd never been involved in anything resembling Matt Cooper's recon of Basir Ahmad-Shah's drug refinery. It wasn't simply creeping through the dark on unfamiliar ground that made the experience unique. Nor was she troubled by the fact that they possessed no search warrants.

Deficient paperwork was nothing, in comparison to what she'd done so far following Cooper's lead. It seemed incredible, but after the initial shooting in Kabul she had been swept along by events that seemed strange beyond measure, surpassing anything in her experience.

And yet Falk felt…what?

Not good, which presumed happiness, but she certainly wasn't encumbered by guilt. She hadn't pulled the trigger on a decent man so far, and as for legal repercussions, she'd begun to feel as if she was beyond the law somehow. Not above it, but caught in a zone where rules mattered less than results.

Or maybe that was just her premonition that she wouldn't make it through the night.

She stood between Cooper and Barialy, silently examining the guarded loading dock where trucks backed up to take on loads of packaged heroin. The last two trucks to leave the plant were smoking wrecks right now, midway between where Falk stood and the Pakistani border.

How much heroin had they destroyed in those ferocious moments on the highway? Had there been a ton? Or double that? Had Falk saved any lives in Europe or the States by killing Carlisle's mercenaries?

Or would torching that much product simply raise the street price of a fix?

"It's one way in," Bolan said, cutting through Falk's speculation with a whisper. "But it may not be the best. Let's see the rest of it."

They moved on, circling warily, marking the sentries as they made their way around the plant. Falk had no way of knowing when their shift change might occur, but every stranger that she saw was one more she might have to kill.

One more who might kill her.

She'd reached her supervisor briefly, trying to communicate with him through crackling static and repeated fades that made it sound as if he might have fallen down a well. He'd cautioned her against returning to the office in Kabul, where it was "raining shit," and urged Falk to get by as best she could with Cooper—whom, her boss said, was "the real deal, five by five."

Amen to that, she thought, then wondered who she might be praying to.

Was there a deity that sanctioned vigilante tactics when the System failed? If so, did He have any kind of rule book Falk could study, that would help her find her way?

Too late.

She cleared her mind to focus on the target. From her background research, Falk knew it had been constructed in the 1960s as a slaughterhouse, where cattle, sheep and goats were butchered twelve hours per day, six days per week. The plant had closed after the Russians invaded Afghanistan in 1978, and stood empty throughout the ten-year occupation. Sometime around 1990, it had been converted to its present use. Taliban zealots closed it again in 1997, but coalition troops had cleared the way for reactivation in 2001.

How many millions had Basir Ahmad-Shah banked since then, from this single refinery? Falk knew the plant wasn't his only one, although it was the largest and the most productive. Closing it for good would be a victory, she thought.

No matter who got hurt in the process.

She'd seen five guards so far. One stationed at each corner

of the factory, and one more on the loading dock. All carried automatic rifles, and they all appeared to be Afghans. Two wore black turbans commonly associated with the Taliban, while three did not. Unless some of them bolted when the action started, she supposed all five of them would have to die.

How many more inside?

Falk didn't want to think about it. They were here to close a heroin refinery, not log a body count. The fact that they would have to spill more blood was inescapable, but secondary to their main objective.

This was war, she thought.

Her law-enforcement colleagues used the term a lot, describing what they did from day to day in the defense of civilized society, but it remained hyperbole for most of them, who never fired a shot in anger during their careers.

Now, Deirdre Falk had crossed the line from talking war to waging it.

And there was no way back.

"One more go-round," Bolan said, almost breathing in her ear. "Then we can pick our spots."

"Spots, as in more than one?" she whispered back.

"It's more efficient that way," he replied. "It helps with the survival odds."

She gave a fatalistic shrug and said, "Okay, then. Sign me up."

*Sherzad, Nangarhar Province*

SHEIKH BASIR AHMAD-Shah smoked thoughtfully, eyes focused on some distant point in space, before he said, "I want the guard doubled on all of our facilities."

"I'll see to it at once," Jamal Woraz replied.

As Ahmad-Shah's favored lieutenant and his strong right arm, Woraz agreed with everything his master said and found ways to transform his orders into flesh-and-blood reality.

Doubling of guards was simple. All it took was men and money in sufficient quantities.

As for their real problem…

"I fear we must begin to look beyond Carlisle and Vanguard International," the sheikh continued. "I never fully trusted the Americans, as you know, and now it seems they cannot even guard my merchandise effectively."

"Shall we dispense with him?" Woraz inquired, hoping that he did not appear too eager.

"Not yet," Ahmad-Shah replied, "but it is always best to be prepared for any circumstance."

"I will update our information on the target's residence and office in Kabul."

"And his associate," Ahmad-Shah said. "The pudgy one."

"Ingram," Woraz said, providing the name.

"If one goes, both must go, to throw the rest off balance."

"What of the intelligence they have collected during our collaboration?" Woraz asked.

"The DEA already recognizes our operation," Ahmad-Shah replied. "So do the National Police, ASNF and CNPA. They ignore us, as you know, because we pay them well to close their eyes. God be praised, there is no longer any Vice and Virtue Ministry."

That government department, thirty thousand strong under the Taliban regime, had been created to enforce bans on popular music, television and videotapes, kite-flying and other forms of "immoral amusement," while harassing men who cut their beards and women who resisted wearing head-to-toe burqas. Woraz himself had slain two of the group's petty tyrants, leaving their naked corpses in the gutters of Jalalabad.

Those seemed like ancient times, since the Americans had stripped the Taliban of its authority and passed the reins of government to more practical men. Still, Basir Ahmad-Shah and those who served him had their share of enemies.

And enemies had to be eradicated.

"Have we made progress in finding Edris Barialy?"

The use of *we* was gracious on the sheikh's part, when Jamal Woraz and his subordinates were doing all the work.

"We have addresses for his next of kin, as do the National Police," Woraz replied.

"Are they in custody?" Ahmad-Shah asked.

"Detained for questioning, without charges. Of course, that does not guarantee that they will ever be released."

"I doubt that they know where he is," the sheikh observed. "Still, we must be apprised of any information the police obtain."

"It is arranged, sir."

"On the other hand, if it were possible for them to be released into our custody, the matter might be more efficiently resolved."

"I can suggest it, but we may face opposition in a matter so public."

"A suggestion is sufficient. What of the Americans, their DEA? The man in charge… What is his name again?"

Woraz supposed it was a test. Ahmad-Shah never forgot the name or face of anyone significant.

"Alan Combs," Woraz replied. "He has been stationed in Kabul since the Americans came. Their rules demand that he retire in three months' time."

"That may be too long to endure him, if he lets his agents violate the law," Ahmad-Shah said.

Woraz missed any irony inherent in his master's comment. Among criminals around the world, it is an article of faith that law-enforcement officers are limited, and rightly so, by regulations governing their conduct in pursuit of felons. Any violation of those rules threatens the balance that permits organized crime to flourish in the shadows.

"We could kill him," Woraz said.

"Indeed we could," the sheikh replied. "What risks do you suppose we might incur?"

Woraz considered it and shrugged. "If he or his superiors already grant their agents freedom to ignore the laws of both Afghanistan and the United States, they can do nothing more against us. It is possible his death may cause them some embarrassment."

"Another benefit," Ahmad-Shah said. "Make the arrangements."

"Yes, sir."

"I am sick of doing nothing while these whoresons make us look like fools."

Woraz offered no reply to that, afraid that Basir Ahmad-Shah might think his answer meant the sheikh seemed foolish in *his* eyes.

Instead he said, "I shall assign our best men to the work in Kabul."

Ahmad-Shah turned to face him with a smile. "If feasible," he said, "I would enjoy a gift of the American's ears."

*Nangarhar Province*

BOLAN PRESSED a button on his wristwatch to illuminate its face and read the time impassively. Another forty-seven minutes remained before it struck the hour of the wolf.

He'd run a risk leaving the others on their own, positioned at strategic points beyond his line of sight. If the refinery's commander should decide to mount predawn patrols, Bolan's companions would be isolated and cut off, forced to evade detection or to defend themselves alone. The greater risk, though, in his mind, is that fatigue would overtake them as they lay immobile, lulling one or both of them to sleep.

He would've bet on Edris Barialy first, to drop the ball. The Afghan lacked Deirdre Falk's law-enforcement training and experience, which would include no end of dreary stakeouts working for the DEA. Still, Falk herself was only human, and the day that had begun for her when Bolan introduced himself in Kabul might have stretched her reserved to their limit.

Bottom line: there was nothing he could do about his comrades now. He couldn't man his post and do his part while creeping through the dark to check on them, make sure they were wide-eyed and ready for the next grim party to begin.

He'd strike when it was time, unless some unforeseen event should force his hand ahead of schedule, and he'd trust the others to support him. If they failed, Bolan would soldier on alone and do his best against the odds.

And if they fell, while Bolan somehow made it out alive, there would be two more ghosts to follow him through the remainder of his lonely war.

God knew he had enough already, but there seemed to be no limit on how many the Executioner could collect. Old friends and allies, adversaries, innocent bystanders. Bolan had them all, and then some.

He could feel them with him now, not in a Sci-Fi Channel kind of way, but watching. Maybe even judging. Was that how it worked when crossing over to the Great Beyond? Were souls judged by the others they had helped or harmed along the way?

Seemed fair, he thought, and put it out of mind.

Bolan had picked the loading dock for his approach, since it was covered by three guards: one in the loading bay itself, two others at the nearest corners of the plant, say eighty feet away on either side. That left Barialy and Falk to deal with one guard each, before they reached their entry points on the northern and eastern flanks of the plant and made their way inside.

At which point, they were flying blind.

The plant was running, so he knew there must be workers—lab rats for refining, maybe peasants hired to do the packaging—but Bolan didn't know how loyal they were to Basir Ahmad-Shah, if they'd resist, or if they would be armed.

He *did* know there would be some kind of manager in place, to supervise, and surplus guards to rotate with the outer sentries. But how many? Were they sleeping now, or maybe eating breakfast, getting ready for a shift change?

All those questions would be answered when he got inside.

Assuming Bolan lived that long.

Hazards inside a drug refinery went far beyond resistance by its posted guards, as Deirdre Falk would know firsthand. They'd skated through the smoke and fumes of burning heroin during the convoy ambush, but inhaling airborne heroin during a firefight was the quickest way Bolan could think of to get killed. Aside from that, ether and other explosive chemicals used in the refining process could be touched off by a muzzle-flash or damned near anything.

Bolan intended to destroy the plant, but he had no wish to be trapped inside it when it blew. Ideally he would do his job and live to fight another day.

And as his wristwatch silently confirmed, that other day had already arrived.

At one time, he had seen the bumper stickers everywhere, reading This Is the First Day of the Rest of Your Life. Then, of course, some smart-ass wag had come along and cashed in with another reading This is the *Last* Day of the Rest of Your Life.

Funny.

But in Bolan's world, each day could wind up either way. No living soul on Earth was guaranteed tomorrow, but in Bolan's line of work, the risks were multiplied exponentially. No actuary in the world would bet on him surviving through another week.

It was a treat to prove them wrong.

And now, he was about to roll the dice again.

# CHAPTER NINE

*Nangarhar Province*

Arzad Mansoor hated call-outs in the middle of the night, especially when he had female company, but when Jamal Woraz commanded him to put his pants on and collect a group of gunmen, Mansoor dutifully obeyed.

He knew Woraz was speaking for Sheikh Basir Ahmad-Shah, and furthermore that Woraz in his own right could crush Mansoor like an insect if he chose to do so.

Thus, Mansoor found himself in the shotgun seat of a Toyota Highlander SUV, speeding through early-morning darkness with three armed men in the backseat behind him and five more in a following vehicle. Still only half awake despite a mug of strong coffee and the urgency of his errand, Mansoor reflected on what Woraz had told him.

And it wasn't much.

A convoy from the sheikh's refinery had been destroyed en route to Pakistan. Now Ahmad-Shah wanted the guard force doubled on his plants and other properties, which he deemed likely targets of attack.

To hear was to obey.

Mansoor had managed to collect his team in ninety minutes, which was good, considering that he'd been forced to call most of them grumbling out of bed. They answered Mansoor's call as he answered the summons from Jamal Woraz, because their lives depended on it, but they were not pleased at the prospect of standing guard outside a factory for God only knew how long.

Mansoor had not asked who destroyed the sheikh's convoy. Policemen would have seized the drugs and vehicles. Destruction meant an enemy who did not shrink from killing.

Which, in turn, could have been any rival narco-trafficker.

Mansoor was not concerned about the "who," or even "why." He cared about *how many,* where they might strike next, and whether he had brought enough men for the job he'd been assigned to do.

Technically, Mansoor was safe. Woraz had ordered him to double the refinery's security detachment, and his team would raise the number on site from ten to twenty men. In realistic terms, however, he was still uncertain that he'd brought enough.

Woraz could not revile him for obeying orders to the letter, but if Mansoor lacked sufficient men and guns to guard the plant, he might be killed.

Hard choices for hard men.

Mansoor turned to his driver, a cutthroat named Karim Hajera, and asked him, "How much longer?"

"Twenty minutes, maybe half an hour," Hajera replied.

Mansoor cursed softly. It was insufficient time for sleep, although a couple of his shooters in the backseat had been snoring almost from the moment they sat.

Jealous, Mansoor rounded on them, raised his voice to snap them out of it, and asked, "Has anyone been out to the refinery before?"

Three heads wagged side-to-side, in silent negative replies.

"Nor me," Mansoor admitted. "So it's unfamiliar ground. We don't know who's expected to show up, or if they're even coming. But if they could take a convoy on the road, despite its guards, they're dangerous."

"How many guards?" one of the backseat shooters asked.

Mansoor could only guess. "Perhaps twenty," he said, "for an important shipment."

"And this was important?"

"They are all important," Mansoor answered.

"Twenty men," Hajera muttered from the driver's seat. "And we have ten."

"Plus ten or more already guarding the refinery," Mansoor reminded him.

His driver shrugged unhappily. "If they killed twenty once, why not kill twenty twice? We should have forty, fifty men, at least."

"You want to call Jamal Woraz and tell him that?" Mansoor produced a cell phone from inside his jacket, offered it to Hajera with a frown. "I have his number on speed dial. Press two. Disturb the man at home, at this hour, and tell him you have doubts about his leadership."

Hajera shook his head. "I do as I am told," he said.

"And with a willing spirit," Mansoor prodded him.

"Of course! I live to serve."

If there was sarcasm behind the words, Mansoor chose not to hear it. His assignment was already tedious enough, and laden with potential risks. He did not need to make it worse by sowing animosity among his men.

"Be ready," he warned all of them, while anxious fingers stroked the submachine gun in his lap. "Remember, anything can happen from the moment we arrive."

BOLAN TIED THE SCARF behind his neck, then raised it in front to cover his nose and mouth. It wasn't a disguise, but rather substituted for the surgical mask he'd neglected to buy in Kabul. It would help with smoke inside the plant, and more importantly, with any cloud of white addictive powder raised by gunfire and explosions while he brought the rat's nest down.

If Falk and Barialy were awake, they would taking similar precautions at that moment, getting ready for their jump-off in—he checked his watch again—two minutes' time.

Bolan was hoping for surprise, but he could only carry it so far. Darkness would cover his approach at first, but lights had burned all night over the loading dock, and when he dropped that guard, the other two were bound to notice. Once the party started, he would need a nifty one-two-three step to prevent a racket that would certainly alert more guards inside the plant.

And even then, he had to breach the place.

Bolan fitted a suppressor to his pistol's threaded muzzle, spinning it in place until the connection was snug. Added weight made the Jericho muzzle-heavy, but Bolan had been using silenced pistols from the first days of his one-man war against the Mafia, and he had learned to compensate.

The problems with suppressors were that few produced a truly "silent" shot, and the gas-bleed that reduced a gunshot's noise also reduced a bullet's velocity. Not much, in most cases, but in some it could make a significant difference.

Especially if the target was wearing Kevlar.

Bolan saw no evidence that any of the sentries in his view were wearing body armor, and he knew it would be out of character for hit men on a basic guard detail. If Bolan's luck held, he could take the three men down before one of them jerked a trigger and announced his presence to the world.

But even if his luck failed, he was going in.

One minute left until H-Hour.

Bolan counted down the seconds, gathering his muscles for the leap and sprint toward the loading dock. He carried the

Israeli pistol in his right hand, with his AKSU-74 reversed in his left, butt forward for an easy hand-off to himself when he had need of greater firepower. The MGL launcher was slung across his back, easily reachable, as were his bandoliers of 40 mm rounds and extra magazines.

Ten seconds.

Bolan pictured Falk and Barialy at their posts, participating in the silent countdown. He had told them to push off at one minute past four o'clock, instead of waiting for any signal on his part. If Bolan was successful, there would *be* no signal. He would reach the loading dock and find his way inside the plant even as Falk and Barialy dropped their men.

And that was critical, because their weapons had no sound supressors.

One minute's grace was all he had, and Bolan hoped that it would be enough.

He felt the hour strike and launched himself at full speed from the shadows that had sheltered him. His footsteps on the dirt and sparse grass thundered in his ears, becoming even louder with his first step onto old cracked pavement, but the sentries still did not appear to notice him.

Another few strides, and the shooter on the loading dock was finally rising out of his trance, groping for the weapon he had propped against the wall beside his metal folding chair.

Bolan fired twice at thirty yards, the classic double-tap, and saw his rounds slap hard against the target's chest, slamming him back against the bricks now streaked with crimson.

A pivot to his left and Bolan faced the second target, sighting down the Jericho's slide for a longer shot. Again he squeezed the trigger twice, saw one slug raise a flap of scalp and bone before the sentry dropped.

One left, and Bolan swung through the three-sixty, facing back toward what had been his right-hand side when he left cover. The third sentry had his rifle shouldered, was about to fire, when Bolan shot him three times on the rise, between his navel and his throat.

With ten rounds still remaining in his pistol, Bolan took the concrete steps three at a time and strode across the loading dock.

A steel door stood in front of him.

Its knob turned in his hand.

GUARD DUTY AT THE DOPE plant was a drag. Ike Skelton wanted to be out hunting the bastards who had killed eight of his friends, along with several times that many of their Afghan colleagues. He could almost taste his hatred for them, and could damn sure feel it churning in his gut, but he was stuck there, babysitting at the factory with Rick Belanger and a bunch of natives that he couldn't even talk to, while the hunt went on without him.

Afghanistan was Skelton's second tour with Vanguard, after eighteen months in Africa. He had been guarding diamond mines on that job, and the miners who were little more than slaves as far as he could tell. The politics were none of Skelton's business, and he had no interest in it, any more than he'd been interested in math or history when he was cruising through high school and junior college as a football star.

He'd fumbled once too often while the scouts were watching, though, and when he didn't make it to the pros his sophomore year, he'd joined the Navy and went through SEAL instead, to test himself. As it turned out, he loved the action but was hungry for a bigger paycheck, so he'd pulled the pin with four years in and found his way to Vanguard International.

Which suited him just fine, except when he got bored and thought that maybe he should go out there and find some action of his own, make something happen if he couldn't find a brawl in progress.

"You want to get some sleep?" Belanger inquired. "I've got another four, five hours in me, if you want to hit the sack."

"I'm bored, not tired," Skelton replied. "Bored *and* pissed off. We ought to be out with the others, not stuck here, sitting around."

"I guess the brass thinks someone might drop by," Belanger said.

"In which case, why send just the two of us?"

"Because the others—"

"Are out hunting. Yeah. I know."

"You've got the itch, man," Belanger suggested. "You just want to get some."

"Goddamned right I do. What's wrong with that?"

In modern military parlance, the time-honored phrase "get some" transcended its familiar usage with regard to sex. Young soldiers hungered for the thrill of action, even mortal combat where they might be killed at any second. It was why they joined the military in the first place—or abandoned it, if there were no wars left to fight.

And yeah, Ike Skelton definitely wanted to get some.

"Best I can do," Belanger said, "is get you drunk and get you laid when this is over."

"Man, there'd better be a woman in there somewhere," Skelton answered.

"Fuck you, buddy!"

"See? I *knew* it. Man, you gotta—"

Skelton almost missed the first shot. Almost, but not quite.

"Hear that?" he asked Belanger.

"I heard something."

"Sounded like an AK." Moving as he spoke, Skelton grabbed his Model 733 Colt Commando carbine.

"Shit. One of the rags out killing shadows," Belanger replied.

"Whatever. We still need to check it out."

His hand was on the break room's doorknob when the first explosion rocked the factory.

IT WAS THE FINAL SIXTY seconds, knowing that Matt Cooper had already made his move to enter the refinery, that tortured Deirdre Falk. She understood the need to wait, and wished like hell that she'd bagged a suppressor for the Mini-Uzi while she had the chance, but Cooper knew his strategy.

She waited, holding down the button on her watch so that its face was constantly aglow, until she got to the ten-second mark and started counting in her head. At *eight*, she checked the safety on her AKSU for the thousandth time or so.

At *six*, she touched her holstered Glock, then made a minuscule adjustment to the Mini-Uzi's shoulder strap, hoping it wouldn't bang against her ribs too much during her dash toward the refinery. Then thought, Who cares? If I get through this night with nothing but some bruises, it will be a freaking miracle.

She rose at *three*, stepped off a beat ahead of time and silently apologized to Cooper for the breach of discipline. As if it mattered.

Cooper was in by now, she guessed. If he had failed, she would have heard the sentries killing him, or there would be some kind of shrill alarm, like during prison breaks. She'd *know* if he had failed—and she'd be running for her life, back to the car and the large rock where Cooper had concealed the keys, in case he didn't make it back but she and Barialy did.

As if.

The door Falk was supposed to try lay straight ahead of her, but her first target was a gunman standing thirty-odd feet to her left. He had his back turned toward her at the moment, giving Falk a fleeting qualm about what she was now required to do.

Fair play, and all.

Screw it.

She broke stride, aimed and shot the stranger once between his shoulder blades and watched him drop, trusting the AKSU's 5.45 mm slug to keep him down.

And they were in the shit now, totally. The plant's brick walls might muffle gunshots, but Kalashnikovs were loud. No way could she expect all of the men inside to miss that noise—or the explosive sounds of Barialy's gunfire on the eastern side of the refinery.

Three shots to drop his man, unless the guard was killing Barialy at that very moment. Falk gave a fleeting thought to veering off her course, running to check on him, but that would be the same as stabbing Cooper in the back, ensuring that their mission failed.

She stood in front of the door, reached for the knob, hoping it would be left unlocked in case the sentry needed to relieve himself or had some other urgent cause to slip inside the plant. She clutched it, twisted and the door eased open silently.

Falk stepped into a hallway lit by caged lightbulbs and closed the door, then pushed the button on the inside knob to lock out anyone who might try slipping in behind her. Cooper was already somewhere in the plant, and Barialy had his own way in.

No one outside the plant was any friend of Falk's.

She moved along the corridor, tracking the sound of voices at its other end. Along the way, she pushed through doors on either side, revealing toilets, storage space for brooms and mops, another room stacked high with plastic bags and tarps, a smaller room of closet size with circuit breakers on the facing wall.

A dozen paces from the door where she had entered, Falk ran out of hallway, forced to choose between a left- or right-hand turn. Most of the noise was coming from her right, excited voices now, so she turned that way, after checking out the other track and making certain no one was about to shoot her in the back.

More doors on either side, before her new route spilled into the main part of the former slaughterhouse. Despite the handkerchief she wore over her nose and mouth, Falk smelled the sickly scent of chemicals used in refining opium to heroin.

Three steps along and suddenly a door flew open on Falk's left. Two men with turbans, beards and automatic weapons spilled into the corridor. They blinked at her, in shock.

"Hey, boys," she said.

And opened fire.

"WE TURN HERE," Karim Hajera announced.

"Finally," Arzad Mansoor muttered, shifting the Spectre M-4 submachine gun in his lap.

The other members of his party all carried Kalashnikov rifles in varied models, but for close-up work Mansoor preferred the Spectre. It was less than fourteen inches long with its butt folder, was the only double-action submachine gun ever manufactured, and its unique double-column magazine held fifty 9 mm Parabellum rounds while measuring no longer than the standard 30-round clip used in comparable weapons.

Mansoor could empty that fat magazine in 3.5 seconds of full-auto fire, shredding anyone who stood against him, and he carried ample spare mags in a canvas shoulder bag. If all else failed, he wore a Walther P-5 Compact semiauto pistol tucked inside his belt, with half a dozen extra magazines weighting his pockets.

The Toyota Highlander ran smoothly over normal pavement, but the access road to Basir Ahmad-Shah's refinery had not been well maintained. Perhaps the sheikh supposed that cargo trucks and Humvees could negotiate the track regardless of its cracked and pitted blacktop—or, more likely, he gave no thought to matter one way or another.

Hajera cursed when they hit a pothole, then accelerated as if to punish the road for his own discomfort. Mansoor considered snapping at him to be careful, but in truth he wished to put the long dark drive behind him, and he didn't care if one of Ahmad-Shah's innumerable vehicles was damaged in the process.

He could always blame Karim Hajera, anyway.

Five minutes on the narrow, rugged access road, with headlights from the second SUV glaring behind them, then Mansoor had his first glimpse of the refinery.

Buildings constructed in pursuit of death were much the same throughout the world. Be it an abattoir, a morgue or mortuary, crematorium or execution block inside a prison, there would be few windows in the walls made out of brick, concrete or stone. No matter how a given architect may decorate his final prize achievement, each would soon display a morbid attitude of gloom.

The drug refinery had been a slaughterhouse; now it produced poison for profit, ultimately killing thousands who enslaved themselves to heroin. Sheep, cattle or addicts. They were all the same.

Mansoor cared nothing for their fate.

He thought himself impervious to suffering and death—but he was still surprised to find a body lying crumpled near the front door, bathed in the Highlander's high beams.

"Who's that?" Hajera asked.

"How in hell should I know?" Mansoor snapped, clutching his submachine gun in one hand and reaching for his door latch with the other as the SUV slid to a halt.

Prepared for anything—or so he thought—Mansoor stepped from the vehicle. At once, he smelled the faint but unmistakable scent of cordite on the air. He did not have to wonder how the man sprawled in front of him had died.

Or who he was, for that matter. The black turban identified him as a member of the Taliban, presumably detailed to help guard the refinery as part of Ahmad-Shah's arrangement with Frozaan Sabeir.

But why was there no living person with the body? How

could those inside the plant have failed to note the slaying of an outer guard?

Unless...

A rattling sound of gunfire reached his ears, muffled by stout brick walls, then Mansoor flinched as an explosion echoed through the plant.

"Hurry!" he shouted to his soldiers as they piled out of their vehicles. "We've just arrived in time!"

But even as he spoke, Mansoor wondered if they had come too late.

BOLAN WAS BRACED for anything as he stepped through the doorway leading from the loading dock into an open space roughly the size of a three-car garage. It was the room where products—be they fresh-killed carcasses or plastic-wrapped kilos of heroin—were racked or stacked for loading onto trucks.

No one was in the room when Bolan entered, and he moved directly toward another doorway opposite the loading bays. That arch was tall and wide enough to let a forklift pass, and in the place of normal doors, long strips of heavy plastic dangled from the ceiling to the floor, resembling a shredded shower curtain. On the other side of that translucent screen, he saw blurred figures moving back and forth, heard muffled voices speaking in a language he could not translate.

It made no difference. He hadn't come to warn or threaten them. The Executioner was there to shut them down.

And he had used his extra minute now. Outside, Barialy and Falk should be making their moves, ceding the critical advantage of surprise.

Bolan holstered his pistol, slipped the AKSU's sling over his right shoulder and unlimbered the MGL launcher. He prodded two strips of plastic aside with its chunky muzzle and scanned the plant's main packing room, where mounds of heroin sat on stainless-steel tables and lines of masked workers used metal scoops to fill up kilo bags, which were then wrapped in oilcloth and sealed.

Across the room, some forty feet from Bolan, stood a pair of guards or supervisors. Both wore pistols on their belts, and the taller one held a Kalashnikov down at his side, muzzle aimed toward the floor. They hadn't noticed Bolan yet, and now they'd missed their chance to stop him.

Bolan raised his weapon, fired and stepped back to one side of the doorway before the HE round exploded in a fiery thunderclap. Its death wind wafted through the plastic streamers, lifting them, while cries of panic filled the packing room.

Bolan switched guns again, slinging the 40 mm launcher as he palmed the pistol grip of his Kalashnikov. He cleared the doorway, checked the supervisors first, and found their mangled fragments scattered up and down the room's south wall. There were no other guns in evidence, so far, but thirty-odd plant workers were stampeding toward the doorway where he stood.

The Executioner sidestepped and let them pass, scanning the ranks as they ran past him, making sure that no armed men escaped. Most of the runners barely glanced at him, their eyes wide with panic as they fled the killing floor.

And now, as the explosions echoes died away, he heard the opposition coming. There had to be a lab somewhere beyond the packing room, where opium was transformed into heroin, with better-educated personnel and other guards. And logic told him there would also be an office, plus a lounge for sentries killing time between their shifts, perhaps even a barracks wing where guards assigned to duty at the plant could sleep.

The piles of heroin around him looked like pristine, million-dollar sand dunes, trucked from exotic islands to dress up a movie set. Bolan intended to destroy it all, but first he had to deal with those whom Basir Ahmad-Shah paid to protect his lethal product.

He had no more than half a minute to prepare, and it would have to be enough. Moving to one of the long tables heaped with white powder, he tipped it over, spilling dope worth millions to the concrete floor. A second table crashed down on its side with Bolan's help, the drifts of heroin replacing sandbags as a bullet-stop, in case he needed cover from incoming fire.

But Bolan didn't plan to hide from his approaching enemies. Instead he'd meet their charge head-on and break it, if he could, then mop up the survivors as they fled.

Unless they killed him first.

## CHAPTER TEN

In his mind, even as he prepared to meet his enemies and kick
the living hell out of them, Ike Skelton was planning what he'd
tell Dale Ingram when the time came. How he'd wriggle out
from under any hint of blame for letting strangers barge into
the plant and trash it.

"Not my fault" was lame and simply wouldn't fly, but he
could argue that Ahmad-Shah's men resented Vanguard's
presence and insisted on sidelining him while they dictated
all security procedures.

And he heard the sneer in Ingram's voice coming back at
him, "Are you so weak you let the rags walk over you? What
do we pay you for?"

Or something similar. And he would say—

A rattling burst of automatic fire blanked out his thoughts
of any subject other than survival. Skelton double-timed in the
direction of the lab and packing room, with Rick Belanger on
his heels.

"We're screwed," Belanger said. "You know that, right?"

"The winner's never screwed," Skelton replied. "Make
goddamned sure we win this thing!"

He smelled cordite and something else, the scent of an

expended HE charge. Most likely a grenade of some kind, though his nose couldn't rule out plastique. And either way, the threat was serious.

Nearing the lab, he met some of Ahmad-Shah's people hastily retreating, firing blindly back along the way they'd come. Before Skelton could ask them what was happening, or where in hell they thought they were going, another blast shook the plant and made all of them duck, seeking cover.

The HE smell was stronger now, coupled with smoke and a gut-wrenching chemical odor.

"Shit!" Belanger said. "That's ether!"

Skelton forgot about the fleeing shooters in a heartbeat as his eyes swept left and right, then locked on a wall-mounted fire extinguisher. It wouldn't help him if a spark touched off the ether fumes, but he could still try to prevent a flash fire in the seconds left before that happened.

"Hold these bastards here," he snapped at Belanger. "Try getting them back in the game."

Skelton snatched the extinguisher from its wall mount, verified that it was designed for fighting chemical fires and yanked the ring that would prevent him from discharging it. Clutching his carbine tight beneath one arm, he took a deep breath, held it and pushed on into the lab.

Even without inhaling, the ether fumes made Skelton's eyes water, blurring his vision as he scrutinized the damage. He didn't need a Ph.D. in chemistry to know the lab was trashed, along with any product that was in the works when the explosion wrecked the place. There was no fire, yet, and he tried to head it off, directing milky spray from his extinguisher toward spreading pools of noxious fluid on the floor and any tables that were still upright.

Beyond the lab, inside the packing room, gunfire still hammered at his eardrums, telling him that some of Ahmad-Shah's soldiers had balls enough to stand and fight. Who they were fighting was a mystery, which Skelton meant to solve as soon as he was satisfied that he'd secured the lab from bursting into flames and blowing all of them sky-high.

In fact, he wasn't satisfied when the extinguisher began to hiss and splutter, running out of foam, but he had done his best. Dropping the empty canister, he clutched his Colt Commando in both hands and shouted back to Rick Belanger, "Get a goddamned move on, will you?"

"Coming!" Belanger replied, and suited words to action, shoving some of Ahmad-Shah's reluctant men ahead of him into the shattered lab.

"The ones who didn't run have someone blocked in there," Skelton explained. "We need to root them out and finish it."

Rick grinned and said, "Let's get some!"

"Fucking ay!"

Skelton was halfway through the entrance to the packing room when yet another thunderclap went off somewhere above him to his left. As he was tumbling backward, dazed, with grit and smoke stinging his eyes, he thought he saw a portion of the ceiling crashing to the floor.

Then something struck his skull and darkness swallowed him alive.

THE NEXT THREE ROUNDS in Bolan's 40 mm launcher were triple-aught buckshot. Crawling along the concrete floor, with bullets whistling overhead, he tried to judge the angle of incoming fire.

Three guns, at least, two on his right flank, one off to the left. Armed guards had poured into the packing room at first, then some had beat a swift retreat when Bolan started to hose them with AK fire. Those who remained behind had rallied now, and they were would do their best to finish him, if Bolan let them have an inch of breathing room.

Glancing upward as he wriggled on his back behind one

of the capsized tables, Bolan was surprised to see mirrors suspended from the ceiling on cables. At first glance, they appeared surreal—some shattered, others dangling precariously where supports had been severed, still others intact—but he soon realized that they had to have been hung for security reasons.

Employee theft was a problem in most modern workplaces, and none more than illicit shops where drugs or other contraband were handled on a daily basis by known criminals. Some cutting plants in the United States and elsewhere forced their mostly female line workers to labor in the nude, thereby preventing anyone from salting her pockets with coke, crank or smack.

Sheikh Ahmad-Shah's workforce was all male, and apparently he didn't relish having them undress. The mirrors—a crude equivalent of the overhead surveillance posts, or "eyes in the sky" employed at all modern casinos—would give supervisors a view of any worker who snorted a hit or tried to hide a pinch of the drug for later.

And now the mirrors that remained after his HE blasts told Bolan he was quickly running out of time.

Two shooters were advancing from his left, the west side of the packing room, firing short bursts at the point where they'd last glimpsed Bolan. A third was closing from his right, or east, and being slick about it. That one held his fire and let the others cover him while making all the noise, perhaps hoping that Bolan wouldn't notice him.

It might have worked, except for Ahmad-Shah's solution to the pilferage dilemma.

Bolan took the two-man party first, rolled out from cover at a point some fifteen feet from where their twin Kalashnikovs were aimed and spitting death. He fired once from a prone position, riddling both of them with buckshot, then jackknifed and powered back across the littered floor, digging with knees and elbows for momentum.

Number three was charging now. He'd guessed approximately where the latest 40 mm blast had come from, and had seen his chance. Still silent, if you didn't count the slapping of his shoes on concrete, he sprinted toward the spot and launched himself into a running broad jump, hurdling over mounds of heroin and the upended table to take Bolan by surprise.

But the assault plan boomeranged when the Executioner fired another buckshot round and caught his would-be killer on the fly—a kind of huge, awkward clay pigeon in a skeet match where the stakes were life and death. Descending in a cloud of crimson mist, the shooter landed awkwardly, twitched once, then moved no more.

One buckshot round remained, with another HE round behind it. Bolan heard excited voices coming from the general direction of the lab directly opposite his present cover. At least one of those voices cursed in English, but beyond that, Bolan could not eavesdrop on their back-and-forth with any certainty.

He had a choice to make, and quickly.

Staying where he was and waiting for the reinforcements to arrive could get him killed. So, too, could rushing them and throwing everything he had against the lab, to flush them out.

Stand pat? Or make a move?

Bolan's experience and nature made the choice for him. He had enjoyed success in past engagements by taking the fight to his enemies, rattling their cages and keeping them off balance. That had been the premise of his strike this night, and Bolan saw no cause from deviation of a tried and tested formula.

As if in answer to his silent thoughts, one of the laboratory voices called, "Come on! Get up here!"

And while that command was clearly meant for someone else, the Executioner obeyed.

EDRIS BARIALY FELT as if he was about to lose his mind. All night, he had wondered what had brought him to this place, to risk his life against strangers for whom killing was a profession and a form of recreation. He could find no answer, other than his personal desire to be someone, to do something that mattered for his country and his family.

Whom, if the wild ride with Matt Cooper should continue on its present course, he feared that he might never see again.

The shooting in Kabul had terrified him, but Barialy had recovered in time to acquit himself well in the convoy ambush. He had been waiting for the sickness to wash over him, leaving him nauseous and guilt-ridden over having taken human lives, but strangely he felt none of that.

What Edris Barialy felt was fear. Of being killed or wounded, possibly. Of being captured by the enemy and tortured to the point of death, for information. Of collapsing in the middle of a fight, leaving his two companions to be overwhelmed and slain.

The latter fear kept him from being paralyzed, and memories of his army training came back to offer vague encouragement, but Barialy still felt reasonably sure that he would die tonight.

And, oddly, that conviction seemed to free him somehow, granting him sufficient courage to proceed.

He had been stationed on the east side of the factory, with one guard to eliminate before he entered through a rusty metal door. The inner floor plan was unknown, meaning that Barialy had no preselected meeting place where he would rendezvous with Falk and Cooper.

He would try to find them somehow, if he could, but for the most part he was on his own. His orders from the tall American were simple: "Raise as much hell as you can. Shoot anyone you see, except the two of us. You've got no other friends in there."

Easy.

He simply had to burst in on a group of homicidal strangers, all well-armed, and then behave like one of the deranged Americans who ran amok at schools and shopping malls, killing everyone he met.

Until they gunned him down.

The outer guard, as it turned out, had not been difficult to kill. He had seen Barialy moving toward the plant, but hesitated and called out to him instead of shooting him on sight. The brief delay let Barialy aim and fire a 3-round burst into his target's body, rather startled at how easily he had performed the execution of another stranger.

The rusty door had opened at his touch, and Barialy had left it ajar as he entered, in case he needed to retreat at speed.

But where would he retreat? To what safe haven could he flee?

Nowhere.

This night, it would be victory or death—and even if his side emerged victorious, he still might die.

Inside the plant, he'd covered three long strides before a door opened in front of him, immediately on his right, and armed men charged into the hall. There was no time to count them, scarcely time to aim at all as he began firing, raking the group from side to side with automatic fire.

They wilted under it, collapsing, but a couple of the stragglers were alert and swift enough to save themselves by ducking back into the room from which they'd come. Afraid to cross the threshold, which they had to have covered with their weapons, Barialy palmed one of the hand grenades Cooper had given to him, pulled the pin as he'd been taught in basic training and sidearmed the bomb through the open doorway.

Scrambling footsteps told him that his enemies knew what he'd done. He crouched beside the door, ready to cut them down as they ran out, but neither one appeared. Instead a thunderously loud explosion shook the hallway, smothering a high-pitched scream.

But Barialy couldn't leave them there, assuming they were dead or crippled. He had to find out for himself, confirm it and ensure that he'd left no one in his wake to creep around and take him from behind.

He took a deep breath, held it and leaped through a screen of drifting smoke into the room beyond. It seemed to be a kind of lounge for plant employees, where they might consume a hasty meal brought in from home, before returning to the line. A hot plate stood atop a folding table, to one side, its coffeepot shattered.

One of the men he'd glimpsed before they turned and fled lay gasping on the floor at Barialy's feet. His abdomen was open, spilling its wet secrets, but his brain still clung to fragile life.

The other man was dead, unmarked except for sooty smudges and the single leaking wound where a sliver of shrapnel had pierced his forehead. He sat against the wall, his eyes open, staring deep into a timeless void.

Barialy considered leaving the gutted man to die on his own, but mercy intervened. Instead of aiming from the shoulder, he leaned over, placed his AKSU's muzzle against the stranger's skull and fired a single shot that sent a tremor up his arm into his shoulder.

Done—at least, in there.

But from the sounds of combat ringing in his ears, there was a battle still to fight, with enemies to slay, companions to find.

Edris Barialy left the death chamber and moved into the slaughterhouse proper.

ARZAD MANSOOR SENT TWO MEN ahead of him, then followed them toward the sounds of gunfire and shouting voices. His fear of Basir Ahmad-Shah propelled him forward, when

Mansoor's brain clamored with alarms that warned him to retreat as fast as he could run.

But flight was not an option. He might die if he continued forward, but if Mansoor broke and ran, the sheikh would track him down and kill him, slowly, in some way that made Mansoor pray for a bullet to the head or heart.

A guard whom Mansoor recognized came scuttling toward his scouts, along the corridor, stopping abruptly with his gun raised at the first glimpse of them. Mansoor's point men almost fired, then, but he called a warning to them, pushing forward to confront the man.

Where had he seen this one before? Mansoor could not remember. Possibly with Ahmad-Shah or with Jamal Woraz. Somewhere, in any case, that let him recognize a comrade here and now.

"You know me?" he demanded.

"Yes." The shaky gunman bobbed his head.

"What's happening?" Mansoor demanded.

"We have been attacked," the guard replied.

"By whom?"

A helpless shrug before the words spilled out of him. "They have rockets or something. All too much!"

"Where are you going?" Mansoor asked.

Another shrug, ending this time in silence.

Mansoor grabbed the gunman by one arm. "Take us to meet them," he commanded.

For an instant Mansoor worried that the guard might disobey, even start shooting, then his shoulders slumped and he reluctantly turned back the way he'd come, moving with zombie steps, as if resigned to death.

Mansoor fell back beside Karim Hajera, put his scouts between the point man and himself as they pressed on along the corridor. Another moment brought them to a doorway screened by hanging strips of plastic, which Mansoor had seen in other factories where meat and vegetables were processed. The peculiar screen did not keep smoke from bleeding out into the corridor they occupied.

"Go on!" he barked at those ahead of him. "What are you waiting for?"

The shaky point man and his scouts pushed through the dangling obstacles and stepped into a smoky swirl of combat. Mansoor felt another urge to run, but it was now too late. The riflemen behind him jostled forward, pushing him across the threshold in a rush that made him hurry to stay upright.

Deafened by the roar of guns, Mansoor added his own noise to the chorus, rushing to join the battle now and meet whatever fate might lie in store for him.

RICK BELANGER GAVE UP on rousing Skelton after two quick shakes failed to revive him. Was he breathing? Did he have a pulse? Belanger had no time to think about it, as the warm blood from a scalp wound bathed the left side of his face.

The blast had been from some kind of grenade, he thought, maybe rocket-propelled, although he hadn't heard the telltale whoosh of an RPG-7. Definitely high-explosive, it had filled the air with shrapnel, either from its casing or from chunks of concrete shattered by the blast.

Ignoring his wound, Belanger edged forward, trying to peer through the smoky doorway to the packing room, seeking targets for his Heckler & Koch MP-5 submachine gun. It wasn't the heaviest piece in the Vanguard arms cache, but he liked its accuracy, its four-position fire selector and its cyclic rate of 800 rounds per minute.

It would do the job for him, if he could only find a target in the goddamned haze.

And there it was!

Belanger saw the furtive movement of a man-size figure coming toward him, aimed for its center of mass and triggered a 3-round burst of 9 mm manglers at fifteen feet. His target lurched forward, stumbled, spilled out of the smoke—

And he saw one of Ahmad-Shah's men on the floor, twitching through his death throes.

Rick looked around, half expecting to find one of the other Afghans sighting down on him now, for payback, but it was even worse than that.

He was alone inside the stinking, smoke-filled lab.

Ahmad-Shah's so-called soldiers had deserted him, fleeing as fast as they could beat feet to some safer portion of the plant.

And where would that be? From the sounds that now echoed behind him, Belanger felt reasonably sure that the refinery had been attacked from several sides at once. That, or Ahmad-Shah's troops were firing at shadows, perhaps at each other.

Belanger wouldn't put anything past them right now.

He was considering a fallback option of his own, when he heard voices drawing closer, muttering in what sounded like Pashto, though Belanger wouldn't have cared to bet his life on it. He wasn't any kind of linguist, more a kick-ass kind of guy who let his fist and hardware do his talking for him when his adversaries couldn't speak English.

Conflicted now, Belanger tried to watch both directions at once, covering the packing room *and* the hallway he'd followed to the lab, before Skelton went down for the count. If he was trapped between two hostile teams, there would be nothing he could do about it. Sell his life dearly, and make each bullet count.

But when the faces started edging through the doorway to the lab, he recognized a couple of them. One—the first to show—had been among the troops who'd recently abandoned him. Some of the rest, he'd seen before when Vanguard's people mixed with Ahmad-Shah's. The absence of black turbans made Rick feel a little better, but not much.

The seeming leader of the pack pushed forward, faced Belanger, and asked him, "Who is responsible for this?"

"Hell if I know," he answered. Nodding toward the late Ike Skelton, he explained, "The two of us were having coffee when it hit the fan. Explosions, autofire, the whole nine yards. I haven't seen one of the fuckers yet."

The new arrival glanced off toward the packing room and said, "They are in there?"

"Some of them, anyway. I hear shooting all over the damned place."

"We start here, then," the take-charge guy replied. "You come with us."

Belanger was about to protest, then the phrase safety in numbers crossed his mind, and he just nodded, rising from his crouch to join the squad. He let half of them go ahead of him, then stepped into the flow, clutching his MP-5 in a death grip.

BOLAN WAS HALFWAY to the laboratory's entrance when his enemies came charging through to meet him. His adjustment to the changing situation was immediate, reflexive, executed without conscious thought.

First, Bolan fired the sixth round from his 40 mm launcher into their surging ranks. Before it blew and scattered the frontrunners like mannequins in a hurricane, he was belly-down on the floor and scooting for cover, finding his grip on the AKSU.

The blast's shock wave washed over him, helped Bolan by concealing him with smoke and pushing more tables in his direction, piling up his cover while the grisly ruin of his frontline adversaries started raining down around him.

Bolan gave no thought to what he had to look like—dusted with heroin, plastered with blood and flesh, the world's worst recipe for God-knew-what unpalatable stew—as he prepared to follow up on his advantage. Rising on one elbow, he surveyed the scene as best he could and found some of his enemies still standing, evidently rallying to try another rush.

And he was reaching for a frag grenade, about to pluck it from his web belt, when staccato sounds of firing echoed from behind his would-be killers coming from somewhere beyond the lab.

Experience had taught him not to get his hopes up in the middle of a firefight, where a disappointment or distraction could be fatal, but he felt a small involuntary pulse of optimism. If the new sounds meant that Falk or Barialy, maybe both, were coming up behind the plant's defenders now, he had at least a fighting chance.

And so it seemed, as some of those who'd been about to rush Bolan turned back and started firing in the opposite direction. The soldier couldn't see if they were taking hits, but he clutched the frag grenade, released its pin and lobbed the bomb through the tattered dangling remnants of the plastic screen that separated lab and packing room.

Five seconds later, when the blast ripped through his opposition's ranks, Bolan was up and running, dropping those who were still on their feet with short bursts from his AKSU. He stopped short of the doorway, crouched beside the concrete wall, and waited for the firing on the other side to sputter out and die.

When silence had descended for a moment, Bolan called out, "Falk? Are you out there?"

"Right here!" her now-familiar voice came back. "And I've got Edris with me."

"Are we clear beyond this point?" Bolan inquired, rising to stand upright.

"Unless somebody's hiding in a closet that we haven't found," Falk answered.

"Okay, come through then. But watch out for anybody playing dead."

He waited in place while Falk and Barialy crossed the killing pen, examining the bodies sprawled around their feet. Most obviously wouldn't rise to fight again, but certain ones revealed no wounds on casual inspection. Bolan had them covered all the way, watching for any sign of life among the fallen as his comrades cleared the lab.

"What now?" Falk asked him through her wilted mask when they were together in the packing room.

"Now," he replied, "I burn it down."

He broke open the MGL's rotating cylinder, extracted the spent casings and reloaded it with thermite rounds. He likely could've done the job he had in mind with two or three, but Bolan loaded six, just to be thorough.

"Time to go?" Falk asked.

"I'm right behind you," Bolan said, and nodded toward the door through which he'd entered the plant a lifetime earlier. "It should be clear, but don't let down your guard."

"No fear of that," Falk said.

When they were clear, Bolan shouldered the MGL and fired a white-hot round into the ruins of the lab. Before his second shot, he backed off to the doorway fronting the loading dock, then lobbed another thermite canister into the midst of all that scattered smack.

He left the door open behind him, feeding flames with oxygen, and padded down the stairs descending from the concrete platform. Falk and Barialy trailed him as he walked around the plant, firing more thermite rounds through windows situated high up near the factory's roofline, one shot for each side of the factory.

"That's it," he told them finally. "There won't be much left when the fire department gets here, if they come at all."

"Who'd call them?" Barialy asked.

"You've got a point."

They started back through star-shot darkness, toward the

point where they'd left the Toyota Avalon. When they were roughly halfway there, Falk asked him, "So what's next?"

"You get some shut-eye while we travel," he responded.

"Travel where?"

"To visit Basir Ahmad-Shah."

# CHAPTER ELEVEN

*Harry S. Truman Building, Washington, D.C.*

Hal Brognola was rarely summoned by anyone, and he had *never* been called from his office on Pennsylvania Avenue to the complex located at 2201 C Street NW. Some pundits called it Foggy Bottom, but that nickname properly applied to the entire low-lying neighborhood, located west of downtown Washington on the Potomac River.

It was Brognola's first call-out to the U.S. Department of State, more specifically the Diplomatic Security Service, where he had an appointment he hadn't requested with a deputy assistant undersecretary named Xavier Manning.

Brognola couldn't help wondering if anybody ever called him X-Man.

Manning's personal assistant—what they'd called a secretary until sometime in the nineties—had phoned Brognola's office to announce that Manning would be pleased to speak with him in one hour, precisely. Since he'd never heard of Manning and had not sought any kind of face-to-face with anyone from State, the big Fed had suggested that there had to be some mistake. The PA had replied, in no uncertain terms, that all would be explained when Brognola met Mr. Manning.

Nine o'clock. Sharp.

Brognola had walked the halls of State on various occasions in the past, but never really got a feel for diplomatic work. In his view, buttressed by a world of evidence and countless covert jobs that had been thrown his way when talking failed, diplomacy consisted of equal parts bluffing, bravado and bullshit. The "good" it accomplished came with a price tag attached and was seldom—if ever—permanent.

Color him skeptical *and* curious, to find out why his presence was commanded by the X-Man.

Brognola identified himself to security guards in the lobby and received a laminated visitor's pass that he clipped to his lapel. Instead of simply giving directions and turning him loose, one of the guards escorted him to a bank of elevators and rode up with him to the fourth floor, then led the big Fed along a hallway that reminded him of every high school he had ever seen, until they reached a door with Manning's name engraved on a plastic insert sign.

The escort didn't knock before he ushered Brognola across the threshold and presented him to Manning's personal assistant, a ginger-haired Midwestern type whose look contradicted his sonorous telephone voice. The PA checked his watch, dismissed the escort and directed Brognola toward a row of three mismatched plastic chairs.

A minitable set in front of them offered *Forbes*, *Newsweek* and *People* magazines, but Brognola preferred to leave his mind uncluttered by the doings of the rich and shameless. He had arrived three minutes early and supposed Manning would make him wait for starters, as a petty demonstration of authority. Brognola had decided he would leave at 9:05 and let the ginger boy explain his absence to the boss, but the PA passed him along at nine o'clock precisely.

Manning's office had a view of the Potomac and Virginia on the western bank, but from the photos mounted on the other walls, it seemed that Manning leaned toward ogling photos of himself with famous men and women. While his suit changed from one snapshot to the next, his squint and rigid smile were constant, as if someone had transferred Manning's head into dozens of scenes with the high and mighty.

The man himself was not impressive at first glance. He had a Woody Allen look about him, stripped of anything resembling a sense of humor. Here was one, Brognola thought, who took himself extremely seriously and demanded that subordinates do likewise.

Manning introduced himself and pumped the big Fed's hand once in a clammy grip, then half turned toward a larger man whose face reminded Brognola of a spray-tanned cottage cheese sculpture. He couldn't tell which lumps were scars and which were blemishes, but focused on the matte-black marble eyes.

"Mr. Brognola," Manning said, "allow me to present Wedge Crocker."

Brognola assumed his ears were playing tricks on him until the other man remarked, without a hint of levity, "I came between my parents."

Stumped for a reply, he shook the second stranger's rough, cold hand.

"Wedge has been kind enough to join us from BISN," Manning said, then added, "That's the Bureau of International Security and Nonproliferation."

"Great," Brognola said. "I'm all for both."

Instead of laughing as he sat behind his desk, Manning nodded with solemn gravity and said, "We hope that's true."

"Well, since we've cleared that up…"

"Please, sit," Manning said.

This time, Brognola's choice was a single chair, positioned in front of Manning's desk as if he were a rowdy
student summoned to the principal's office for a tongue-
lashing, or worse. Crocker sat off to one side of the desk,
facing Brognola from Manning's side. The man from Justice
half expected him to grab a steno pad and start taking notes.

He sat and waited silently, giving Manning nothing of
himself. The silence stretched between them for a moment,
deepening the X-Man's frown, until at last his host said, "I
suppose you wonder why you're here."

Brognola shrugged and said, "I thought we'd get around
to it eventually."

"Mr. Brognola, we—by which I mean Wedge and myself,
along with our superiors and theirs—are concerned about
some of your recent actions."

The big Fed cocked an eyebrow at his host and said, "I see."

"Do you?" Manning's frown deepened.

"Well, no. You probably hear this a lot, but I have no idea
what you're talking about," Brognola stated.

Manning tented his fingers and peered across them,
through his gold-rimmed trifocals. "Let me speak plainly
then," he said.

"It couldn't hurt."

"I—*we*—have reason to believe that you have been
meddling in certain sensitive areas—international realms,
shall we say?—which far exceed your jurisdiction and your
competence."

"Ah. And you believe this…why, again?"

"Our sources are reliable," Wedge Crocker interjected.

"Then you won't mind naming them," Brognola said.

"No can do," Crocker replied.

"I guess we're done here, then."

Brognola was already on his feet and moving toward the

office door when Manning called out from behind him, "Where do you think you're going?"

"Back to Justice," Brognola replied, "where no one needs refresher courses on the Sixth Amendment."

"You don't need a lawyer here," Crocker said.

"Next time, read the whole thing," Brognola replied. "I'm entitled to confront all my accusers, if I'm charged with anything."

"This isn't a grand jury," Manning said.

"It feels more like an inquisition," Brognola informed him.

"Let's try again, shall we? Please, sit and hear us out."

Reluctantly, Brognola sat. He showed them eyes of stone.

"We are concerned," Manning began afresh, "over recent events in Afghanistan."

"You should be," Brognola replied. "The Taliban's still running wild, and you've got more civilian deaths around Kabul these days than in Baghdad."

He left drugs out of it deliberately. If Manning and his sidekick were about to argue Vanguard's case, he'd let them walk into the trap.

"You're right on all counts," Manning said. "Despite the triumph of a free election, I admit the occupation hasn't gone as well as we had hoped."

"Good luck with that," Brognola said.

"You understand our problems, over there," Manning continued. "And as a fellow bureaucrat—please, no offense—you know the limitations on our government's resources. Sometimes, economy demands employment of civilian contractors in varied situations."

"We don't have that luxury at Justice," Brognola observed. "We get by with the FBI, the DEA and ATF."

"And they're all very capable, I'm sure," Manning allowed.

"Unless somebody interferes with them," Brognola said.

"Not sure I follow you," Manning stated.

"Well, let's take a hypothetical. Suppose the DEA was on a smuggler's case, about to lock him up and throw away the key, when someone from another branch of government stepped in to help the bad guy wriggle off the hook. You see how that can be damned frustrating."

X-Man blinked and said, "There's no need for profanity."

"Sorry." Brognola beamed. "Sometimes my manners are for shit."

The angry color rose in Manning's face, but he controlled himself. While he was chewing nails, Crocker said, "The thing that troubles us is a report that Justice may be running unauthorized programs from Kabul, harassing and endangering valued contract employees of this department."

"A report?" Brognola said. "I'd like to see it."

"I misspoke. Call it a rumor, if you like."

"I don't like rumors," the big Fed replied. "Who are these valued contractors? And why would Justice be interested in them?"

The black eyes in the whey-face pinned him. "Why don't we all cut the s— The nonsense? Can we do that? State officially objects to any unauthorized Justice programs you may be running in Afghanistan or *contemplating* there. That comes all the way from the top. I hope it's clear enough for you."

"It's crystal-clear," Brognola said, rising to his feet. "I can assure you without fear of contradiction that Justice has no *unauthorized* programs running in Kabul, or anywhere else. And *that* comes from the top. Have a good one."

Brognola felt them staring daggers at him as he left, couldn't resist a sly wink at the ginger boy who manned the waiting room, but wiped it off his face before he met his escort in the outer corridor.

He had a problem now, perhaps a leak, and Brognola knew he would have to deal with it before it dumped them all into a world of hurt.

*Vanguard International Branch Office, Kabul*

THE CALL WOKE Clay Carlisle at 5:08 a.m., twenty-two minutes ahead of his bedside alarm clock. He did not fumble his way to consciousness by slow degrees, but came awake within an instant, through a combination of experience and training.

And he recognized the caller's grim voice instantly.

"Deputy Minister," he said. "Good morning, sir."

"I would not say that it is good, so far," Habib Zarghona replied.

"May I inquire as to the difficulty?"

"First," Zarghona said, "I must know if this line is perfectly secure."

"On my end, yes," Carlisle replied. "We sweep it every two hours, around the clock. I obviously can't vouch for your own connection, sir."

"That bit is my concern. I place this call on behalf of a mutual friend in Sherzad."

Basir Ahmad-Shah's swarthy face flashed into Carlisle's mind as he replied, "I understand."

"There was another…incident, last night."

"Aside from the equipment breakdown in Nangarhar Province?" Carlisle asked.

"It is related, I assume," Zarghona said. "But, yes. A separate incident, and far more serious."

Carlisle could feel his stomach tighten as he asked, "And that would be…?"

"The factory," Zarghona answered.

"What about it?"

"It has been destroyed."

Carlisle was speechless for a heartbeat. He had men at Ahmad-Shah's refinery. Only a pair of them, last night, but still…

"Is this confirmed, sir?" he inquired.

"Consider it a fact. My men are on the scene, investigating as we speak."

Grilling survivors, he supposed, assuming there were any.

Carlisle tried for a casual tone as he asked, "Were there any witnesses to the event?"

"Peasant employees only," Zarghona said. "We've detained two who were found in the vicinity. They may lead us to others. No one in authority survived."

"But those you have in custody—"

"Are talking gibberish," Zarghona said. "It seems they either saw nothing, or else they were too frightened to absorb any details. My people will encourage them to concentrate."

Carlisle knew what that meant, and he could almost pity them. Almost. But at the moment he required hard and reliable intelligence. Descriptions of the people who had staged the raid, for starters. And beyond that…

"I will help in any way I can, of course," he told Zarghona. "My resources are at your disposal."

"I believe," Zarghona said, "that those responsible for your equipment breakdown must be deemed responsible for this event, as well. Do you agree?"

"It's likely, sir," Carlisle replied.

"And you still think this Matthew Cooper is behind it, with the agent you identified?"

"Her name is Deirdre Falk. I wouldn't say *behind* it, sir. They seem to be the frontline troops. There will be other hands pulling the strings."

"In the United States?"

"Perhaps," Carlisle agreed.

"That is your venue, is it not?" Zarghona asked. "Your so-called field of expertise?"

"It is, sir."

"Then I would suggest you master it and solve this problem. "Kill it at the root, before it slips completely out of our control."

"Yes, sir. I under—"

But the line was dead. Zarghona didn't wait to hear Carlisle agree with him or promise to obey.

The flush of anger passed in seconds flat. Carlisle cradled the telephone receiver, then immediately lifted it again and hit speed dial.

*United States Embassy, Kabul*

LEE HASTINGS FROWNED at Russell Latimer and said, "I wasn't expecting to see you again so soon."

"No, sir. I'm afraid our situation has taken a turn for the worse."

Hastings felt a small, unpleasant stirring in his gut, as if some restless parasite was looking for a hasty exit.

"Worse?"

"In spades, sir. Have you heard the news out of Nangarhar Province?"

"No. We've been swamped with preparations for a visit from the Secretary of State. Why don't you fill me in?"

Latimer did precisely that, sparing none of the grisly details. When he'd finished, Hastings thought he knew how a deer had to feel, trapped by headlights in the middle of a road, at midnight, with a semi-trailer rushing to destroy it.

"Jesus Christ!" he swore. "How many dead is that now?"

"I'm not sure about the factory," Latimer said. "Let's be conservative. Say sixty and counting, with the original men in Kabul."

"This is incredible! Impossible!"

"And yet, it's happening," Latimer replied.

"How do we stop it?" Hastings asked the spy.

"Sir, you were going to investigate the DEA connection in this thing and see—"

"I *did* look into it," Hastings said, interrupting Latimer. "I spoke to Alan Combs, agent in charge of operations in Kabul, and dropped the name you gave me. Combs denied that he had anyone named Cooper on his staff, of course, which may be true. I got the feeling he was pleased to see things shaken up a bit."

"More than a bit, at this point, sir."

"Yes, quite."

"We're talking arson, explosives, mass murder. In a word, terrorism. The PR damage alone, if Combs or his agents are linked to that kind of activity, well…"

Hastings could see it now. A scandal that dwarfed Iran-Contra, congressional hearings and FBI probing of personal lives. His career would be a total loss. Hell, he'd be lucky if he didn't end his life in prison.

Swallowing hard, he asked Latimer, "What do you suggest?"

"The way I see it, sir, there are two ways we can proceed. One is for you to challenge Combs officially, demand a full accounting of the DEA's activities, no stone unturned. Of course, that leads you through a minefield. If the General Accounting Office finds out you hold stock in Vanguard—"

"Yes. I understand."

And the GAO was the least of his problems, right now. They could only report back to State and recommend censure. The damned FBI could arrest him and send him to jail.

"What's the alternative?" he asked.

Latimer's shrug was almost casual. "They're running black ops," he replied, "so we do likewise. Hit 'em on the down-low."

"Russell, I don't speak Ebonics."

"Sir, I'm saying we fight fire with fire. It's dirty, but if handled properly, there'll be no comebacks. You'll be safe and sound, while all the blame falls on those nasty narco-traffickers."

"Don't tell me any more about it," Hastings ordered. "Need to know, right?"

"Absolutely right, sir."

Latimer's smile reminded Hastings of a grinning skull.

*Stony Man Farm, Blue Ridge Mountains, Virginia*

THE FLIGHT HAD TAKEN fifteen minutes to arrange, and the best part of an hour to complete in a Bell 427 helicopter. Now, Brognola walked across Stony Man's helipad through a swirl of rotor wash, his shoulders slumped as much by care as by caution.

Aaron Kurtzman met the big Fed, flanked by Barbara Price, the Farm's mission controller. Both wore grim faces.

They barely spoke until they reached the War Room and were locked inside it, huddled together at one end of a conference table that could seat twenty in a pinch.

"I pray you're wrong about this," Kurtzman said.

"There still may be some explanation that I haven't thought of," Brognola replied. "If you come up with one, I'd love to hear it. In the meantime, it *appears* that someone's dropped a dime on me—on *us*—to State. Specifically, the Diplomatic Security Service and the Bureau of International Security and Nonproliferation."

"Rings a distant bell," Kurtzman said.

"Bottom line, there's no good reason they should know that I exist, much less call me in for a grilling on running unauthorized programs in Kabul."

"They said that?" Price asked.

"Not *just* that," Brognola replied. "I'm suspected of harassing their valued contract employees."

"Meaning Carlisle and Vanguard," Kurtzman said.

"Who else?" Brognola agreed.

"I can see why you'd think that we're leaking."

"What else can I think? They didn't get it from a White House briefing or the *Washington Post.*"

"Carlisle has eyes and ears all over," Price reminded him. "At Langley and the Hoover Building, inside Congress, maybe at the NSA. Whatever he's been told, it didn't have to come from here."

"There's something else we should consider," Kurtzman said. "Vanguard hires former cops and military personnel, almost exclusively. The ones who've worked with us in various capacities don't vanish when they get their discharge papers. Sure, they take an oath of secrecy, but Carlisle could have one of our ex-blacksuits on his payroll, or a G-man who's retired and singing for his supper."

"Shit!" Brognola said, with feeling. "That's been preying on my mind from the beginning, but we've been damned lucky. Still, an ex-employee or associate can't spill the beans on what we're doing now. We've kept a solid lid on Striker's mission in Kabul."

"The same as always," Price replied.

"If not more so," Kurtzman agreed. "Even most of those we've got here at the moment don't know anything about this job. You didn't even brief him at the Farm."

"So, what, then?" Brognola demanded.

"We can rule out educated guesswork," Kurtzman said. "Even if Carlisle has someone on his payroll who served at the Farm—hell, even if he has a dozen of them—they can't play connect-the-dots without the dots. If someone's leaking, that means someone in this room or…"

"Back in Washington," Hal said.

"Start with whoever wanted this job done, originally," Price said. "Then consider those around that person, with intimate knowledge of his or her business. If it isn't one of us, it must be one of them."

"I'll have to go back to the source," Brognola said, "and

pin him down. Meanwhile, run triple-checks on all outside communications to and from the Farm, to put an old man's mind at ease."

Brognola wasn't looking forward to the next step, but he knew that it was one he'd have to take alone.

And if it meant the end of his career, or worse, he'd be prepared for anything.

But one way or another, he would make it right.

*Nangarhar Province, Afghanistan*

BOLAN SAW NO POINT in debriefing his companions after their attack on the refinery. They'd been together at the finish, and the place was out of business. Bolan hadn't gone in seeking any information, and besides, there'd been no time or opportunity for Falk to question anyone.

Therefore, job done. For now.

They set to cleaning weapons, working by dawn's light on a side road midway between the plant and Sherzad. At the same time, Bolan took inventory on their stock of ammunition, noting that he'd used up slightly more than half his 40 mm rounds so far. Twelve left, and they still had sufficient ammo for the other guns to carry out the next phase of his plan.

Beyond that, if they needed to restock, Bolan supposed there'd be no shortage of arms dealers who would resupply them for a price. The trick, as always, would be dodging cops and soldiers while they made the buy.

"Who's looking for us now, do you suppose?" Falk asked.

"The National Police, for sure," Bolan replied. "Maybe the ASNF or the CNPA. Vanguard, of course, and Ahmad-Shah's people. The CIA could be involved. I'm not so sure about the FBI."

"It's nice to be wanted," she told Bolan, smiling. Then asked, "Who do you think will find us first?"

"With any luck," he answered, *"we'll* find *them."*

"About that," Falk said, frowning at the field-stripped AKSU lying with its parts spread out in front of her. "Sorry I can't be certain where we'll find the sheikh. He switches off between his places in Sherzad and Mihtarlam, to keep the opposition guessing."

"Sherzad's closer," Bolan said. "We'll try there, first. If no one's home, we'll go to Mihtarlam."

"After the other stunts we've pulled," Falk said, "he'll have an army waiting for us."

"Probably," Bolan agreed.

"It doesn't worry you?"

"I plan around the odds," Bolan replied. "But I don't let them paralyze me. Naturally, I'd prefer it if Ahmad-Shah had someplace he likes to go and kick back by himself, but—"

"That won't happen," Falk said. "Too many people want to kill him, and he knows it. He won't set foot outside his walled estates without a dozen bodyguards. Business associates and politicians, doctors, girlfriends—everybody comes to him."

"Which means, I have to do the same."

"You mean, we have to," Falk corrected him.

"About that…"

"Stop right there," Falk said.

"I haven't—"

"I know where you're going with it," she pressed. "You want to dump us and go on alone, right? What's the excuse? Belated chivalry? You can't be worried that I'll slow you, after all we've just been through together."

"No," he granted. "But it's getting worse. And if I make it past Ahmad-Shah's people, I still have to deal with Vanguard. That's another army in itself."

"You think I'm scared?" she asked.

"You should be."

"Well, okay. Maybe I am, a little. But we've beaten them

three times already. This is no time to have second thoughts, my friend. We're in the shit, and there's no turning back. We either move ahead or stop and drown in it."

"That's me," Bolan replied. "The two of you still have an out. Go back to Kabul. Call your supervisor. Meet him some-where—preferably at the embassy. Say anything you have to, to get off the hook. Tell them I took you hostage, put you in the car trunk and you didn't see a thing. The other side won't have a witness who can contradict you."

Falk shook her head, clearly exasperated. "Jesus! First, you do your best to get me killed, now, you're insulting me."

"How's that?" Bolan asked.

"By believing that I'd run and leave you in the middle of this by yourself, when we both know you're only here because of me."

"I'm here because Clay Carlisle's smuggling heroin," Bolan replied.

"And who discovered that?" She tapped her own chest with a fist and said, "Yours truly, that's who. Anyway, I can't go back to shuffling papers after this, pretend none of it ever happened in the first place. Not my style. Sorry, you're stuck with me."

"What if I made it an order?" Bolan asked.

"Get real! I'm DEA, not IMF or whatever you are. You don't rank me. Besides, I've probably been fired by now, which makes me a civilian free agent."

"Okay, you sold me," Bolan said, half turning to face Barialy. "And what about you?"

"The worst thing I can do for any of my family or friends is to go home and contact them," Barialy replied. "I will be hunted for the rest of my life, unless we destroy the hunters."

"Right, then," Bolan said. "Sounds like a plan."

# CHAPTER TWELVE

*Shar-e-Naw, Kabul*

Red Scanlon knew that he was lucky to be alive, much less still on the Vanguard payroll, but he couldn't help hating the limitations of his new assignment.

Okay, sure. He understood why he was on probation after screwing up what should've been a relatively simple job and losing the eleven men assigned to him, including one of Vanguard's own. He still felt bad for Eddie Franks, though truth be told, he thought the rest of them were shit.

If they'd been fast and tough enough to match the stranger when he drew down on them, Scanlon wouldn't be assigned to visit gun shops now and ask about their customers. He'd be out hunting with the others, who—

No, wait. That wasn't right, either.

If Scanlon's team had bagged the stranger and his DEA contact as planned, there'd likely be no hunt in progress. No one would have jacked the convoy yesterday or taken out the heroin refinery.

When he thought about all that had happened because of his team's botched-up snatch job, Scanlon had to rethink his position. Framed in that perspective, it surprised him that Dale Ingram hadn't sent someone to take him out while things were plummeting from bad to worse.

He still might do that, Scanlon realized, if Scanlon gave him any reason to remember and regret the mercy Clay Carlisle had shown.

In that light, checking gun shops didn't seem so bad.

And here came number seven on the list, so far. As Scanlon's car turned off Shar Ali Khan onto a side street, he could see the target halfway down. It was supposed to be a pawnshop, and he guessed the owner made a fair living legitimately, but his real high-ticket merchandise was tucked away somewhere inside, well out of sight.

More power to him, Scanlon thought.

If firearms by the millions weren't found everywhere throughout Afghanistan, the big boys wouldn't need Vanguard to cover them and Scanlon might not have a job that had been sweet and easy, until yesterday. He might be humping through the Congo or Rwanda, maybe hunting Red guerrillas in the Andes or on East Timor.

Who needed that shit, anyway?

His driver double-parked outside the pawnshop, confident that any local cops who happened by would not mess with a car displaying Vanguard International decals on the windshield and rear window.

His driver was an Afghan doubling as interpreter for Scanlon's sweep. His backseat shooters, just in case, were Vanguard all the way: a blond named Harry Smathers and a tattooed skinhead Scanlon barely knew, named Mickey Flack. They pushed into the shop and met the owner coming out, around a long display case filled with jewelry and watches.

Scanlon spoke through his interpreter, saying, "Tell him we've got nothing to pawn. We're here to talk about his other business."

The proprietor played dumb, of course, pretending that he didn't know what Scanlon meant. What else was he supposed to say, with three white faces glaring at him?

"Tell him," Scanlon said, "that I mean guns. We don't care what he sells or whether it's against the law. We aren't police. But we *are* looking for an American who may have been a recent customer."

Something clicked behind the merchant's eyes as Scanlon's man translated what he'd said. A sly thought, swiftly muzzled, but Scanlon had seen it peeking out.

The answer came back negative again, with an apologetic attitude.

"He's lying," Scanlon said to no one in particular.

"How can you tell?" Flack asked.

"It's in his eyes," Scanlon replied.

"Something you didn't see the last six places?" Smathers asked.

"That's right."

He wasn't taking any shit from these guys over gut instinct, which any soldier ought to understand.

Scanlon stared the dealer down and told his driver, "Tell him that we'll pay for information if it's accurate. And he'll pay, if it's not."

That message registered, but still the older man played dumb.

"Okay, then," Scanlon said. "We know the guns are here. Let's find them, first, then ask him one last time. Harry, this place is closed for renovations."

"Right."

Smathers went back to lock the door and turn around a hanging sign that none of them could read. It stood to reason that the side facing the street when they came in said Open or something similar, and that the flip side would read Closed.

In any case, Red Scanlon didn't really give a damn.

They hauled the old man into his backroom, feet barely

grazing the linoleum before they dropped him on a cluttered metal desk and started ransacking the place. They hadn't trashed more than a couple thousand dollars' worth of merchandise before the dealer squawked and pointed to a door in the west wall, concealed behind a hanging tapestry.

"A basement." Scanlon beamed. "It figures. Mickey, check it out."

Flack spent less than a minute down below, returning to announce, "Old man's got hardware up the ass."

"Not yet," Scanlon said. "But he may have, if he doesn't smarten up."

Scanlon drew his pistol, aimed it at the dealer's face and told his translator, "Ask him again. We're looking for a recent customer. A tall American, with murder in his eyes. There may have been a woman with him. He has one last chance to talk."

The old man stared at Scanlon for a moment, then began to weep.

And told them everything.

*United States Embassy, Kabul*

AFTER TWENTY-SIX YEARS with the U.S. federal government, first as an FBI agent, then rising through the ranks at DEA, Alan Combs had learned to recognize whether a summons from one of his bosses portended a pat on the back or a kick in the ass. Sometimes they split the difference and made it a knife in the back.

This day, the summons from Lee Hastings smelled like pure bad news.

For one thing, the vice consul had never previously shown the slightest interest in Combs, the DEA, or any aspect of law enforcement that didn't involve tracking suicide bombers. For another, the timing was rotten. Combs couldn't imagine any kind of commendation coming out of the events that had begun with gunfire in the Sharh-e-Khone, continuing with the destruction of a drug convoy and one of Basir Ahmad-Shah's main heroin refineries.

Combs looked upon those incidents as good news, even if the folks responsible had broken several dozen laws, but others with more influential friends than he possessed would take a different view.

So, he was ready for the worst as he announced himself to the vice consul's pretty young receptionist. His hands were clean. The worst that they could do was put him out to pasture, and retirement might turn out to be a blessing in disguise.

Hell, what disguise, if it relieved him from the task of hunting scumbag narco-traffickers all day, while scumbag politicians did their best to wipe out any gains he made?

"The vice consul will see you now."

Combs resisted the urge to shout, "Whoopee!" He winked at the lady, instead, and was pleased when she blushed.

I've still got it, he thought. For the moment, at least.

Hastings wore a diplomatic smile as he shook hands with Combs—the kind that, with a twitch of some obscure muscle, can easily become a scowl or sneer. In no case was it ever trustworthy.

"Alan, please have a seat!"

They hadn't spoken five words in three years, but he was on a first-name basis with the high and mighty now. Another grim portent.

"You must be wondering what brings you here," Hastings said.

"It was e-mail," Combs replied.

"Of course. I mean, the purpose of my invitation."

Combs kept quiet, making Hastings work for it.

"It's come to my attention," the vice consul said, "that you may have a...shall we say, a personnel problem?"

"I don't know what you mean, sir," Combs replied. A simple lie, to bait the hook.

"Indeed? You have an agent on assignment here, I understand, named—" Hastings paused to peer at something written on a memo pad "—um, Deirdre Falk. Is that correct?"

"Yes, sir."

"Yes. And I understand that she's dropped out of touch."

"How do you understand that, sir?"

"Excuse me?"

"I've filed no reports to that effect," Combs said. "I'm curious about your source of information."

"Is that relevant?"

"Extremely," Combs replied. "If I've got leaks, I need to plug them. On the other hand, if someone's circulating rumors, I should squelch it. Either way, it's time to kick some ass."

"We don't retaliate for whistle-blowing, Alan. You should know that. It's the law."

"A whistle-blower's someone who exposes government malpractice, sir. They do it publicly."

"I leave interpretation to the courts. Now, is it true or not that Agent Falk has broken contact with your office?"

"False, sir."

"Did you say false?"

"Yes, sir."

"When was the last time you heard from her?"

Combs frowned, stalling with a pretense that he was leafing through some mental dossier. After the better part of sixty silent seconds, he replied, "I couldn't say for sure."

"Well, there you have it!"

"Have what, sir?"

"You can't recall the last time that you spoke to Agent Falk. I'd call that unacceptable."

"Because you don't know what we do."

The diplomatic smile edged toward sneer mode as Hastings said, "Enlighten me."

"Without discussing a specific case, I'm sure you understand, sir, that investigating, penetrating and dismantling major drug cartels involves substantial risk to agents in the field and their informants. There are times when contact with the office is both inconvenient and potentially life-threatening."

"You're saying that this Agent Falk is on some kind of undercover mission? Is that it?"

"I can't discuss that, sir."

"You *will* discuss it, Mr. Combs!"

"No, sir. If you have any further questions in that vein, you can express your interest to the attorney general's office. If you need the number, sir, I have it in my files."

"Your insubordination has been duly noted, Mr. Combs," Hastings replied through clenched teeth.

"Was there something else, sir?"

"No. I'd say you're finished here."

"In that case, sir, you have a super day."

*Arlington National Cemetery, Virginia*

HAL BROGNOLA'S SECOND State Department meeting of the day required a venue more discreet than Foggy Bottom. Arlington had served him well for meetings with Mack Bolan, and he trusted that 290,000 silent heroes would respect his privacy again today.

The man he'd come to meet was highly placed. His comments appeared regularly on the front pages of the *Washington Post* and *The Times*—New York, Los Angeles or London, take your pick. He wasn't in direct line of succession for the presidency, but his advice had persuaded more than one commander in chief to take dramatic action in foreign lands.

The man went nowhere without bodyguards in these perilous times, but they knew when to keep their distance and forget the faces they glimpsed in passing.

No leaks there. And yet...

"You say we have a problem," he observed after he shook Brognola's hand. The bodyguards stood fifty yards away, but still Brognola and his contact kept their backs turned toward the watchers.

"One of us is in a leaky boat," Brognola said. "I'm double-checking my end as we speak. You'll be among the first to know if I find anything amiss."

"But you don't think you will," the other said.

"No, sir. I don't."

"This has to do with our most recent conversation, I assume?"

"It does."

There was no need to mention Clay Carlisle or Vanguard International. The substance of their last discussion—which had been the first in several months—was mutually understood.

"That's troubling, to say the least."

"In spades, sir."

"I only know two others who are privy to the matter," the contact explained. "One brought the job to me, initially. I think we can eliminate him as a suspect."

"Probably," Brognola said. "Unless he's also sharing his concerns with someone else."

"Unlikely, but it's something I can check on when we're finished here." The contact frowned. "The other person, well, I'd hate to think it's possible. I've known him, trusted him, nearly as long as I've been in the diplomatic service."

"It's the same with my people. Something like this, I start with personalities and gut instinct, but I still look for opportunity and motive."

"Yes. Of course, you're right. We can't leave any stone

unturned. Not only for this task, important as it is, but for any collaborations in the future. Everything depends upon security."

"Agreed, sir."

"If you have specifics for me…"

"Wedge Crocker," Brognola replied. "Xavier Manning."

"I know both of them," the other man replied.

"I was called to meet with them this morning. They're concerned about 'recent events in Afghanistan,' more specifically, DOJ 'meddling in sensitive areas' that 'exceed my jurisdiction and my competence.'"

"Sounds like you're quoting."

"Give or take an adjective."

"That's troubling," the contact said. "They'd be aware of any major incidents, of course. But linking them to Justice, much less to you directly… Yes. I'd call that worrisome."

"I can't imagine anyone on my end knowing those two characters. It's possible, of course, and I'll pursue it thoroughly. But, still…"

"It sounds like someone tattling in my house," the other said. "Your point's well taken."

"It's never easy," Brognola observed. "Whichever way it goes."

"You're right." A quirky smile lit up the other man's face. "I have an added disadvantage, since I can't make people disappear."

"Sometimes they do the right thing on their own initiative," Brognola said.

"It's nice to think so, anyway."

"Sorry to drop this on your plate, with all the rest you have to handle."

"Nonsense! *I* dumped this on *you,* as I recall," the contact said. "It's only fair that I should clean up any mess in my backyard."

"Maybe there'll be another explanation," Brognola suggested, not believing it.

"I'll keep my fingers crossed. Meanwhile, how is it going over there?"

"I think we're making progress."

"Well, that's something, isn't it?"

"About the best I ever hope for, sir."

"I'll see you, Hal."

"Yes, sir."

They parted company, the man from State returning to his bodyguards and limousine, while Hal Brognola lingered for a few more moments with the shades of heroes.

Pondering the best way to dispose of a traitor.

*Rika Khana, Kabul*

FROM THE U.S. EMBASSY, Alan Combs moved on to a scheduled lunch with one of his several CIs in Kabul. Confidential informants were critical to the DEA's work—as to every other branch of law enforcement worldwide—and Combs courted his with the zeal of a suitor wooing a prospective bride.

At least, until he had the information he required.

Once they were on the hook, it was a different game entirely. Combs milked his CIs for every bit of valuable data they possessed, tracking the leads they gave him until he could build cases against the dealers they identified. He paid for useful information, sure, but if a CI decided that he was worth more than the budget would bear, Combs showed the flip side of the coin.

A CI who got pushy, too demanding, could expect a firm reminder that he had no other friends in town besides the DEA. A hint that he was squealing, even if it came third-hand from some street junkie, was enough to get a CI killed in most unpleasant ways.

Combs played that card only when nothing else would work, and he had never followed up the threat with actual exposure of a DEA informant, but some of them bought the farm, regardless. He could think of eight or ten, offhand, whose grisly and protracted deaths still haunted him.

But even they were useful, in their way.

Word gets around, and the CIs who worked for Combs— or those who'd serve him later, for a list of motives that included greed, fear and revenge—soon realized that when they shook his hand and closed the deal, it was forever. They would serve the DEA until they died or quit the druggy life and were no longer useful to the agents who employed them.

The CI Combs planned to meet for lunch that day was called Osman Sabour. He was a strong midlevel cog in Basir Ahmad-Shah's machine, trusted with information on deliveries, the disposition of selected rivals—and Ahmad-Shah's use of Vanguard International employees to ensure that shipments reached their destinations safe and sound. It was Sabour who had tipped Deirdre Falk to that relationship in the first place, and the rest was history.

Now, Combs thought, maybe so am I.

Lee Hastings hadn't frightened him. The worst that any diplomat could do to Combs was get him reassigned or fired. No, it was Falk that Combs worried about, since she was off the books, running with a wild bunch that appeared to take no prisoners.

In one respect, it was a fantasy that Combs had treasured since he joined the FBI so many years ago. Each time he saw a bad guy skate on technicalities or some bizarre interpretation of the law, he'd wished there was a righteous vigilante out there somewhere, like Charles Bronson in the *Death Wish* movies. Shooting fast and straight, no doubt that he was targeting the right punk every time.

But that had only been a fantasy, until somebody higher

up the ladder of command suggested that his Vanguard problem might be solved by "intervention" with "irregular techniques." Combs hadn't fully understood—or, so he told himself now that the stiffs were piling up—but he had gone for it.

Why not?

When all else failed, and money talked louder than any judge or statute on the books, why should pure Evil be allowed to have its way? Combs wasn't one of those who railed against the System—hell, he was a living, breathing part of it—but there were times when it broke down or was diverted from its normal course by wealthy, bloodstained hands.

The stranger who had led Falk on her wild ride through the gates of hell was touted as an antidote to that disease. Combs didn't know his real name, had no clue who paid his salary, where he'd come from or where he'd go when this was finished. If he lived.

Combs didn't want to know.

Sometimes, it was reward enough to tip the scales in favor of the good guys or to at least make sure they were balanced.

Combs was running late, though not by much. Osman Sabour would have a corner table staked out in the small café where they'd agreed to meet, wearing the trademark sour expression on his face. Combs couldn't wait to hear what Ahmad-Shah's team thought about their recent losses in Nangarhar Province.

Waiting for a break in traffic that would let him cross the street, Combs didn't hear the man step up behind him, touching-close. He felt the strong hand on his shoulder, though, and then the blade that hammered in and out between his ribs, piercing his lung once, twice, three times.

It stunned him that a knife could strike that fast, and then Combs lost that thought as blood rose in his throat, triggered his gag reflex and overflowed his lips. At the same time, a hard shove drove his sagging body from the curb, into the path of fast oncoming traffic.

In the heartbeat left to him, Combs knew that someone else would have to close the Vanguard case. His own file had been closed, his ticket canceled.

He was history.

*Sherzad, Nangarhar Province*

BOLAN DROVE PAST the gates of Basir Ahmad-Shah's walled compound, noting that they weren't constructed from wrought iron, as was the case with many affluent estates. Wrought iron was decorative, stylish, but it granted passersby visual access to what lay beyond the gate.

And what a sniper could observe, he could bring under fire.

Ahmad-Shah's gates reminded him of something from a movie. Maybe *Fort Apache,* with John Wayne. A drive-by couldn't tell him whether there was steel beneath the dark wood paneling, but either way, he couldn't see inside the property.

Reluctantly, Bolan ruled out the Dragunov. He'd hoped to use the sniper rifle here—if nothing else, to whittle Ahmad-Shah's security detachment—but he saw no point in carrying a long-range weapon when he stormed the compound. As to how he'd manage that…

"How do we get inside?" Falk asked, as if reading his mind.

"I'm working on it," Bolan said.

The compound's eight-foot walls were topped with coils of razor wire instead of the more traditional broken glass set in concrete favored by wealthy recluses from Turkey eastward, to the Indian subcontinent. He couldn't tell if the coils were electrified, but from what Bolan saw of the wall on his first pass, it offered no handholds. There were no convenient trees looming beside it, for an agile ninja-type to climb.

"I'm thinking we should not do this," Edris Barialy said from his backseat spotter's post.

"We could give up," Falk said. "Or we could give the bastard what he wants and let him choke on it."

Bolan frowned. "And what he wants is…?"

"Us. What else?"

"Keep talking."

"You most likely have his private number," Falk went on. "And if you don't, I do. One of us calls him—I was thinking you'd be best for that—and tells him Carlisle's people have a present for the sheikh. Those nasty people who've been ruining his day are in the bag, and they're alive. Smart money says Ahmad-Shah will be chomping at the bit to meet us, grill us, spend a few days sending us to hell a half inch at a time. Takers?"

It was an audacious plan. Bolan was sorry that he hadn't thought of it before Falk did.

The cautious warrior said, "It might work, but I see potential problems."

"Break them down," Falk said.

"First, Ahmad-Shah may not want to do business with an underling. If he demands to speak with Carlisle personally, we can scratch the plan. He'd recognize a partner's voice."

"In which case," Falk replied, "we're only out the price of a phone call. But I think he'll be eager to believe he's won. He definitely won't suspect his enemies are dumb enough to waltz in through his gates. As far as Carlisle goes, give it a shot. Say he's handling the clean-up. You can pass for someone from his inner circle. Third-in-charge, whatever."

"Maybe," Bolan answered. "In which case, we need new wheels. Vanguard may use sedans on stakeouts, but they wouldn't transport prisoners to Ahmad-Shah's doorstep in anything smaller than a Humvee."

"You're right," Falk said. "And I think I know where to get one."

"Oh? Where's that?" Bolan asked skeptically.

"I thought we'd strive for authenticity," she said, grinning.

"Go on."

"What better than to borrow one of Carlisle's own Hummers?"

"Sounds great," Bolan replied. "But by the time we drive back to Kabul and bag one, if they're not all on the street, Ahmad-Shad might decide he likes the weather better in Mihtarlam."

"That would be a problem," Falk said, "if the wheels I had in mind were parked in Kabul."

"Let's cut to the chase," Bolan advised.

"Okay. Vanguard has people in Sherzad. Not many, just an outpost, but they have at least one Hummer. We can drop by, borrow it. Hell, we could even use their phone to call the sheikh, in case he's got Caller ID.

As Bolan glanced at Falk, her grin became a full-blown smile.

## CHAPTER THIRTEEN

*Vanguard International Outpost, Sherzad*

Carlisle's place in Sherzad was more of a barracks than a branch office, comprising a three-bedroom house on the outskirts of town. A black Hummer, recently polished, occupied the dwelling's covered carport.

Bolan's drive-by didn't prove that anyone was home, but he assumed the Hummer wouldn't be there if the nest was empty. Now his task would be to find a way inside and silence Carlisle's guns-in-residence without raising a ruckus to alarm the neighbors.

All he needed was a plan, audacity and luck.

A sneak-around might work, except that it was broad daylight, and Bolan knew that in the present circumstances, at least some of Carlisle's soldiers in Sherzad would be on full alert.

And the best way to slip one past them, even for a second, was...

"I hope you're carrying your badge," he said to Falk.

"Never leave home without it. Why?"

"I'm thinking we should raid the place."

"Say what?" she asked.

"Knock on the door, badge them, and ask to have a look around."

"Yeah, that'll work," she scoffed.

"I'm betting it will get the door open," Bolan replied. "That's all we need."

"Sounds like a half-baked scheme to me," Falk said.

"And your alternative would be…?"

She frowned and shook her head. "Sure, why not? Let's drop in for a jolly chin-wag. What the hell."

That's where audacity came in.

Bolan parked on the street in front of the house and rolled out of the driver's seat, joining Falk and Barialy on the strip of dried-up grass that passed for a sidewalk. He let Falk lead, pacing her on the right, while Barialy took her left flank. On the doorstep, after briefly searching for a doorbell that did not exist, Falk hammered on the door with her fist.

Bolan heard feet shuffling toward the door inside. A peephole opened at eye-level and a male voice growled from hiding.

"Who are you?"

Falk badged him through the peephole and responded, "DEA. We have some questions for the owner of this property."

Her move masked Bolan as he drew his 9 mm Jericho with its sound supressor attached. Their trio stood and waited while a muffled debate ran its course on the door's other side.

At last the gruff voice said, "Get lost."

"Sir," Falk replied, "if I leave now, I'll be coming back in fifteen minutes with a team of agents from the ASNF and the CNP. I don't mind going that route, if it's really how you want to play it."

More muffled discussion from inside. Then, "Say again what you wanted."

"A half dozen questions. That's all."

"About what?"

"I doubt you want me shouting all your private business through the door," she said. "In fact, forget it. I'll go fetch the home team with their battering rams."

"Hang on, for Christ's sake! Just a friggin' minute!"

Bolan hung on, and heard the dead bolt open, followed by the rattling of multiple security chains. The door opened three inches, to reveal a slice of glaring Anglo features.

"Lemme see those creds again," the mercenary demanded.

"Love to," Bolan said, and shot him through the left eye from three inches, taking out the back half of his target's skull.

He charged in while the body was still tumbling through a waterfall of crimson. Caught another shooter grappling with a stubby MP-5K submachine gun that he hadn't cocked before.

Too late.

The second nearly silent round from Bolan's Jericho punched through the mercenary's forehead, dropping him before he had a chance to prime his weapon. Bolan stepped around him as the dead man fell, first to his knees, then forward, on his ruined face.

A third merc came out of a room on Bolan's left, pistol in hand and tracking into target acquisition. The Executioner hit a crouch and put two muffled shots into the gunman's chest, slamming him back into a plaster wall that shuddered from his body's impact. Falk rushed forward through the cordite reek and snatched the weapon from the fallen shooter's hand.

They searched the rooms together, Bolan leading with his silenced weapon while his two companions watched his back and covered other doorways, just in case. They came up empty, and began to let themselves unwind as Falk went back and closed the open door that faced the street.

Had any neighbors seen the action going down?

If so, would they risk getting mixed up with police?

No time to waste.

Bolan spotted a telephone in the kitchen, palmed the receiver and began to tap out a number.

*Basir Ahmad-Shah's Home, Sherzad*

SHEIKH BASIR Ahmad-Shah was editing a mental list of enemies and rivals when he heard a muffled rapping on the stout door to his private chamber. It was rather startling how that list had grown in recent years, with his increasing affluence, but he supposed that was always the case.

Great men became the focus of great hatred. It appeared to be a fact of life.

Which of the enemies whom Ahmad-Shah had failed to kill, thus far, possessed the strength and will to raid his convoys and obliterate his largest heroin refinery? No names immediately came to mind, but he was working on it when the knock distracted him.

He scowled, then made his face deadpan and said, "Enter."

Jamal Woraz obeyed, ducking his head in an approximation of a bow before he closed the door behind him. He held a cordless telephone in his left hand.

"Someone wishes to speak with you," Woraz declared.

*"Someone?"*

"From Carlisle's office, I believe."

"Why the uncertainty?"

"I do not recognize his name, sir. But he has good news."

Ahmad-Shah considered refusing the call, incensed that Clay Carlisle would leave direct communication to some underling Woraz had never heard of, but the lure of good news proved irresistible after the sheikh's humiliating losses.

He received the telephone as if the very act of holding it was drudgery, somehow beneath him. There was no trace of familiarity or warmth in Ahmad-Shah's voice as he asked, "Who is this?"

"Fred Kovacs, sir, with Vanguard International. Mr. Carlisle sends his apologies for being out-of-office, but he didn't think you'd want to wait before hearing the news."

"What news is this?" the sheikh inquired.

"We've caught the people who were tearing up your operation. Some of them, at least," the caller quickly added. "These three are the ones who shot our guys in Kabul yesterday, for sure."

"What of…the rest?" Ahmad-Shah asked.

"Mr. Carlisle thought you might like to question them yourself. Or, we can do it for you, if you'd rather not be bothered."

"No!" the sheikh replied. "I will receive them gladly."

"As to that," the caller said, "where do you want them? I'd have thought the plant, but since that's gone—"

"Where are they now?"

"Right here," the stranger answered. "In Sherzad."

There was no holding back the smile that cracked Basir Ahmad-Shah's face. Without a vestige of the hesitation normally required for thought, he asked, "You know my residence?"

"Yes, sir. Sure thing."

"I will receive them here," the sheikh instructed.

"Excellent. We'll be at your gate with the delivery inside of half an hour."

"Please convey my thanks to Mr. Carlisle. I look forward to discovering if we have other adversaries still at large, or if his thoughtful gift completes the set."

"He's working on it, sir. I'm sure he'll be in touch, ASAP."

The line went dead before Ahmad-Shah could reply, and while that rudeness modified his smile a bit, in the direction of a subtle frown, he did not let it trouble him. In his experience, Americans were brash and thoughtless at the best of times. And the more courteous they seemed, the more likely it was that they were lying.

Setting down the cordless phone, he faced Jamal Woraz and asked, "You heard the message first?"

"Yes, sir. Forgive me. I did not wish to disturb you if—"

Ahmad-Shah waved off the apology. He suddenly felt generous.

"Make ready to receive our guests, Jamal," he said. "Have all in readiness downstairs when they arrive."

The prisoners would not appreciate his private dungeon, but the sheikh suspected that he would enjoy their tenancy enough for all concerned. Before he finished with them, there would be no secrets unexplored. Between screams, they would tell him what he had to know.

And after that, the rest would all be sport.

BOLAN DROVE THE HUMMER, Falk in the backseat, with Barialy trailing in the rented Avalon. They'd switched most of their gear from the Toyota to the larger vehicle before they left Clay Carlisle's not-so-safe house in Sherzad. Their stockpile now included three MP-5Ks and stacks of ammo magazines they'd liberated from the Vanguard arsenal, one of them resting on the empty seat to Bolan's right, the other two in back with Falk.

Their plan was basic. It required one stop, a block short of the narco-smuggler's walled estate, where Barialy parked and locked the Avalon, then dived into the Hummer's wide backseat. Power buttons controlled the windows all around, so he and Falk could fire from either side while Bolan drove the heavy vehicle.

But first, they had to get inside the compound.

Even with the Hummer, Bolan knew he couldn't ram Ahmad-Shah's gates aside to force entry. He thought his call had done the trick, but it was always dicey when you couldn't see the other player's eyes and judge his physical reaction to a con.

They might be seconds from a lethal trap, and if it played that way, well, there was nothing he could do about it. Death was always waiting, somewhere down the road.

Bolan slowed to ten miles per hour, approaching the gates to Ahmad-Shah's walled compound. "Last chance to abort," he advised his companions.

"What, and miss the party?" Falk replied.

"We must proceed, I think," Barialy said.

"Okay, then," Bolan said. "Be ready when the gates open. We're playing it by ear from there."

"Hard entry from the start?" Falk asked.

"Depends on Ahmad-Shah. I'd like to get in closer to the house before the shooting starts, but if we get a hassle from the gate guards, we can take them down."

"We hope so," Barialy said, as if speaking to himself.

Falk glanced at him, then told Bolan, "If they look in the car, they'll wonder where the Vanguard muscle is."

"We'll let that be our guide," Bolan replied. "They're bound to have an English-speaker on the gate for this. If I can't talk us through without a search, we'll have to go for broke."

"All right," she said. "Let's do it."

Bolan heard his passengers cocking their weapons in the backseat. He already had his MP-5K cocked, ready to rip, resting beside his AKSU carbine and the MGL grenade launcher. He wasn't dressed in combat gear, in case he had to pass inspection from the sentries, but his bandoliers were puddled in the footwell for the Hummer's shotgun seat.

He didn't have to tap his horn when they arrived. The moment that his headlights touched the gates, the portal started opening as if the gates were photosensitive. Bolan waited, with one hand on the wheel and one resting upon the SMG's smooth pistol grip.

Bolan waited until the gates were open wide enough to let

the Hummer pass, then eased down on the gas pedal and moved the boxy vehicle forward. He saw the guards immediately, two on either side, with automatic weapons in their hands. Not slung, but primed for action at a second's notice. Bolan studied them through tinted glass and wondered how much armor Vanguard's Hummer had in place.

Ten feet inside the gates, he braked, removed his left hand from the Hummer's steering wheel, and found the button that would lower his window.

DEIRDRE FALK CLUTCHED the twin grips of the MP-5K SMG she'd liberated from the Vanguard hangout with sufficient force to make her fingertips go numb. Her AKSU and the Mini-Uzi lay beside her, with the third MP-5K.

Edris Barialy had preferred to trust his folding-stock Kalashnikov over a new gun he had never fired. He occupied the far end of the Hummer's wide backseat, almost against the right-hand door, legs jiggling nervously as he sat waiting for the drama to unfold.

Falk was surprised to find herself almost relaxed. Whether the shooting started now, or five minutes later, she understood that she faced yet another life-threatening challenge, the kind that had become almost routine since she'd first shaken hands with Matthew Cooper in the Sharh-e-Khone. Falk wasn't getting used to it, exactly, but the dread had lessened somewhat.

She was growing numb to bloodshed.

Like her fingertips.

Falk made a conscious effort to relax her grip on the SMG as Cooper's window powered down. One of the guards on that side of the Hummer crouched slightly, as if to peer inside the vehicle. Falk saw him frown—confused by the empty passenger's seat?—but she missed the question he fired at Cooper.

"In the back," Bolan told him.

His eyes met Falk's in the rearview mirror, and he gave a barely perceptible nod.

*Here we go.*

Falk waited for her window to descend, lowered by Cooper's hand on the command console. She had to focus now, couldn't glance over to check Barialy's attitude of readiness. As soon as any of the gunmen peered into the back and saw no captives under heavy guard, the jig was up.

And now, a bearded face was peering at her through the half-open window, dark eyes blinking in surprise at what they saw, or didn't see. The guard half turned, opened his mouth to speak, and Falk triggered a 3-round burst into his ear.

Some of the splash-back stained her blouse—already long past saving by a normal laundry—but she let it go and scanned the field for other moving targets. Cooper's man was down and out, tattooed across the chest by automatic fire, and Barialy's AK chattered noisily behind her as the Hummer lurched into acceleration mode.

It was a mad dash for the big house now, with Cooper's foot pressed to the floorboard and the Hummer growling like some kind of prehistoric monster as it charged along the driveway then veered off across a neatly-tended lawn.

Make that a gauntlet, as the sheikh's men opened up with everything they had, from sidearms and Kalashnikovs to an RPG-7. Falk saw the rocket-propelled grenade coming, but she barely had time to curse before Cooper cranked hard on the wheel and swerved off to the right. The projectile flew past on Falk's side, close enough that she felt her hair singe, and whooshed on to detonate behind them when it struck the compound's wall.

"Think that'll bring the cops out?" Falk asked no one in particular.

"One problem at a time," Bolan replied, still firing through his open window while he drove left-handed and the Hummer started taking hits.

Jesus, let there be armor, Falk thought.

And there seemed to be. The slugs striking the Hummer's doors weren't coming through—not yet, at least—although it sounded as if several dozen maniacs with baseball bats were hammering the vehicle. The tinted windshield frosted over with a web of cracks, but didn't buckle.

On the other hand, they couldn't fire through open windows and expect to be protected from incoming fire. Falk felt a bullet slip-slide through her windblown hair before it ripped into the Hummer's ceiling. Another hit the nearest window post and shattered, tiny fragments stinging her like red-hot pinpricks.

"Shit!" she snapped. "If we don't make it to the house soon—"

And before she had a chance to finish, Cooper hit the brakes, the Hummer fishtailing as it slid to a halt, halfway across a spacious patio with awnings, flagstones and a red-brick deep-pit barbecue.

Cooper was out and moving as the Hummer's engine died. Behind her, she heard Barialy bailing, firing as he ran around behind the vehicle.

Last one inside's a rotten corpse, Falk thought, and snatched her backup guns, then leaped out of the car.

JAMAL WORAZ WAS WATCHING from the ornate ground-floor windows of Basir Ahmad-Shah's mansion when the firefight started. Something twisted in his gut as automatic fire cut down the sentries on the gate before the Hummer roared along the driveway and across the broad front lawn. Its fat tires scarred the turf, while other guards began to pepper it with small-arms fire.

Woraz spun toward a pair of soldiers flanking him, but they were already in motion, bawling orders, spreading the alarm. Whichever guards were not already covering the house, including those asleep after a night patroling dark and silent grounds, would soon be rushing to the exits with their weapons.

Woraz hoped they would not be too late.

The Vanguard call had clearly been a trick, and he had passed it on to Ahmad-Shah, but the decision to invite the enemy inside had been the sheikh's alone. Now the perimeter was breached, and while a single Hummer could accommodate no more than eight or ten armed men, the open gates placed Ahmad-Shah's entire compound at risk.

Woraz keyed the transmission button on his compact two-way radio and barked at anyone who might be listening. "The gates! Someone must close the gates immediately!"

No one answered, which could mean that none of the defenders had his radio switched on, or that all of those still living had their hands full at the moment, trying to eradicate the enemy.

Woraz drew his Walther P-1 pistol from its armpit holster. It was one of ten thousand semiautomatics donated to Afghanistan's security forces by the German government in January 2006, of which more than a hundred were diverted to Sheikh Basir Ahmad-Shah. In form, it was identical to the classic P-38 carried by Wehrmacht officers in World War II, reissued during modern times as the P-1.

The pistol helped, but Woraz did not feel prepared to rush outside and face the enemy himself. Instead, he thought, his place was with the sheikh, protecting Ahmad-Shah—and, by extension, safeguarding himself.

Retreating toward Ahmad-Shah's private study, Woraz met some of the nightshift guards, fumbling with clothes and weapons as they spilled out of their quarters. He snapped orders at them, sending them to reinforce the troops outside, while he moved on to join his master.

Ahmad-Shah was just emerging from the study, carrying a Spectre submachine gun, when Woraz got there. Wild-eyed, he demanded, "What is happening, Jamal? Has Carlisle turned against us?"

"Who can say?" Woraz replied. "The damned Americans—"

His thought remained unfinished as the blast of a grenade or rocket shook the house. Woraz had seen one of the guards fire at the Vanguard Hummer with an RPG and miss, just moments earlier. Now he could only wonder if the fool had tried again and struck the house instead.

If not, it meant the enemy had weapons far more powerful than submachine guns or Kalashnikovs.

"We must get out while there is time," Ahmad-Shah said.

"I'll find someone to drive the limousine," Woraz replied.

"To hell with that! Go get Farouk!"

Of course!

Farouk Tarana was Ahmad-Shah's private helicopter pilot, and the last man in the world to risk himself in combat with invaders. Unless Woraz missed his guess, the man would even now be hiding in his small bedroom on the third floor.

Leaving the sheikh to guard himself, Woraz turned and sprinted toward the staircase.

BOLAN HAD EMPTIED one MP-5K magazine before he drove the Hummer onto Ahmad-Shah's veranda, and he keyed the window button, raising his, before he switched the empty mag out for a fresh one. And the reflex action saved his life as two slugs struck the driver's window, starred it but did not come though.

"Jesus!" Falk said behind him. "That was close!"

"It's getting closer," Bolan answered fatalistically as he

slung bandoliers over his head, slipped both arms through the slings of backup weapons, and prepared to take it EVA.

"Through the glass doors to the house," he told his friends, then grabbed the door handle, lifted and lunged into the killing ground.

This time, the MP5K saved him. Its cyclic rate of fire—900 rounds per minute—was a hundred rounds per minute faster than other SMGs in the same series from H&K, although its short barrel reduced muzzle velocity from 1,300 feet per second to a "mere" 1,219. He'd set the little weapon for full-auto fire but milked the trigger with an expert's touch, producing 3- to 5-round bursts upon command.

And who could stand in front of him without body armor?

Not the pair of shooters who had rushed to take him on the patio, so hasty that they came prepared with pistols only for the battle of a lifetime. Bolan dropped them both with short bursts to the chest and left them twitching on the flagstones as he moved toward the house.

Bright sunshine on the patio prevented him from seeing any critical details or movements in the spacious room beyond. Charging the glass doors that already stood half open, Bolan swept the room with 9 mm fire and heard a pained cry from one corner, giving his unseen target a quick second dose.

He hit the floor rolling on deep-pile shag carpet that smelled of some chemical cleanser, coming to rest behind a long sofa covered in leather. It wouldn't stop bullets, but might slow them. Either way, any cover was better than none.

Bolan was ready, waiting, when his two companions followed him into a rec room whose expensive furnishings included video and pinball games, a jukebox and a giant flat-screen TV set, now bullet-punctured and forever dark. A gut-shot figure occupied one corner, curled up where he'd fallen by a rack of free weights. Bolan didn't see him moving at the moment, nor was any weapon visible, but he'd be one to watch.

They had to clear the rec room in a hurry now, with reinforcements gathering outside to follow them, and soldiers in the house using each moment they were granted to improve hasty defenses. Bolan caught Falk's eye, mouthed, "Time to go," and rose from cover with the AKSU carbine in his right hand and the MP-5K in his left.

The huddled figure moved as Bolan neared his corner of the rec room, headed for its only interior doorway. The Executioner gave him three more rounds that splashed the matte-black weights with crimson, and a Micro-Uzi slipped from lifeless fingers over there.

One less to think about as they moved on in search of bigger prey.

Behind him, Falk and Barialy covered their advance with rounds fired toward the patio and yard beyond. Shooters out there would be returning fire and following on foot as soon as they believed that it was reasonably safe, but logic told him that they'd try to minimize the damage to their master's palace.

Bolan, on the other hand, felt no such contraints.

He reached the exit from the rec room, met a shooter coming down the hallway to his left and emptied the SMG into his startled opponent, then dropped it. He could only use so many weapons in a firefight, and that still left three, including his pistol.

Bolan cleared the exit, beckoned Falk and Barialy past him, then turned back to face the glass doors and veranda. Short of stopping where he was, he couldn't block pursuers absolutely—but he had a decent chance to slow them.

He unslung his MGL and two rounds from the 40 mm launcher, angled upward toward the point where wall met ceiling, just above the broad glass doors. The twin projectiles did their job, dropping a portion of that ceiling to obstruct the entryway—and, in the process, causing one whole side of Ahmad-Shah's mansion to sag, as if a giant had sat on the roof.

"Not bad," Falk said. "We'll have to find another exit, though."

"After we turn up Ahmad-Shah," Bolan replied, and struck off to his right along the hallway, tracking human game.

## CHAPTER FOURTEEN

Basir Ahmad-Shah was on the verge of panic when he heard voices and footsteps drawing closer to the open doorway to his private study. Even with the din of battle on the floor below him, he could not mistake the sounds of two men, maybe three, advancing toward his sanctuary.

Crouched behind his massive desk, he clutched his Spectre submachine gun, ready to unleash its fifty rounds in one wild burst if enemies breached his study. He was on the verge of firing when he recognized Jamal Woraz and the pilot, Farouk Tarana, coming through the doorway,

Ahmad-Shah rose from his hiding place, then staggered as another blast vibrated through the floor beneath his feet. He worried that the house might fall around his ears at any moment, but he dared not show his fear to Woraz, if he planned to let his chief lieutenant live.

An underling who glimpsed his master's weakness was a mortal adversary in the making. Ahmad-Shah could never trust Woraz again, if he had any reason whatsoever to suspect Woraz believed he was incapable of dealing with his enemies.

Already thinking toward the future, Ahmad-Shah addressed the pilot first, putting an edge of steel into his voice.

"Farouk," he said, "we must preserve our family's command structure. You understand?"

"We're leaving?" the pilot asked, cutting to the bottom line.

"We are. Is all in readiness?"

"The helicopter has full tanks. I need a few minutes of preparation, prior to takeoff. And, of course, we have to reach it through…all that."

As Tarana spoke his final words, he gestured vaguely toward the study doorway and the sounds of combat echoing from the ground floor.

"We should begin at once," Woraz observed.

Ahmad-Shah cringed at the idea of running down the stairs into a storm of gunfire. And, in fact, despite his confidence that he would never need emergency escape routes, he had made allowances for that scenario.

"The ladder, then," he said.

Tarana looked confused, but Woraz smiled in understanding. "We should hurry," he remarked.

Ahmad-Shah moved immediately to the study doorway, steeled himself and peered into the hallway. Glancing left, then right, he saw no guards—and, more importantly, no enemies.

Trusting Woraz and the pilot to follow, he moved along the corridor with brisk, determined strides. Each step he took emboldened Ahmad-Shah, making him feel as if he had redeemed himself with a display of courage in adversity. Woraz would not think him a coward now.

But Ahmad-Shah might kill him after this was all behind him, just in case.

The ladder was concealed in Ahmad-Shah's bedroom, a hedge against attackers who might raid the compound while he slept. Attacks in broad daylight, unless the raiders were police whom he could bribe, had never seriously crossed his mind. Thus, he could only make his exit from a bedroom window, rather than his study or the fourteen rooms located on the mansion's second floor.

The sheikh's suite was located at the far end of the hallway, at the south end of the house. Unfortunately it was not adjacent to the compound's helipad, since Ahmad-Shah preferred a garden view and did not wish to have his sleep disrupted if the chopper was required to fly without him for some reason at ungodly hours.

They had to reach the bedroom, take the custom-made rope ladder from its hiding place inside a window seat, attach it to the hooks concealed by hanging drapes, and then descend to ground level without being picked off by snipers. From there, they had to run halfway around the mansion to the helipad and board the waiting chopper, wait while Tarana ran his preflight checklist, and hope that none of the raiders had noticed.

How many were now on the grounds?

Ahmad-Shah didn't know, and in a sense, he didn't care. It only took one man, one bullet, to destroy him. Even if a thousand raiders swarmed over the compound, only one would claim the prize for snuffing out his life.

But if he managed to escape, he'd make them pay.

Thoughts of revenge kept Basir Ahmad-Shah from trembling as he ran along the hallway toward his bedroom, begging God for an opportunity to save himself.


BOLAN CHARGED THROUGH the doorway to a formal dining room and found cover behind a massive ornate cabinet displaying china edged with gold. There was another entrance at the far end of the room, now occupied by two or three defenders armed with automatic weapons who were obviously pledged to stop him here and now.

Falk followed Bolan through the entrance at his back and slid beneath a dining table built for thirty guests. Behind her, Barialy dived headlong into the same cover.

Their worm's-eye view beneath the table gave Falk and Barialy a fair line of fire toward the opposite door, but that could work both ways, permitting their opponents to return fire at the same angle. Granted, the doorway shooters suffered from a disadvantage in the face-off, but a single lucky burst— or a grenade—could shift the balance, while depriving Bolan of his two allies.

Before one of the snipers had a chance to score, he swapped the 40 mm launcher for his AKSU, braced himself, then rose and fired a round downrange, angling to strike the door jamb on the left side of the portal. When it blew, one shooter vanished in a cloud of smoke and plaster dust, while his companion yelped in pain and started to return fire, lurching out from cover when he should have turned and run.

Falk and her sidekick cut him down with short bursts from the floor, waiting to see if any other troops emerged to threaten them at once. When none appeared, Bolan advanced and felt the others following, trusting them to watch out for Ahmad-Shah's defenders closing on their heels.

Where would they find the man in charge?

Without a floor plan for Ahmad-Shah's house, they'd have to search it room by room—unless they found someone willing to finger his employer in return for Bolan's one-time-only promise of a deal.

Give up the sheikh and live. Hang tough, you die.

It was a long shot, but compared to scouring three floors with forty, fifty rooms while fighting off the home team and waiting for the police to show, it sounded like a plan.

Bolan explained it, tersely, while they hustled through a kitchen large enough to serve an upscale restaurant and eased into a pantry larger than many New York apartments. Falk looked skeptical, while Barialy's face was deadpan. Neither raised an alternate suggestion.

So, the plan was threefold now. Keep looking for the man

in charge, while fighting off his loyal defenders *and* bag some of those defenders for hasty interrogation as they went along.

Simple as falling in an open grave.

The next two guys they met gave Bolan no chance to negotiate. They burst out of a doorway, firing as they came, and only stopped when Bolan stitched them both with 5.45 mm rounds that left them coughing blood before they died.

Too bad.

Bolan was angling through a parlor, toward a massive staircase, when two more defenders started their descent. A third remained above, on the second-floor landing, to fire through the railing.

Bolan hit a flying shoulder roll with bullets pecking at the marble floor around him, leaving Barialy and Falk to deal with the upstairs sniper while he took the shooters on the staircase. Both were firing from the hip toward where he'd been a heartbeat earlier, revealing shocked expressions when he cut their legs from under them and spilled them tumbling down the steps.

Falk and Barialy hosed the third shooter with autofire and flattened him, while Bolan raced forward to disarm the others, snatching rifles away from them and frisking them for sidearms, tossing their pistols after the long guns. In another moment, both lay sprawled in their own blood and staring up at Bolan.

He called Barialy to his side, eyes never leaving the two wounded captives for an instant as he said, "Okay, now. Ask them if they want to live or die."

JAMAL WORAZ WAS SWEATING freely by the time he reached Ahmad-Shah's private suite. A smell of smoke wafted along the corridor, and he envisioned hungry flames devouring the walls and carpeting downstairs. Gunfire and echoing explosions drove sharp spikes of pain into his ears.

They reached the door they sought and Ahmad-Shah pushed through it. Woraz braced himself, unsure what they would find across the threshold. True, it seemed their enemies were all downstairs, but how could he be sure? If some had scaled the outer wall, or landed on the roof from helicopters, say...

The helicopter!

How would they escape if it was damaged and unable to take off? The sheikh had many cars, of course—most of them bulletproof, to some extent—but driving over the chaotic battleground outside did not appeal to him.

Worse yet, he'd ordered that the gates be closed. What if they were? Who would the sheikh order to leave the safety of the car and open them?

At that moment Woraz made up his mind to drive the car if they were forced to flee by land. He would not stand on ceremony and require Tarana or some other subordinate to take the wheel. Let *them* be shot. Woraz would save himself.

And Basir Ahmad-Shah, of course.

If that was also possible.

Inside the lushly furnished bedroom suite, Ahmad-Shah ran directly to a window near his massive bed, bent to the window seat below its sill and opened its hinged top. Reaching inside, he lifted out a rolled rope ladder that had wooden rungs. Twin ropes dangled from one end of the ladder, linked to large steel rings.

Ahmad-Shah closed the window seat and stood, holding the ladder, as he snapped at his companions, "Hold the drapes."

Woraz knew what he meant, although Tarana clearly had no clue. Leading the pilot by example, Woraz grabbed the curtains on Amad-Shah's left and pulled them well back from the window, to expose a steel hook mounted on the wall. Ahmad-Shah slipped one of the ladder's shiny rings over that hook, then waited for Tarana to bare the other one and make the set complete. Another second filled with muttering apologies saw that job done.

Now, Ahmad-Shah lifted the lower window sash as high as it would go, then reached through with an arm and punched the window's screen. It took three blows before the mounted screen buckled enough to loosen, then fell off into the yard below.

That done, the sheikh peered through the open window, searching the immediate vicinity for enemies, apparently detecting none. Growling with effort, Ahmad-Shah propelled the coiled rope ladder through the window, whence it rattled out of sight against the south wall of the house.

The sheikh picked up his submachine gun, turned to face Woraz and said, "You first. Farouk goes next. I follow when the ladder is secured."

Woraz saw his employer's index finger on the Spectre's trigger. He did not protest. Ahmad-Shah would protect himself at any cost, and why not?

Given half a chance, Woraz would do the same.

But now clearly was not the time.

He leaned out through the open window, glanced in both directions, and saw no one watching as he braced himself for the attempt. A quick pat reassured him that he had not lost his pistol, then Woraz surveyed the window, realized that he could never make it with the window seat in place, and dragged the obstacle aside. That let him step over the windowsill from floor-level, instead of two feet off the floor, which put his hip against the upper window sash and made escape a virtual impossibility.

And even now, despite the large size of the window, it still wasn't easy. Woraz had to bow, thrust one leg out the window, straddling the sill, and try to find one of the ladder's rungs with that foot, though he could not see it. All the while, the window sash scraped painfully across his spine and shoulders, while the windowsill pressed on his crotch.

He found the rung at last, then had to brace himself with

both palms on the sill, back aching where the window sash cut into him, and raise his other leg at a near-impossible angle, first pressing the thigh and knee to his chest, then easing his foot backward, blindly, to join the other on its ladder rung.

If Woraz lost his grip now, he would plummet to the earth below, after first smashing his head against the window sash. With any luck, he thought, he'd be unconscious when he hit the ground, breaking his legs, pelvis and spine. Or, better yet, someone might shoot him while he clung there, with his buttocks protruding into empty space.

Somehow, he made it, gasping, sweating through his clothes. Woraz shifted his grip from windowsill to ladder, and began his swaying, dizzying descent.


EDRIS BARIALY DID as he was told, asking the wounded men in Pashto, "Do you wish to live?"

Both blinked at him as if he was insane, then one of them— the gunman on his right—replied, "How many camels fucked your mother?"

It was Barialy's turn to blink, surprised rather than angry.

"What was that?" Bolan asked.

"He's in pain. I'll ask again," Barialy said.

And he did. To which the gunman answered, "Do you sleep with this unclean woman? Are you both diseased?"

"Time's wasting," Bolan said.

Tasting the bile on his soft palate, Barialy said, "He won't cooperate."

Cooper leaned slightly forward, shot the cursing man between his eyes, then turned his pistol on the sole survivor, saying, "His turn."

"Do you wish to live?" Barialy asked one more time.

"What must I do?" the frightened shooter asked.

"Tell us where we can find Sheikh Basir Ahmad-Shah."

"I haven't seen him since—" The glint in Barialy's eye told

the informant he should try another tack. "Upstairs!" he blurted. "The second floor! He has an office there, also his sleeping quarters. If he's in the house, which I don't know, look there!"

Barialy translated for Bolan, who asked, "Is he lying?"

"I doubt it."

"Let's move, then."

Falk and Bolan started up the staircase in a rush, taking the steps two and three at a time. Before he followed, Barialy told the wounded soldier, "You are free to go."

The dazed man glanced down at his shattered, bloody legs and whooped a laugh that instantly turned into weeping. Barialy left him there, to live or die alone, and followed his companions to the mansion's second floor.

They raced along the corridor, meeting no opposition, since the guards had all apparently rushed out to meet the enemy below. Ten yards from the staircase, they checked an open door and saw what had to be Ahmad-Shah's private den or study, decorated to his taste from boar heads on the walls down to a pipe rack filled with pricey, ornate smoking implements.

But there was no one home.

"You want to try to find the bedroom?" Falk inquired.

"We might as well."

"Which way?" she asked.

"I can't imagine he'd be sleeping any closer to the stairs than this," Bolan replied. "On toward the far end of the hall."

And there, a door stood open, as if waiting for them, but they paused to check each one along the way for Ahmad-Shah, and to prevent concealed gunmen from popping out behind them as they passed. None yielded anything but rumpled beds and general disarray.

At last they reached the open door and stepped across its threshold, Bolan in the lead as usual. The sheikh's bedroom was larger than the house where Barialy had been raised with his four siblings, easily four times the size of his apartment in Kabul.

And it, too, seemed to be unoccupied.

"The window," Bolan said, and ran immediately to the only one of four that stood open.

Barialy took a moment to identify the metal rings with ropes attached as part of an escape ladder, then recognition hit him like a swift punch to the gut.

"We've lost him," he declared.

"Not yet," Bolan replied. "He had to go somewhere."

And saying that, he vanished through the window, scrambling like a monkey down the ladder, to the ground below.

BOLAN KICKED OFF from the wall and dangling ladder halfway down, and landed in a crouch on grass surrounding paving stones. One path circled the house, while yet another veered off toward a garden filled with shrubs and flowers.

He had scanned the garden from Ahmad-Shah's bedroom window and had seen no one concealed there. Bolan's quarry had gone east or west, circling around the mansion, passing out of sight before he arrived.

As Falk touched down beside him, Bolan asked himself where Ahmad-Shah would go, what would he seek?

Escape.

On land, the sheikh could either run or ride. Bolan had seen cars parked outside the mansion, and he guessed there had to be others tucked away somewhere, perhaps in one or more garages.

On the other hand, if he was anxious to escape right now, with minimal engagement...

Bolan turned to Falk as she was helping Barialy off the swaying ladder. "Do you know if Ahmad-Shah owns any kind of aircraft?"

"There's a Learjet," she replied. "At least two helicopters—"

Bolan didn't wait to hear the rest. He might be wrong, but

if he wasn't, every second counted. Once the sheikh was airborne, Bolan couldn't hope to catch him, and the hunt would have to spread worldwide. It could take years, assuming that he *ever* found his target.

Falk shouted after Bolan, "What the—? Oh, my God! Come on, Edris! Hurry!"

Bolan ran, the 40 mm launcher slapping heavily against his ribs with every stride, and scanned the ground ahead of him for enemies. As he ran past one window, someone in the house fired at him, missed, then reaped a whirlwind of full-auto fire from his companions following behind him.

There'd been no sign of a heliport when they drove into the property, meaning that it wasn't in front of the house or around the north side, where he'd parked the Hummer on Ahmad-Shah's veranda. They'd scrambled down a ladder at the south end of the mansion, which left west.

Bolan picked up his pace, rounded the final corner and beheld the chopper on its concrete pad, already warming up, its rotors turning lazily, accelerating by degrees toward lift-off speed. Three shooters stood between him and the airship, spread out in a fragile skirmish line, while someone in a pricey suit climbed up inside the chopper and prepared to close the hatch behind him.

Bolan dived headlong onto the turf as bullets rattled over-head. He spared a fleeting thought for Falk and Barialy, under-standing there was nothing he could do for them, then started fighting for his life.

His AKSU stuttered, short bursts parceled out among his adversaries as the flaming muzzle tracked from left to right across the field. One shooter twitched and fell, still firing toward the sky as he went down. The second started running backward, tripped on his own feet and tumbled through a clumsy backward somersault while Bolan shifted to confront his standing comrade.

Number three was good, but not quite good enough. He fired a trifle high, his bullets riffling through the air a foot above where Bolan lay prone on the grass. The snake's-eye view was good enough for Bolan, squeezing off a burst that stitched his target from the groin up to his throat and punched him over backward in a lifeless sprawl.

Now, number two had found his feet and he was running toward the helicopter, panicked into suddenly forgetting his immediate orders. Bolan, rising, hit him with three rounds in the back and then forgot him, while the corpse slid facedown over grass like someone finishing a home run in a zombie baseball game.

The helicopter had his full attention now, and it was lifting off. Bolan emptied his AKSU's magazine to no effect, then swung the 40 mm launcher off its shoulder sling and brought the sight up to his eye. He scarcely had to aim, at that range, but he didn't want to blow it, either, through a sudden burst of overconfidence.

The MGL had four rounds left in its revolving cylinder: two buckshot, two HE. Bolan held steady as he squeezed the trigger four times in succession, aiming for the cockpit and the passenger compartment just behind it, leaning hard into the weapon's recoil for consistent aim.

He saw the chopper's windscreen shatter and implode, showing the pilot's bloody, screaming face, with two more peering anxiously over his shoulder from the rear seats. Then, the HE rounds went off with a concussive force that rocked Bolan back on his heels like a man in a wind tunnel, hair blowing back from his face.

He was retreating, double-time, before the fuel tanks detonated in a roiling cloud of orange flame, pouring thick black smoke into the Afghan sky. The chopper's blazing wreckage settled on its landing skids, long rotor blades drooping like wings on a gigantic, dying dragonfly. Fire spread around the

helicopter, eating at the lawn, as Bolan turned away and faced
his two companions.

"Time to go," he said, "if we can still get out of here alive."

IN FACT, IT WASN'T ALL that difficult. Their stolen Hummer,
after all the hits that it had taken, still stood solidly on run-
flat tires. Its engine fired the first time Bolan pressed the
starter button, and he had no problem steering through a broad
U-turn.

Reaching the vehicle had been a challenge, forcing Bolan
and his friends to kill another eight or nine of Ahmad-Shah's
defenders, but the home team—what was left of it—seemed
to be losing heart. Bolan could not have said whether they
knew the sheikh was dead, but those inside the house made
no concerted effort to pursue the Vanguard vehicle, or even
fire on it as it fled the scene.

They cleared the gates with only scattered fire behind them,
most of the bullets missing completely. Bolan turned back
toward the point where they'd left the Toyota Avalon, accelerating as he buzzed his window down and listened for approaching sirens.

Nothing yet.

How long would a response take to the home of Basir
Ahmad-Shah? Bolan assumed the sheikh had bribed local
police, but that would be to look the other way and close their
eyes to criminal activity, not rush to Ahmad-Shah's compound
at the first sign of trouble. It could even work against the
sheikh now, when his gunners needed help, if the authorities
delayed responding to alarms, in hopes that Ahmad-Shah
would solve his own problems, clean up his own mess at the
compound.

Bad for him, Bolan thought. Good for us.

He found the rented car where they had left it, seemingly
untouched, and transferred from the Vanguard ride to the

Toyota. Bolan left the Hummer idling in the middle of the
street. Whatever happened to the vehicle from that point on
held no interest for him at all.

When they had traveled half a mile, Falk heaved a sigh and
said, "I can't believe we freaking pulled it off!"

"We're not done yet," Bolan replied. "At least, I'm not. You
two have done a lot more than I counted on, so if you want to
pack it in…"

"No need to be insulting," Falk advised him. "What else
did you have in mind?"

"There's still Vanguard," he said. "And Clay Carlisle."

# CHAPTER FIFTEEN

*Kabul International Airport*

Afghanistan's only terminus for international civilian flights, also known as Khwaja Rawash Airport, stood nine miles from downtown Kabul. Constructed in the 1970s, it closed in 1997 after Western sanctions on the Taliban restricted air travel. It reopened in October 2001, with the U.S. invasion of Afghanistan, restricting traffic to American military flights and NATO's International Security Assistance Force. Removal of United Nations sanctions in early 2002 reopened Kabul International, but it was still run by U.S. soldiers and ISAF members, chiefly officers of the Romanian air force. Japanese contractors began construction of a new $35 million international terminal in November 2006, while domestic fliers were relegated to the airport's older facilities.

Approaching Kabul International in one of Vanguard's Humvee limousines, Clay Carlisle knew that story and dismissed it from his mind. His only focus, at the moment, was on getting out as fast as possible, before the roof caved in and buried him alive.

Or dead.

Carlisle supposed that Basir Ahmad-Shah had not awakened that fine morning with a premonition that he would be dead by lunchtime. Ahmad-Shah had been a wise old desert fox, but he'd revealed no psychic talents in the time Carlisle had known him.

Which was over now, as sure as hell.

Carlisle still didn't know who'd have the balls or troops to tackle Ahmad-Shah on his own ground and live to talk about it, but he didn't plan on lingering to read about it in the next day's newspaper. Smart money said that he was next in line for whoever had taken out the sheikh, and he could think about it later.

From a nice, safe distance.

Three thousand, four hundred miles should be good, for a start.

"You understand exactly what I want?" he asked Dale Ingram, who sat stone-faced on the seat beside him, separated from his boss by Carlisle's briefcase.

"Absolutely," Ingram said. "I'm clearing out the Kabul office, getting rid of anything that I can ship, e-mail or carry with me on the plane tomorrow. A skeleton crew stays in place for the troops, but all major decisions will issue from Antwerp."

"Correct," Carlisle replied. "If all goes well, I'll see you there tomorrow night."

"And if it doesn't?" Ingram asked, shooting his boss a sidelong glance.

"I'm not a fortune-teller, Dale. You know what scripture says about trying to tell the future with the aid of unclean spirits."

"Yes, sir."

"Still, only a fool fails to be educated by experience. We face a strong and ruthless enemy today. So far, we haven't even managed to definitively identify him—which I find incredible—and all the losses have been ours. In your place, I would shake the filth of Kabul from my shoes as soon as possible. In fact, I am."

"Yes, sir."

Carlisle suspected there was attitude behind the bland words, but he wouldn't make an issue of it. No one who was left behind to clean up a collapsing outpost ever liked it. That would be a symptom of insanity. He understood Ingram's desire to leave on Carlisle's private plane, that afternoon, instead of waiting for the next day's flight, but rank still had its privileges.

"About the product…" Ingram said, then left his comment hanging there, unfinished.

"Never fear," Carlisle replied. "Nature and commerce both abhor a vacuum. Someone will replace our late supplier, probably before the week is out. We'll make a new deal and the traffic will return to normal when our enemies have been eradicated."

"Yes, sir."

"You sound worried, Dale."

"Aren't you?"

"Tides change. I'm putting on the pressure where it counts, in Washington. We have too many friends *and* know too many secrets for the powers that be to turn their backs on us."

"On *you,* you mean."

"O, ye of little faith."

"It wears thin, Clay."

"What does?"

"This holier-than-thou routine," Ingram replied. "We rent out mercenaries and we smuggle heroin. No matter how I put that underneath a microscope, I don't see Jesus in the details."

Carlisle felt the angry color rising in his cheeks as he turned to face Ingram.

"Are you questioning my faith?"

"No, sir. I understand that you believe. But how it brought you to the place we're in is anybody's guess. If anybody understands it, I have yet to meet him. And I'll tell you without fear of contradiction that most people absolutely question your beliefs. I've heard them use the 'H' word, and they didn't bother whispering."

"The 'H' word?"

"Hypocrite."

"I see. And do you share that view?"

"No, sir. But I'm beginning to suspect that you're…confused."

Carlisle pinned Ingram with a glare. "Are you prepared to do your job here, as I've outlined it, or not?"

"Of course, I am."

"There's no of course about it, Dale. You're either with me or against me."

"Clay, I'm with you. But it's getting harder all the time."

Carlisle relaxed a bit and said, "We'll talk about that when we meet in Antwerp. For the moment, just accept that I may have a handle on the situation. Can you do that?"

Ingram nodded.

"It's all good, then," Carlisle said. Facing toward his driver, at the far end of the stretch Humvee, he called out, "Can we try to make that flight sometime today?"

*Harry S. Truman Building, Washington, D.C.*

XAVIER MANNING WASN'T SURE if he should be flattered or worried, excited or biting his nails to the quick. A command appointment with the Undersecretary of State surely meant he'd been noticed. But was that a good thing?

The great man's personal assistant offered no clues when Manning introduced himself. Her smile was minimal, polite, revealing no concern for him of any sort. The word *dismis-*

*sive* came to mind, and Manning found himself resenting her, although they'd never met before.

He sat and waited, paging through a back issue of *Orbis,* published quarterly by the Foreign Policy Research Institute. None of the words made sense when Manning tried to focus on them, so he gave up and faked it, pretending to read. It was a struggle not to glance at his watch and keep track of the time, but it would have betrayed him. Above all else, he had to be cool.

At last, the PA muttered something to the tiny microphone suspended on a stalk in front of her glossy lips, then told Manning, "You may go in now."

Not even a "sir" to send him on his way?

He frowned, thinking, This can't be good.

And he was right.

The undersecretary stood in front of a window facing the Potomac, hands clasped at the small of his back. He didn't turn as Manning entered, speaking to the river as he said, "Sit down."

No greeting, no handshake, not even "please."

The undersecretary turned at last, crossed to his desk and stood behind it, staring down at Manning in his plain, uncomfortable chair. His gaze reminded Manning of a judge's—or a hangman's."

"So," the undersecretary said. "I understand you have an interest in Afghanistan."

"Sir?"

"More specifically, some rumor of an operation Justice may be running over there?"

Panic threatened to strangle Manning. "I'm not sure I follow, sir."

"Have you enjoyed your time here?" the undersecretary asked.

The change-up took him by surprise, but Manning answered, "Yes, sir. Very much, sir."

"All good things must end, they say."

"Sir? I don't—"

"Start with Crocker. Did he drag you into this? Was it the other way around?"

"Sir, if I knew—"

"The time for playing dumb is over, Xavier. I mention that, in case you're not just playing and you really are as fucking stupid as you look to me right now."

The epithet shocked Manning into momentary silence. When he found his voice again he said, "Sir, if I may explain…"

"It's why you're here," the undersecretary said. "Confession won't save your career, of course. But it might keep you out of prison, if you're lucky. It might even save your life."

"Sir, I thought—"

"I wouldn't give a flying fart in space for what you *thought*," the undersecretary interrupted. "Tell me what you know, and be damned quick about it."

"Yes, sir," Manning said, feeling the tears well in his eyes.

And he began to spill his guts.

*Vanguard International Branch Office, Kabul*

AFTER HIS NINE-MILE DRIVE back from the airport, sweating all the way from nerves, the air-conditioning inside the Vanguard office complex was a sweet relief. He shed his jacket first, then called the troops together for a minibriefing, to make sure that all of them were on the same page.

No one was shocked by Carlisle's exit. His official residence was still a Maryland plantation outside of Washington, and he'd already been in Kabul for a week before the trouble started. If they held the timing of flight against him, no one let it show.

Why not get out? Were any of them anxious to remain?

They listened silently while Ingram told them he, too,

would be leaving in the morning, after he'd put everything in order. Business as usual was the order of the day, with everyone on full alert against attack until their enemies had been identified and finally eliminated. Those who stayed behind could count on a substantial bonus in the form of hazard pay.

If they survived.

He didn't add that part, of course. Why make things worse?

When he had finished boosting their morale, Ingram retreated to his private office and began the task of purging files he dared not leave behind for hostile eyes to read. Most of the sensitive material was on computer now, which saved on paper and made packing up the whole lot easier, but time was still required to sort through files, burn those he needed onto CDs, and delete them from his hard drive.

But deletion wouldn't be enough, of course.

Modern computers never really erased anything. Deleted files were set aside and overwritten by new data, but the FBI and DEA had personnel and programs that could scour a hard drive, search through layers of data and retrieve files that had been "erased" with most or all of their contents intact.

Unless, that was, the hard drive had been wiped completely clean or lifted out and physically destroyed. The quickest method was exposure to a powerful electro-magnet, like the one now sitting on Dale Ingram's desk, waiting for him to plug it in.

When he was finished burning files in, say, an hour or two, he'd activate the magnet, place it next to his PC, and leave it overnight to do its sly, subversive work. By the time Ingram made his next run out to Kabul International, his hard drive would be squeaky-clean.

How did that old song put it?

Like a virgin.

He was crashing, felt it coming on him as he sat behind his desk, downloading files and burning them. He might have two

CDs when he was finished, nothing much for any Customs declaration. If a touchy officer suspected he was smuggling kiddy porn, a quick glance at the files would put most minds at ease.

And if they wanted to read any further, well, he made a mental note to have a lawyer standing by and ready, just in case.

Ingram took a break and popped a Xanax, washed it down with ice-cold beer, and then returned to his appointed task. Carlisle would be airborne by now, likely somewhere over Bamian province and winging northwestward, toward Turkmenistan, the Caspian Sea and the lush sanctuary of Europe.

Ingram, who generally did not enjoy flying, still looked forward to that journey with anticipation. Eighteen hours, give or take, and he would truly shake the dust of Kabul from his shoes.

His last exchange with Carlisle raised the prospect of another, more unpleasant conversation when they met again, but Ingram would confront that problem when it came. In Carlisle's present state, he might even forget Ingram's harsh words about his faith.

But if Dale Ingram was about to be jobless, at least he would perform his duties properly until the ax fell.

And with backup copies of the files he'd burned, he might have a surprise or two in store for Carlisle, after all.

*Crossing into Kabul Province*

BOLAN DROVE the Toyota Avalon while Deirdre Falk and Edris Barialy slept. They need rest, after the battle in Sherzad and what had gone before it, just as Bolan needed solitude to put his thoughts in order for the next phase of their strike.

He knew there was at least a fifty-fifty chance that those in charge of Vanguard's office in Kabul would flee as soon as they found out that Basir Ahmad-Shah was dead. Leaving would be the smart thing. Fly away and let your staff run things as usual, until Afghan authorities or someone else cleaned up the mess and made it safe for high-end CEO types to return.

That was the smart thing. But was Carlisle smart?

Or was he stone-cold crazy?

If he chose to stand and fight, Bolan might end it here, aside from any mopping up that still remained at home. Brognola would decide how that should play out, in the end. He might not want a mess in Washington, and that was fine.

Bolan had no illusions about putting Vanguard out of business, when a thousand other private military contractors—called "PMCs," for short—were standing by, ready to do the same damned things. His lonely war had never been about purging the Earth of evil. The history of Homo sapiens ruled out any such miracle.

Bolan was simply dealing with the predators he met, one at a time. Making things marginally better on a small scale, step by step. And shot by shot.

He felt Falk wake beside him, shifting slightly in her seat. She kept her eyes closed for another moment, maybe trying to recapture something she had dreamed, or simply to postpone the next dose of reality.

It never worked.

"Nightmares?" Bolan asked, when her eyes opened at last.

"Nothing I can remember," she replied. "How do you deal with it?"

"Experience, I guess," Bolan replied. "Some folks take it harder than others."

"You saying I'm a hard-case?" Falk inquired.

"Just different," he answered. "Not a girly-girl."

"Gee, thanks. That's *so* much better."

"You know what I mean. You didn't freeze or fall apart. You stepped up like—"

"A man?"

"A soldier."

"Oh. Well, thanks, I guess." She watched the landscape pass, then said, "You know, there were a few times there, I figured I was dead."

"A few times there, we nearly *were,*" Bolan confirmed.

"But you get up and do this every day," Falk said.

"Not quite. But you get used to some of it."

"I'm not sure I could," Falk replied.

"No reason you should have to. After this…"

She waited for him to complete the thought, then asked him, "What?"

"I won't pretend your life at DEA will necessarily go back to how it was before this started."

"If I even have a job at DEA, you mean."

"My people may be able to come up with something," Bolan said, feeling himself creep out along a shaky limb.

"Let's see how it plays out first, shall we?" Falk turned from the window, adding, "Who knows? I may just decide to quit and join the freaking Peace Corps."

"You'd be good at it," he said.

"Oh, sure. As long as I could pack my Uzi."

"You'll be needing it for one more job, at least," he said. "If you're still up for it."

"Carlisle?" she asked, and smiled. "You kidding me? I wouldn't miss it for the world."

*Over Turkmenistan*

CLAY CARLISLE's Learjet 60 cruised at an altitude of forty thousand feet, holding steady at a speed of 486 miles per hour. With a range of 2,800 miles, he would be landing first at Athens, to refuel, then flying on another 1,300 miles from there to Antwerp International Airport. With ground time in

Greece, that meant the better part of ten hours spent traveling before he truly felt secure.

But as Carlisle was well aware, ten hours could change everything.

Ingram might save the day, though Carlisle was inclined to doubt it. Their last conversation had exacerbated doubts he'd experienced for some time now about his Number Two. If Ingram did not share his faith in God and Vanguard's mission, ultimately, why should Carlisle keep him on the payroll?

Firing Dale would be a tricky proposition, granted, since he knew where countless bodies were buried, both literally and figuratively. Ingram's contract included a generous severance package, but would it be enough to keep his lips sealed, when he'd had some time to brood about his time with Carlisle and the way they parted company?

Of course, there were alternatives.

Carlisle was hesitant to think about that now. He had the aircraft to himself, excluding the flight crew and two armed guards who wouldn't speak unless the boss asked one of them a question, and he needed to relax.

The past two days had drained him. From the starting gun in Kabul to the destruction of Basir Ahmad-Shah's drug refinery, Carlisle had reeled from one blow after another, failing in every attempt to contain and destroy his still-unknown enemy. Worse yet, his overtures in Washington—where he had lavished so much money on the "right" connections—had proved nearly fruitless.

Carlisle had a name—Harold Brognola—but it wasn't one he recognized, and so far he had no idea where it would lead him. Brognola was a former G-man, who had parlayed his experience and contacts into an office job at Justice.

Doing what?

That was the point where Carlisle's questions ran head-on

into a stout brick wall. Somebody "thought" Brognola was involved in covert operations. Someone else "suspected" that he ran some kind of black-ops group but couldn't prove it. Carlisle had one of his people on the case, but now they'd fallen out of contact and he couldn't seem to find out why.

Rumors amounted to a kind of currency in Washington. A few panned out, became explosive scandals or at least prime blackmail ammunition, while the vast majority were first exaggerated, then forgotten.

Carlisle didn't mind using a rumor for some kind of leverage, when that was feasible, but he preferred to deal in facts. If this Brognola person *was* a covert operator with some kind of grudge against the Vanguard operation in Afghanistan, Carlisle needed to find out why, who'd put him up to it, the whole nine yards.

But it appeared that he would have to wait on that, until he landed back on U.S. soil. Until then, he would have to treat the symptoms rather than the cause of the disease that plagued him, hoping that his men would bag one of their enemies and gain more information than they presently possessed.

Meanwhile, he needed sleep.

Carlisle donned one of the blindfolds that he carried every time he had to fly for a protracted length of time. A pair of earphones piped a flow of gospel music to his weary brain.

By the time the sweet peaceful voice had finished singing "What a Friend We Have in Jesus," Carlisle was fast asleep and dreaming of a better day when all his enemies would fry in hell.

*Kabul*

BOLAN DROVE PAST the Vanguard office once again, unsure of what he'd find. Clearly, the place wasn't abandoned, but it didn't seem to be on full alert, either.

Of course, appearances could be deceiving.

"What's the plan?" Falk asked as they cruised by and kept on going, following the flow of eastbound traffic.

"Only two ways we can play it," Bolan answered. "Flush them out, or take the game inside."

"I like Plan A," Falk told him, "if you've got a way to make it work."

That was the rub. What would it take to roust the Vanguard team out of their bunker headquarters? A bomb threat might've done it in the States, but after the attacks they'd suffered recently, he thought they'd be more likely to conduct a private search of the facility without exposing anyone to further peril on the street.

Same with a fire alarm, which Bolan couldn't fake in any case, unless he was inside Vanguard's facility. As for a sniping, even if the tiny windows he could see weren't bulletproof, their bright metallic finish rendered anyone inside the place invisible to spies outside.

"Can't think of any way, offhand," he answered.

"Shit. I was afraid of that," Falk said. "So how do we get in?"

"Only two ways I can think of," Bolan told her. "The direct approach, or something sneaky."

"By direct approach, you mean…"

He shrugged. "Carlisle's been looking for us since his people screwed up yesterday. They know you two, and one of them's seen me. We show up on their doorstep, I suspect they'll ask us in."

"Or kill us where we stand," Falk said.

"It's possible," he granted. "But that means more racket and a mess they might have to explain. Inside, we're at their mercy."

"Which, to me, makes it a bad idea," Falk said.

"It could go sour," he admitted.

"So what kind of sneaky business did you have in mind?" she asked.

"A variation on the theme," Bolan replied. "Edris and I deliver you."

"Uh-huh. So far, it sucks."

"We can't expect to break in," Bolan said. "I mean, we'd need C-4 or something similar to blow the door or make one of our own, *after* we get beyond the barricades and outer wall. I just don't see that happening."

"But you could waltz me in there…how, again?"

"Role camouflage," he said.

"Which means?"

"Show them what they expect to see, then wait until they drop their guard and run with it."

"What is it they'd expect to see?" Falk asked.

"Maybe corrupt police delivering a prisoner," Bolan replied.

"And I can't be one of the cops because—"

"You need the XY chromosome," he finished for her.

"Great. And you?"

"I'm male," Bolan said. "I can do some touch-up work, let Edris do the talking, and with any luck, we're in."

"Sounds easy," Falk replied. "Why am I not convinced?"

"We still need props," he told her. "We can't use this car, for instance. One look through their CC cameras, and they'll know that it's not official."

"Ah. So we'll need a police car."

"And two uniforms," Bolan replied.

"It just keeps getting better."

"If you've got a better plan in mind, I'm open to it. Fire away," Bolan said.

"Hell, you know I don't," she said.

"Okay, then. What we need to do is find two cops, borrow their uniforms and wheels, then we're all set."

"And you know how to do that?" Falk inquired.

"I might, at that."

## CHAPTER SIXTEEN

Hijacking a patrol car and a pair of uniforms was tricky, in light of Bolan's private vow that he would never kill a cop. No matter how corrupt or brutal a specific law-enforcement officer might be—and he had met some of the worst during his war against the Mafia—Bolan regarded all police in general as "soldiers of the same side," and had promised to himself that he would die or spend his life in prison rather than stain a badge with blood.

That said, he didn't *want* a bloody uniform. And there were many ways to take a target out of action without using deadly force.

Bolan found the cops he wanted in the Rika Khana district, loitering around a bus station. He couldn't tell if they were on a coffee break or operating some peculiar kind of stakeout, and he didn't care.

Two men in uniform. One vehicle.

He did the math and smiled at the result.

His plan relied on Falk and Barialy for its first phase. They would brace the cops, Falk badging them, while Barialy translated her spiel. The story, in a nutshell, was that she'd located an important fugitive and needed the immediate assistance of police to nab him in the men's room of the bus depot. Since every second counted, there'd be no time for the officers to radio for backup or report what they were doing.

If they tried to stall, Plan B meant pulling guns, disarming them in broad daylight and forcing them into the backseat of their cruiser, but the risks involved made Bolan very hesitant to try that route. In fact, he'd already decided that he'd rather scrub the snatch and find a different pair of cops—or make a new plan for assaulting Vanguard headquarters—than risk a shootout with patrolmen on the street.

Bolan watched through a bus depot window as Falk and Barialy made their approach. The two cops looked confused at first, then nervous. They went through some back-and-forth with Falk, one pointed toward their cruiser's dashboard-mounted radio, but finally they yielded and began to follow her inside.

Bolan was waiting in the men's room when they reached it, thankful that it had been unoccupied when he arrived. The officers would be there within seconds, Barialy leading them, and Falk would guard the door against hapless intruders while the issue was resolved, one way or another.

Barialy was first through the door, but the two cops pushed past him, both reaching for guns as they yelled at Bolan in Pashto. He tried a bewildered expression for size, then charged as Barialy drew his old Webley revolver, swung it hard against the skull of one patrolmen, and the cop went down.

Not out, but down would do for a start.

Bolan's man had his pistol half drawn from a clumsy flap holster that looked good on parade and shielded guns from dust or rain, but which was never meant for fast draws. Bolan hit him with a swift jab to the solar plexus, emptying his lungs, then grabbed the wrist of his gun arm, twisted, relieved his adversary of the weapon.

Extra pressure on the wrist evoked a gasp and put his

captive on one knee, his head bowed in pain, his neck offered for the chop that sent him off into oblivion. At the last second, Bolan pulled his punch, used but a fraction of the force that would have snapped his opposition's neck and made his snooze time permanent.

Behind him, Barialy had subdued the second officer with two more cracks across the skull. There was some bleeding from the downed man's scalp, but nothing serious. And nothing on his shirt, so far, as Bolan was relieved to note.

"Be careful stripping him," Bolan advised. "You can't ring Carlisle's doorbell looking like you've just been in a bar fight."

Neither of the khaki costumes was a perfect fit, but they would serve their purpose. Bolan left the officers unconscious, stripped down to their shorts and handcuffed in two separate toilet stalls, each gagged with his own sweaty undershirt. They would raise muffled hell when they woke up, and might be noticed even sooner, but he only needed ten or fifteen minutes to reach Vanguard's office.

After that, whatever happened would rely in equal parts on will, audacity and Fate.

*Vanguard International Branch Office, Kabul*

RED SCANLON WAS WORRIED. He'd begun to feel as if the ship was going down and those in charge were lying about it to save their own asses. Clay Carlisle was already gone and now Dale Ingram was going through his office like a dying man preparing for his last yard sale.

But Scanlon wasn't going anywhere.

Carlisle had made that clear before he flew the coop smiling and offering his compliments to those who did their duty in adversity. He spoke of those who'd made the final sacrifice but couldn't quite recall their names, nor was there time for any questions as he hurried out the door to make his flight.

This place feels like the Alamo, Scanlon thought, and he didn't feel like playing Davy Crockett, but what choice was left to him? Wasn't it his fault, basically, that all this shit had happened in the first place?

If he'd nailed the DEA bitch and this Cooper spook first time they met, how much of what had followed might have been avoided altogether? Would the brass be running for their lives and leaving chaos in their wake?

Maybe. But Scanlon didn't think so.

It came down to him. His failure at a relatively simple task had set the stage for the disastrous convoy ambush, the attack that leveled Basir Ahmad-Shah's refinery and Ahmad-Shah's assassination at his home. Even supposing that the Falk bitch and Matt Cooper weren't the only ones involved, Scanlon believed that bagging them before they had a chance to put their heads together would have thrown the whole damned plot offkilter, maybe canceled it entirely.

Now he'd never know.

But he would always bear the stigma of his failure.

"Hey, Red!" the doorman, Bobby Jackson, called to him as Scanlon wandered by his post. "You gotta see this, man."

"What is it?"

"Somethin' gonna make your day, bro," Jackson said.

"I doubt that very much," Scanlon replied, but when he saw the CCTV monitor he thought it might be true.

Two cops were at the outer gate, holding a prisoner between them. Even with her head down and her hair all mussed around, Scanlon knew Deirdre Falk immediately.

"What the hell?"

"They wanna bring her in, man. Say they heard there's some kinda reward. It's not my call, of course, but if it was—"

"Open the gate!" Scanlon snapped. "Get her ass in here before those lazy bastards change their minds and take her back downtown."

"Will do."

Jackson keyed the electric gate and watched the monitor with Scanlon, making sure that no one else tried sneaking in behind the two cops and their prisoner. Before the gate was fully closed again, Scanlon was on his way to the front door, ready to greet the woman who had trashed his life.

The short walk seemed to take a long time, as if Scanlon had stepped into a time warp or a movie slow-mo sequence. He reached for his pistol, then thought better of it and left it holstered. There were two men on the door, and with the Afghan cops escorting Falk, he didn't expect any trouble.

If five men couldn't handle one woman, Scanlon reckoned it was time to pull the plug and find himself a new profession. Maybe something in the field of fashion design or interior decoration.

He found his men waiting at the door, looking to him for permission to open the locks. Scanlon nodded and told them, "Let's do it."

The door swung open, and it felt like slow-mo time again as Scanlon flicked his gaze from Falk to her escorts. The tall one on her left looked damned familiar now, without a cap screening his face, and what about the other one.

He saw their submachine guns rising, knew Falk wasn't handcuffed when she whipped a Mini-Uzi out from underneath her blazer, leveling the piece at him.

Red Scanlon's final thought before the point-blank autofire began was *Jesus! Not again!*

FALK FIRED A SHORT BURST at the middleman and left his flankers to the boys in uniform. It would be wrong to say the Vanguard soldiers never knew what hit them, but they definitely had no time to bitch about it, much less to defend themselves. They fell together, almost tangled on the threshold, forcing Falk to jump across the one she'd killed while one of her companions slammed the stout front door behind them.

Things got a little hazy after that, with darting figures, drifting plaster dust, the panic of inhabiting a real-life killing game where no score registered except survival and you couldn't start from scratch again if you were killed.

The Vanguard complex was just that—complex, a maze of offices and cubbyhole workstations, storage closets, conference rooms and lavatories, a communications center, sleeping quarters and an armory. As soon as their first shots were fired, alarms began to blare through every room and corridor, alerting anyone who'd missed the their noisy entrance that an enemy had breached the fortress.

Falk didn't know how many people were inside the complex, or which ones were armed. She didn't know if they had other exits, but assumed there had to be some way to escape if things went wrong and access to the front door was cut off. Vanguard dealt in security, and no place with a single access point could ever truly be secure.

Moving from room to room, firing on those who fired at her, Falk didn't really care if some of them escaped. Unless, of course, the fugitives included Clay Carlisle and/or his second in command, Dale Ingram. All the rest were pawns. Gunmen and secretaries, technogeeks and bean counters. Whether they lived or died this day depended on the depth of their commitment to defending Vanguard headquarters against Falk and her friends.

She made a near-fatal mistake with one of Carlisle's secretary-types, turning away when the young blonde rose from behind her desk with empty hands raised high and said, "Don't hurt me! Please!" When Falk was halfway through her turn, she saw the looker's hand dart back behind her, clutching at a handgun she had hidden there.

It looked to be a Walther PPK, but Falk wasn't concerned

with caliber or nomenclature. Cursing bitterly, she stitched the blonde with four rounds from her SMG that dropped her out of sight behind the desk. She saw blood, and thus was satisfied that there had been no Kevlar in between her slugs and tender flesh.

Your call, she thought, retreating from the office now vacated by its only living soul, as she moved on to find new targets. When she'd emptied the Uzi's magazine, Falk ditched it, took another from her pocket, slammed it home and went on with the hunt.

The worst part of it was that it no longer felt unusual. She'd come to terms with bloodshed. It seemed normal, now.

And that, Falk told herself, was probably a damned shame.

THE FIRST THREE GUARDS were easy, but it got worse after that, with shooters popping out of office doors and stairwells, a braying alarm that nearly drowned out the gunfire, and flashing emergency corridor lights that could trigger seizures in an epileptic.

Bolan felt as if he were fighting inside a 1970s disco, until he remembered that disco was dead. And he would be, too, if he let the flashing lights and sound effects distract him from his enemies.

His main target was Clay Carlisle—or, failing that, someone who could direct him to the man in charge of Vanguard International. It would be nice if he had time to question Carlisle, get the names of certain friends in government who'd profited from Vanguard's crimes, but that might be a flight of wishful thinking.

Cutting off the serpent's head was still job one. Whatever else he managed to accomplish in the process would be icing on the bloody cake.

On his left, a howling figure leaped out an office cubbyhole, brandishing some kind of knife or letter opener. It almost seemed a shame to shoot him, but the Executioner had no time for an unarmed combat demonstration at the moment, so he pumped a 5.45 mm round into the target's chest and left him twitching on the floor.

He couldn't say if Vanguard's personnel were desperate or dedicated, but it came down to the same thing in a killing situation. Like a swarm of cornered rats, they fought with grim determination for their turf.

Bolan lost track of his companions in the melee, trusting them to watch out for themselves. His liberated uniform had a useful effect on some of his opponents, causing them to stop and do a blinking double-take while Bolan cut them down.

It was an edge, but he was still outnumbered, and the fire-fight definitely could go either way.

As if to emphasize that fact, two shooters opened up on Bolan from the doorways of opposing offices some thirty feet ahead of him, with one on each side of the corridor. He bellied down on slick linoleum and groped for one of the grenades he'd stuffed into his trouser pockets when they'd switched from the Toyota to the marked patrol car.

Bolan yanked the pin and made his pitch, wobbling the lethal egg down range. Its ovoid form prevented it from rolling in a straight line, but he didn't care which way it swerved, as long as it had ample distance from him when it blew.

Head down, he heard one of the shooters cry a warning, but it came too late. The frag grenade exploded, riddling walls and ceiling with its shrapnel and providing a convenient smoke screen for Bolan's assault. He was up and moving before the last shock wave had passed, jogging along one wall and covering both doorways through the haze of smoke.

In one, a slow shooter was sprawled against the jamb, leaking from shrapnel wounds to face, throat, chest and legs. Bolan fired an insurance round into his forehead, then spun toward the closer doorway and stepped through it.

His second adversary was shaken but bouncing back from it when Bolan faced him, sighting down the barrel of his AKSU carbine. The stranger growled at him and lunged for the weapon he'd dropped when he fell, giving Bolan all the time he needed for the 3-round burst that finished him.

Leaving the office, Bolan turned left, covered three paces, then heard an elevator chime. He faced it as the door slid open on a pair of crew-cut suits with desert tans and faces locked in matching grimaces. At the sight of Bolan, both raised pistols, but he had the drop on them and put them down with two short bursts before the elevator's door hissed shut again.

The lift carried his thoughts upstairs, where the CEO was most likely to have his office, and Bolan started looking for the service stairs. He found them seconds later, shooting a husky wrestler-type to reach them, and began to climb.

DALE INGRAM TRIED to think of any time he'd been this frightened in his life, and came up blank. Once, as a young street agent with the FBI, he'd been involved in the arrest of a Most Wanted fugitive, but other G-men did the heavy lifting, kicking in the doors, disarming the offender, cuffing him and dragging him outside. Ingram had been part of the team—much like the guys who handed wrenches to the real mechanics in the NASCAR pits—but he had never fired a shot in anger.

And he didn't feel like starting now.

He blamed Carlisle for bugging out and leaving him to deal with the minutiae of packing up the office, at the very time when enemies were most likely to raid the goddamned place and slaughter everyone inside. He could have left some junior member—hell, an intern could've done it—but Carlisle had ordered Ingram to remain behind and see to it himself.

Hoping for something just like this, perhaps?

Stuffing his briefcase in a frenzy, Ingram couldn't make

himself believe that. Carlisle was a bastard, no two ways about it, but if he had wanted Ingram dead he would've had his goons perform the execution, dump Dale's body in the Afghan desert for the jackals and the vultures to devour. Why take chances with a hit-or-miss third-party execution that might never happen?

Call it shitty luck, then. Like the day Ingram had signed with Vanguard in the first place.

No, it hadn't been all bad. He'd seen the world and grown rich in his role as Carlisle's hatchet man, but there had been a price attached. Despite his boss's sermonizing, Ingram wasn't sure if he believed in souls and all the rest of it. But he'd lost something at the same time he was fattening his bank accounts with Carlisle's cash.

Who would've thought he'd wind up as a drug dealer and an accomplice to mass murder, after all his years in law enforcement? Sometimes Ingram stood in front of his mirror and didn't recognize the man reflected there.

It was too late for psycho-babble bullshit, though. Between the clamoring alarms, gunfire and the occasional explosion, Ingram knew the place was coming down around him. Even if his people won the fight, he couldn't stick around and try explaining any of it to the police. He would be lucky if they only locked him up and threw away the key.

Ingram looked around his office, seeking anything important that he might have missed while he was shoveling CDs and papers into his briefcase. He saw nothing and latched the case, patted his pockets to confirm the presence of his car keys, then retrieved his jacket from its wall hook. Finally, reluctantly, he drew the pistol that he hadn't fired in three years from its holster on his hip.

There was a decent chance that he would meet some kind of opposition on his way to the underground garage. In which case, he would finally discover what the locker-room discussions he had listened to for years on end was all about. The so-called thrill of combat. Facing down an enemy who was prepared to kill you. Shooting first and asking questions later.

Ingram thought that he could handle it. Firing at human targets was a reflex, ingrained by his training at the FBI Academy, though never actually used against a felon. It was point-and-click, like using a computer, but with lethal consequences if your system crashed.

He checked the corridor, considered trying for the elevator, then thought better of it and turned left, in the direction of the service stairs. Two flights to reach the ground floor, two more for the basement where the office kept its various civilian vehicles. There should be guards down there, but if they had been lured away, he had a key card that would raise the heavy metal gate that kept intruders from the motor pool.

No sweat.

But Ingram *was* sweating and copiously as he moved along the hallway with the briefcase in his left hand, pistol in the right and held against his thigh, its muzzle pointed toward the floor.

The last thing he expected was a woman's voice behind him, calling out his name.

He turned, started to raise his weapon, but the automatic rifle pointed at his face dissuaded him. He recognized the woman holding it, although he'd only seen her face in photographs.

The damned bitch from DEA.

And she was smiling as she closed the gap between them, saying, "Glory be. Dale Ingram, as I live and breathe."

BOLAN MET THEM on the stairs, descending as he moved up toward the second floor. His first glance framed only the big man, coming down, and Bolan recognized him from Brognola's CD photo lineup even as he checked the hands of Carlisle's second in command for weapons.

He saw Falk behind Ingram as she announced, "He's clean. You want to grill him here, or find Edris and walk him out?"

Bolan was weighing options when the staircase door opened below him and he spun toward target acquisition with his AKSU, easing his pressure on the trigger when he saw another faux policeman jogging up the stairs to join them.

"There are dead men in the elevator," Barialy said, "but something told me you would find your way upstairs."

Bolan made his decision, turning back to Ingram with a move that jammed the AKSU's muzzle underneath the captive's chin.

"Where's Carlisle?" he demanded.

"In the wind," Ingram replied. "You missed him."

Bolan read the dismal truth behind those frightened eyes and made his choice. It would take time they couldn't spare to search the building's other floors for someone who had almost certainly escaped.

"You understand the cost of lying?" Bolan asked.

Ingram shrugged, apparently resigned to whatever Fate held in store for him. "He's gone. I'm here. You want to kill me, get it over with and go to hell."

"We like your company," Bolan replied. "You're coming with us." He turned to Falk. "Car keys?"

She spun a key ring on her left-hand index finger. "These were in his pants. Not much else, though."

Bolan retrieved the ring and recognized the BMW logo on its fob. "Parked below?" he asked Ingram.

Their captive nodded. He didn't seem to care what happened next, but Bolan didn't wholly trust his melancholy funk.

"Don't kill him, if he tries to run for it," he cautioned Falk. "Kneecapping's good."

"I'm looking forward to it," she replied.

Bolan and Barialy led the way downstairs, past the ground floor and two flights farther on, until they reached a door labeled Garage. It opened, and they stepped through into near-silence, where the reverberations of the battle overhead, still sputtering along without them, barely registered. Fluorescent ceiling fixtures lit the rows of shiny private cars and corporate Humvees parked carefully in rows, which made up Vanguard's office motor pool.

"Where is it?" Bolan asked, holding the keys in front of Ingram's face.

"Down to your left. My name is on the wall."

"Here's how it works," Bolan informed him. "If there's someone on the gate, you talk us through or take the first shot in the skirmish. If there's no one there, you let us have the code, key card, whatever it may be."

"No problem," Ingram said.

They found his BMW 3 Series sedan parked in a slot with "Mr. Ingram" stenciled on the wall in front of it, and piled into the car with Bolan driving, Barialy in the shotgun seat, Falk and their prisoner in back. It took a circuit of the underground garage to get them pointed toward the exit ramp, where Bolan saw a lonely, nervous-looking guard on duty.

"Here you go," he said as they rolled toward the rifleman. "Decide whether you want to live or die."

As Bolan braked beside the sentry, Ingram powered down his window and leaned out to tell the man, "We're clearing out. Open the gate!"

The sentry snapped, "Yes, sir!" and ran to do as he was told, slapping a button on the wall to activate the barred gate's overhead controls.

A moment later they were clear and rolling up the short ramp to a surface street, then turning left away from Vanguard headquarters and toward the Shash Darak district. They'd traveled half a mile or so before Ingram spoke again.

"Mind if I ask you where you're taking me?"

"We need to have a private talk," Bolan answered. "I've got someplace in mind where we won't be disturbed."

"Should I be worried?" Ingram asked.

Bolan considered it, met Ingram's dark eyes in the rearview mirror and replied, "That all depends on whether you intend to lie or tell the truth."

# CHAPTER SEVENTEEN

*Qale'h-ye-Bal Hisar, Kabul*

Falk helped transfer their hardware from the smaller Avalon to Ingram's BMW, then returned to the backseat where Ingram waited for her, under Barialy's gun. When they were rolling once more, toward the destination she had helped select, the ex-vice president of Vanguard spoke for the first time since they had cleared the underground garage.

"I have to give you credit, Agent Falk," he said. "With your two friends, here, you've inflicted much more damage than I would've thought was possible."

"You live and learn," she answered without facing him.

"Indeed. Well, some do. I suspect that I may not live long enough to learn from this particular experience."

"You play the game, you take your chances," Falk replied.

"Of course," Ingram agreed. "I wonder if your supervisor, Agent Combs, would feel the same? Would he say that the game was worth its cost? I mean, if he *could* feel?"

That drew Falk's eyes to Ingram's face. "What do you mean?" she asked.

"Well, obviously… Oh, my goodness! You've been out of touch, I take it. You don't know."

"Know what?"

"About your chief," Ingram replied.

Falk clenched her fist and said, "Don't make me ask the goddamned question three times."

"No, no. Why be petty? I assumed you knew, of course."

"Ingram…"

"Your agent Combs is dead. Some kind of traffic accident, I understand. Or, maybe not."

Her first swing caught him in the mouth as he began to smirk, splitting the lower lip against his teeth and snapping back his head. Before Ingram could raise a shielding hand or gasp in pain, she struck twice more, nailing one eye and doing her utmost to break his nose.

Bolan delayed a beat, then asked, "Is everything okay back there?"

"We're fine," Falk said. "I'm just telling a friend goodbye."

"Try not to kill the messenger before we've had a chance to question him," Bolan said.

"Right. I hear you," Falk replied, and caught him watching from the rearview. "It's okay. I promise."

"Well, I'm not okay!" Ingram blubbered. "You ask me to help you and—"

"Correction," Bolan interrupted him. "First, we're not asking anything. We're giving you a chance to help yourself by giving us the information that we need to put your boss where he belongs. You've got no free walk coming, either way."

"That's hardly an incentive, is it?" Ingram answered. "I believe plea bargains are traditional."

"With the police and courts," Bolan replied. "We're handling this a different way."

"And if I told you where you could lay hands on twenty million dollars cash? To split in any way you choose?"

"I'd have to recommend you save your breath for the important questions," Bolan answered. "Starting now."

When Ingram took the hint and offered no reply, Falk said, "I want to know what really happened. You say 'traffic accident,' I automatically think murder."

Ingram dabbed blood from his swollen lips and said, "That would be my guess, too."

"Your guess?"

"Vanguard was not involved."

"And you expect me to believe that?"

"You'll believe what pleases you," Ingram said. "I can only tell you what I know to be a fact."

"So, who's responsible?"

"I understand that you already visited him, in Sherzad."

"You're blaming Ahmad-Shah?"

"*He* blamed *you*, Agent Falk. And being frustrated in his attempts to reach you, well, he turned upon the man he felt must be responsible. And it would have to be a man, of course. Our friend Basir wouldn't believe a woman could possess such strength, much less initiative."

Tears stung Falk's eyes as she replied, "You're saying I killed him."

"Oh, please. Don't be ridiculous. Wasn't it Combs who gave you this assignment in the first place? Was he so weak that he would let you run amok without his supervision, or at least tacit permission?"

Falk had no response for Ingram, so he slipped into a phony accent to complete his thought.

"Shit happens, girlfriend. It's on bumper stickers, so it must be true."

It took every ounce of Falk's iron will to keep from punching him again, and timing helped. She was still struggling with herself when Bolan slowed the car, then stopped and said, "We're here."

*Vanguard International Branch Office, Antwerp, Belgium*

CLAY CARLISLE LEANED BACK in his swivel chair, propped his feet on a corner of his spacious desk and thought, This is more like it.

In Antwerp it wasn't one hundred degrees in the shade, and the wind wasn't constantly blowing sand against his office windows. Some of his fattest bank accounts were close at hand.

And no one was trying to kill him.

At least, not yet.

Carlisle had telephoned Kabul as soon as he was settled into his quarters in Antwerp. He'd wanted to smooth things over with Dale Ingram, at least on the surface, and satisfy himself that Ingram was doing his job. It troubled him when he discovered that the office numbers, both public and private, were all "out of service." Worse yet, the operator babbling at him in broken English couldn't offer any cogent explanation.

He had called Lee Hastings next, connecting with the diplomat's sat phone and thus circumventing the embassy's switchboard. Hastings had been edgy, hadn't wanted to spare any time for Carlisle, but he'd finally explained that there was "trouble" at the Vanguard office in Kabul.

"I don't have any details yet. We're looking into it," Hastings had said, and broke the link without the courtesy of a goodbye.

Carlisle sipped from a large glass of cranberry juice and considered his options. He would assume, for argument's sake, that the Kabul office was a write-off. If Ingram was alive and capable of getting to a telephone, he would have called to break the news himself.

Under the circumstances, Carlisle hoped that he was dead, that he and all the covert data he'd been ordered to retrieve had gone up in a ball of white-hot flame. Because if he was still alive and talking to the wrong people, it could cause further problems down the road.

Where would the enemy strike next? And when?

There was an outside chance that Carlisle's tormenters were only interested in Afghan heroin and his connection to the late Sheikh Basir Ahmad-Shah. If that was true, then fleeing Kabul might have solved his problem.

But he didn't really think so.

Deirdre Falk was one thing, representing DEA, but she had brought some kind of supersoldier into Kabul from outside. Perhaps even from Washington, although the evidence for that conclusion was by no means clear. Even if Falk was satisfied to let it drop with Kabul, would "Matt Cooper" feel the same?

Carlisle considered calling Washington, then checked the time and realized that those who had the power and the motivation to assist him would have gone home for the day. He had their private numbers, naturally, but those would register on phone bills that could be retrieved by federal agents and investigative journalists, which did not suit his purposes.

The following day should be soon enough to speak with those who owed him favors—and whose very futures might, in some cases, depend upon Carlisle's continuing survival. From the onset of their long and lucrative relationships, he'd made no secret of the fact that if he was betrayed, if he went down through treachery, he would not take the fall alone.

He would relax tonight, enjoy his first good sleep in— what?—two days. Or was it three?

And he would tackle all his problems with renewed vigor tomorrow, first thing in the morning.

Let the unknown supersoldier try to find him, if he managed to get out of Kabul with his skin intact. Clay Carlisle wasn't finished yet, by any means.

He still had several tricks left up his sleeve.

And he had Jesus in his corner, giving him the will to persevere.

*Qale'h-ye-Bal Hisar, Kabul*

THE WAREHOUSE WAS ONE of several hundred crammed along the riverfront, smaller than most, but capable of storing and off-loading several tons of cargo if employed to full capacity. In fact, however, it was rented by a paper company that fronted for the DEA, employed for different purposes as need arose.

This day, it would serve as a dungeon.

Dale Ingram, already battered and bloodied, was visibly nervous as Bolan's team marched him into the warehouse and locked out the rest of the world. His mood did not improve when he was shown a simple metal folding chair and told to sit.

"If you intend to kill me—"

"I'm considering it," Bolan told him honestly. "You've caused a world of misery, exporting heroin to Europe and the States. Offhand, I'd say it's your job to persuade me you should live."

Ingram stared back at him through one good eye, the other swollen nearly shut from Falk's knuckles. The man was shaky, but he still maintained a measure of control.

"If all you wanted was to waste me," he replied, "you could've done it at the office, or at any point after we left. You must want something."

"Information," Bolan said. "Answers to some specific questions would be helpful, but I won't pretend to guarantee a free pass for your crimes."

"So, it's the soft-sell, eh?" The swollen lips managed a smile of sorts. "Go on and ask, then. What the hell."

Bolan glanced up at Falk, standing behind their prisoner, and chose his first question to suit her.

"In the car, you said that Ahmad-Shah put out the contract on Falk's boss. Was that the truth?"

"I can't be positive," Ingram replied. "As you can probably imagine, DEA agents aren't very popular in new, improved

Afghanistan. I *can* say that the contract didn't go through me. If Carlisle set it up, he tasked somebody else with handling the details, and I just don't see that happening."

"But he'd be glad the job was done," Falk said.

"Of course. Why not? You've spent the past two days upsetting several multimillion-dollar apple carts, lady. There's a price attached to courage, as you've learned."

Bolan saw Falk's fist clench again and stepped in with another question.

"Carlisle. You said he's in the wind. Where was he going?"

"Vanguard's branch office in Antwerp, if he wasn't lying to me. As to whether he'll stay there…" A shrug. "Your guess would be as good as mine, at this point."

"Why Antwerp?" Bolan asked.

"It's our main European office, full security, et cetera. The rest are minor cubbyholes in half a dozen capitals. Clay thought of Switzerland, at first, but Belgium's cheaper and it has its own nice banks. London and Paris are nearby. What's not to like?"

"I'll need floor plans," Bolan said.

"Not a problem, but I won't pretend my drawing skills meet any kind of draftsman's standard."

"Legible should do the trick," Bolan replied. "Now, as to Vanguard's contacts in Kabul—"

"I don't know most of them," Ingram said, interrupting him. "A place like this, junior executives drum up their own native connections. Sometimes, even soldiers try the cloak-and-dagger game, if they want to show some initiative. Across the province, there are hundreds—"

"Top men only," Bolan said, his turn to interrupt. "I want your contacts at the U.S. Embassy and in the Afghan government."

"You ask a lot," Ingram observed.

"You have a lot to lose."

"Sure. What the hell. Who cares, eh? I know two men at

the embassy. One of them's Russell Latimer, the CIA's deputy station chief for Kabul. He's the one I normally talk to, if Vanguard needs a helping hand."

"The other?"

"Lee Hastings, vice consul," Ingram said. "We've met, but never had a private conversation. You could say he's Carlisle's man. A go-to guy, as long as money goes his way."

"And on the native side?" Bolan asked.

"Only one who counts," Ingram replied. "Habib Zarghona at the Ministry of Justice."

"I know him," Falk said. "Well, know of him. He's number two at the ministry's inspections division."

"That's him," Ingram said. "Are we done now?"

"Antwerp floor plans," Bolan said, reminding him.

"Oh, right. Somebody have a pencil, then? Some paper? As I said, it won't be art, but it should do."

Bolan watched Ingram go to work, still undecided whether he should live or die.

*Department of Justice, Washington, D.C.*

BROGNOLA HAD BEEN WAITING for the call, not sure when it would come—or even, truly, whether it would come at all. In Washington, some matters were resolved without a paper trail or any public notice that a problem had existed in the first place. Troublemakers vanished from their offices and left a legacy of rumor, typically reluctant to discuss it when they surfaced somewhere in the hinterlands, in jobs that everybody knew would never take them back to Wonderland.

And sometimes, they just vanished.

It was rare, but Brognola could think of half a dozen cases in his decades of involvement with the FBI and Justice. Sweeping things under the rug sometimes included taking out the trash.

The call came through as he was getting ready to evacuate his office for the evening. He had his jacket on, was reaching for the hat he sometimes wore because he liked it and it suited him, despite the shifting tides of modern fashion. When he recognized the shrill tone of his private line, he got it on the second ring.

"Hello?"

"I've solved our problem," the familiar voice announced. "It's being handled."

"Do I want to know?" Brognola asked.

"The two you gave to me were hatchet men with aspirations, serving someone higher up. We've come to terms with their misjudgment. Both will be severely penalized. Transferred outside the country...for a start."

Brognola frowned at that, wondering, but he had to ask. "And Mr. Higher-Up?"

"Your chauvinism's showing, Hal. Why take for granted that it was a mister?"

"You don't mean—"

"I feel a resignation coming on," the caller said. "Might take a day or two, but in the meantime, she'll be closely monitored."

"And afterward?"

"You'd probably have grounds for prosecution, but I'm not sure anyone would benefit from the publicity surrounding any sort of trial."

"No, sir."

"I'm thinking tight surveillance for a while, and then...who knows? Three-fourths of all fatal accidents happen at home."

Brognola swallowed and asked, "Where did she get the information?"

"Your end's clean," the caller said. "There is—or *was*—a leak at Langley."

"Shit! Again?"

"Needless to say, it is a matter of concern. I think the leak's a one-off, now contained, but we'll be looking into it like a proctologist on crystal meth. No stone unturned."

"Sir, if I need to take some kind of action at—"

"I don't believe that's necessary, at the moment, but you know the price of liberty."

"I do," Brognola said.

Eternal vigilance, as Andrew Jackson once declared.

"Words to the wise," the caller said. "Sleep well, but lightly, my old friend."

"Thank you. And good night, sir."

"Oh, and about those transfers out of country. You should get a postcard soon, with the addresses. Just in case you want to drop the boys a line."

Brognola set the telephone receiver back into its cradle, while a wave of mixed relief and apprehension flooded through him. It was good to know he didn't have a mole at Stony Man, of course—and terrible to know the CIA had sprung *another* leak, after the first had nearly doomed the Farm and everything it had accomplished, or might possibly accomplish in the future.

There would always be bad apples, sure, as long as governments were run by human beings, but where some were useless drones and others might embezzle cash, the worst endangered lives.

The three who'd been exposed were paying now, and Brognola or someone else would cancel out their tabs before much longer. In the meantime, though, the very fact of their existence reinforced his fear of other traitors still unknown, or yet to turn against their friends.

*Enough!* he told himself.

For now, at least, it was enough.

He reached out for the phone again, to give the team at Stony Man some good news for a change.

*Qale'h-ye-Bal Hisar, Kabul*

"THIS IS THE BEST that I can do," Dale Ingram said. He held the ballpoint pen and pad of notepaper until Bolan retrieved it and examined his drawings.

"Should do the trick," Bolan acknowledged as he skimmed the list of security devices installed at Vanguard's Antwerp field office.

"Okay, then. I've done my part," Ingram said. "So what comes next?"

Bolan removed the perforated sheets of paper, then returned the pad and pen to Ingram.

"Now," he said, "you write and sign a statement spelling out Carlisle's connection to the drug trade. Make it quick and only hit the highlights. You can fill in gaps and details when you talk to the DEA."

"I see." Ingram looked glum. "So now you just expect me to confess, stroll off to prison with a big smile on my face? Or maybe turn state's evidence and help you lock more people up? Jesus, who's even going to be left for trial, when you get through with them?"

"It's hard to say," Bolan replied. "Sometimes I drop a stitch or two."

"And if they're dead, I just incriminate myself? Is that the game?"

"You did that when you joined Carlisle in fielding mercenaries, handling murder contracts, smuggling heroin. Were you expecting a free pass?"

"I'd hoped for some consideration," Ingram said.

"And you received it," Bolan said. "You're breathing."

"And for how long, if I go along with what you're asking now? How long before some tattooed Aryan or crooked guard gets paid to shut me up for good? The people I just named for you are elephants, okay? They don't forget a thing. And if you kill them all, their comrades and their cousins *still* remember. I'm as good as dead, inside a cage."

"The Feds can take precautions," Bolan said.

"Oh, sure. A life in solitary sounds inviting. Maybe I can go the Joe Valachi route and spend my last twenty years on an army base somewhere. How about a barracks in Wyoming or Alaska, eh? Sound good to you?"

"Depends on the alternative," Bolan replied.

"You recognize the name Abe Reles, friend?"

"He rolled over on Lepke and Murder Incorporated, back in the day," Bolan said.

"The very same. Remember how he wound up?"

"Not offhand."

"Guarded by four plainclothes detectives in a Coney Island hotel room," Ingram said. "One night, he went out the window. Two cops were asleep, they said. The other two said Reles loved practical jokes. They claimed he made a rope of sheets and planned to wriggle one floor down, then sneak back and surprise them. Poor sap lost his grip and fell, they said. Years later, on his deathbed, Lucky Luciano told reporters that the cops were paid to help Abe pull his little stunt— without the rope."

"There's still WITSEC," Bolan replied. "They've never lost a witness who observed the rules and kept his nose clean."

Ingram nodded. "Right. I'm sure you're right. Well, hey, before I start my memoirs, have you got a toilet in this place?"

Bolan nodded to Barialy. "Walk him over, will you?"

"Certainly."

Ingram rose stiffly from his chair, turned toward the slender Afghan with a smile—and suddenly lunged forward, snatching Barialy's big Webley revolver from his belt. Bolan's 9 mm semiauto filled his hand, sights locked on Ingram's chest.

"You won't need that," the prisoner informed him as he raised the Webley to his temple. "I'll take care of it."

The big .455's report sounded like thunder in the cavernous garage.

THE RIVER AT THEIR DOORSTEP, called Rhudkhane-ye-Kabul, offered a simple means of dumping Ingram's corpse. Bolan and Barialy checked for witnesses, then walked it out and dropped it in the water, watching while it sank into subsurface currents and was swept away. If no one snagged it on a fishing line or anchor chain, the body might continue on downstream for some 430 miles, until the Kabul River spilled into the Indus near Attock, in northern Pakistan.

Bolan suppressed an urge to wish the dead man bon voyage.

Inside the warehouse, Deirdre Falk was mopping up. There hadn't been much mess, all things considered, and she'd nearly finished by the time Bolan and Barialy came back from their visit to the riverbank.

"It's weird," she said, putting the mop away. "A guy like that, connected, filthy rich, I would've thought he'd lawyer up and tough it out. Even with a conviction, he could stall imprisonment for years with the appeals."

"Ingram's connections all revolved around his old days in the FBI and the new gig with Vanguard," Bolan said. "He's toxic for the Bureau, once the news breaks on his Vanguard deals, and Carlisle wouldn't let him have the time of day if he thought Ingram was a rat. I wouldn't be surprised to learn that Vanguard owned his home and had some kind of backdoor access to his bank accounts."

"Still, checking out like that..."

"Some people can't take prison," Bolan said. "Some crack from the embarrassment alone."

"Okay, so what's next?" Falk asked. "The red-eye flight to Antwerp?"

"Not tonight," Bolan replied. "I need to scout some targets for tomorrow, when I finish cleaning house."

"You don't mean—"

"Someone has to do it," Bolan cut her off. "We've got a diplomat involved in smuggling heroin, a spook from Langley working as some kind of a coordinator, and a native big shot covering their action at the local Ministry of Justice."

"We can report them," Falk suggested.

"Right. To whom? Supporting accusations with what evidence, again?"

"You must know someone back in Washington," Falk said. "Or, I could tell the DEA director. After what they did to Alan—"

"After what a dead sheikh did to Alan," he corrected her. "There's nothing to connect Hastings or Latimer to any of it, and the DEA has no jurisdiction over Habib Zarghona."

"Jesus, Coop! You don't know what you're asking."

"I'm not asking anything," Bolan replied. "In fact, I'd recommend that both of you bow out right now. Find someplace safe and go to ground. Or, better yet, get out of the country completely."

"While you just waltz into the U.S. embassy to waste the vice consul?"

"That's not exactly what I had in mind."

"Ah. So you've got a plan?" she asked.

"I'm working on it," Bolan said.

Falk sighed and said, "You'd better run it past me, just in case."

# CHAPTER EIGHTEEN

*Bagh-e-Qazi, Kabul*

The meet had been a total waste of time for Russell Latimer. The contact who had claimed that he could finger Deirdre Falk's sidekick, this Barialy character, had weaseled out when Latimer got in his face, demanding details. When it turned out that the little shit was simply angling for a handout, Latimer had knocked him down and crushed his right hand underfoot.

There was a price attached to screwing with the CIA. See how the little weasel liked eating his curry with the same hand ritual ordered him to use wiping his ass.

The violence had been invigorating, but a letdown followed close behind it once the sharp kick of adrenaline began to fade away. Latimer needed information, not the pleasure he derived from kicking some damned peasant's ass.

And he was nowhere close to getting it.

His station chief was spitting mad, the man who pulled their strings from Langley wanted answers yesterday, and Latimer was striking out, no matter what he tried. Things just kept getting worse, and now he wondered what the crazy bastards he was hunting could devise to top their raid on Vanguard's local headquarters.

How many dead over the past day and a half? One hundred? Two? He'd lost count, and it didn't really seem to matter anymore. The body count had passed that magic point where deaths ceased to be tragedies and turned into statistics.

Latimer had almost reached his car when he noticed the woman standing behind it. She had her back turned, but her hair, clothes and attitude told him she wasn't an Afghan. Was it mere coincidence that she was standing by his car, or was she waiting for him? And if so, what could she want?

Latimer closed the gap between them, was about to speak, when suddenly the woman turned to face him and his questions vanished in a heartbeat.

Putting on a smile for Deirdre Falk, he said, "Good timing. I've been hoping we could talk."

"Sounds like a plan," she said. "Let's take a ride."

Better, he thought, and said, "That's cool. I see you found my car."

As Latimer was fumbling in a pocket for his keys, Falk drew her jacket back on the right side and let him see the pistol holstered there.

"We'll take mine," she replied.

"You think this is a good idea?" Latimer asked.

"Feels right to me," she said. "If you'd prefer to argue, we can finish it right here."

Her eyes, the flat tone of her voice, told Latimer she wasn't bluffing.

"No need to be touchy," he advised her. "Where's your ride?"

"Back there," she told him, nodding without breaking eye contact. "You go ahead, and I'll direct you."

"Suits me fine," he lied.

He followed her directions, turned into a nearby alley

where a BMW waited with a man behind the wheel, another watching Latimer from the backseat.

"You're riding shotgun," Falk informed him as she stepped around to get the door for him.

It was his last chance for a break, but what chance was there? If he tried to run, Falk had a clear shot at his back, and if he turned on her the men would take him down in nothing flat. He shrugged and tried to make it sound like he was joking when he asked, "Is this a one-way ride?"

"That all depends on you," Falk said.

She closed his door when Latimer was settled in, then sat in the backseat behind him. Instinct told him that she'd drawn her gun to cover him. Latimer faced the driver as the BMW rolled out of the alley.

"Matthew Cooper, I presume?"

"Today, I am," the wheelman said.

"You've raised a lot of hell, my friend."

"I'm not your friend," Bolan replied. "The ones you chose belong in hell."

"You ever read the Good Book?" Latimer inquired. "It says, 'Judge not.'"

"I'm not a judge," the driver told him. "I'm the executioner."

Latimer forced another nervous smile and said, "I must've missed the trial."

"You were distracted, covering for narco-traffickers," Bolan said.

"Sometimes national security is complicated," Latimer replied.

"And sometimes it's a smoke screen for corrupt scumbags."

"So you're a fan of speaking plainly, then," Latimer said.

"I am. And here's your deal. It's nonnegotiable, and the offer's good for thirty seconds."

"Shoot—no pun intended."

"You can pay your tab right now, or make a phone call. Fix a public meeting with your boss, and maybe walk away."

"My boss?"

"Lee Hastings," Cooper said. "You don't get any points for playing dumb."

"Okay. When you say maybe walk away—"

"It means you'll have a script to follow. If you deviate, ad-lib in any way, you're history."

"And you'd know that because…?"

"I'll have you wired."

Latimer got it now. He could put Hastings on the spot and likely "volunteer" to testify against him afterward, or join the hundred-something others who'd already bought the farm since Falk and Cooper started their rampage.

The man from Langley swallowed hard and said, "You've got a deal."

### United States Embassy, Kabul

LEE HASTINGS TOOK THE CALL at 9:05 a.m. and recognized the caller's voice immediately. Taking care to say nothing that might incriminate him, Hastings asked, "What's going on?"

"I've been out working on that thing we talked about, you know?" Russ Latimer replied. He understood the rules for speaking on an open line that might be monitored.

"And are you making any progress?" Hastings asked.

"It looks that way," said Latimer. "In fact, I have something I need to show you, when you have some free time."

"Show me? I don't follow you."

"I can't exactly spell it out. You follow?"

Hastings didn't appreciate the agent's tone. He was entitled to a measure of respect, particularly from subordinates. And yet, the spook did have a point. Nothing of any consequence could be discussed on open lines outside the embassy.

"My schedule's pretty tight," the vice consul replied. "We're in the middle of a crisis, as I'm sure you realize."

"And I might have a handle on it for you," Latimer suggested. "But I can't just walk it through the gates."

Hastings glanced at his desktop calendar—which, despite what he'd told Latimer, had no serious appointments listed prior to lunchtime—and said, "Very well. If you can meet me in one hour, we can talk."

"Perfect," said Latimer. "You know the Istiqlal Minaret?"

"I've seen it," Hastings said.

"I'll meet you in the park west of the tower."

Hastings hated all the cloak-and-dagger bullshit, but he seemed to have no choice.

"I hope this isn't all a waste of time," he said, letting his tone supply the warning.

"I think you'll be pleasantly surprised," Latimer said, and broke the link.

Damned CIA, Hastings thought, as he set down the telephone. More trouble than they're worth.

Or, maybe not, if Latimer had solved their problem. Hastings could make no sense of the agent's cryptic comments on the telephone, but it was always possible that Latimer had made some kind of breakthrough in their efforts to identify "Matt Cooper" and locate his group of renegades.

Hastings spent fifteen minutes clearing off his desk, then had his personal assistant page a driver from the motor pool. The driver would be armed, of course—a bodyguard-chauffeur who could be trusted not to see or hear a thing that wasn't need-to-know. Their vehicle, a jet-black Lincoln Town Car, would be bulletproof, with tinted glass and run-flat tires.

It was a twenty-minute drive through crowded Kabul streets to reach the park that framed the lofty Istiqlal Minaret. He knew that *istiqlal* meant "independence" or some such, and guessed the mosque with its imposing tower had received that name either to celebrate departure of the Brits in 1919 or the Soviets in 1989.

As if Lee Hastings gave a damn.

"I'm going for a stroll," he told the driver. "Keep your eyes peeled, right?"

"Yes, sir!"

Lee Hastings stepped out of his sleek armored cocoon and moved into the park, looking for Russell Latimer and looking forward to good news.

THE RUSSIAN SVD—short for *Snayperskaya Vintovka Dragunova,* or Dragunov sniper rifle—weighed ten pounds with its PSO-1 telescopic sight and loaded 10-round magazine in place. It was a newer model, with the classic wooden furniture replaced by black polymer moldings, but was otherwise identical in form and function to the weapon designed by Yevgeny Dragunov in 1958 and used to this day by active-duty troops in Russia and twenty-six other countries.

The rifle's telescope let Bolan track his moving target from a range of just over 450 yards, roughly one-third of the SVD's maximum effective range. He'd gone for distance in this case, to maximize his chances of escape, while leaving Falk and Barialy to control the site downrange.

Latimer had grumbled while they "wired" him, switching out his tie clip for a cheap one Bolan had bought for thirty Afghanis—about sixty cents—from a Kabul street vendor. It featured a tiny stainless-steel airplane, and Latimer believed that it contained a tiny microphone that would transmit his conversation with Lee Hastings to a tape recorder hidden in some nearby vehicle.

It was a ruse, of course. There'd been a decent chance that Latimer would balk at helping Bolan execute Lee Hastings, but he understood the world of double-crosses and betrayal very well. The trade-off he'd assumed Bolan was offering, his life for evidence that would destroy Hastings, was something Latimer could recognize and grasp without undue alarm.

Without suspecting that his own time had run out.

Bolan watched Latimer approach Hastings. The diplomat was fairly bold, standing some thirty paces from his car. Bolan supposed the bodyguard behind the Lincoln's wheel was watching every angle of approach, most likely with a weapon drawn and ready in his hand. He might be cursing the employer who made life and the performance of his job so difficult.

But it was almost over.

When the diplomat and spy were face-to-face, Bolan focused his sights on Hastings, framed the face he'd never seen on television or the front page of a newspaper. He didn't know what might've made Hastings betray his country and the most basic of common moral codes. But, then again, what difference did it make?

Bolan had picked his sniper's nest with care, atop a three-story apartment house that faced the park and the imposing minaret. He hadn't stretched it out to test the SVD's limits, recalling the design peculiarity that left the first two inches of his rifle's twenty-four-inch barrel without rifling lands and grooves. It might not matter, even with an unfamiliar weapon, but Bolan preferred to take no chances in the crunch.

He placed the crosshairs of his sight on the target's hairline, allowing for a quarter-inch drop at 450 yards, and sent a 7.62 mm slug hurtling downrange at 2,723 feet per second. Impact came half a second after Bolan squeezed the trigger, when a burst of crimson filled the eyepiece of his scope.

Russ Latimer recoiled from sudden, ugly death, turning to run as the vice consul's out-of-work bodyguard sprang from the Lincoln Town Car. Bolan could've let the shooter from the embassy complete his work, but didn't trust a man he'd never seen before to do it right.

Bolan had planned his second shot well in advance. He'd

known that Latimer would bolt, and guessed the frightened agent wouldn't run back toward the spot where Deirdre Falk and Edris Barialy had released him from their stolen BMW. That meant he would veer either to the north or south, running toward Bolan or away from him in something that approximated a straight line.

Which made it simple.

Bolan lined up on the runner's gasping mouth, squeezed off, and put the bullet through his Adam's apple, nearly severing his head. Latimer may have known what hit him, but he had no time to think about it as the stunning impact slammed him over backward, down and out.

The bodyguard stopped then, turned back and sprinted for the cover of his vehicle. There'd be a radio inside it, for communication with the embassy, but Bolan would be gone before the first sirens began to wail.

He had the rifle packed before the bodyguard could find his frequency, and by the time the halting message was delivered, spreading shock waves through the embassy, Bolan was on the move, relaxing in the backseat of Dale Ingram's BMW with Falk behind the wheel.

"Still want Zarghona?" she inquired.

He met her gaze, reflected in the mirror, and replied, "Why not?"

HEADQUARTERS FOR THE Ministry of Justice stood on Malek Ashgar Street, directly opposite the Afghan Ministry of Foreign Affairs. Habib Zarghona, deputy director of the Taftish branch, had a prestigious corner office on the fifth floor, with a view of Park-e-Zarnegar and the Republican Palace.

On most days, he enjoyed that view.

This day was not a normal day.

The city spread in front of him had become a place of menace, filled with unseen, unknown enemies. Zarghona wondered if he was secure, even within his own office. The window glass was bulletproof and yet…

The sudden shrilling of his telephone, though a familiar sound, startled Zarghona into flinching from the noise. He cursed, embarrassed by his own timidity, and lunged for the receiver as if he would strangle it.

"Hello!"

Of course, it was his personal assistant, sounding hesitant and cautious as he said, "A call for you, sir."

"Well, who is it?"

"A Jamal Woraz. Shall I tell him—"

"I'll take it!" Zarghona snapped. "Put him through."

How was it possible? Zarghona had assumed Woraz was killed along with Basir Ahmad-Shah, in the Sherzad attack. For him to call Zarghona at the ministry was a bizarre breach of their standard protocol.

The line clicked and Zarghona said, "Why are you—"

"Calling your official line?" an unfamiliar voice cut in. "Alas, I fear you've been deceived."

"Who is this?"

"One concerned about your welfare, let us say."

"Explain yourself!"

"A civil tone would be more helpful," the stranger said, "but I understand you have been under stress. Now, I'm afraid it will get worse. You've heard the news?"

"News? What news?" Zarghona asked, truly angry now.

"About Lee Hastings."

Taken by surprise, Zarghona parroted the name. "Hastings?"

"Your contact from the embassy of the United States."

"I don't know what you're saying. Who is—"

"If I am mistaken," the caller said, "then it won't concern you that he's dead."

Zarghona bit off his intended answer, shelved the vain denial to inquire, "Dead, how?"

"A sniper's bullet. If it's any consolation, he did not appear to suffer."

Turning from the large expanse of window glass, Zarghona rushed around his desk and crouched behind it, shielded from the world outside.

"Why tell me this?" Zarghona asked, dropping his voice to something like a whisper.

"So that you can save yourself," the stranger said. "You're not entirely without friends, Habib. Not yet."

"Why should I fret over the death of an American?"

"No reason," the mocking voice said, "if I'm mistaken about your relationship to Hastings. Still, if those who killed him think you were his friend, they may not listen to your plea of innocence."

"Who are you? I demand to know—"

But he was shouting at a dial tone now, with no one on the other end to hear him. Slowly, Habib Zargona raised his head to peer across his desktop, toward his office window. When a full minute had passed without a bullet's impact on the glass, he rose, cradled the telephone receiver and considered what he should do next.

First, he would check to find out if the caller had been lying about Hastings. He found the number for the U.S. Embassy and dialed it, waited for the switchboard operator to respond, then gave his name and title, asking that she put him through to Hastings.

With a small hitch in her voice, the operator said, "I'm sorry, sir. The vice consul is unavailable. If you would care to speak with his assistant or a deputy—"

"When can I speak to Mr. Hastings?" Zarghona asked.

"I'm afraid that won't be possible," she answered. "Sir, there's been…an incident. The vice consul is no longer—"

Zarghona broke the link, fighting a surge of panic.

It was true. Hastings was dead, murdered, over his ties to Clay Carlisle and Basir Ahmad-Shah. The caller who had warned him, posing as the late Jamal Woraz, had to somehow be involved in those events. Details were not important at the moment.

If the killers could reach Ahmad-Shah, storm Vanguard's office *and* take out a senior member of the U.S. consulate in Kabul, they could reach Habib Zarghona. In an instant, he decided that the only way to save himself was to get out, put as much distance as he could between himself and his would-be assassins.

Zarghona reached toward the desktop intercom, then reconsidered. He would leave alone, driving himself, sharing his destination with no one. In fact, he would decide where he was going after he was on the road, keeping the secret even from himself until the final instant.

He would leave at once, with nothing but the clothes he wore, the pistol on his hip, the cash and credit cards he carried in his billfold. There was no more time to waste.

Crossing the outer office, passing his surprised assistant's desk, Zarghona said, "I'll be back soon. Hold any calls."

The lie would buy him time, at least a little.

Whether it would save his life or not, Zarghona couldn't say.

"HERE COMES OUR pigeon," Deirdre Falk announced. "Driving himself."

"Don't spook him," Bolan replied from the backseat.

"It's not my first time following a mark," she said, easing the BMW into midtown traffic.

"How'd the other tails turn out?" he asked.

"I always get my man," she said.

Granted, it *was* her first time on a drive-by hit, if Cooper had a chance to pull it off. She knew he wouldn't want to blast

Zarghona on a crowded city street, but if the choice came down to that or letting him escape, she'd leave the call to Cooper.

He'd done well enough, so far.

Their route took them into Charrah-e-Saderat, the district south of Embassy Row and Kabul's main government buildings. She couldn't guess where Zarghona was headed, rolling south along Shir Ali Khan, then southeast on Salang Wat and south again on Asmayi. For all she knew, he could be leaving town, rolling toward some hideout she'd never heard of, where he hoped to tuck himself away, ride out the storm.

Too late, she thought. We've got you.

The game of cat-and-mouse continued for another quarter mile, until Zarghona slowed and turned into a short driveway beside a modest house.

"Looks like the best chance that you'll have," Falk said.

"I'll take it," Bolan answered as his window powered down.

Falk stopped the BMW at the mouth of Zarghona's chosen driveway, raising both hands to cover her ears while Barialy did likewise. Behind her, Bolan aimed his 40 mm launcher through the open window and began to fire.

The first round struck the rear of Zarghona's sedan and exploded. A second round burned through the roiling smoke cloud from the first blast and finished its work, spewing chemical fire.

Falk heard the screams, even with both ears covered, and she turned to see Zarghona lurching from the wreckage, hungry flames swarming over his form from scalp to shoes. Vaguely aware that she was chanting curses, willing her defiant eyes to look away, Falk jumped when Cooper fired twice more, his buckshot mercy rounds ending the screams.

She clutched the steering wheel and stood on the accelerator, only slowing when Cooper's voice, his warm hand on her shoulder, cautiously reminded her that they were trying to avoid police.

"Okay," she said. "I'm cool."

And wished that it was true.

*Bagram Air Base, Parvan Province, Afghanistan*

IT WAS AN ODD but fitting place in which to say goodbye. Afghanistan's primary U.S. air base was twenty-seven miles north of Kabul, maintained by the Army's 101st Airborne Division, with supporting units from the 455th Air Expeditionary Wing of the U.S. Air Force, plus other Army, Marine Corps and Navy units on hand.

A sat-phone call to Hal Brognola in Washington had cleared their way for entry to the base, where their equipment was sequestered pending the arrangements for their booking on the next flight out.

Or, rather, some of them.

A UC-35A Cessna Citation would take off within the hour, bearing Bolan and Falk on the first leg of their long journey to Belgium. They were sharing the flight with a brigadier general, but didn't expect much give-and-take small talk in flight.

And they were leaving Edris Barialy behind.

It was inevitable, and while Falk appeared to understand that, she was sweating out the final separation. She reminded Bolan of an anxious mother, sending off her firstborn to begin his studies at a world-class party school.

Except that Barialy would be staying in Afghanistan, where parties often ended in a bloodbath.

They'd discussed the possibility of taking him along to Antwerp, but the powers that be had vetoed it on the expected grounds. Specifically, they didn't need a Pashto translator in Belgium, where the official languages were Dutch, French and German. Furthermore, their own mission was deemed risky enough, without dropping an armed, undocumented Afghan into the mix.

And so, case closed.

But Falk didn't like it.

"It's not fair," she said. Her new mantra, repeated at two-minute intervals.

Bolan said nothing this time, let her fume at herself without offering poor consolation. He had no solutions, but focused instead on the deal that Barialy had been offered by the DEA.

The agency wanted to place him in protective custody, pending his testimony in a string of trials that were expected to send shock waves through the corridors of power in Afghanistan. The top-flight players might be dead, but all of them had left subordinates, accomplices, the kind of hangers-on who often found themselves swept up and prosecuted in the wake of scandal. Barialy knew them, had observed their criminal activities firsthand, and he could put them all in prison.

If he lived that long.

That was the rub, of course. But since the DEA was highly motivated, seething at the murder of their man in Kabul with apparent CIA complicity, Justice was offering a level of protection formerly reserved for top-ranked KGB defectors during the cold war.

And after all the trials, if Barialy stuck it out and did his part, the State Department had agreed to ease his passage from Afghanistan to the United States, if that was what he wanted. There was guilt behind it, as Brognola had explained, but Bolan didn't care. In his world, motives mattered less than end results.

But Falk was having trouble with saying goodbye.

He left her to it, guessing she'd be ready when their flight was called in forty-seven minutes. If she wasn't, Bolan was prepared to leave without her. He would track Carlisle and do the job himself.

As he had done so many times before.

# CHAPTER NINETEEN

*Department of Justice, Washington, D.C.*

The sat-phone call came through as Hal Brognola cursed the cup of steaming coffee that had burned his tongue. It meant his lunch would taste like tinfoil, but he had no one to blame except himself for gulping it.

He hoped he wasn't lisping from the tiny blisters as he grabbed the phone and said, "Hello?"

"It's me," the deep and long-familiar voice informed him.

"So, you're clear?"

"Airborne," Bolan replied. "No hitches, thanks to you."

"My pleasure. Setting up a flight's the easy part."

"And we'll be bouncing out of Turkey?"

"Right. NATO's Incirlik Air Base. They're expecting you and setting up a hop to SHAPE in Belgium."

The Supreme Headquarters Allied Powers Europe— SHAPE, for short—was NATO's central military command, located at Casteau, Belgium. Bolan and his DEA companion would be landing there and picking up a car, driving the final fifty-seven miles due north to Antwerp.

"Sounds good," Bolan observed. "I have something in mind that might be useful when we hit the ground."

"What's that?" Brognola asked.

"I'm guessing that our guy will be concerned about his trade routes, now that there's been interference at the source."

Brognola thought that *annihilation* might have been a better term, but kept it to himself.

"I'm with you so far," he replied.

"And I was thinking," Bolan said, "that someone ought to touch base with his various connections on this end, to let them know he's having problems with supply and transport."

"Just in case they want to help him out," Brognola said.

"Or something."

"Right. Which means you'll need the names and contact numbers."

"If you've got them," Bolan said.

"Not at my fingertips, but I imagine it can be arranged. I'll ask Bear and call you back, ASAP."

"It might be easier if I call you," Bolan replied. "You think an hour's long enough?"

"Should be."

"I'll call you then," Bolan said, and the line went dead.

It was a risky plan, the big Fed realized. But if it worked, it could destroy Vanguard's connections in the world of heroin once and for all. With any luck, somebody else might even pull the plug on Clay Carlisle before Bolan could do the job himself.

Brognola speed-dialed Stony Man, ID'd himself and asked for Aaron Kurtzman. When his man came on the scrambled line, the big Fed spelled out what he needed, then sat back and listened while Kurtzman repeated it for confirmation purposes.

"You want the names, home addresses and private phone numbers of major heroin importers working out of Antwerp, with a side order of Brussels. Not just Belgians, but whoever's dealing top weight in the country. Russians, Turks, Frenchmen."

"Throw in the triads, if you find some," Brognola suggested. "Maybe the Nigerians. Can do?"

"It shouldn't be a problem," Kurtzman said. "I can't predict how many will turn up, but we're cross-referenced seven ways from Sunday. Names and nationalities, locations, type of contraband. It's covered."

"Great. How long?"

"For two cities in Belgium? Say ten minutes. Did you want it faxed or e-mailed?"

"E-mail's good," Brognola said. "It saves me scanning for a text transmission."

"Cool. I'll get right on it."

"Thanks, Bear."

*"No problemo."*

Kurtzman beat his own best estimate, sending the list at the eight-minute mark. Antwerp produced four names, while Brussels added three. Out of the seven, four were native Belgians. The remainder included a Sicilian, a Turk and a Ukrainian.

None were the kind you'd like to irritate.

Unless, perhaps, you were the Executioner.

Bolan called back exactly on the hour mark. Brognola recognized his voice and said, "I've got your shopping list. How do you want it?"

"Can you text it through?" Bolan asked.

"Not a problem."

"Great," Bolan replied. "I'll log it in and make some calls, see what develops."

"What's Plan B, in case your guy's moved on?" Brognola asked.

"We follow," Bolan said. "We're in it to the end."

"It could get dicey if he makes it home," the big Fed said.

"Any way it plays," Bolan replied, "we need to finish it."

"I know. Stay frosty, eh?"

"You know it," Bolan answered, and the line went dead again.

Brognola cradled the receiver, wishing he could heed his own advice.

*Casteau, Belgium*

NATO's SUPREME HEADQUARTERS Allied Powers Europe had been located in France until 1967, when French President Charles DeGaulle launched his second term in office by attempting to gain control over placement of U.S. nuclear weapons in France. Failing that, DeGaulle announced that changes in the field of geopolitics had "stripped NATO of its justification" for integrating European military forces, demanding that all foreign powers vacate French soil by April 1969. SHAPE beat the deadline by two years, moving its headquarters to Belgium in April 1967. Since 2003 its role had expanded, making SHAPE in fact the headquarters of Allied Command Operations for military dispersal worldwide.

And it was handy for a bit of undercover work, from time to time.

Flying on military planes to military bases meant that Bolan and Falk weren't required to leave their hardware behind in Kabul. They arrived fully armed and ready to rumble, except for the car they'd find waiting on touchdown.

He had placed his seven calls while airborne over the Aegean Sea and Greece, connecting with his target in each case by dropping names and dangling bait. To each in turn, he gave the same message with subtle variations, playing off the individual's response and attitude, sowing distrust among the predators.

The three Belgians were Aloys Leclercq, Dietger Maes and Jens Verhoeven. None admitted knowing Clay Carlisle, nor had Bolan expected anything resembling spontaneous confessions to a total stranger on the telephone. They started with denial and insistence that he had to have dialed the wrong number, then listened silently as Bolan ran down details of Carlisle's recent unpleasantness, including the disruption of his trade routes and the sudden death of his supplier, Basir Ahmad-Shah.

The listeners might be forgiven if they thought he was suggesting that Carlisle had played a role in Ahmad-Shah's demise. Maes came the closest to admitting a connection with the chief of Vanguard International, mouthing a quiet "thank you" as he broke the link.

The Sicilian, Luca Maranzano, was less cordial, twice suggesting that the unknown caller should go screw himself. And still he listened to the end of Bolan's spiel before he cradled the receiver.

Kemal Serhan was the Turk. He chuckled throughout most of Bolan's recitation, asking half a dozen times, "What does this mean to me?" It might mean nothing, after all, but Bolan seized the opportunity, fouled Carlisle's nest—and, maybe, gave encouragement to a competitor whose market share of heroin in Western Europe had been undercut by new Afghan production.

The Ukrainian, one Olek Boyko, claimed to understand no English beyond yes and no. He put the call on speakerphone and muttered unintelligibly while his house interpreter translated Bolan's words. When Bolan finished, the interpreter said, "Do not call again this number, please," and hung up on him.

But the message had been registered.

If only one or two of those he'd called were customers of Carlisle's, Bolan counted it a job well done. All seven would have contacts in the drug trade, some of whom might benefit from Bolan's information, all of whom would likely spread the word through Antwerp, Brussels, and beyond.

If Carlisle had remained in Belgium, and if he was looking

for a way to cut his losses, maybe find a new supplier who would keep his trade routes open while he shopped around for partners in Afghanistan, his job would now become more difficult.

Perhaps impossible.

The Vanguard boss might find himself adrift, with hungry sharks already circling.

And if not, if it was all a waste of time, he still had to survive the Executioner.

*Vanguard International Branch Office, Antwerp, Belgium*

FROM HIS BEDROOM WINDOW overlooking Ernest Van Dijck-kaai, Clay Carlisle had a panoramic view of the Schelde River winding its way through the heart of Antwerp. No one on the street below or on the passing boats could see him watching them, since all the windows in the Vanguard wore an outer layer of thin metallic film that turned them into copper-colored mirrors.

Safe at last.

Or was he?

Carlisle, although never quite a soldier in his own right, was a self-made scholar in the field of military tactics. He was perfectly aware that once his enemies had driven him out of Afghanistan, the smart move on their part would be to follow him and try to capitalize on that initial victory.

Of course, that would require the other side to find out where he'd gone, then follow him across the intervening miles from Kabul to Antwerp, pinpoint his specific location and make the hit in spite of his security arrangements.

All of that was possible, of course, as lightning strikes and a fatal impact from a falling meteor were possible. But was it likely?

Carlisle wondered.

On the downside, he'd had nothing but bad news from Kabul since he left. Carlisle now realized that raiders had invaded Vanguard's office there, that they'd slaughtered most of its personnel, and that Dale Ingram was missing. Whether he'd escaped or not meant nothing to Carlisle, unless the weakling had been captured and interrogated.

If that was the case, then Carlisle could assume the hostiles knew he'd flown to Antwerp. They might even have his street address or his unlisted phone number.

So, what?

It would take time for them to get out of Afghanistan and follow him, especially if they were linked—as he suspected—to the slaying of Lee Hastings in Kabul. That news had made the global circuit, thanks to CNN, while Carlisle's days of loss and suffering were swept under the rug.

The talking heads suspected that America's vice consul in Kabul was killed by members of al Qaeda, and while that was also possible, Carlisle was reasonably certain that they had it wrong.

Especially since he'd received the news about Habib Zarghona being blown up, fried and shot outside a home belonging to one of his mistresses. That hit had "Matt Cooper" written all over it.

Whoever he was.

Carlisle planned to solve that riddle, if it took the rest of his life.

"Which it might," he muttered, and smiled at his own show of wit.

Believing as he did that Ingram might have squealed, Carlisle could stump his enemies by clearing out of Belgium and returning to the States. He owned six ranches there, scattered from South Dakota to Wyoming, each of them a mini-fortress where it would require a full-scale military blitz to root him out.

But Carlisle still had work to do in Antwerp. He had bridges to mend, nervous associates who needed reassurance now that Basir Ahmad-Shah was dead and their supply of heroin was temporarily restricted. None of those he'd come to meet were noted for their patience or refinement, but the trait they shared in common was that all were businessmen. They might be stone-cold killers, but they kept a sharp eye on the bottom line.

And when it came to killing, Carlisle was no slouch himself.

So he would have his meeting, calm the restless natives and address the prospect of competitors trying to poach on his preserve. Kemal Serhan would be the one to watch, in that respect. He already had pipelines into Belgium, France and Britain, but his product couldn't match the quality or quantity of Afghan heroin since 9/11. Carlisle could expect Serhan to take advantage of his late misfortunes if the Turk saw any opportunity at all—and he might have to deal with that directly, if it proved to be a major problem.

One less Turk. Who cared?

And if it sparked hostilities, Carlisle believed that he could field more guns than Serhan's people could, despite his recent losses in Afghanistan.

Recruits were joining Vanguard every day, seeking adventure and a chance to see the world without subsisting on the lousy paychecks signed by Uncle Sam. Soldiers of fortune were a dime a dozen in the current buyer's market.

If there'd ever been a time to be a private warlord, this was it.

Smiling at last, Carlisle began to dress for his meeting. Armani should do nicely, he decided, with a touch of Glock for balance.

What the hell?

With friends like his, Clay Carlisle always dressed to kill.

*Flemish Brabant, Belgium*

DRIVING NORTH FROM Mons, toward Antwerp, Deirdre Falk handled the Peugeot 4007 mini-SUV as if she had been driving it forever. Cooper occupied the shotgun seat, a heavy canvas duffel bag between his feet containing some of their hardware. The rest was in the Peugeot's trunk.

With half a dozen silent miles behind them, Falk decided it was time to break the ice. "So, are you happy with the various reactions to your calls?" she asked.

"It's too early to say," he answered. "There's a chance that some of them don't know Carlisle or haven't dealt with him. That kind of problem's built into the scattergun approach."

"But you still think you scored some hits." This time, it didn't come out sounding like a question.

"Some of them took more time to blow me off than I'd expect, if they had no connection to Carlisle. A couple of them sounded worried, but they covered it."

"You think they'll take him out?" she asked him.

"We can hope," Bolan said, "but I doubt it. They're more likely to ask questions about Ahmad-Shah, who killed him, whether Carlisle has another source who can deliver major weight. That kind of thing."

"Too bad," Falk said. "I wouldn't mind if someone else took up the slack this time."

"You still might get your wish. But don't count on it."

"Well, it's a new day anyhow," she said, forcing a smile. "I haven't murdered anyone in Belgium yet. I'm looking forward to it."

"Deirdre, you can still drop out of this."

"And tell the DEA director that I'm ready for appointment as his second in command? You think my old job's even waiting for me, after they hit Alan Combs? I'm toast, my friend. I may as well be buttered on both sides."

"It may not be that bad," Bolan suggested.

"Women's prison? What the hell. Worse comes to worst, I can catch up on all of those kinky experiments I never tried in college, right? I'm looking on the bright side here."

"You weren't the one who set this thing in motion. Neither was your station chief," Bolan replied. "You know it had to start upstairs."

"And when has anyone upstairs been shy about off-loading blame on folks downstairs? I'd say it was the norm, not an exception to the rule."

"I'm only saying that you may have friends you're not aware of at the moment."

"Maybe they can let me check out early, with a fraction of my pension. I can always go the PI route. Investigate divorces, missing persons. Hey, the sky's the limit."

"Don't start planning your retirement yet," Bolan advised. "If you're coming with me, I need you focused on Carlisle until we're finished with him."

"Never fear," she said. "He'll have my full attention. Still, I can't help wondering."

"About?"

"Edris. Any way you look at it, we left him hanging. If he still had Combs to cover him, I'd rest a little easier. But who'll replace him? How long will it take to find somebody for the job? Suppose the new guy doesn't like CIs?"

"In that case," Bolan said, "he never would've lasted in the DEA."

"Okay, I'll grant you that. But what if he's a shit who doesn't care what happens to them? What if—"

Bolan cut her off, saying, "From what I saw, your guy is a survivor. He'll most likely work it out, and if he sees it isn't working, he can always split."

"Unless they kill him first," Falk said.

"Unless that, sure. You want to guarantee he lives forever, I suggest you give it up. Nobody ever has. Nobody ever will."

"You sure know how to give a pep talk, Matt," she said.

Falk gave up talking then, and focused on the highway leading toward their fate.

Whatever that might be.

## Antwerp

THE HIGH-RISE OFFICE building stood on Quinten Matsijslei, facing the green triangle of the Stadspark and its man-made lake resembling the outline of a long-necked dinosaur. There was no sign or name plate on the building, other than its street number. Inside the lobby, even the directory mounted against one wall gave no hint as to what most of the building's tenants did to earn their keep.

Clay Carlisle's limousine was double-parked just long enough to unload seven buff young men in stylish suits, their jackets cut with extra room for burly shoulders and the compact automatic weapons slung beneath their arms. They formed a living shield for Carlisle as he stepped out of the limo, closed around him and permitted no one to approach him as they swept through the revolving door.

Carlisle was fashionably late, not as a power play, but to ensure that all the men he planned to meet would be in place ahead of him, with any bodyguards they'd brought along. He left one guard in the lobby, to watch out for late arrivals by suspicious characters, and let the other six convey him toward the bank of elevators. There, they chose a car, filled it without allowing anybody else inside and rode up to the ninth floor without speaking.

Every modern elevator came equipped with cameras for security. It was no stretch of the imagination to assume that microphones were added for the benefit of listeners who sought an edge in various negotiations, where the stakes ranged from mere cash to life and death.

On nine, Carlisle found troops resembling his own lined up along the corridor. Most of the men were nondescript, a certain type that ran toward scars and menacing tattoos, but he identified the Turks without much difficulty. They were shorter, generally darker than the others. All of the shooters studied Carlisle's men, assessing them, while his mercs did the same.

If anything went wrong inside the meeting room, there would be bloody chaos in the corridor outside.

Unfortunately, if that happened, Carlisle likely wouldn't live to see the show.

Carlisle had been expecting three men, but he found four waiting for him in the conference room. The Belgians, rivals Aloys Leclercq and Jens Verhoeven, had submerged their mutual animosity to sit on one side of the table, facing Kemal Serhan and a stranger Carlisle recognized from photographs but hadn't met.

Because the meeting had convened at his request, Carlisle's chair waited at the table's head. Smiling, he moved to take his seat, greeting three of the delegates by name, then pinned the fourth man with his eyes and asked, "Who's this?"

Kemal Serhan replied, "Is Olek Boyko. He's a friend of mine. We started talking and I asked him to come with me. I am hoping that you do not mind."

The Turk's smile mocked Carlisle, daring him to object. Carlisle replied, "Of course not. Bring your friends and neighbors if you like, Kemal. I thought we were discussing business, but it seems I was mistaken."

"Olek does the same business," Serhan explained.

Carlisle ignored the Turk and asked Boyko directly, "What business is that?"

Boyko responded with a lazy shrug. "Whatever governments deny their people, I supply it."

"More specifically?"

"I understand we came to speak of heroin."

"You wouldn't be an undercover cop, by any chance?"

Boyko spit out a barking laugh, but Carlisle saw the Belgians trading nervous glances on his left.

"You make the joke," Boyko replied, grinning with little lizard's teeth. "You want to see my jail tattoos?"

"I'm not impressed with body art," Carlisle said. "I could have Karl Marx inked on my ass and still not be a Communist."

"You saw that movie, eh?" Boyko inquired. "The *Eastern Promises*? It makes some stupid people think is easy for police to infiltrate *vorovskoy mir.* That is a serious mistake."

*Vorovskoy mir.* Thief's world.

Carlisle knew the name Russian gangsters applied to their outlaw milieu, just as he knew that the Ukrainian was no policeman. Still, he'd asserted control of the meeting and cast doubt on the drop-in delegate he hadn't invited.

But he wasn't finished yet.

"Should I expect other surprises?" Carlisle asked the room at large. "I ask three friends to meet with me in private, and a man I've never seen before shows up. What else should I expect now? Hidden microphones and cameras? Is there a secretary in the closet, taking notes?"

The Belgians blanched, while Kemal Serhan scowled.

"You chose the room," Serhan reminded him. "Perhaps we should be worried about spying, yes?"

"Explain that," Carlisle ordered.

Serhan bristled at his tone and said, "We are not children, Mr. Carlisle. All of us are knowing what has happened in Afghanistan this week. Your merchandise, your office, your supplier—*poof!* All up in smoke. You have no drugs to sell. Perhaps you think to make a profit selling us instead."

Carlisle could feel the tide shifting. It was against him

now, and if he wasn't very careful it could draw him out to sea, where he would drown and disappear without a trace.

"I'm glad you've finally subscribed to CNN, Kemal," he said. "But there's a problem with believing everything you see and hear. Ninety percent of what the media reports is either skewed to make a point or fabricated from thin air."

Four pairs of eyes were riveted on Carlisle, waiting for him to explain. He kept them hanging for half a minute longer, then resumed speaking.

"It's true that terrorists have recently inflicted certain damage on my network in Afghanistan. Some of you knew my friend, Sheikh Basir Ahmad-Shah, who fell before their guns. He will be missed, but he was not unique. If any of you know the first thing about geopolitics, you realize that the law of supply and demand reigns supreme. Addicts need heroin, and there are more of them each day. Afghanistan produces better heroin, in larger quantities, than any other nation on Earth. That will not change with one man's death, or with a thousand."

"So you have a new connection, then?" Serhan inquired.

"I'm in negotiations as we speak," Carlisle lied smoothly. "And I'm confident that everyone I've dealt with in the past will be well satisfied. As for new customers…I guess we'll have to wait and see."

"That's gratifying news, indeed," Leclercq said.

"Most gratifying," Verhoeven agreed.

"If true," Boyko said. "But it takes time to complete arrangements, yes?"

"A week or two, at the outside," Carlisle replied.

"How many millions are we losing in a week or two?" the Ukrainian asked.

"In your case," Carlisle answered, "since you've never been my customer, it would be zero."

"I am not so selfish to think only of myself," Boyko replied. "And for my friends around this table, I propose to cover Mr.

Carlisle's—what you call it, short-fall?—for however long it takes him to resume deliveries. I pledge this with my friend, Kemal."

Carlisle couldn't object without losing the Belgians, so he smiled and said, "I thank my new friend for his generosity, and hope that no one's clients suffer from the change in quality."

"You're pleased to make a joke of me?" Boyko inquired.

"By no means. All I am saying is that when you've had the best, it's hard to settle for second-best, third-best…whatever."

"You *are* insulting me!"

"I don't know you from Adam," Carlisle lied. "You say you're not a cop, okay. Kemal supports you. Now you take offense because I don't know if your product is on par with mine? You need to get a grip on those emotions, friend. This is a business, not a high-school drama club."

"Maybe I send you sample of my merchandise, to show you how it is," Boyko said.

"I don't use it," Carlisle said, "but if you need a chemist who can analyze it for you, I can recommend several."

"We have agreement, then," Leclercq said before the verbal sparring match could escalate. "Kemal and Olek will supply our needs until Mr. Carlisle is able to resume deliveries. Okay? Good. Done."

Carlisle was furious, but kept it off his face as he shook hands around the table and prepared to join the others for a grand buffet in celebration of their pact. He'd been the victim of a bloodless coup, edged out in favor of Serhan and Boyko.

Still, he clung to hope.

What he had said about Afghanistan was true enough. Carlisle needed to find a new contact, perhaps one of the drug lords who had hated Basir Ahmad-Shah, and strike a new bargain. When he resumed deliveries in Europe, there'd be opposition from Serhan and Boyko, but he'd deal with them as he had dealt with other enemies.

Scorched earth.

His time would come, but here and now was not the place to start a war.

Particularly when he still had one to finish with his unknown enemies.

# CHAPTER TWENTY

Bolan drove twice around the block where Vanguard's office overlooked the Schelde River, then nosed his car into a parking garage one block from the target, at the corner of Ernest van Dijckkaai and Vlasmarkt Reyndersstraat. He found a space on the third level, parked and switched off the Peugeot's engine.

Bolan and Falk had the cavernous garage to themselves as they left the car, footsteps echoing. It was a gray and drizzling day outside, perfect for raincoats that would cover slung weapons, pockets heavy with spare magazines. Bolan considered carrying the 40 mm launcher, but decided it would make him look like Quasimodo as he hiked back to his target through the rain. He compromised by clipping frag grenades along his belt.

Hats were the crowning touch: a fedora for Bolan and something slightly larger for Falk. The spitting rain made them entirely natural.

"All set?" he asked.

Falk shrugged inside her drooping coat and said, "As ready as I'll ever be."

They found the stairs and started down the six flights that

would take them to street level, speaking softly so their voices wouldn't carry past the stairwell.

"There should be no problem in the lobby," Bolan said. "Vanguard has one floor out of nine, and Carlisle doesn't own the building."

"But he's bound to have security," Falk said. "Especially after Kabul."

"There'll be cameras, for sure," Bolan agreed. "The hats and raincoats ought to help, but if they spot us going up, we'll deal with it."

They had to share the wet sidewalk with shoppers and a crush of working people bustling off to lunch. Bolan was thankful for the crowd that covered them, in case Carlisle had spotters on the street outside his office building.

Once they crossed the threshold, it would be a different game entirely.

"Now I wish we'd called ahead, to see if Carlisle's even there," Falk said.

Bolan repeated what he knew she knew. "We can't trust anything they'd tell us. If he's in, would anyone admit it? If he's gone, would anybody tell us where he went? We have to check it out ourselves."

"I know. Ignore me, will you? I'm just tired of living in a shooting gallery."

They walked north through the rain, toward Haverstraat and Carlisle's office building, where the Vanguard CEO maintained a suite of rooms for sleepovers when he was visiting Antwerp. With any luck, they'd find him watching TV, catching up on news from Kabul, or negotiating nooners with one of his secretaries.

Then again, he might be in the wind.

Bolan had tried to check on private flights departing out of Antwerp International within the past twelve hours, but so far he'd gotten nowhere. Carlisle could have flown the coop in Vanguard's jet and he'd be none the wiser. The attack he was about to stage could be a monumental waste of time.

But he would never know unless he tried.

At last they stood outside the tall glass doors, swarmed by pedestrians on every side. Bolan was pleased to see a small stream of them trickling into Carlisle's lobby. Falk plunged in ahead of him, and Bolan let two other women rush the doors with their umbrellas raised before he followed her.

Vanguard monopolized the seventh floor. Bolan and Falk bypassed the elevators—which were bound to have surveillance cameras and might require a special key to stop on Carlisle's floor, where armed guards lay in wait—moving beyond the bank of polished metal doors to find the service stairs.

Bolan did not expect live guards, and thought motion detectors might be too much trouble on a staircase used by everyone from janitors to secretaries sneaking cigarettes. As for surveillance cameras, they were so small these days that he could search for hours without finding one that tracked his every move.

Since neither one of them could fly, it was a chance they'd have to take.

He hadn't spotted any Vanguard sentries in the lobby by the time they reached the stairwell and slipped through its stout fire door. Falk offered him an almost wistful smile and whispered, "Here goes nothing," then began to climb.

"YOU'RE LEAVING when, sir?" Eric Dawson asked.

"Right now," Clay Carlisle told his Antwerp office supervisor. "Have my car and personnel ready to roll within five minutes. I've already called ahead to warn the flight crew."

"As you wish, sir," Dawson said, turning away to make the necessary calls.

In fact, nothing had gone as Carlisle wished it to for days.

After the bloody business in Afghanistan, he'd hoped to reassure his European partners, buy himself some time to re-establish trade routes from the East, but he'd been ambushed at their meeting by Kemal Serhan and Olek Boyko.

Now he had to find a new supplier in Afghanistan, nego-tiate new rates, *and* plot a fitting retribution for the rivals who had stabbed him in the back. Carlisle had two inform-ers inside Serhan's syndicate, if they could still be trusted, but he'd need intelligence on Boyko, too, before he made his move.

When he struck, his action needed to be swift, decisive, ruthless, and the damage suffered by his enemies had to be irreparable. He needed to destroy them, leaving no doubt in the minds of his remaining allies or potential future custom-ers that Clay Carlisle and Vanguard International were forces to be reckoned with.

But first, he needed to go home.

He felt as if the squalor of the Middle East had soaked into his body through its pores, infecting him with a contagion that no scalding shower could remove. He needed time and room to breathe, to think without a constant yammering of alien ideas and dialects distracting him.

And there were problems to investigate at home, as well.

His latest calls to Washington were not being returned. Assistants of the men he paid to do his bidding made excuses, offered their condolences, muttered vague explanations with-out saying anything. Carlisle wondered what he would find when he landed in Washington.

Now he intended to find out.

"All ready, sir, in the garage," Dawson informed him.

"Good. My overnight bag's in my suite. Have someone fetch it, will you?"

"Right away, sir."

*This* was how things ought to be, with flunkies snapping

to attention when he spoke, obeying his commands as if they were decrees from God Himself.

Carlisle offered a silent prayer of contrition for that blasphemy, secure in the knowledge that his Savior would forgive him anything. The Lord knew that Carlisle's every move was directed toward His greater glory, by purging the world of heretics and inferiors. The means and tools were immaterial.

Carlisle saw one of his gorillas coming with the overnight bag. Dawson shook his hand and wished Carlisle a peaceful flight, then watched him board the elevator with his soldiers.

Going down.

For the transatlantic crossing, Carlisle couldn't use the Learjet 60, which would run out of fuel a thousand miles from home and drop him in the drink. Instead he would be flying in Vanguard's Bombardier Challenger 600, with seating for nineteen passengers, which had a range of 3875 miles— sixty-three more than he needed for the hop from Antwerp to Washington, D.C. Being a cautious man, he had allowed for headwinds and delays upon arrival, scheduling a stop in London that would let the crew refuel and shave 190 miles from the line-of-sight journey, leaving the aircraft with 206 air miles to spare.

Now all he had to do was to reach the airport in one piece, board his flight without incident and put Europe behind him for a while. Once he was home, Carlisle would start the grueling task of rebuilding his empire, punishing his enemies and letting everyone on Earth know he was still in charge.

BOLAN AND FALK WERE on the seventh flight of stairs, approaching the fourth floor with no sign of a camera yet, when Bolan heard the scraping of a door somewhere above them, followed by the racket of descending feet.

Two people, unless Belgium grew them with four legs. He couldn't tell if they were male or female, though the footsteps sounded heavy, hurried. No one spoke as they descended, either being cautious or saving their breath for the stairs.

Bolan drew his Jericho pistol, muzzle-heavy with its suppressor attached, and thumbed back its hammer. He held the gun down by his thigh, half concealed by a fold of his raincoat, waiting to see if the folks on the stairs overhead needed killing.

Who would use the stairs this time of day?

Custodians should work at night, unless they had repairs to finish. Normal office staff would use the elevators, unless they were sneaking off to steal a moment for themselves in the midst of a workday. He didn't want to blast two sneaky smokers or a pair of undercover lovers, so he waited, hard eyes covering the fourth-floor landing.

Almost there.

He saw the legs first, stylish slacks and black shoes polished to a mirror shine. A heartbeat later Bolan faced two young men in their late twenties or early thirties, sporting near-identical crew cuts. Both filled their suits with muscle, strained their ties with stout necks.

Soldiers in disguise?

They didn't recognize him—couldn't have—but something sparked inside their eyes and Bolan's hand was rising with the Jericho before the new arrivals started reaching for their own concealed weapons. He fired twice, easy head shots from a range of fifteen feet or less, then stepped aside as they came tumbling down to join him on the landing between three and four.

"They weren't expecting us," he told Falk. "We're still good to go."

"Let's find out what they're carrying," she said, and pulled aside one open jacket, then the other.

One of the dead mercs had worn a heavy Desert Eagle autoloader, the .357 Magnum version, in a custom shoulder rig.

The other had a Mini-Uzi tucked inside his belt at the small of his back.

"My little friend," Falk said as she retrieved the SMG. Smiling at Bolan, she said, "What the hell. I may as well have two."

Bolan removed the Desert Eagle from its holster, checked the magazine to verify a full load of nine rounds, with one more in the chamber, and found room for it under his belt. It tugged his pants down on one side a bit, but Bolan guessed he wouldn't have to carry it for long.

The started climbing once again, burdened by extra steel and two more deaths. Bolan wondered how Falk was taking it, behind her fleeting smile, and knew that it was better not to ask.

Sometimes, in combat, soldiers wore a fragile mask of courage. They were fine while there was something to be done—killing the enemy, reloading weapons, beefing up defenses—but they broke down if they had to stop to think about it, focus on the things they'd suffered, seen and done.

He didn't know if Falk was in that place, or if she was really as tough as she seemed. Either way, Bolan didn't plan to risk upsetting her internal balance.

Bolan heard Falk breathing heavily beside him and decided they should take a moment when they reached Carlisle's floor, rest up and catch their breath before they stepped into the dragon's lair.

What difference could another minute make?

STANDING WITH COOPER on the landing, Deirdre Falk felt like Ma Barker or Bonnie, from Bonnie and Clyde. She was packing four guns, nearly bowed with their bulk and the weight of their spare magazines, psyching up for a fight where a shitload of people were going to die.

"When we go in," Bolan whispered, "you'll have to cover everything at once. All sides. The door likely has some kind of alarm attached, most likely silent, so they can dispose of an intruder privately."

"We need to think about the cops," she said. "Antwerp's not Kabul. No one who hears guns will hesitate to drop a dime."

Bolan nodded and said, "We're absolutely on the clock. Five minutes maximum, I'd say, to find out whether Carlisle's here or not."

"And kill him, if he is," she said.

"Unless we see a chance to take him out alive, for questioning."

Falk remembered Dale Ingram's interrogation and decided that she didn't feel like trying to arrest Carlisle. What was the point, when nothing that he said under the gun could ever be used against him or anyone else?

Not in court, anyway.

Funny, the path a person's mind took when she's seen life from a different angle, cutting through the red tape with a cleaver.

"Right," she said. "I'm ready, if you are."

Both of them couldn't clear the door at once, so Bolan took the lead, Falk close behind him, almost stepping on his heels. They separated in the hallway, one taking each side and moving forward in a crouching scuttle-run that made Falk feel as if she'd joined a SWAT team.

Better.

When they cleared the stairwell, there was only one man in the corridor, retreating with his back turned toward them, disappearing through an open doorway. Bolan followed him, while Falk began checking the offices on her side of the hall.

Inside the first, a barrel-chested man with iron-gray hair sat ramrod-straight behind a cluttered desk. Falk showed him her Kalashnikov and asked him, "Where's Carlisle?"

He blinked and answered, "Who the hell are you?"

"My answer first," she said, then shot him when he yanked a desk drawer open on his right and reached inside.

At the same time she heard another AK stutter somewhere down the hall. Cooper, she hoped, getting acquainted with the Vanguard troops.

Falk left the office and its former occupant, to find people emerging from a dozen doors along the hallway to her left. There'd also be another corridor on nine, she calculated, running parallel to that in which she stood, with other rooms now occupied by secretaries, mercs and God knew who else, scrambling for their telephones, their guns, their panic buttons.

Great, she thought, and raised her autorifle, squeezing off a burst that raked the left side of the hall. One of her targets fell, while half a dozen others ducked back, out of sight.

Falk knew that she would have to root them out, one at a time.

And time was something that she didn't have to spare.

CLAY CARLISLE SIPPED grape juice as his limousine rolled out toward Antwerp International Airport. He felt better than he had in days, relaxing at the thought that he would soon be safe at home.

"Safe," however, was a relative concept these days. Regardless of income or status, it remained a fact of life that nearly anyone could be killed anytime, anywhere, if the would-be assassin was willing to give up his own life achieving that goal.

Good luck, Carlisle thought as he drained his glass. You'll have to catch me first.

As if on cue, his cell phone rang. Frowning, he drew it from his pocket, checked the Caller ID display and saw E. Dawson printed there.

So, Eric had forgotten something during Carlisle's rush to leave the office and get out of Antwerp. That was no surprise.

Carlisle thumbed down a button to accept the call and

raised the cell phone to his ear. His lips were still forming the words, "What is it, Eric?" when the crack of an explosion echoed from the small phone in his hand.

"Eric? *Eric!* What's going on there?"

Someone, maybe Dawson, shouted something at Carlisle, but it seemed as if the caller's telephone was held at arm's length from his lips. Or maybe it was the explosive sounds of combat that were drowning out his words.

Carlisle heard automatic weapons firing in the background, interspersed with pistol shots and what he thought were shotgun blasts. Another echoing explosion smothered the small-arms reports, and there were fewer weapons firing back when they resumed.

Carlisle stared at his phone and pressed another button to confirm Caller ID. Instead of Dawson's name, he saw a phone number displayed and recognized it as belonging to the Antwerp Vanguard office.

He could feel the short hairs bristling on his nape, raised by the distant sounds of men in mortal agony, dying while he sat in his limo, listening.

Carlisle switched off the telephone and stuffed it back into his pocket. Leaning forward, elbows on his knees, he shouted at his driver, "Get me to the airport! *Now!*"

THE YOUNG MAN had been hiding underneath a desk when Bolan found him, dragged him out and pressed the AKSU's muzzle to his forehead, singing flesh. Trembling, the captive winced but made no sound.

"You have one chance to live," Bolan informed him.

"Where's Carlisle?"

"He's gone!"

"When did he leave?"

"Within the last ten minutes. Shit, you prob'ly passed him in the lobby."

"No, I didn't."

"Maybe out through the garage, downstairs."

Bolan put pressure on the rifle as he asked, "Gone *where?*"

"Away, man! How'n hell would I know? Ask the D-Man."

"Who's that?"

"Dawson! The manager! Eric Dawson!"

Bolan hauled the young man to his feet and ordered, "Take me to him."

"Christ! With all this going on, I don't know where he is."

"We'll look for him together," Bolan said, propelling his new human shield toward the cubicle doorway.

"Suppose he already got out?"

"Your bad luck," Bolan said.

No one immediately challenged them as they entered the hallway. Bolan kept a firm grip on his captive's collar, following the staffer as he turned left, moving through a haze of dust and acrid smoke.

Alarms were clamoring, but the gunfire had subsided for the moment. Bolan couldn't tell if the surviving Vanguard staff had fled the premises or if they'd gathered somewhere to prepare a counterthrust. Worse yet, he had lost track of Deirdre Falk and didn't have a clue where he should look for her, alive or dead.

Bolan's reluctant guide stopped at the doorway to an office on their left. The door displayed a plastic name plate reading Eric Dawson, Manager.

"Don't stand on ceremony," Bolan said, and gave the kid a shove.

"Hey, man, if he's in there—"

"We'll know it in a second."

"Shit!" He grabbed the knob and turned it, opening the door a crack as he said, "Mr. D? I need to—"

Dawson's first shot struck the young man high and outside, spinning him toward Bolan with a stunned expression on his face. A second hit him as he fell, somewhere around the waistline.

Bolan was counting shots as he slammed through the doorway in a crouch, spraying the room with 5.45 mm rounds. He stitched a sofa, filing cabinets and the desk where Eric Dawson, Manager, stood leveling an automatic in both hands. The Russian FMJ rounds shattered Dawson's pelvis, shredding his intestines, slamming him against the nearest wall before he slid to a seated posture on the floor.

Bolan was instantly beside him, kicking Dawson's pistol out of reach, saying, "I'm here for Carlisle."

"Guess you blew it," Dawson gasped, half smiling through a smear of crimson foam that stained his lips. "Long gone."

"Gone where?"

"Back home. The States. You lose."

"Goddamn it!"

Bolan half turned toward the office doorway at the sound of Falk's voice. She was standing with a Mini-Uzi in each hand and an expression on her face that mirrored failure.

"So, we missed his ass again," she said. "After all this. I don't freakin believe it! Can we race him to the airport?"

Bolan shook his head. "Too many cops. And with a private plane, he's got no wait for takeoff."

"Shit! Tell me some good news for a change, will you?"

Before Bolan could answer, scuffling footsteps sounded from the corridor outside. Falk turned and raised her right-hand submachine gun, triggering a short burst toward some target Bolan couldn't see. A strangled cry and thud of impact on the floor told him she'd scored.

"The good news," Bolan said, "is that there's nowhere he can hide. Not in the States. Not on the planet."

Falk met Bolan's gaze, then nodded.

"We should probably get started, then," she said.

"Step one is getting out of here alive," Bolan reminded her.

"I guess we'll have to ditch the toys," she said, raising matched Uzi's as she spoke.

"Only if you intend to board a flight."

"Good thing I don't leave home without my passport, eh?" Her smile looked weary, worn.

Bolan was halfway to the office doorway when Eric Dawson raised a frail voice from behind him.

"Wait! Can't leave…like this…"

"You're right," Bolan agreed, and put a mercy round between his eyes.

Stragglers had cleared the stairwell by the time they reached it, leaving only the two mercs Bolan had shot and one clerk-type who'd fallen in his rush to clear the battlefield, tumbling downstairs to break his neck.

As they descended, Falk and Bolan shed their weapons, extra magazines and Bolan's solitary spare grenade. The Executioner unscrewed his pistol's suppressor but kept the pistol. He had phony FBI credentials to explain it if they were accosted by police, as Falk had her legitimate ID to justify the Glock.

They couldn't carry either weapon on a transatlantic flight, unless Falk chose to fill out reams of paperwork at Antwerp International and risk detention or at least further delays. Bolan wasn't concerned about the flight or landing on the other side, however.

He was thinking past the last leg of their intercontinental journey, toward his meeting with Clay Carlisle somewhere on their native soil.

It had been long delayed.

Too long.

The Executioner could hardly wait.

# CHAPTER TWENTY-ONE

*Treasure County, Montana*

Clay Carlisle watched the sun rise over Rattlesnake Butte, away to the east of his rambling farmhouse. Rose-colored hues slowly gave way to brighter shades of red and orange, as if a battle raged on the horizon and had set the sky on fire.

Treasure County was the third-smallest county in Montana, at 979 square miles, and had the second-smallest population with 861 registered inhabitants. It had been named in 1919 to attract new settlers, but the PR campaign had obviously failed.

That was fine with Carlisle, who owned roughly one-third of the county and called the shots for half its leading businesses. He loved the open spaces, couldn't get enough of Big Sky Country, even though his duties as the president and CEO of Vanguard International kept him away from home most of the time.

But not this day.

From Antwerp, he'd stopped off in Washington to find out what was happening to his network of well-placed friends, and found the nation's capital in turmoil. Most of it wouldn't rate a mention in the media, although the suicide of a high-ranking State Department official had made front-page news across the country.

They were blaming it on "clinical depression" that had somehow gone unnoticed and undiagnosed during the late diplomat's entire career of some twenty-odd years—and that was fine with Carlisle, too. The last thing that he needed being aired in public was the truth, for God's sake.

Not that he was clear on that himself.

His network had been breached somehow. His main mouthpiece and champion at State was dead and privately disgraced. Her hatchet men were being scattered to the winds with transfers that could only be interpreted as punitive. Somewhere along the way, while Carlisle had been fighting for his life in Kabul, someone on the home front had screwed up big time.

The Antwerp office was a bloody shambles, more dead there and screaming headlines calling for investigation and indictment of his company, perhaps Carlisle himself. Belgian police still didn't have a clue to help them work out what had happened, and Carlisle could definitely sympathize.

He was still puzzling over that himself.

This time last week he had been on top of the world. America's champion, beloved by conservative politicians nationwide, renowned as the world's number-one private military contractor. Today his operations in Kabul and Europe were trashed, his covert friends were being hounded out of Washington, and Carlisle still wasn't sure who had set the dogs on him.

But he intended to find out, oh yes. If it was the last thing he did in his life, he would track down and punish those who'd tried to ruin him.

The Bible spelled it out in Deuteronomy 32:35: "To me belongeth vengeance and recompense; their foot shall slide in due time: for the day of their calamity is at hand, and the things that shall come upon them make haste."

But sometimes, even God Himself could use a little help. Clay Carlisle lived to serve.

Another line he loved, although it came from Ben Franklin's *Poor Richard's Almanac*, rather than from Holy Scripture: "God helps those who help themselves."

Amen.

Carlisle had been helping himself for as long as he could remember, and God had never let him down. His recent setbacks were a challenge and a disappointment, granted, but he understood that every faithful servant of the Lord was tested now and then.

He planned to pass the test with flying colors.

For a start he'd brought two dozen of his best mercs to the ranch and placed them on guard in eight-hour rotating shifts. Meanwhile his agents in the field and a small army of computer geeks were working overtime to find out who'd betrayed his team in Washington. Exiled survivors of the network weren't cooperating yet, he would find a way to overcome their reticence, whether it took brute force or bags of cash.

Carlisle would have his answers, one way or another. And when all the vital information was within his grasp, it would be payback time.

Someone would weep for their attempt to bring him down.

Someone would *bleed*.

But first, Carlisle would have his breakfast. Two eggs over easy, crispy bacon, sausage, gravy over fried potatoes, Texas toast and fresh-brewed coffee. Just like Mama used to make.

Stomach growling, Carlisle rose from his seat on the long porch and went inside the house.

He'd lived to see another sunrise, and today he would begin the process of recouping losses, settling scores, reclaiming every corner of his life.

THE RIFLE WAS A DPMS Panther LR-308B custom job. The "LR" stood for long range, as in sniping, and its .308 Winchester loads had an effective range in excess of one thousand yards. With 180-grain Nosler partition high-energy rounds, each bullet would leave the Panther's muzzle at 2,740 feet per second, delivering 3,000 foot-pounds of destructive energy.

The piece vaguely resembled its M-16 forebears, but it had been modified with an eighteen-inch 4140 chromium molybdenum barrel, fluted to reduce vibration and improve accuracy. The Panther weighed fourteen pounds with its telescopic sight and 19-round magazine in place, plus a suppressor on the muzzle to retard tracking of its location by potential targets.

The sound suppressor would decrease Bolan's effective range by a hundred yards or so, but he was willing to accept the compromise. In any case, he'd need to be a good deal closer to his primary objective when he finished picking off the guards.

He'd hiked in overland the night before, navigating with infrared goggles and a handheld GPS unit to avoid pitfalls and unwelcome detours. Carlisle's vast ranch wasn't fenced, but the land *was* patrolled by armed men in Jeeps, while others walked their beats around the house and outbuildings. If it wasn't exactly a hardsite, Bolan thought it was the next best thing.

But now he was inside, lying atop a low ridge running northeast to southwest, six hundred yards from Carlisle's farmhouse. Peering through the scope, he watched the sentries make their rounds, breaths pluming in the early morning chill.

Bolan knew his first targets should be the roving hunters in their jeep. Mobility made them more dangerous than any of the foot soldiers, and there was no doubt in his mind that they would have a com link to the house, either with cell phones or a two-way radio. That meant that he would have to drop them both before one of the pair could sound a general alarm and summon reinforcements.

Spotting the jeep at seven hundred yards, he tracked it for a quarter mile until an unexpected opportunity presented itself. He saw the vehicle slow then stop beside an ancient cottonwood where the shotgun rider dismounted and circled around with quick strides, out of sight no doubt to answer a call of nature. The driver waited for him, gazing off across the landscape, drumming restless fingers on the steering wheel.

Bolan adjusted his scope for elevation and projected bullet-drop at the selected range, then found his mark and held it steady. He inhaled deeply, released the breath and lightly stroked the Panther's trigger before drawing in another.

Downrange, three-quarters of a second after firing, Bolan saw the driver's head explode, resembling a melon with a cherry bomb inside it. There'd be no sound but the sloppy noise of impact to announce the kill at that distance, and the dead man's companion didn't seem to notice that.

A minute later he was back, smoothing his fly and strolling toward the Jeep until he saw the mess awaiting him and froze. By that time, Bolan had him sighted in and round two was already hurtling toward its mark.

The rider vaulted backward, like a stuntman in the movies yanked by cables that the audience will never see. In this case, though, it was slamming through the sternum and the heart behind it that propelled him through a tumbling backward somersault, coming to rest beneath the cottonwood.

The merc had watered it a moment earlier, now he would nurture it with blood.

The Jeep was idling but its parking brake was set. It could sit there and run in place until its fuel ran out, for all that Bolan cared.

He turned cold eyes back toward the house and waited for another target to reveal himself.

CLAY CARLISLE LOVED crisp bacon. There was something to the way it crumbled in his mouth, combining burned and salty flavors all at once, that made him close his eyes and sigh.

Of course, he loved ham, too. Along with pork chops, ribs, pork tenderloin—to hit the bottom line, hog meat in any form except for pickled pig's feet, which he had been raised to shun as poor people's food.

He was on the verge of ordering more bacon from the kitchen when one of his morning sentries burst into the dining room without a by-your-leave, red-faced and grimacing.

"Boss! Quick!" he blurted. "We're under fire!"

Carlisle half rose, then caught himself and asked, "What do you mean?"

"Sniper! We've got one down, at least."

"Who's down?"

"Kowalski, sir." The lookout had regained a bit of his composure. "Head shot, but the looks of it. He's dead, for sure."

"Where's Harrigan?"

"Not answering," the merc replied.

Jim Harrigan was Carlisle's captain of the guard, well paid to supervise security arrangements at the ranch and make Carlisle's retreat impregnable. He was on call around the clock. It was unthinkable that he would not respond to an emergency alert.

If he was able to respond.

Now on his feet, breakfast forgotten, Carlisle snapped, "Call in the Jeep."

"No answer there, either," the red-faced messenger informed him.

It was impossible—unthinkable—for Harrigan *and* the roving Jeep patrol sentries to fall out of touch. Brushing past the nervous guard, en route to the nearest gun closet, Carlisle said, "Get on the horn and rally everyone who *does* answer. I want them all together on the front porch now. Then roust the others out of bed and get them down here, armed and ready to kick ass."

"Yes, sir!"

Carlisle's latent paranoia had conditioned him to be prepared for an attack no matter where he was, regardless of the day or time. He couldn't have explained exactly who or what he feared—the government, commercial rivals, friends or relatives of those he had destroyed financially or physically, perhaps a troop of aliens from outer space—but he always kept weapons close at hand.

His destination, at the moment, was a closet in the hallway leading from the dining room to his ground-floor study. It contained a rack of long guns—two assault rifles, two shotguns, one scoped hunting rifle—with some pistols hanging on the wall immediately to his left, and Kevlar body armor dangling on his right.

Carlisle reached for the Kevlar first, pulling a vest over his head and fastening the Velcro straps beneath his arms on either side. Next he retrieved a Glock 21 pistol, chambered in .45ACP, and tucked it under his belt at the small of his back. Carlisle's final selection, a Steyr AUG, ranked among the world's finest and most dependable assault rifles, officially adopted by the U.S. Customs Service and the armies of twenty-two foreign countries.

Carlisle spent another moment filling his pockets with spare magazines—black plastic for the Glock, clear plastic for the Steyr—until he felt his trousers straining at their seams.

He was as ready as he'd ever be.

A sound of muffled footsteps overhead, coupled with voices shouting back and forth, told Carlisle that his off-duty defenders had been roused and were responding to their battle stations. Even if some unknown enemy had slaughtered all his other troops outside, he still had seventeen remaining to protect him.

Carlisle waited for them at the bottom of the staircase, hoping it would be enough.

IN FACT, THE OUTER sentries were all dead, as Carlisle rallied his survivors in the farmhouse. Bolan waited for the reinforcements to emerge and make a recon of the scene, and Carlisle didn't disappoint him.

Two men dressed in denim jeans and work shirts took the point, one covering the other as they exited the front door and sprinted across the porch, seeking the cover of a Dodge Ram 1500 pickup parked off to the west side of the farmhouse.

Bolan let them reach it, hunker down beside the truck and offer him a pair of stationary targets as they planned their next move, unaware that they were totally exposed from his position on a low rise, four hundred yards out from the house.

A small adjustment to the scope and Bolan dropped them with a one-two punch that snuffed the second shooter's life before he realized the first was down. They fell together, tangled in a loose embrace, beyond mortal embarrassment.

How many left inside?

He'd have to wait and see.

Five minutes passed before the next two shooters showed themselves. They'd obviously come out through an exit somewhere at the rear, beyond his line of sight, one circling the house in each direction, east and west. The west-side hunter surfaced first, and died with one of Bolan's bullets in his brain just as he recognized the fallen bodies of his friends.

Ten rounds remaining in the Panther's magazine before Bolan had to reload. He watched and waited, saw the east-side shooter peek around that corner of the house and held his fire, encouraging the man to think that he was safe.

His target took the bait, edged farther out from cover and collapsed as Bolan drilled him through the chest. Dying, his index finger clenched around the trigger of his SMG and fired a wasted burst across the farmyard.

Bolan waited five more minutes, then laid the Panther aside and shouldered his backup weapon, an AT4 portable antitank weapon manufactured in Sweden by Saab Bofors Dynamics. The one-shot, disposable AT4 had replaced American-made M-72 LAW rockets in NATO's standard arsenal with a heavier punch, delivering high-penetration rounds that could pierce twenty-four inches of rolled homogenous armor on modern battle tanks.

So a farmhouse provided no challenge at all.

Bolan lined up his shot with the forty-inch, fifteen-pound launcher, sent its fin-stabilized rocket downrange, and watched the front of Carlisle's rural home erupt into billowing flames. Before the shock waves of the first blast had receded, Bolan raised his second AT4 and fired its charge into the holocaust he had created, then discarded it, as well.

Were those screams coming from the blazing ruins of the farmhouse or the normal sounds wood made as it was burning? From a distance, with a mild but steady wind blowing across the battlefield in front of him, Bolan could not be sure.

He waited with the Panther's stock against his shoulder, muzzle pointed toward the funeral pyre. When first one man and then another lurched out of the maelstrom, wreathed in flames, he sent them mercy rounds to end their suffering and left their slack forms smoking in the yard.

And finally he saw the target he'd been waiting for.

Clay Carlisle came around the west side of the house, limping past the bonfire that had been his home, veering around the Dodge Ram pickup that was burning now, after a flaming section of the wall had toppled onto it. He wore a Kevlar vest over a shirt with one sleeve missing and its tails untucked. His slacks bore stains of soil or soot, and blood was smeared across his lower face, as if someone had ground his nose into a wall.

In short, he looked like hell, but he was on his feet and carrying a Steyr AUG assault rifle, scanning his property with manic eyes and smiling through the blood.

Shouting.

It took Bolan a moment to realize that Carlisle was bellowing scripture.

"'Whoso sheddeth man's blood, by man shall his blood be shed,'" Carlisle bellowed, then fired a short burst from his Steyr.

"'Prepare slaughter for his children for the iniquity of their fathers, that they do not rise, nor possess the land, nor fill the face of the world with cities!'"

And another burst.

Bolan had heard enough.

He wasn't sure what kind of vest Carlisle was wearing, but he tested it at three hundred yards with a shot to the chest. The impact knocked Carlisle down and kept him there for a moment, then the Vanguard boss began to wriggle, testing arms and legs, before slowly clambering to his feet.

Still grinning. Still shouting.

"'Go ye after him through the city, and smite. Let not your eye spare, neither have ye pity. Slay utterly old and young, both maids, and little children, and women.'"

As Carlisle stooped to retrieve his rifle, Bolan's last shot struck him in the forehead and released whatever madness had possessed him in a crimson halo. Carlisle seemed to blink once, though it may have been an optical illusion, then his knees buckled and he collapsed.

Bolan lay where he was for several seconds longer, listening to hungry flames, then rose and started back the way he'd come, putting that place of death behind him.

# EPILOGUE

## Arlington National Cemetery

"THIS WAS A SURPRISE," said Deirdre Falk. "Well, I mean two surprises. Seeing you surprised me, but I never knew that Alan was a vet."

"They're all around you," Bolan said. "In daily life, I mean."

"Well, sure. But we were stuck in Kabul for the better part of three years and he never mentioned it. Is it just me, or does that seem a little odd?"

"A lot of us did time in uniform," he said. "Some mention it to make a point, or play it up for personal advantage. Others wouldn't talk about it for a million dollars."

"Sure, I get it. And on you it shows. But Alan? He was a Marine, if you can believe it. They tell me now that he saw action in Grenada."

"There you go. A man with secrets," Bolan said.

The graveside turnout wasn't large. Besides Falk and himself, there were a couple of suits from DEA headquarters, a Marine color guard, a sister of the deceased with her slouching teenage son—and Hal Brognola.

"Least I could do," he'd said while shaking Bolan's hand when he arrived.

The funeral had not been widely advertised, none of the media had picked it up, and Bolan was relieved to find no cameras hovering. He'd been prepared to beg off if the place had been a circus, knowing Falk would understand, but now they'd had their moment, parting with a friend of hers whom Bolan never met.

Although his whole life seemed to hinge on death—preventing it, inflicting it, learning new ways to make it happen—Bolan rarely went to funerals. He'd never been one to commemorate his fallen enemies, and when he lost a friend, the circumstances normally precluded any kind of ritual.

He'd chosen to attend this one because he thought it might help Deirdre Falk somehow, and he was relatively certain that they'd never meet again.

After the casket had been lowered and the mourners were dispersing, Falk told Bolan and Brognola, "I don't know if you've heard this or not, but I've been asked to stick around at DEA. On track for a promotion, they're suggesting, if I keep my nose clean."

"You're surprised?" Brognola asked.

"Damn right. They could be prosecuting me, you know. Instead, it's like someone behind the scenes was pulling strings."

"In Washington?" Bolan said with a smile. "Hard to believe."

"I was just wondering, okay?" Falk said. "In case there's anyone I need to thank for anything. Besides my life, that is."

Brognola shrugged and said, "Can't help you there."

"Not me," Bolan replied. "I've never been the backroom caucus type."

"Well, if you're sure…"

"Will you be staying?" Bolan asked her.

"I'm not sure yet. But I'd be a fool not to consider it. Keeping my nose clean doesn't mean I couldn't try to change things, right? Maybe cut some red tape from time to time."

"I'm not the one to ask," Bolan reminded her.

"Okay."

Brognola sensed the mood and ambled on without them, toward a line of waiting cars.

"Hey, look," Falk said. "I don't know whether I'll be running into you again or not."

"I wouldn't count on it," Bolan said.

"No." Her eyes had gone misty again, as they had done beside the grave. "That's what I thought."

She placed a hand on Bolan's shoulder, rose on tiptoe and kissed him lightly on the lips.

"Thank you," she said. "For keeping me alive. For everything."

"My pleasure," Bolan said to her retreating back.

And meant it.

# TAKE 'EM FREE

## 2 action-packed novels plus a mystery bonus

## NO RISK

### NO OBLIGATION TO BUY